The Devil's Garden

Richard Montanari is the Top Ten *Sunday Times* bestselling author of *The Rosary Girls*, *The Skin Gods*, *Broken Angels*, *Play Dead* and *The Devil's Garden*, as well as the internationally acclaimed thrillers *Kiss of Evil*, *The Violet Hour* and *Deviant Way*.

Richard Montanari

The Devil's Garden

arrow books

Published by Arrow Books 2010

1 3 5 7 9 10 8 6 4 2

First published in Great Britain in 2009 by
William Heinemann
Random House, 20 Vauxhall Bridge Road
London SW1V 2SA

www.rbooks.co.uk

Addresses for companies within The Random House Group Limited can be found at:
www.randomhouse.co.uk/offices.htm

The Random House Group Limited Reg. No. 954009

A CIP catalogue record for this book
is available from the British Library

ISBN 9780099538684

Typeset by SX Composing DTP, Rayleigh, Essex
Printed and bound in Great Britain by
CPI Bookmarque Ltd, Croydon, CR0 4TD

The Devil does not always wear boots — he sometimes comes barefoot.
—Estonian proverb

The Devil's Garden

PROLOGUE

Elena Keskküla knew they would come at midnight, bathed in the blood of ancients, just as she had known so many things in her fifteen years. As the *ennustaja* of her village – a fortuneteller and mystic whose readings were sought by believers from as far away as Tallinn and St Petersburg – she had always been able to glimpse the future. At seven she saw her family's small potato farm overrun by vermin. At ten she saw Jaak Lind lying in a field in Nalchik, the blackened flesh of his palms fused around the face of St Christopher. At twelve she foretold the floods that washed away much of her village, saw the peat bogs choked with dead livestock, the bright parasols adrift on rivers of mud. In her brief time she had seen the patience of evil men, the heartbreak of motherless children, the souls of all around her laid bare with shame, with guilt, with desire. For Elena Keskküla the present had always been past.

What she had not seen, what had been denied the terrible blessing of her second sight, was the torment of bringing lives into this world, the depth to which she loved these children she would never know, the grief of such loss.

And the blood.

So much blood . . .

*

He came to her bed on a warm July evening, nearly nine months earlier, a night when the perfume of rue flowers filled the valley, and the Narva River ran silent. She wanted to fight him, but she had known it would be futile. He was tall and powerful, with large hands and a lean, muscular body marked with the tattoos of the villainous *vennaskond*. Drug lord, usurer, extortionist, thief, he moved like a wraith in the night, ruling the towns and villages of Ida-Viru County with a ruthlessness unknown even during Soviet occupation.

His name was Aleksander Savisaar.

Elena had first seen him when she was a child, standing in the place of the grey wolf. She knew then that he would come to her, enter her, although she was far too young at the time to know what it meant.

At morning he stole away as quietly as he had come. Elena knew he had left his seed in her, and that he would one day return to reap what he had sown.

Over the many months that followed, Elena saw his eyes every waking moment, felt his warm breath on her face, the cruel power of his touch. Some nights, when the air was still, she heard the music. Those who whispered of him said on these nights Aleksander Savisaar would sit on Saber Hill overlooking the village, and play his flute, his long fair hair blown back by the Baltic winds. They said he was quite learned in Mussorgsky and Tchaikovsky. Elena did not know of these things. What she did know was that many times, when his song soared over the valley, the lives within her stirred.

On a late winter midnight the babies came, two of them perfect girls, one stillborn, each wrapped in a thin veil, the true sign of the second sight.

For Elena, consciousness came and left. In her fever dream she saw a man — a Finn by his dress and manner and accent, a man with fog-white hair — standing at the foot of the bed. She saw her father bargain with this man, take his money. Moments later, the Finn left with the newborns, both children swaddled in a black woolen *tekk* against the cold. On the floor, near the fireplace, he left a third bundle, bloodied rags in a lifeless pile. Her maternal instincts battling her dread, Elena tried to rise from the bed, but found she could not move. She wept until her tears ran dry. She wept for the terrible knowledge that these babies, the progeny of Aleksander Savisaar, were gone. Sold in the night like so much chattel.

And hell would be known.

She sensed him before she saw him. At dawn he filled the doorway, his shoulders spanning the jambs, his aura scarlet with rage.

Elena closed her eyes. The future raced through her like a furious river. She saw the severed heads on the gateposts at the road that led to the farm, the charred and battered skulls of her father and brother. She saw their bodies piled in the barn.

As morning crested the hills to the east, Aleksander Savisaar dragged Elena outside, the blood between her legs leaving a ragged red streak in the snow. He placed her against the majestic spruce behind the house, the tree around which Elena and her brother Andres had wrapped ribbons each winter solstice since they were children.

He kissed her once, then drew his knife. The blue steel shimmered in the morning light. He smelled of vodka, venison, and new leather.

"They are mine, soothsayer, and I will find them," he whispered. "No matter how long it takes." He brought the edge of his razor-sharp blade to her throat. "They are my *tütred*, and with them I will be immortal."

In this moment Elena Keskküla had a powerful vision. In it she saw another man, a good man who would raise her precious daughters as his own, a man who had stood in death's garden and lived, a man who would one day, in a field of blood far away, face the devil himself.

PART ONE

ONE

On the day Michael Roman realized he would live forever, five years after the last day of his life, his entire world went pink. A pastel pink at that: pink tablecloths, pink chairs, pink flowers, pink crepe banners, even a huge pink umbrella festooned in smiling pink bunnies. There were pink cups and plates, pink forks and napkins, a plate piled high with frosted pink cupcakes.

The only thing keeping the property from a listing with Candy Land Realty was the small patch of green grass barely visible beneath the maze of aluminum folding tables and plastic chairs, grass that would surely never be the same.

Then there was that other vision of green. Departing green. The money.

How much was all this costing again?

As Michael stood behind the house, he thought about the first time he had seen it, and how perfect it seemed.

The house was a three bedroom brick colonial, with buff-colored shutters and matching pilasters, set far back from the winding road. Even for the suburbs, it was isolated, perched atop a slight hill, embraced by a stand of sycamores, shielded from both the road and neighbors by a waist-high hedgerow.

Behind the house was a two-car garage, a gardening shed, a wide yard with a latticework trellis. The lot gave quickly to the woods, sloping down to meet a meandering creek, which ran toward the Hudson River. At night it became eerily silent. For Michael, having grown up in the city, the change was hard to take. At first the isolation had gotten to him; Abby too, although she would never admit it. The nearest houses were about a quarter-mile in either direction. The foliage was thick, and in summer it felt like living in a giant green cocoon. Twice over the past year, when the power had gone out in a storm, Michael felt as if he was on the moon. Since that time he had stocked up on batteries, candles, canned goods, even a pair of kerosene heaters. They could probably survive a week in the Yukon if they needed to.

"The clown will be here at one."

Michael turned to see his wife crossing the yard, carrying a plateful of pink frosted cookies. She wore tight white jeans and a powder blue *Roar Lion Roar* Columbia University T-shirt, along with a pair of drugstore flip flop sandals. Somehow she still managed to look like Grace Kelly.

"Your brother's coming?" Michael asked.

"Be nice."

Abigail Reed Roman, thirty-one, was four years younger than her husband. Unlike Michael's working-class childhood, she had grown up on an estate in Pound Ridge, the daughter of a world-renowned cardiac surgeon. Where Michael's patience seemed at times to be nonexistent – his temper usually hovered at a constant 211 degrees Fahrenheit, often rising – his wife ran on an even keel. Until she was cornered. Then there were rodents in Calcutta that bowed to her ferocity. Nearly a decade as an emergency room nurse at New York Downtown Hospital will do that to you; ten years of crack heads, PCP heads, exploded lives, torn people, and broken souls.

But that was another life.

"Did you frost the cake?" Abby asked.

Shit, Michael thought. He had forgotten all about it, which was unlike him. Not only did he do most of the cooking in his small family, he was the go-to guy for all things baked. His *Bienensticke* had been known to make grown men weep. "I'm on it."

While jogging back to the house, dodging pink Mylar balloons, Michael thought about this day. Since moving from the city a year earlier, they had not had that many parties. When Michael was small, his parents' tiny apartment in Queens seemed constantly filled with friends and neighbors and relatives, along with customers from the family's bakery, a symphony of Eastern European and Baltic languages floating over the fire escape and onto the streets of Astoria. Even in the past few years, since his meteoric rise through the district attorney's office, he and Abby found themselves hosting at least a handful of cocktail or dinner parties for well-selected political guests every year.

Here in the suburbs, though, things had slowed down, almost to a halt. Everything seemed to revolve around the girls. Although it might not have been the best career move, Michael found he didn't want it any other way. The day the girls came into their lives, everything changed.

Standing in the kitchen, ten minutes later, the cake frosted and decorated, Michael heard four little feet approach, stop.

"How do we look, Daddy?"

Michael spun around. When he saw his twin four-year-old daughters standing there, hand in hand, dressed in their matching white dresses – with pink ribbons, of course – his heart soared.

Charlotte and Emily. The two halves of his heart.

Maybe he *would* live forever.

*

By noon the party was in full cacophonous swing. Eden Falls was a small town in Crane County, near the banks of the Hudson River, about fifty miles from New York City. Situated north of Westchester County – and therefore further from Manhattan, and therefore more affordable to young families – it seemed to boast an inordinate number of children under the age of ten.

To Michael it looked like every one of them had been invited. He wondered: How many friends can four-year-old girls have, anyway? They weren't even in school yet. Did they have their own Facebook pages? Were they Twittering? Socially networking at Chuck E Cheese?

Michael surveyed the partyscape. In all there were about twenty kids and matching moms, all in some version of J. Crew, Banana Republic, or Eddie Bauer motif. The kids were a constant buzz. The moms were all standing around, cellphones at the ready, chatting softly, sipping herbal tea and raspberry acai.

At twelve-thirty Michael brought out the cake. Amid the *oohhs* and *ahhhhs*, his daughters looked concerned about something, little brows creased. Michael put the huge cake on one of the tables, got down to their level.

"Does it look good?" he asked.

The girls nodded in union.

"We were wondering something, though," Emily said.

"What, honey?"

"Is this organic cake?"

Coming from a four year old, the word sounded Chinese. "Organic?"

"Yes," Charlotte said. "We need organic cake. And guten-free. Is this guten-free?"

Michael glanced at Abby. "Have they been watching the Food Network again?"

"Worse," Abby said. "They've been making me Tivo reruns of *Healthy Appetite with Ellie Krieger*."

Michael soon realized an answer was required. He looked at the ground, the sky, the trees, again at his wife, where he found no shelter. "Well, okay, I would say this cake has *guten*-free properties."

Charlotte and Emily gave him the fish-eye.

"What I mean is," he continued, reaching into his lawyer's bag of tricks. "It has *guten*-absent characteristics."

The girls glanced at each other, in that way that twins have, a secret knowledge passing between them. "It's okay," Charlotte finally said. "You make good birthday cake."

"Thanks, ladies," Michael said, enormously relieved, and also a little disbelieving, considering that this was only the third cake he had made them, and found it hard to believe they remembered the first two.

As Michael prepared to cut the cake, he saw the moms whispering to each other. They were all looking toward the side of the house, fluffing hair, straightening clothes, smoothing cheeks. To Michael, it could only mean one thing. Tommy had arrived.

Thomas Christiano was one of Michael's oldest friends, a man with whom Michael had, in the gaudy plumage of youth, closed every bar in Queens, and not a few in Manhattan; the only man who had ever seen Michael cry, and that was the night Michael and Abby brought Charlotte and Emily home. To this day Michael claimed it was pollen. Tommy knew better.

When Tommy and Michael were in their twenties they'd been a holy terror. Tommy with his dark good looks and smooth lines; Michael with his boyish face and ocean blue eyes. They'd had that Starsky and Hutch, Hall and Oates, swarthy and fair thing down pat. They were both around six feet tall, well dressed, and carried with them the confidence that came with authority. Where Tommy's tastes went to Missoni and Valentino, Michael's went to Ralph Lauren and Land's End. They were the dynamic duo.

But that, too, was a few years ago.

Tommy swaggered across the back lawn, on display, as always. Even at a kid's party, he was turned out – black Armani T-shirt, cream linen slacks, black leather loafers. Even at a kid's party, or *especially* at a kid's party, Tommy knew that there would be a number of women in their twenties or thirties present, and that a certain fraction would be divorced, separated, or separating. Tommy Christiano played the percentages. It was one of the reasons he was one of the most respected prosecutors in Queens County, New York.

The number one spot, the most feared assistant district attorney at Kew Gardens, was Michael Roman.

"Miss Abigail," Tommy said. He kissed Abby on both cheeks, Euro-style. "You look beautiful."

"Yeah, right," Abby said, waving a hand at her battered sandals and frayed jeans. Still, she blushed. Not too many people could make Abby Roman blush. "I look like something that just washed up on Rockaway."

Tommy laughed. "The prettiest mermaid ever."

Blush number two from Abby, followed by a playful slug on Tommy's shoulder. Considering Abby's nearly demented devotion to Pilates, Michael bet it hurt. Tommy would rather die than show it.

"White wine?" she asked.

"Sure."

As soon as Abby turned her back and headed to the house, Tommy rubbed his shoulder. "Jesus *Christ* your wife is strong."

"Try playing touch football with her. We always have paramedics standing by."

Over the next half-hour, a number of people from the mayor's office and Queens County DA's office made their perfunctory appearances. Michael was a bit flattered and more than a little surprised when Dennis McCaffrey, the district attorney himself, showed up with a pair of outlandishly big teddy bears for the girls. Michael had recently been to a party for the deputy mayor's five-year-old son, and at that gathering Denny McCaffrey — a nineteen-year veteran of the elected position, and the most politically savvy man Michael had ever met — only brought a rather puny Beanie Baby penguin. It seemed that, as Michael's reputation as the hottest ADA in the city grew, so did the size of the plush toys for his children.

At one o'clock the entertainment arrived in the person of a tall, feathery woman who went by the professional name Chickie Noodle the Clown. At first Michael thought she might be a little too long in the tooth for a kid's party, but she turned out to be a trouper, with more than enough energy and patience to deal with twenty little kids. In addition to the balloon-twisting, face-painting, and something called the Merry Madcap Olympics, there was also the obligatory piñata. The kids got to select which one they wanted, a choice that came down to a shark piñata and a butterfly piñata. The kids chose the butterfly.

Two questions instantly arose in Michael's mind. One, what kind of clown buys a piñata in the shape of a shark? And two, perhaps more importantly, what kind of kids wanted to pick up a plastic bat and beat the crap out of a butterfly?

Suburban kids, that's who. They should have stayed in Queens where it was safe.

At two-thirty the pony clopped onto the scene, and there was near pandemonium as Chickie Noodle was left spinning in the dust, holding a stack of cardboard cone hats. One by one the kids got to ride an indifferent Shetland named Lulu around the perimeter of the backyard. Michael had to admit that the act was pretty good. The owner of the horse, the guy who led the animal, was a short, kindly looking cowpoke in his sixties, replete with droopy white mustache, bow legs, and a ten gallon Stetson. He looked like a Shetland-sized Sam Elliott.

At three-thirty it was time for presents. And *man* were there presents. Michael considered that he and Abby would be buying reciprocal gifts for every child at the party during the next year or so, a suburban *kid pro quo*.

Midway through the consumer love fest, Abby picked up a pair of small square boxes, read the card. "These are from Uncle Tommy."

The girls ran over to Tommy, arms extended. Tommy knelt down for a pair of big kisses and bigger hugs. It was his turn to blush. Despite two brief marriages, he had no children of his own. He was godfather to both Charlotte and Emily, a position he took with the solemnity of an English archbishop.

The girls zipped back to the table. When they got the wrapping paper off the small boxes, and Michael saw the logo on the sides, he did a double take. The second glance was unnecessary. He'd know that logo anywhere.

"Yaaaay!" the twins cried in unison. Michael knew that his daughters hadn't the slightest idea what was inside the boxes, but that didn't matter to them. The boxes had been wrapped in shiny paper, the boxes were for them, and the pile of birthday swag was growing exponentially.

Michael looked at Tommy. "You bought them iPods?"

"What's wrong with iPods?"

"Jesus, Tommy. They're *four*."

"What are you saying, four year olds don't listen to music? I listened to music when I was four."

"Four year olds don't *download* music," Michael said. "Why didn't you just get them cellphones?"

"That's next year." He sipped his wine, winked. "Four is too young for cellphones. What kind of parent are you?"

Michael laughed, but it occurred to him that his daughters weren't all that far off from cellphones and laptops and cars and dating. He barely survived them going to preschool. How was he going to handle the teen years? He threw a quick glance at Charlotte and Emily, who were tearing into a new pair of presents.

They were still little girls.

Thank God.

By four o'clock the party was winding down. More accurately, the parents were winding down. The kids were still jacked sky-high on cookies, chocolate cake, Kool Aid, and ice cream.

As Tommy prepared to leave, he caught Michael's eye. The two men gathered at the back of the yard.

"How's the girl?" Tommy asked, lowering his voice.

Michael thought about Falynn Harris, the quiet girl with the sad angel's face. She was the star witness — no, the only witness — in his next homicide trial. "She hasn't spoken a word yet."

"The trial starts Monday?"

"Monday."

Tommy nodded, taking it in. "Anything you need."

"Thanks, Tommy."

"Don't forget Rupert White's party tomorrow. You're coming, right?"

Michael instinctively glanced at Abby, who was cleaning the frosting off a neighborhood boy's face, neck, and arms. The kid looked like a chubby pink fresco. "I have to clear it with command and control."

Tommy shook his head. "Marriage."

On the way out, Michael saw Tommy stop and talk to Rita

Ludlow, a thirtyish divorcee from the end of the block. Tall, auburn-haired, shapely, she had probably populated the day-dreams of every man under ninety in Eden Falls at one time or another.

Not surprisingly, after just a few seconds of chatter, she handed Tommy her phone number. Tommy turned, winked at Michael, swaggered off.

Sometimes Michael Roman hated his best friend.

Because the invitations said noon to four, when they heard the car doors slam out front, it could only mean one thing. Abby's brother Wallace was making his regal entrance. He was not just fashionably late. He was fashion*ista* late. Which was all the more ironic, considering his past.

Angel-hair thin, freckled and balding, Wallace Reed was the kid in high school who ironed his book covers, the kid who would have played triangle in the school band if he hadn't gotten smoked in the audition and ended up playing *second* triangle.

Today he was chairman of WBR Aerospace, pulling down something north of eight figures a year, living in a McMansion in Westchester, and summering in one of those sea-foam green Gatsby places in Sagaponack featured in *Hamptons Magazine*.

Still, despite his card-carrying status in Nerds Anonymous, Wallace had romanced an astonishing array of beautiful women. Amazing what a few million dollars can do for your image.

This day his *belle du jour* didn't look a day over twenty-four. She wore a Roberto Cavalli halter dress and a pair of burgundy ballet flats. This according to Abby. Michael wouldn't know a ballet flat from a flat tire.

"Now here's a woman who knows how to dress for cake and Kool Aid," Abby said, sotto voce.

"Be nice."

"I'm going with Whitney," Abby whispered.

"I'll take Madison." It was a running five-dollar bet they had.

"There's my favorite sister," Wallace said. It was the standard line. Abby was his only sister. He kissed her on the cheek.

Wallace wore a bright plum Polo, razor-creased beige chinos and green duck boots. Barney gone LL Bean. He gestured to the girl. "This is Madison."

Michael could not look at his wife. He just couldn't. The twins came running over, sensing fresh chum.

"And these must be the girls of the hour," Madison said, getting down to the twins' level. The girls did their shy act, fingers to lips. They hadn't figured out the woman's gift-potential yet.

"Yes, this is Charlotte and Emily," Abby said.

Madison smiled, stood, patted the girls on their heads, like they were schnauzers. "How *adorable*. Just like the Brontë sisters."

Abby shot a desperate glance at Michael.

"Right," Michael said. "The Brontë sisters."

Here was a party-pause longer than the one where Rock Hudson came out of the closet.

"The authors?" Madison said, blinking, incredulous. "The British *authors?*"

"Of course," Abby said. "They wrote . . ."

The second longest pause.

"*Wuthering Heights? Jane Eyre?*"

"Yes," Abby said. "I simply adored those books growing up. So did Michael."

Michael nodded. And nodded. He felt like a bobble-head doll in the back window of a car with busted shocks.

The girls circled the four adults. Michael could almost hear the theme from *Jaws*. Presents from Uncle Wallace were like the Oscars. Best picture was always last.

"You ready for your gifts?" Wallace asked.

"Yes!" the girls chanted. "Yes we *are*!"

"They're out front."

The girls made a move to rocket across the yard, but instead waited for Wallace, taking him by the hand. They were no dummies. They knew how to work their quarry. Even though Charlotte once said Uncle Wallace smelled like pickles.

"He said *they're* out front," Michael said, once they had disappeared around the corner. "*They're*. As in *they*."

"I know."

"He did not buy them bikes. Please tell me he did not buy them bikes. We talked about this."

"He promised me, Michael. No bikes."

Getting your daughters their first grown up bicycles was an important thing, a father-daughter thing to which Michael Roman was greatly looking forward. He was not going to let a millionaire who wore *eau de gherkin* take that away from him.

When Michael heard the *yay* come flying over the house, his heart sank. Moments later he saw his daughters come racing around the corner in their matching pink motorized Barbie Jeeps.

Oh, Jesus, Michael thought.

They're driving *already*.

Twenty minutes later the final few guests gathered in the driveway. Thanks were proffered, cheeks were kissed, promises were made, and teary little ones were bundled into SUVs – the party was over.

On the back patio, Charlotte and Emily shared a piece of chalk. They drew a hopscotch pattern on the concrete. Emily found a suitable stone in the flower garden, and the girls played a full game. As usual, they did not keep score, neither wanting to best the other in anything.

When they tired of the game, they began to draw something else on the concrete, an intricate figure of a big blue lion with a long curling tail. They worked in silence.

At six o'clock, as deep violet clouds gathered over Crane County, New York, their mother called them inside. The little girls rose, looked at their drawing. They each whispered something to the other. Then, in their private way, they hugged, and went inside.

Twenty minutes later it began to rain; huge gobbets of water falling to earth, soaking the grass, giving life to the spring garden. Before long, small ponds pooled on the patio, and the symbol was washed away.

TWO

SOUTH-EASTERN ESTONIA

The valley was silent the morning he left, as if in its stilled branches, its songless robins, its hushed streams and posing wildflowers, it knew there would soon be change.

The tall man in the black leather coat stood at the split rail fence that surrounded the main section of his property. He had already shuttered the structure, armed its systems, and programmed its photosensitive lighting grid. From the outside the dwelling – although not a large house by any means, not by the standards of the young "minigarch" Russians who had begun to buy property throughout Estonia – appeared to be a sturdy but humble building. Inside, in its heart, in the heart of its builder and owner, it was a fortress.

The tall man picked up his two leather bags, shouldered them.

It was time.

As he began to make his way down the two-mile gravel lane that wound through the hills, Rocco, the Italian mastiff, found him at the first turn. Rocco had been rooting in a log, it seemed, and smelled of rot and compost and feces. The aroma filled the tall man with an instant and indefinable melancholy. Soon the other five dogs emerged from the forest and fell into a rhythm next to him. The dogs were nervous, excited, sad, leaping on each other, onto him. They sensed he was leaving, and like all dogs, felt he was never going to return. The wolf-hound, Tumnus, already over a hundred pounds, was getting too large for such antics, but on this day – this day for which the tall man had so long waited – it was permitted.

The entourage made the final turn toward the gate. Rounding the bend, the man considered the boy who lived at the edge of the village, the boy who would let himself onto the grounds each morning to feed and water and groom the animals in his absence. The tall man trusted the boy. He trusted few people.

When he reached the gate he unlocked it, stepped through, re-armed it. The dogs all sat on the other side, shivering in the moment, softly keening their sorrow. The smallest of them, the alpha male pug named Zeus, put a paw to the chain-link fence.

The rented Lada Niva was parked on the side of the road, keys in the ignition, as promised and paid for. Except for automobiles belonging to the tall man, no vehicle had ever driven the two miles up to the house. No other vehicle ever would. The silent weight alarms deployed just beneath the surface of the gravel lane, along with the gossamer thin trip wires strung throughout the property – all at forty-eight inches from the ground, lest the dogs trip them – were sufficient warning. The perimeter had yet to be breached. Perhaps it was more the man's reputation that spoke to any would-be interlopers than anything electronic.

If the alarms were triggered in his absence, the boy next door, Villem Aavik, a growing and muscular fourteen, knew what to do. The boy, whose father was killed in the war in Bosnia, was strong and smart. Aleks had trained him to shoot, which had come to the boy with difficulty, having lost a finger in a foundry accident. He also taught the boy how to read the hearts of men. He would one day be a master thief, or a politician. As if there were a difference. Perhaps the boy, like the tall man, would be *vennaskond*.

The tall man placed his shoulder bags in the trunk, slipped inside the car.

He looked down the road, and began to feel the exhilaration one feels at the onset of a journey, a journey that had long been in the planning, a journey that would find for him his very soul.

In the silence and darkness of the womb there were three.
  Anna, Marya, and Olga.

Four, the tall man thought. His girls were *four years old* now. He had not slept fully or soundly since the night of their birth, had not drawn one breath of God's air, had not stopped looking.

Until now.

He had finally located the man who had been there that morning, the white-haired Finn who walked the shadows of his dreams, the man who had stolen his daughters. He would meet the man in Tallinn, find out what he needed, and a reckoning would be known.

The tall man turned to look one last time at the intricate wrought iron gate – a gate bearing the complex metalwork of a blue lion surrounded by oak branches, the national symbol of Estonia – and his house on the hill, the structure now obscured by trees ripe with leaf and blossom. He believed the next time he saw this place his life would be different. The sky would be clearer, the air twice as warm. There would be sweet voices singing in the forest, children's voices.

He touched the crystal vial hanging from a silver chain

around his neck, the small glass bottle filled with Olga's blood. There it gently clinked against the two empty vials.

With his daughters, his beloved *tütred*, the tall man believed he would live the prophecy of Koschei the Deathless, believed he would live forever.

No. It was more than a belief. Much more.

Aleksander Savisaar *knew*.

THREE

Two hours after the party ended, after the crowd had departed and the mess had been cleared, Michael and Abby sat their daughters down for a solemn talk about the ground rules regarding their new little cars: no driving anywhere near the street, helmets always and, most importantly, no driving after more than two glasses of grape juice.

Michael thought his line was funny; Abby was not amused. She was not all that happy with her brother.

Michael pushed the cars to the double garage. The evening was quiet. The evenings were *always* quiet here. Through the trees he could just make out the lights from the Meisner house a quarter-mile north.

He tried to find parking spots for the little pink Jeeps in their already cramped garage. When he moved a pair of old bi-fold doors, he saw it. It was the sign from the window of the bakery. As always, it dragged his heart and mind down a long corridor of remembrance.

When Michael's parents Peeter and Johanna Romanov immigrated to the United States from Estonia in 1971 the world was a very different place. The Soviet Union was still twenty years from collapse, and the process of escaping an Eastern Bloc country was both dangerous and expensive.

They settled in Astoria, Queens, in a small apartment over a shuttered retail store on Ditmars Boulevard near Crescent Street.

In July 1973 Mikhail Romanov was born at Queens Hospital. The next day Peeter applied to have the family's last name changed to Roman, figuring that, as the Cold War still raged, his son would not be served well by such a Russian-sounding name, especially one so patrician.

Two years later, with a credit union loan, Michael's parents bought the retail space beneath their apartment, and opened a bakery. Word quickly spread among the local Estonian, Russian, and eastern European residents of the neighborhood. On a block that boasted both Greek and Italian bakeries there was now a place where one could purchase fresh brown breads, gingerbreads, *piroshkis, rugalah* and, every Easter, their beloved *kulich*. Patrons no longer had to travel to Rego Park for their *kartoshka*.

But what made the Pikk Street Bakery special – the shop was named after the street in Tallinn on which Peeter had proposed to Johanna – was its old-fashioned wooden shelves, its linen tablecloths, its luminous display of candy bins stuffed with an unbounded selection of gaily wrapped confections, which turned the place into every child's fantasy.

Perhaps what made it even more special, especially for the young mothers in the neighborhood, was Johanna Roman's exquisite Estonian lace. Michael's fondest memory of his mother was her sitting on the fire escape in spring and summer, her steel needles blazing, chatting with neighbors, her tapestry bag at her feet, the tote with an Estonian cottage embroidered on its side. Booties, blankets, hats, sweaters, especially her delicate Haapsalu shawls – Johanna always gave away whatever she knitted.

Her nickname for Michael – a private nickname, one Johanna

never uttered in front of Michael's friends on the block — was *nupp*. A nupp was a particularly difficult maneuver in knitting, one that required the left-hand needle to penetrate five stitches. Some women in Johanna's circle called it "Satan's contribution to knitting," but Johanna Roman always meant it as a term of endearment.

Good night my little nupp, she would say to her handful of a son.

Michael always slept well.

In 1980, on a blustery winter day, Michael arrived home from school to find a stranger in their small kitchen above the shop, a large rockpile of a man, with a wide forehead, zinc-colored eyes, and a deeply cleft chin. He wore a pilled woolen coat and boots gone round at the heel. He ate sardines from a can. With his fingers.

The man was Solomon Kaasik, his father's childhood friend from Tartu. Peeter Roman had sponsored the man's voyage to America.

Every Sunday, for many months, Solomon would come for Sunday dinner, often with a small present for Michael, never without something to add to the stew. He would drink Türi vodka and smoke cigars with Michael's father well into the night. Some evenings he would play chess with Michael, sometimes letting the boy win.

In the spring of Michael's eighth year, Solomon ceased visiting. Michael missed his loud laughter, the way he would throw him on his broad shoulders with ease. Finally Michael asked. His father did not answer him, but eventually Johanna took Michael aside one day and told him that Solomon had fallen in with some bad people, the local *vory*. Michael was not sure what the *vory* were exactly, but he knew to be afraid of them. After much nagging, Peeter told Michael that Solomon had gotten involved in the robbery of a bank in Brooklyn, a robbery where people had died. He said Solomon was now in a place called Attica and he was not coming back for a long time.

Although deeply saddened by these events, Peeter Roman visited Solomon often. When Michael turned nine, his father talked the guards into letting Michael see Solomon. To Michael, Solomon looked thinner, but harder. He had new markings on his arms. He no longer smiled.

On July 4, 1983, just a few weeks before Michael's tenth birthday, he sat in the window overlooking Ditmars Boulevard. Below him, neighborhood kids threw cherry bombs, M80s, fired bottle rockets. Michael was forbidden to leave the house unaccompanied by his parents – there was always a story of a child losing a finger, an eye, something worse – so Michael leaned as far as he could out the window, the smells of spent gunpowder filling his head. The shop closed at seven PM. Every few seconds Michael would glance at the clock. At seven sharp he ran down the stairs.

At first he thought he had mistakenly taken the back stairs, for he heard none of the familiar sounds – the pans being washed and put away, the sound of the Hoover being run, doors locked, register closed out. But he *was* on the front stairs, and the shop was quiet.

Something was wrong.

Michael crouched on the stairs and looked into the shop. The plastic OPEN sign had not been turned around on the door. The neon display in the window still glowed.

By the time Michael rounded the platform at the bottom of the steps, he saw it. It was a picture that would live in his mind and heart forever.

The bakery was covered in blood.

Behind the counter, where his mother always stood, chatting with customers, filling white boxes with pastries and rolls, her laughter a sweet song soaring over the sounds of traffic on the street, the entire back wall had been painted crimson. The cash register had been pulled from the counter, and lay on its side, emptied, like a gutted dog. Michael saw his father's creased brown shoes, ever covered in white flour, sticking out from behind the main oven, all around them thick dots of scarlet in the spilled sugar.

His heart black with fear, Michael crossed the room to where his mother lay bleeding. She did not open her eyes, but in the moment before she died she whispered softly to him.

"Zhivy budem, ne pomryom."

It was an old Russian phrase meaning *If we will be alive, we will not die.*

Only much later would Michael learn what had happened. He would learn that two young men – not neighborhood men, Ukrainian men from somewhere called Red Hook – had come into the shop and demanded money. Once they had everything in the register, they cold-bloodedly shot Peeter and Johanna Roman. The sounds of the gunfire were masked by the sounds of the fireworks. While Michael sat upstairs, resenting his parents for being so old fashioned as to not let him play with fireworks, they lay below him, his father dead, his mother dying. Even at the age of nine he vowed to never forgive himself.

The police investigated the crime, but after six months or so the case went cold. Michael was taken in by cousins. He withdrew completely in his grief and sorrow, into the worlds of Jack London and Zane Grey. He didn't speak for nearly a year. His grades suffered and he grew terribly thin. In his eleventh year he began to come out of it, and it was during that summer that news came to his household. Michael overheard his cousins talking of a grisly discovery made by police. It seemed that two men were found hanging from a girder beneath the Hell Gate Bridge near Nineteenth Street. The men were naked, brutally beaten, and had their genitals removed. Carved into their chests were two numbers: 6 and 4.

The address of the Pikk Street Bakery was 64 Ditmars Boulevard.

When Michael turned eighteen, and began what would become monthly visits to play chess with Solomon Kaasik, a tradition the two men maintained for many years, he walked into the room, met Solomon's lupine eyes and, with a slight nod of Solomon's great jaw, Michael knew. It was Solomon who had put the hit on the two men. Although Solomon could have revealed this many years earlier, he had waited for the right time. He had waited until Michael was a man.

It was in this moment that Michael Roman considered, for the first time in his life, the true heart of justice, both old world and new.

Twelve years later, on a frigid Bronx thoroughfare, when his world exploded and white fire rained down around him, Johanna Roman whispered to her son once more, this time from beyond the grave, and Michael realized that these things were one and the same.

Abby was prone on the bed, reading the *Daily News*. In the corner of the room was a five foot pile of presents. Sitting on the bed, Michael kissed her on the back of her neck. Michael Roman loved the back of his wife's neck.

"Man, look at all this loot," he said. "Maybe we should have a party for them four or five times a year."

"You just want one of the iPods."

It was true. Michael was still using his battered Sony Walkman. And listening to the New York Dolls to boot. He had to get with the times. "You know me too well."

"It's a living."

"Are they asleep?"

Abby laughed. "They ate a pound of sugar. They'll fall asleep sometime in August."

"I suppose I have to call and thank your parents."

Michael was kidding, and Abby knew it. Dr Charles and Marjorie Reed were in Austria, or Australia, or Anaheim – it was hard to keep track of them. But they had sent checks for Charlotte and Emily, $10,000 each, earmarked for their college funds. Abby's parents had always been a bit cool toward Michael. They were never crazy about their blue-blood daughter marrying a lawyer, especially a civil servant lawyer. But if Michael had to choose between seeing them, or padding his daughters' college fund, there was no contest.

"I'll let your conscience be your guide on that one," Abby said.

Michael flopped back onto the bed, turned on his side, facing his wife. "Do you think they had fun?"

"Four year olds always have fun, Michael." She stroked his hair. "They would've had fun with a cardboard box and a broken frisbee. Besides, the party wasn't for them, you know."

"It wasn't?"

Abby rolled her eyes. "My love, you are *so* naive."

"Who was it for?"

Abby turned to face him. His skin was clear and pale, with the lightest powdering of freckles, her eyes the color of semi-sweet chocolate. She had her ash-blond hair pinned up, but some of it had escaped, and now softly framed her face. She still looked at least five years younger than she really was, but her experience – the practice of holding life and death in her hands for almost a decade – had brought something to her eyes that spoke more of wisdom than age. She still gave him butterflies. "It was for all the other mothers on the street, of course. It's a competition."

"What kind of competition?"

Abby sat up, energized. "Okay," she began, counting it off. She'd obviously given this some serious thought. "Number one. The catering. Did we have expensive catering – as in did we just go with the hot dogs, mini-burgers, and pizza – or did we spring for the chocolate fountain? Two. Do we have eucalyptus outdoor furniture or did we go for the teak? Three. Do we have an in-ground or above-ground pool? Four. Did we have a band or just the clown –?"

"I have to tell you, that was one weird frickin' clown," Michael said. "Miss Chicken Noodle 1986."

"I think she was non-union."

"But we did have a pony. Don't forget the pony."

"The pony was a big plus."

"Even though he crapped in the azaleas."

"Ponies will do that."

"Man," Michael said. "I had no idea about any of this."

Abby touched his cheek. "My city boy."

Michael glared. "City boy? *City* boy? Didn't you see me with the Weed Eater out there this morning? There is not a man in any one of the five boroughs who can handle a piece of lawn maintenance equipment like that."

Abby smiled *the* smile, the one that always started a shiver somewhere around Michael's forehead and traveled to all regions nether. "Yeah, well," she began, moving closer, looking at his lips, "I've always said you were a man who could handle his equipment."

Michael smiled, kissed his wife on the nose, got up, bolted into the bathroom, brushed his teeth. When he came out, Abby was sitting up in bed. The only thing she wore was a beautiful navy blue silk tie. It still had the price tag on it.

"That's the one?" Michael asked.

Abby nodded. It was a ritual for them. Before every big case she would buy him a new tie, a lucky charm to wear during his opening statement. She had not failed yet. With Abby's magical neckwear Michael had a 100 per cent conviction rate.

"Professor Roman?" Abby asked, gently unknotting the tie and placing it on the nightstand.

"Yes, Nurse Reed?"

"I was wondering if I could ask you a question."

Michael pulled off his shirt. He now had on just a pair of light green hospital scrubs. "Of course."

"Which of the Brontë sisters' books would be your favorite?"

Michael laughed. "Well, let me think about this for a second." He slipped out of his scrubs, under the sheets. "I'd have to say my favorite would be the one about Jane Eyre's sister Frigid."

Abby snorted. "Frigid Eyre?"

"Yes. It's the story of a homely English girl's quest for sexual adventure."

Abby shook her head. She put her arms around Michael's neck. "I can't believe we never made the connection. Charlotte and Emily. I mean, how many years of higher education do we have between us? Fifteen?"

Of course, for Michael, this was not a rare occurrence. He was twenty-nine before he realized that the ABC song was the same melody as "Twinkle, Twinkle Little Star". In his time he had once prepared a closing argument in a homicide case in less than an hour – with a vicious hangover, no less – and could recite the contributors to Black's Law (Eighth Edition) by rote. But the subtleties of "Twinkle, Twinkle" were lost on him.

The subtleties of Abby Roman's body, however, were not.

*

Midnight. Michael stood in the doorway to the girls' room. Abby had been right. The girls were both still awake. He entered the room, kneeled between the beds.

"Hi, Daddy," Charlotte said.

"Hi ladies," he said. "Did you guys have fun today?"

They both nodded in unison, yawned in harmony. Sometimes they were so different in their outlooks, their problem-solving skills, it was as if they were not even related. Charlotte with her ability to divine logic from chaos. Emily and her sense of color and flair for the dramatic. Other times, most of the time, they seemed to be of one mind, one heart, even more so than the connections that bound most twins.

Michael glanced over at the corner of the room. Their little table was set for tea. It was, as always, arranged for three people. They never put a stuffed bear or bunny in the third chair. It was always just empty. It was one of the many mysteries that were his daughters.

He turned back to the girls as Charlotte pushed a strand of hair from her eyes. She crooked her finger, beckoning Michael forward, as if to share a secret. He leaned between the two girls. They often did this when they wanted to tell him something together, an exercise that often ended with a kiss on each cheek. The kiss part was supposed to be a surprise.

"What is it?" Michael asked.

"*Ta tuleb*," the two girls said softly.

At first Michael thought he misheard them. It sounded as if they'd said "tattoo" or "the tool." Neither interpretation made sense. "What did you say?"

"*Ta tuleb*," they repeated.

Michael leaned back, a little surprised. He looked back and forth between his daughters, at the four big blue eyes in the soft blush of the nightlight. "*Ta tuleb*?"

They nodded.

The phrase brought Michael back to his early childhood, to evenings above the Pikk Street Bakery, nights when he would be reading comic books while he was supposed to be doing his homework. When his mother, looking out the kitchen window, her long steel knitting needles in hand, saw Peeter Roman turn the corner onto Ditmars Boulevard, she would yell "*ta tuleb!*" up the stairs, and Michael would immediately get back to his studies.

"What do you mean?" he asked.

Charlotte and Emily looked at each other, shrugged, slipped under the covers. Michael took a moment, still a bit bewildered. He tucked the girls in, planted kisses on their foreheads.

On the way out of the bedroom he stood at the door for a moment, thinking.

Ta tuleb was an Estonian phrase.

His daughters did not speak Estonian.

Michael walked into the small room on the first floor that served as his office, flipped on a light, opened his briefcase. He studied the photograph of Falynn Harris. She was only fourteen.

Falynn was the daughter of Colin Harris, a Long Island City florist who had been gunned down two years ago in April, murdered in cold blood by one Patrick Sean Ghegan. Ghegan, along with his younger brother Liam, were the demon spawn of Jack Ghegan, a former mid-level Queens mobster currently doing life-plus in Dannemora.

Falynn, who was sneaking a cigarette behind the store, saw the whole thing go down through the back window. She was so traumatized by the horror of the crime she had not said a single word since. And she was the state's star witness.

Michael Roman had won RICO cases, had prosecuted some of the most hardened career criminals ever to pass through the New York state legal system, had successfully tried two death penalty cases, including the infamous Astrology Killer, had more than once reached for something that far exceeded his grasp, only to thrive. But this one was special. And he knew why. He had lobbied long and hard to get it.

The question was: Could he get Falynn to talk to him? In the next forty-eight hours, with the specter of Colin Harris standing over them, could he get her to remember?

If we will be alive, we will not die.

Coffee. He needed coffee. This was going to be a long night.

On the way to the kitchen he stopped at the foot of the stairs and glanced up at the slightly ajar door to his daughters' room.

Ta tuleb, he thought.

It was an Estonian phrase that meant: *He is coming.*

As Michael Roman entered the kitchen and took the French press out of the cupboard, a question flitted around his mind like a gypsy moth drawn to a light bulb.

Who is coming?

FOUR

Aleksander Savisaar stood in the center of the bustling square. It was an unseasonably warm evening, the lilies were pregnant in bloom, and Viru Tänav Street was a carnival of the senses.

He walked a few blocks, sat at a small outdoor café, ordered tea, watched the girls walk by in their springtime dresses, each a long-petalled flower. He had been in many ports in his time, from Kabul to Moscow to a brief tour in Shanghai. His business affairs had taken him many times to Helsinki to Riga to St Petersburg and beyond, yet he was never happy in a city, any city. He could tolerate it all for a few days. Perhaps a week. Sometimes, if his needs were met, he found himself flourishing. But he was not, nor ever would be, at home in any urban setting. His place was the forest, the valley, the hills.

The city of Tallinn sat on the northern coast of Estonia, on the Gulf of Finland. As the capital, it was one of the most completely preserved medieval cities in the world. Since the fall of communism in 1991 it had become one of the more cosmopolitan destinations in the Baltics, with its world class symphony, its thriving tourist business, and even a burgeoning fashion market.

Aleks had driven the E20 route to Narva, in central Estonia, past the rusting relics of Soviet occupation, past the ramshackle buildings, failed collectives, the rusting cars and farm machinery, the slag heaps and stilled conveyor belts.

He then took a small commuter plane from Narva to Tallinn, which meant he'd had to leave a good many things behind. These days, even in small airports, on small airlines, security was quite rigorous.

It was not a problem. He had connections all over Estonia. And he had business. A business that had been a smoldering ember in his heart for four years.

The Schlössle was a small elegant boutique hotel in the heart of the old town. Aleks checked in. He showered, shaved, dressed in a dark suit, open-collar, starched white shirt. He called the concierge, arranged for a table at the Restaurant Stenhus.

He had three hours before he had to meet Paulu. Before then, he had to make a purchase.

The shop was an old stone front on busy Müürivahe Street. The small leaded glass window facing the street offered an elegant display, a single sterling silver place setting, washed with a mini-spotlight. In the lower left-hand corner was a hand-painted sign, lettered in gold leaf:

VILLEROY TERARIISTAD

To the right of the thick oaken door was a brushed-chrome panel with a small button. Aleks pressed the button. Moments later the door buzzed softly. He stepped inside.

The interior was long and narrow and quiet, with gleaming glass display cases on both sides, an elevated counter at the rear. It smelled of polished wood, glass cleaner, and the sharp redolence of honing oils. As Aleks made his way to the rear he surveyed the merchandise. The knives were from all over the world, in all manner of styles – hunting knives, stockmen's knives, Indian kukri. The display case on the right held more exotic wares. Here there were boot knives, diving knives, tanto and throwing knives, the showy but deadly butterfly knife, even a section devoted to neck knives, which were designed to be worn in a sheath around one's neck.

On the walls were racks of gleaming scissors, kitchen cutlery, straight razors, and other tonsorial wares. Overhead, reaching toward the center of the aisle, in the fashion of a trellis, was a dazzling display of swords – military, ninja, medieval and Viking, as well as samurai katana.

As he reached the rear of the shop a man stood and emerged from behind the counter. He was in his sixties, with pewter grey hair, sloping shoulders. He was at least a head shorter than Aleks's six-three, and meticulously dressed in charcoal woolen slacks, white broadcloth shirt, and highly polished oxfords. The ring on his left hand said he was married. The signet on his right hand said he was an alumnus of Moscow University.

"Kas sa räägid inglise keelt?" Aleks asked, inquiring in Estonian if the gentleman spoke English. Aleks was fluent in five different languages, including Russian, German and French.

The man nodded, folded his hands expectantly on the counter.

"You have an impressive selection here," Aleks said.

"Thank you," the man replied. "And how may I be of assistance today?"

"I am looking for a knife, something suitable for both city and forest. Something of great utility."

The man thought for a moment. He gestured to his left. "I'm sure we will have something to please you." He walked behind the counter, reached beneath the glass, removed a display rack. There, presented on a rich burgundy velvet, were a half dozen folding knives. Aleks lifted them one by one, feeling their weight, their balance. He opened them all, trying the action. After giving them their due, he replaced them.

"All fine quality," Aleks said. "But I am looking for something special."

The man returned the rack beneath the case, glanced at Aleks. "I am intrigued."

"I am looking for a Barhydt."

The man drew a quick breath in reaction, recovered. "I see."

Jan-Marie Barhydt was a limited edition armorer from Holland, an artisan of the first order. He produced some of the finest and most sought after knives in the world.

"I'm afraid this is something quite expensive," the man said. "We are a small, humble shop. We don't carry these items."

The dance, Aleks thought. Always the dance. He held the man's gaze for a moment, then reached into his pocket and removed three money clips, each clasped around a stack of different currency. Euros, US dollars, and Estonian kroon. He placed the three stacks on the counter, like an expensive shell game.

For a few moments, no words were spoken. The man glanced briefly toward the door, and the street beyond. They were indeed alone. He placed his right forefinger on the stack of euros. Aleks put the other currencies away, unclipped the bills. He counted off 3,000 euros, roughly 4,500 US dollars. "If one of these items were to be available here," Aleks said, "would this be adequate compensation?"

The man's eyes flashed for a moment. "It most certainly would," he said. "Would you excuse me?"

"Of course."

The man disappeared into a back room, emerged moments later. In his hand was a beautiful walnut case. He opened it. Inside was a thing of beauty, a stunning specimen of craftsmanship. The blade was hot-blued Damascus, as were the bolsters. The scales were premium white mother of pearl, the titanium liners were anodized purple, the back bar was inlayed with four pieces of abalone. It was an authentic Barhydt.

"I shall have this," Aleks said.

"Very good, sir." The man brought the box to the rear of the store. He slipped the polished case into a felt bag, drew closed the gold twine. Moments later he walked around the counter carrying a handled shopping bag with VILLEROY TERARIISTAD on the side. He handed the bag to Aleks.

Before leaving, Aleks looked at his watch, a gold Piaget he wore on his left wrist, the crystal facing in. Being a purveyor of fine things, Aleks knew the man's eye would be drawn to the timepiece. What Aleks wanted the man to note was not the expensive piece of jewelry, but rather the elaborate tattoo on Aleks's wrist, the black star peeking out from beneath his shirt cuff.

When Aleks glanced up at the man, the man was looking at him directly. Aleks did not have to say a further word.

There was no box, no bag. There was no Barhydt. No money had changed hands, no commerce had been conducted. In fact, the tall man with the pale blue eyes and small ragged scar on his left cheek was never there.

Paulu was *vennaskond*, a fellow thief. But *vennaskond* were not merely thieves, they were brothers, and adhered to a strict code. Steal from one, you steal from all. A *vennaskond* was never without someone at his back.

In his early thirties, Paulu was slight of build, but quite

robust, with fast movements and a nervous energy that never allowed him to keep still. He had grown up in the city and was therefore never at peace, never at rest. He wore his black hair straight back. A pair of gold hoops ringed his right ear lobe. He displayed his tattoos with unabashed pride on his forearms and neck.

They met on a secluded section of the western shore of Lake Ülemiste, just a few miles south of Tallinn city center. The main airport was on the eastern side, and every few minutes another plane roared overhead. The two men spoke in Estonian.

"When will he arrive?" Aleks asked.

"Eleven. They say he is quite punctual."

"What did you tell him?"

"Not much," Paulu said. "I told him you have a daughter, a daughter who is pregnant with the child of a Lithuanian. I told him you were in the market to sell the baby."

"And you are certain he is the man who made the deal to sell my Anna and Marya?"

Paulu nodded. "Through his minions, he made the deal. He has been in the black market for children for many years."

"Why haven't I found him before?"

"He is expensive and secretive. There are many people afraid of him, too. I had to meet with three other men first. I had to pay them all."

This angered Aleks, but he pushed the feeling back. Now was not the time for anger. "He will come alone?"

Paulu smiled. "Yes. He is this arrogant."

Ten minutes later, bright headlights split the darkness. A vehicle topped the hill; a candy red American SUV with chrome wheels. The sound system blasted Russian rap.

Another gaudy *vory*, Aleks thought.

"That is him," Paulu said.

Aleks reached into his pocket, pulled out a rubber-banded

roll of euros. He handed it to Paulu, who pocketed the roll without looking at it.

"Where do you want me?" Paulu asked.

Aleks nodded to the hill to the west. "Give this five minutes. Then go."

The smaller man hugged Aleks once – a man he had never met before this night, a man to whom he was bound in ways even deeper than blood – then slipped onto his motorcycle. Moments later he was gone. Aleks knew he would watch from the nearby hill much longer than five minutes. This was the *vennaskond* way.

When Paulu's bike was out of sight, the SUV cut its lights. The man soon emerged. The Finn was big, nearly as tall as Aleks, but soft in the middle. He wore a tan duster, cowboy boots. He had thinning ice white hair to his shoulders, a yeasty, wattled neck. He wore red wraparounds at night. He would be slow.

His name was Mikko Vänskä.

Vänskä smelled of American cologne and French cigarettes.

"You are Mr Tamm?" he asked. *Tamm* was Estonian for *oak*. They both knew it was not a real name.

Aleks nodded. They shook hands cordially, lightly. The distaste between them was thicker than the smell of spent airplane fuel in the air.

"I understand you have something to sell," Vänskä said.

Some*thing*, Aleks thought. This was how this man thought of the children, of Anna and Marya, as if they were objects, some sort of commodity. He wanted to kill him right there and then.

Vänskä reached inside his coat, extracted a pack of Gitanes, put one between his lips. He then took out a gold lighter, lit the cigarette, drew on it deeply. All quite dramatic and unimpressive. All leading up to a discussion of money.

"There are many expenses on my end," Vänskä began, as expected.

Aleks just nodded, remained silent.

"I have traveled a good distance to be here, and there are a number of people – highly placed people – who must be paid." At this, Mikko Vänskä removed his sunglasses. His face was bone-pale, with dark smudges beneath his eyes. He was a drug addict. Aleks surmised meth.

"What is your profession?" Vänskä asked.

"I am a farrier," Aleks replied. While it was true that he shod his own horses, there was something in the tone of his reply that told Vänskä it was not exactly the truth. The man ran his hand through his greasy white hair. He looked out over the lake, then back.

"You do not have a child to sell at all, do you?"

Aleks just stared at the man. It was answer enough.

Vänskä nodded. He smiled, crushed out his cigarette with the toe of his boot. He used the movement to slide back the hem of his coat. The move was not lost on Aleks.

"Do you know who I am?" Vänskä asked.

"I do."

The man shifted his weight. Aleks relaxed his massive shoulder muscles, poised to strike. "And yet you waste my time. You do not do this with Mikko Vänskä. Tallinn is *my* city. You will learn this."

Aleks knew it was pointless trying to finesse men like Vänskä. They looked at him as if he were some sort of rube, a provincial from south-eastern Estonia. "Let us just say it is a tragic character flaw."

Mikko laughed, a raspy sound that echoed among the trees. "I am going to leave now," he said. "But not until you pay me for my time. And my time is very expensive."

"I think not."

Vänskä looked up. It was clear he did not hear this sentiment often. Before he could make a move or a reply, Aleks had the man off his feet, face down on the muddy earth, the air punched from his lungs. An instant later Aleks had the man's weapon removed from the holster at the small of his back. It was an expensive SIG P210. He continued to pat him down, found nothing else. He lifted the dazed Vänskä back up to his feet.

"The question now is, my Finnish friend," Aleks began, his face just a few inches from Vänskä's, "do you know who *I* am?"

A tic in the man's lower lip betrayed his fear. He remained silent as he caught his breath.

"I am Koschei," Aleks said.

The man smirked, then realized that Aleks was serious, and probably insane. This made him twice as dangerous.

"This is a myth," Vänskä said. "Koschei the Deathless. A tale for children and old women."

Aleks lifted the SIG, chambered a round. He handed it back to Vänskä. Vänskä took it in a snap, leveled it at Aleks, his hands shaking. "Fuck you, *vittu!* You do not come to Tallinn and talk this way to me. You do not lay your fucking *hands* on me."

Aleks shrugged, took a backward step. "Then you have no choice but to shoot me. I understand."

"*What?*"

Aleks slapped Vänskä across the face. Hard. So hard the man stumbled back a few steps. His lower lip began to bleed. Hands trembling violently now, Vänskä cocked the weapon.

Again Aleks slapped the man; this time a rotted tooth flew from Vänskä's mouth. Vänskä put the gun to Aleks's forehead and pulled the trigger.

Instead of a loud report, there was only the small, impotent echo of metal on metal. The weapon had jammed.

For a moment, Tallinn fell silent. No traffic, no airplanes.

Just the sound of the water lapping onto the shore of Lake Ülemiste.

With lightning speed, Aleks lashed out with his left hand, striking the man just beneath the solar plexus. Vänskä dropped the weapon, clutched his heaving stomach. A gush of yellow vomit flew from his mouth. Aleks picked up the SIG and threw it into the lake.

When Vänskä caught his breath, Aleks slipped the Barhydt out of its sheath, opened it to its fearsome length. Vänskä's eyes bulged at the sight. Aleks touched a finger to the perfect steel. It seemed to disappear in the blackness of the night.

"You should know this about me, Mikko Vänskä. I am a man who asks a question just one time. I will ask you a question. You will tell me the truth. Then we will part company."

Vänskä tried to stand tall. His shaking knees prevented this. He remained silent.

"Four years ago, just before Easter, you brokered the illegal adoption of two newborn Estonian girls," Aleks said. "The girls were stolen from their mother's bed in Ida-Viru County. All this I know to be true. Who was your contact on the other end?"

"I don't know what you're talking about."

Aleks brought the knife up with a movement so fast it seemed a mere distortion of air. At first, Vänskä did not know what happened. A second later, it was all too clear. The man in front of him had slit open his left eye. Vänskä fell to his knees, blood gushing between his fingers, his shrieks echoing across the ancient hills. Aleks knelt, covered the man's mouth. The snarl of another jet soon covered the screams.

"A man can live with just one eye, yes?" Aleks asked when the roar had trailed to silence. "He cannot live without his heart." Aleks held the tip of the blade over the man's chest.

"A man," he said. His breath came in small, wet gasps. His face was spider-webbed with blood. "His name is Harkov. Viktor Harkov."

"A Russian?"

Vänskä nodded.

"He is in Russia?"

The man shook his head. Blood flicked from the open wound. "He is in New York City."

The United States, Aleks thought. He had never imagined this. Anna and Marya were now American children. It would take a lot to undo this. And getting them out presented a whole new set of problems. "New York City is a big place," Aleks said. "Where is he in this city?"

For a moment it appeared as if Vänskä was going to go into shock. Aleks cracked an ammonia capsule beneath his nose. The man choked, took a deep breath. "He is in a place called Queens, New York City."

Queens, Aleks thought. He knew someone in New York City, a man named Konstantine Udenko, a man with whom he had served in the federal army. Konstantine would help him find this Viktor Harkov.

For a moment Aleks studied Vänskä's face, or what was visible beneath the gloss of fresh blood. He believed him. He had little choice. He put his gloved hands under the man's chin, stared into his remaining eye. "You told me what I needed to know, and I now consider you to be a wise and honorable man. I am going to let you live." Aleks brought his face close. "But I want you to tell your associates of me, of this man from Kolossova who is to be taken seriously, a man who cannot be killed. You will do this?"

Another slow nod.

"Good." Aleks helped the man to his feet. The man was heavy, and offered no aid, but Aleks's arms and back were powerful. He handled him with ease. "Which is the nearest hospital?"

Vänskä hesitated. He had not expected this. "West Tallinn Central. On Ravi Street."

"I have a car," Aleks said. He pointed to the crest of the hill. "Just around the bend. I will take you. Do you know the way?"

"Yes."

"Can you walk?"

The man took a few moments, found his center. "I . . . I think so."

Aleks glanced over Vänskä's shoulder. He saw the moon reflecting off the glassy surface of Lake Ülemiste. He recalled the way the Narva River shimmered on warm summer nights in his youth, glimpsed from the window of his stifling stone room in the orphanage, how he had always wondered what lay at either end.

He thought about his little girls, about this man in front of him. The wrath ignited within him as . . .

. . . *the acrid smell of burning flesh hangs over Grozny, a damp, red blanket of death. In this hellish moment, as death rattles around him, he feels his destiny, the centuries he has lived, the centuries yet to come. He sees the farmhouse at the top of the hill. He hears the cries of the dying animals and . . .*

. . . the man's arrogant words.

You have something to sell?

Aleks turned. In one nimble motion, he spun 360 degrees, the torque of the movement, combined with his strong legs and back muscles – as well as the exquisite steel of the Barhydt – caught Mikko Vänskä just below his jaw, nearly severing his head from his body. The arterial spray launched nearly ten feet as the man chicken-stepped. Aleks then plunged the knife deep into the man's groin, bringing it up with great strength. He pulled it out and finished with a lateral slash forming a T.

Vänskä's bowels spilled into the night, pink and black and foul as the man himself. He was dead before he hit the ground. Steam rose from the ropy entrails.

Aleks took a moment, closed his eyes, sensing the man's soul on its journey. He always gave this moment its due. In the distance, in the silent canopies of the forest, a murder of crows stirred, awaiting its moment.

Ten minutes later Aleks walked to his car, and drove back to the center of the city. Tallinn was coming alive, and he would take full advantage of its charms.

Harkov, he thought. *Viktor Harkov of Queens, New York City. I will meet you very soon.*

The next morning Aleks awoke early, showered, dressed casually. He had rolled Mikko Vänskä into a large canvas tarpaulin, weighted his body with stones, and sank him in Lake Ülemiste. It would only be days before the man floated to the surface, but by then Aleks would be long gone.

Over breakfast, he logged onto the Internet and began to plan his week. He purchased an e-ticket to New York. He made arrangements for lodging in New York, and arranged to ship what he could not bring with him – including the Barhydt, and more than one hundred thousand US dollars in cash – via International FedEx. He returned to his room, packed everything into a FedEx box, and dropped it off with the concierge.

He may not have been at home in the city, but he availed himself of every progress, every advancement. Laptops, cellphones, wi-fi, online banking.

Over his final cup of coffee he searched the web for Viktor Harkov. He found him with ease. Viktor Harkov, Esq., was the owner of a firm called People's Legal Services. He printed off the information at the hotel's business center, making sure he erased all files and the cache from the hotel's computer. He slipped the data into his carry-on bag.

During a layover in London's Heathrow Airport Terminal Five – while luxuriating in the British Airways Terraces lounge, the area set aside for those traveling business class – Aleks allowed himself a massage in the Elemis spa.

Three hours later he sat in the section of the lounge overlooking his gate, a tumbler of Johnnie Walker Black in hand. He glanced down, saw Elena's face swim up from the depths of the clear amber liquid. He recalled the first time he saw her, standing in the grove where he had seen the grey wolf, already an *ennustaja* of her village at the age of seven.

He wondered: would Anna and Marya look like Elena? Would they have the same beguiling blue eyes, the same milky skin?

He reached into the breast pocket of his suit coat. He took out the three crystal vials held on an exquisite gold chain. One of the vials was filled with blood. Two were empty. He slipped the chain around his neck.

Three girls, Aleks thought. *The legend of Koschei and the prince's sisters. Anna, Marya, and Olga. When all their blood was at long last his, they would live forever.*

He looked out the window at the lights of Heathrow's runways. Cities, he thought. How he hated them, and all that they have spawned. Now he was heading to the most important city in the world.

An hour later he settled into his seat on the plane, the power within him beginning to grow.

She was petite and pretty, with a generous mouth and slender, boyish hips. She wore a stiff white blouse, navy skirt. She seemed to be in her late thirties, although her hands suggested she might be older.

"Can I get you something?"

They had been airborne for two hours, served a gourmet meal. The crew had dimmed the lights.

Aleks looked around the Club World cabin of the large, powerful Boeing 747-400. He knew all too well about societal divisions in life. The small group who had stood in a separate, fast-moving line at Heathrow, the select few who had been welcomed aboard with a warm towel and glass of champagne, looked at each other with an understanding that they were all in this together, a cut above those who traveled coach, chosen all.

Aleks glanced back at the woman. She was not a flight attendant. She was a fellow passenger. "I'm sorry?"

She pointed over her shoulder, spoke in a hushed voice. "From the kitchen. Club World passengers have access to the galley, you know. Would you like some juice, or a glass of wine?" She held up her own empty glass.

What a world, Aleks thought. Your own kitchen on a plane. "I'm fine, thank you."

The woman eyed the seat next to Aleks. Business class had individual seats, side by side, facing in opposite directions. The seats flattened into beds, and could be fashioned into dozens of positions. The seat next to Aleks was unoccupied. The woman clearly wanted to sit and chat for a while.

"My name is Jilliane," she said, extending a hand.

Aleks smiled a disingenuous smile. He was traveling under one of his three passports. This identity was Jorgen Petterson. He introduced himself, carefully crafting his accent.

"My friends call me George," Aleks added. When it was clear the woman was not going to leave, he gestured to the seat next to him. Before she sat down, she picked up the small pile of papers Aleks had put there. He had meant to put them back in his bag. He must have dozed off.

Jilliane arranged herself on the seat, smiled. Despite the dim light, Aleks could see her teeth were white and even. She had dimples, a flawless complexion. She glanced around the cabin, back.

"This is all quite posh, isn't it?" she said. Aleks could smell the sweet-sour breath of alcohol.

"Yes."

She tapped a manicured nail against her wine glass, perhaps searching for a portal into the conversation. "Do you travel to New York often, George?"

Questions, Aleks thought. He had to be vigilant. If he said he came to New York often, she may ask him other questions. "This is my first time."

Jilliane nodded. "I remember my first time in the city. It can be a bit overwhelming. I live there now, but I grew up in Indiana."

"I see." Aleks was beginning to regret asking her to sit down.

Before she could respond, she pointed at the swing-out table on Aleks's side of the partition. "What are these?"

She was referring to a pair of marble eggs sitting on the table. The eggs were actual size, intricately carved to depict the ancient Russian legend of an egg inside a duck inside a hare, the fable of Koschei the Deathless. Aleks had had them carved in Kaliningrad. He had forgotten to put them back into his carry-on bag. He wished the woman had not seen them. It was a mistake.

"These are for my precious *brorsdotter,*" he said. "For Easter."

Jilliane looked puzzled.

"I'm sorry," Aleks said. "They are for my nieces. I am from a town called Karlskrona. It's in south-eastern Sweden."

Jilliane picked up one of the eggs, a little mystified. She put it down, getting to the point. "Do you like music, George?"

"Very much," Aleks said. "I play a little."

Her eyes lighted. "Really? What do you play?"

Aleks waved a dismissive hand. "My instrument is the flute. I kneel a thousand feet below Gaubert and Barrère."

"Oh, I'll bet you're just as good as those guys.''

Those guys. He remained silent.

"What about jazz?"

"I am quite a fan," Aleks said. "Chet Baker, Charlie Parker, Oscar Peterson. There is not that much to choose from for the flute, but I have played some of Charles Lloyd's arrangements. To no great acclaim, I'm afraid."

Jilliane nodded. She didn't know Charles Lloyd from Lloyd's of London. She hesitated for a moment, looked over her shoulder, back. Most of the cabin was asleep.

"Look, there's this jazz place I go to, not too far from where I live. I think you'd like it a lot." She took her pen out, and grabbed a cocktail napkin off his tray. "They play a lot of jazz like Kenny G."

My God, Aleks thought. *Jazz like Kenny G.*

She whispered, "I'm free all weekend, George."

She gave him her number.

Long after Aleks had spirited the napkin away, and Jilliane had returned to her seat, he glanced at his watch. They were somewhere over the Atlantic.

He wondered what Konstantine would look like. The last time he had seen the man he had been standing over the body of a Chechen soldier, the dead man's heart in one hand, a half-eaten pomegranate in the other. If one did not know Konstantine, it might have looked as if he was eating human flesh.

Aleks *did* know him, and it was entirely possible.

He settled into his seat, the thoughts of his past set aside. For now, he slept.

Five hours later he awoke from a dream, a vision of Estonia, a fantasy of sun sparkling on the river, of yellow flowers in the valley, of children running through the pines. *His* children.

Moments later, the jet began its slow descent to JFK International Airport.

FIVE

Abby Roman stared at the young man in disbelief. He looked about nineteen or so, drove a tricked-out Escalade with tinted windows, spinner hubcaps, and a vanity plate that read YO DREAM. A real class act. He looked a little threatening, sitting high in the SUV, but that was just part of the white boy thug routine. Abby glanced at the girls. They were in the back seat of the Acura, still strapped in. They were both listening to audiobooks that Michael had downloaded onto their new iPods. Charlotte was lost in *A Bear Called Paddington*. Emily was giggling at something called *Alexander and the Terrible, Horrible, No Good, Very Bad Day*. The windows were rolled up. They wouldn't hear anything, if there was anything to hear.

Let it go or stand down, Abby?

She glanced at her watch. She had forty-eight hours off at the clinic, and at least sixty hours of things to do, but that had never stopped her from getting in the face of some asshole.

Not yet, anyway.

She may have grown up in Westchester County, she may have had a horse named Pablo — named after Neruda, of course, not Picasso — and studied ballet at the Broadway Dance Center, but she had spent nearly ten years in the city, all of them as an ER nurse, and there was a principle at work here.

She pulled the handbrake, and got out of the car.

When the kid emerged from the Escalade he turned out to be about five-four – baggy jeans, T-shirt, backwards Mets cap. *The bigger the SUV*, Abby thought. He clicked the remote-control lock button on his key ring, locking the Cadillac with a toot of the horn. Just one more thing to endear him. He turned to do his pimp-roll into the market, staring at his cellphone, God's gift in a pair of Nike Jordan Six Rings.

"Excuse me," Abby said, at least twice as loud as necessary.

The kid glanced over, pulled the earbuds from his ears. He looked at her, then to his left and his right. She could only be talking to him. "Yeah?"

"Got a question for you."

The kid looked her up and down now, perhaps realizing that, for a woman around thirty, she was in pretty good shape, and maybe, just maybe, he was going to hook up here. He half-smiled, raised his eyebrows in anticipation. "Sure."

"Are you fucking *crazy*?"

Exit the smile. Exit most of the blood from his face. He backed up an inch. "Excuse me?"

"You did that for a parking space?"

For a moment the kid resembled not so much a deer in the headlights, but a deer that had just been run over. "Did what?"

"Endangered my *life*. The lives of my *children*." A little dramatic, Abby realized, but so what.

The kid glanced at the Acura, at the girls. "What . . . what are you talking about?"

Abby took a deep breath, tried to calm herself. This kid was completely clueless, as expected. She put her hands on her hips. "All right," she said. "One more question."

Another step back. Silence.

"When was the last time you saw me?" Abby asked.

The kid did some kind of ape-math in his head. Apparently,

he came up with nothing. "I've never seen you before in my life."

Abby moved in, her finger out front. "Pre*cisely* my point. I was about to turn into that space and you jammed into it right in front of me. You didn't even look. You didn't even *see* me." Abby clocked it up now, the angel of death on a tear. "You're so caught up in your damn MP3, cellphone, text message, Jay Z gangsta-wannabe world, you can't see anything past the end of your fucking 37th Avenue Serengeti knock-offs."

The kid looked at the ground. So they *were* fake. He looked up. "What . . . what do you want me to do about it?"

"I want you to move your truck."

The kid grimaced. Abby knew the word *truck* would get under his skin.

"It's not a truck. It's an Escalade."

Wow, Abby thought. An Escalade driver with attitude. How rare. "Whatever. I want you to get inside, start it, and move it."

The kid looked around. There were no parking spaces for about a hundred feet in any direction. "Where should I go?"

Abby glared her answer at him, as in, *who gives a shit?*

For a second, the kid looked like he was going to stand his ground. He glanced at the front window of the Acura. On the dashboard was a parking permit for the Queens County DA's office, a large rectangle of laminated plastic that, despite the mayor's efforts to curtail, generally allowed ticket-free parking on everything up to and including sidewalks.

The kid glanced at his laceless Nikes for a moment, weighing the options. He conceded. He pressed the button, unlocked the car, and with a movement somewhat slower than the glacier that had carved out the Niagara Escarpment, rolled back, and slipped inside. Driving down the aisle he executed his gangster lean, gave Abby one final glance in the rear-view mirror but did not — as Abby had expected — give her the finger. Obviously, he still had to go inside the store, and was not quite prepared for Round Two. Besides, who would get Mom's nutmeg if he left?

Abby got in her car, pulled into the spot, the thought of NEW YORK AXIOM #208 giving her a warm feeling all over, that being:

Parking spaces fought over are much sweeter than parking spaces earned.

She unbuckled her seatbelt, checked her purse, making sure she had her wallet. Before she could open her door there was a query from the back seat. It was Emily.

"Mom?"

Abby turned around. Both girls had the earbuds out of their ears, and their iPods turned off. How did they learn these things so quickly?

"Yes, sweetie?"

"Who was that boy?"

Abby had to laugh. *Boy*.

God she loved her girls.

The city was every photograph he had ever seen, every film, every song, every postcard. Aleks had taken a cab from JFK Airport to a section of midtown Manhattan called Murray Hill.

If he had been a tourist, he could see himself taking in the wonders of New York for a week or more. He looked at the booklet. The UN Building, Grand Central Station, the Statue of Liberty, Central Park, the Flatiron Building, the Guggenheim Museum. There was much to see.

But he was not a tourist. He had business here. The most important business of his life.

*

The Senzai Hotel was located at East Thirty-Eighth Street and Park Avenue. The pictures on the website had not done the place justice. The floor was marble, the ceilings were high, the brass appointments were subdued. Before leaving Tallinn, Aleks had had his hair cut at the airport salon. He knew that all styles were served in a city like New York, and it would take something pretty outrageous to stand out, but he did not want to take any chances. At just over six-foot three, with shoulder-length sandy hair, dressed all in black, he might attract some attention. So now he looked like a tall European businessman in town for a meeting. In many ways, this was true.

He checked in. The girl behind the desk was Japanese, about twenty-five. She had small streaks of gold in her lustrous black hair.

She greeted him warmly, moved with grace and efficiency, an attention to detail Aleks had not only anticipated but expected. It was one of the many things he admired about Japanese culture, another being how much was expressed in a non-verbal way. He sometimes lived in silence for weeks at a time, and he appreciated this.

After running his credit card, she asked after his immediate needs. In his best Japanese – which was quite meager, the product of a brief study he had made before visiting Tokyo on R & R in the federal army – he told her he was fine for the moment. She smiled again, pushed forward his electronic key. He took it with a slight bow, which was returned, and headed toward the elevators. Before he had taken two steps the concierge approached and told him that a FedEx package had arrived for him, and that it would soon be brought up to his room. He tipped the man, and took the elevator to the eighth floor, slid his electronic key into the lock, and entered his suite.

The room was small, but tastefully appointed. In the closet

were slippers, a pair of terry cloth robes, an umbrella. He had selected the hotel for a number of reasons, not the least of which was that it featured a rooftop garden.

After he unpacked, there was a knock at the door. A bellman handed him his package.

Aleks tipped the young man, locked and chained the door. He flipped on the television – it seemed to be some sort of show where people were locked in a house with each other, people who seemed to hate each other – and opened the box. Everything was intact. He removed the pair of passports, the cash, the Barhydt from its bubble-wrap cocoon.

After a shower, he dressed for the day, then took the elevator to the roof.

Although far from the tallest building in sight, the view was nonetheless exhilarating. He had been in a number of cities, but was never inclined to follow the tourist route, visiting the observation decks of the Eiffel Tower or the Triumph-Palace in Moscow or Frankfurt's Commerzbank Tower. The view from above did not interest him. It was the view into a man's eyes that told him everything he needed to know.

Stepping to the edge of the roof, a rush of warm air greeted him. Below the traffic on Park Avenue hummed. To the left was the massive Grand Central Station, a legendary place about which he had read and heard his whole life. So far, New York seemed rife with legend.

He glanced around the rooftop and, seeing he was alone, opened his flute case, lifted the instrument to his lips, and began to play "Mereschitsja" from Rimsky-Korsakov's *Kashchey the Immortal,* pianissimo at first, then building to a crescendo. The notes lifted into the morning air, and drifted over the rooftops. When finished, he returned the instrument to its leather case, glanced around the rooftop once more. He was still alone. He took out the Barhydt, touched the razor-sharp tip of the blade to his right forefinger. A glossy drop of blood appeared.

Aleks tilted his finger just as the breeze died down. The drop of blood fell toward the street, disappearing into the rushing city below, forever marking this place as one with him. It was his ritual, to stain the battlefield with his blood. He knew that, in this place, some were going to die. He owed them this, to mingle his blood with theirs.

"I will find you, my hearts," he said, closing the knife. "I am here."

The Stop & Shop on Tall Pines Boulevard was crowded with locals stocking up for the long weekend. As always, the girls insisted on pushing the cart. They lined up, each grabbing a portion of the handle and, as Abby watched them roll down the produce aisle, she realized that it wasn't so long ago that they couldn't even move the cart a foot without help. Now they did it with ease.

Abby clicked off the items on her list, with Charlotte and Emily on point, gathering things from the lower shelves.

As they waited at the deli counter, Abby noticed that both girls were humming a song, a song that sounded vaguely familiar. Was it a classical theme? Was it on the audiobooks they were listening to? She couldn't put her finger on the tune, but it sounded so melancholy, so wistful, that she suddenly felt a chilly shiver of disquiet. It seemed a portent to something, although she had no idea what.

Abby shifted her attention to the Muzak. It wasn't anything classical. It was an instrumental version of an old Billy Joel song.

"What are you guys singing?" Abby asked.

The girls stared up at her, and for a moment they looked as if they were disengaged from the present, as if they were not in a store at all, but rather rapt by another moment. They both shrugged.

"Did you guys hear it on the radio or on your iPods?"

They both shook their heads. A moment later they seemed to snap out of whatever mini-trance they were in.

"Can we get macaroni and cheese?" Charlotte asked, suddenly brightening. She wasn't talking about the Kraft variety. She was talking about the prepared kind. This store had an amazing prepared food section, and offered a three-cheddar ziti. Lately, it seemed, Abby was taking full advantage of the prepared food counters. She wanted to cook for her family every night – she really did – but it was so much easier to buy it already made.

"Sure," Abby said. "Em? Mac and cheese okay?"

Emily just shrugged. The girls were so different in many ways. Charlotte was the schemer. Emily floated.

They got their cereal (Captain Crunch for Charlotte, Cheerios for Emily); their peanut butter (smooth and crunchy respectively), their bread (they both agreed on multigrain for some reason; Michael thought it tasted like tree bark).

While they waited in line, Abby cruised the tabloids.

"Can we get Peppermint Patties?" Emily asked.

Abby wanted to say no. But how could she resist all *four* of the prettiest blue eyes in the world? Sometimes the magic was too strong to resist.

"Okay," Abby said. "But just one each. And you can't eat them until after dinner tonight. Okay?"

"Okay," in tandem. They took off for the candy aisle. A minute later they returned. Emily carried the goods. She put them in the cart. There were three Peppermint Patties.

Again with the three, Abby thought.

"Sweetie, I said one each," Abby said. She picked up one of the candy bars. "Did you bring this one for me?"

No answer.

"Okay, let's get one more," Abby said. "One for Daddy. Then we'll have enough for all of us."

It seemed like this was getting to be a standard routine and speech. It wasn't like the girls were leaving out Michael in the equation. Abby had watched them interact with other kids many times. They were always generous with whatever they had to share. This was an early lesson from both her and Michael.

On the other hand, the girls were only four. She couldn't expect them to be math wizards yet.

The Eden Falls Free Library was a small, ivy-laced brick building near the river, a Mid-Hudson design that also was home to the Crane County Community Theater.

Despite the fact that the girls were getting somewhat proficient at the computer, Abby was scared to death of leaving them alone online. So, at least once a week, time permitting, she took them to an honest-to-God, brick-and-mortar library. She had spent a great deal of time at the Hyde Park Library as a girl, and she would not deny the experience to the girls. There was something about the feel and smell and heft of books that no computer monitor could supply. Neither Charlotte nor Emily ever wanted to go. An hour later, neither wanted to leave.

As the girls settled into the children's section, Abby heard an EMS siren approaching the library. As a trained RN, it caught her attention. It had always been so. From the time she was a child, she had been expected to go to medical school, to follow in her father's footsteps and become a surgeon. Dr Charles Reed knew his son Wallace did not have the discipline or temperament for heart surgery, or even the rigors of residency, but felt his only daughter did.

Abby had gotten as far as her freshman year in pre-med at

Columbia when, one night, on an icy sidewalk in the East Village, she slipped and broke her wrist. While being treated in the emergency room at New York-Presbyterian Hospital, she watched the ER nurses in action, and knew that this was what she wanted to do, to work the front lines of medical care. Part of her had to admit that she knew it would get under her father's skin, but when she switched over to the Columbia School of Nursing, she knew she had made the right decision. It took Charles Reed most of the ensuing thirteen or so years to get over it, if he ever did.

As the EMS ambulance passed the library, Abby flashed on the night, five years earlier, when she met Michael.

She had been on for almost twelve hours that day. The ER wasn't busier than usual — that night there had been only one gunshot victim, along with a handful of domestics, including one that had ended in the husband, a fifty-nine-year old man who apparently had received a Westinghouse steam iron to the side of his head for saying to his wife, as a prelude to sex: "Yo, fatso, get *with* it."

At midnight an EMS arrived at the door. As they wheeled in the unconscious patient, the paramedic looked into Abby's eyes, his post 9/11 thousand-yard stare in place.

"Bomb," the paramedic said softly.

All kinds of things raced through Abby's mind. All of it terrifying. Her first thought was that the city had been attacked again, and this was just the first of the victims. She wondered how bad it was going to get. As the other two nurses on duty prepped a room, Abby stepped into the waiting room. She flipped the television channel to CNN. Two guys yelling at each other about the mortgage crisis. No attack.

When she stepped into the triage room, she saw him.

Michael Roman, the man who would become her husband, the love of her life, supine on the gurney, his face powdered with black ash, his eyes closed. She checked his vitals. Steady pulse, strong BP reading. She studied his face, his strong jaw, his fair complexion and sandy hair, now coated.

Moments later he opened his eyes, and her life changed forever.

In the end he had a slight concussion, a small laceration on the back of his right hand. Days later, when Abby saw the photographs of the car bombing, and what it had done to the nearby building, she, like everyone else, was amazed that he wasn't killed on the spot.

The siren faded into the distance. Abby glanced at her watch, then over at the children.

The girls were gone.

Abby sprang to her feet. She walked over to the children's section, looking behind all the low stacks, the festive displays for books on Easter and Passover. She stepped into the ladies restroom. No Charlotte, no Emily. She went down to the lower level, the section that had the DVDs and CDs. Sometimes she and the girls picked out movies here in the Family section. There she found four children, none of them her own. Quickening her pace, she returned to the ground floor, and was just about to speak to one of the library assistants when she looked down one of the long stacks in the adult section and saw them.

Her heart found its way back into her chest. The girls were sitting side by side, at the end of the stack of books. They had a large, coffee-table sized volume across their laps. Abby walked down the aisle.

"Hey, ladies."

They looked up at her.

"You guys shouldn't run off like that. Mommy got a little worried."

"We're sorry," Charlotte said.

"What are you reading?" Abby got down on the floor with the girls. She sat between them, took the book from Emily. She glanced at the cover.

Russian Folk Tales and Legends.

"Where did you find this?" Abby asked.

Emily pointed to the bottom shelf of a nearby stack.

Abby returned to the page at which the girls had been looking. On the left was a large color plate, an intricate woodcut of a fairy tale figure, a tall, skeletal man with a pointed chin, rabid eyes, and gnarled fingers. He wore a black velvet robe and tarnished crown. To the right was an index to stories about Koschei the Deathless. Abby skimmed the next few pages, a little unnerved.

There were a number of variations on the legend, it seemed. One version included a prince and a grey wolf; another was about a firebird. One thing they agreed upon, though, was that Koschei was an evil man who terrorized the countryside, primarily young women, and could not be killed by conventional means. This was because his soul was separate from his body. As long as his soul was safe, he could not die. Except for one way, according to one of the variations. If he was stabbed in the head with a needle, it would be curtains for the big ugly guy. But only if the needle was broken.

Nice kid's story, Abby thought. Right up there with *Charlotte's Web.*

The good news was that her daughters couldn't yet read.

Back in the car, heading home, Abby realized she couldn't get the melody the girls had been humming at the grocery store out of her head. She knew it – recalled the piece of music the way you sometimes remember a face, like a person who was present during something important in your life: wedding, funeral, graduation. It was so melancholy, Abby doubted it was a wedding. The song was too gloomy.

She realized the only way to get a song out of her head was to replace it with something else. She flipped on the radio, dialed to a Nineties oldie station. Good enough.

Twenty minutes later they pulled into the drive. The sun was out, and the girls were giggling over something secret, as they often did. As Abby unloaded the groceries she'd found that the mysterious tune had left her, but for some reason the sense of unease had not.

PART TWO

SIX

The borough of Queens is the largest of the five boroughs of New York City, and the city's second most populous. It sits on the westernmost section of Long Island, and is home to both LaGuardia and JFK airports, as well as the US Open for tennis. At one time or another the borough had been the residence of a number of celebrities, both famous and infamous, including Tony Bennett, Martin Scorsese, Francis Ford Coppola, and John Gotti. It was by far the most culturally diverse borough, boasting more than one hundred nationalities.

The office of the district attorney, a modern ten-story building located in Kew Gardens, looked as if it had been built by five different architects and builders, composed of a series of additions added in different eras, a pastiche of style, materials, and methods. One of the busiest DA's offices in the country, it was home to more than three hundred attorneys, and five hundred support personnel.

The Major Crimes, Investigations, Trials, Special Prosecutions and Legal Affairs divisions of the office were responsible not only for the prosecution of arrest cases brought to the office by the New York City Police Department and other law enforcement agencies, but also for proactively seeking out wrongdoers and aggressively undertaking investigations of suspected criminal conduct.

The DA's office, too, boasted its own stars. Frank O'Connor, a former Queens District Attorney, figured prominently in the 1956 Alfred Hitchcock film *The Wrong Man*.

To some, mostly those who were not inside the elite divisions of the office, the building was called the Palace. Those who did work in Major Crimes never did anything to discourage the practice. And while a palace can really only boast one king – in this case it was the District Attorney, Dennis R. McCaffrey – it can have a number of princes.

When Michael Roman, inarguably the most favored prince at the bar, arrived at the Palace on the day before the Ghegan trial was scheduled to begin, there were only a handful of people. If Saturdays turned the New York legal system into a ghost town, Sundays rendered it virtually barren. Only the newest and most ambitious young attorneys, along with royalty like Michael Roman, ventured into the office. The second floor was all but deserted.

As much as Michael enjoyed the buzz and noise of the office when it was in full swing, he had to admit he liked having the place to himself. He did his best thinking on the weekends. There was a time when the DA's Homicide division was located in a dumpy little building in Jamaica that looked like a check-cashing store and, for a number of prosecutors, Michael included, it was almost a pleasure to try cases out there, off the beaten path, away from the boss's scrutinizing eye.

After five years of working in these trenches, vaulting his way up from the Intake Bureau to the Felony Trial Bureau, Michael cemented his reputation with the trial and conviction of the Patrescu brothers, a pair of vicious drug dealers who had cold bloodedly murdered six people in the basement of a fast food restaurant in the Forest Hills section of Queens. Michael and Tommy Christiano had worked nights and weekends on that case, backed by a capital investigation team with hundreds of detectives from the DA's office and the NYPD.

Marku Patrescu was currently serving six life sentences in the Clinton Correctional Facility, better known as Dannemora. His brother Dante, who had pulled the trigger, had been executed that March. After Dante's sentence was carried out, Michael began to hear interesting stories from DAs all over the city. It seemed that apprehended suspects, in a wide range of crimes – rapes, assaults, robberies – cited the Patrescu execution as a major reason not to carry a weapon, or use a weapon in their possession during the commission of a felony. It was this sort of evidence of cause and effect for which prosecutors live.

The same team that worked tirelessly to convict the Patrescu brothers helped put Patrick Sean Ghegan behind bars. Ghegan's trial began in just over twenty-four hours. Michael had everything in place – the ballistic evidence tying Ghegan's weapon to the crime, a line-up that positively identified Ghegan as the man who had been observed threatening Colin Harris in his florist shop, along with surveillance camera footage that showed Ghegan entering the store moments before the murder.

The only thing Michael did not have, not in the sense he needed, was Falynn Harris, the daughter of the slain man. Falynn, whose mother had died in a car accident when she was only six, had not spoken a single word since the day she saw her father die in a hail of bullets.

Today would be Michael's last opportunity to get Falynn to talk.

Michael knew why he was so driven on this case. It was hardly a secret around the office. Falynn's story was not that different from his own. He had ridden shotgun on every detail leading up to the prosecution, had walked the evidence through the firearms unit, had personally interviewed everyone involved. Michael Roman was known throughout the Palace as the kind of prosecutor who liked to tie down evidentiary details even before charges were returned.

Michael had already met with Falynn six times, once bringing her to his house in Eden Falls, hoping that spending some time with Charlotte and Emily and Abby might open her up. No such luck. Each time she sat, curled into a ball, completely closed off from the world, embraced by the cold arms of grief.

Unless there was a continuance, today would probably be Michael's last chance to prepare her for testimony. She had been subpoenaed by the defense, the judge had already ruled on the matter, and whether Michael liked it or not, she was going to take the stand.

She looked younger than fourteen, even younger than she had the last time Michael had seen her. She was slight and gamine, with light brown eyes and curly chestnut hair. She wore faded jeans and a burgundy sweatshirt, battered Frye boots, at least three sizes too big for her. Michael wondered if the boots had belonged to her father, if she had wadded-up paper towels in the toes.

Then there was that face. The face of a sad angel.

Falynn had been staying at a foster home in Jackson Heights since the murder. Michael had asked for a patrol car to pick her up and bring her to the office. He met her at the back entrance.

As they rode up to the second floor, Michael tried to plot his strategy with the girl.

He knew that if he could get her to open up in court, get her to look into the face of each juror – just once, just one heartcinching time – he would put Patrick Ghegan on the gurney with a needle in his arm. And he knew why he wanted this so badly.

As they walked down the hallway Michael watched her. She was observant, smart, ever aware of her surroundings. He knew she saw the Christmas lights that ran along the wall where it met the ceiling, lights no one had bothered to take down for more than five years.

They walked through the small outer office into Michael's office. Michael gestured to the sofa. "Would you like to sit here?"

Falynn looked up. The slightest smile graced her lips, but she remained silent. She sat on the sofa, drew her legs under her.

"Would you like a soda?"

Silence.

Michael reached into the small refrigerator next to his desk. Earlier in the day, the only things inside had been a single can of club soda and a bottle of Absolut. When Michael first met Falynn she walked in the room holding a diet Dr Pepper, so this morning he ran out and bought a six-pack of the soda. He hoped she still liked it. He popped a can out of the plastic, handed it to her. She took it and, after a minute or so, opened it, sipped.

Michael took the chair next to her. He would give it a few minutes before trying again. This was their routine. In their six meetings, Falynn had listened to everything he had said, but said nothing in response. Twice she had begun to cry. The last time they met, at Michael's house, he had simply held her hand until it was time for her to go.

"Can I get you anything else?" Michael asked.

Falynn shook her head, and curled into a ball at the end of the old leather sofa. Michael thought about how the mayor of

New York City had once sat in the same place, toasting Michael's success, a place now occupied by a young girl who might never breach the shell of heartache and sadness that surrounded her. He had never seen anyone so shut down in his life.

He glanced at the file in his lap.

Since her father's murder, Falynn had run away from her foster home three times. The last time she was picked up for shoplifting. According to the police report, Falynn walked into a Lowe's and shoplifted a package of peel-and-stick decals, the kind you put on the walls in a kid's room. The decals were yellow daisies. When she walked past the security pedestals she set off the alarm.

According to the report, the security guards gave chase, but Falynn got away. The guards called the police, gave them a description. An hour later Falynn was found by the police, sitting beneath an I-495 overpass, a place known as a refuge for the homeless. According to the report, Falynn was polite and respectful to the officers, and was peacefully taken into custody.

The report also stated that police found the stolen decals stuck on the concrete columns under the overpass.

Michael watched her. He had to start talking. He had to give this another try. Because if Falynn did not testify, there was only a fifty-fifty chance that Ghegan would be convicted on the scientific evidence. Even ballistics could be impeached.

"As you know, the trial starts tomorrow," Michael began, trying to sound conversational. "I'll be honest with you, the defense attorney in this case is very good at what he does. I've seen him work many times. His name is John Feretti and he is going to ask you tough questions. Personal questions. It would be great if we could go over some of this before tomorrow. If we could get your story out first, it will be a lot better."

Falynn said nothing.

Michael felt he had one last lever. He sat silently for a while, then stood, crossed over to the window. He shoved his hands in his pockets, rocked on his heels, chose his words carefully.

"When I was really small we lived over on Ditmars, in this small second floor apartment. You know Ditmars Boulevard?"

Falynn nodded.

"I had my own room, but it wasn't much bigger than my bed. I had a small second-hand dresser in the corner, a closet next to the door. The bathroom was down at the end of the hall, by my parents' bedroom. Every night, right around midnight, I always had to go to the bathroom, but I was scared to death of walking past my closet. See, the door never closed all the way, and my father never got around to fixing it. For the longest time I was sure that there was something in there, you know? Some kind of monster ready to spring out and get me."

Falynn remained silent, but Michael could tell she knew what he was getting at.

"Then one day my father installed a light in that closet. I kept that light on for the longest time. Months and months. Then one day I realized that, if there ever was a monster in there – and I'm still not convinced there wasn't – the monster was gone. Monsters can't stand the light."

Michael turned to look at Falynn. His fear was that he had put her to sleep with his admittedly ham-handed analogy. She was listening, though. She was still curled up in a ball, but she was listening.

"If you testify tomorrow, you'll be shining a light on Patrick Ghegan, Falynn. He will be exposed, and everyone will know who and what he is. If you testify we'll be able to send him away, and he won't be able to scare anyone or hurt anyone ever again."

Falynn did not look up at him. But Michael saw her eyes

shift side to side, saw the wheels begin to slowly turn.

Michael glanced back out the window. A few minutes passed, minutes during which Michael realized he had taken his best shot, and failed. He envisioned this broken young girl sitting on the witness stand, devastated by the murder of her father, adrift on an ocean of sorrow, unable to say a word. He saw Patrick Ghegan walking out of the courtroom a free man.

"Everything is so ugly."

Michael spun around. The sound of Falynn's voice was so foreign, so unexpected, Michael thought for a moment it had been in his head.

"What do you mean?" he asked.

Falynn shrugged. Michael feared for a moment that she was going quiet again. He crossed the room, sat near her on the couch.

"What's ugly?" he asked.

Falynn picked up a magazine, began plucking away at the mailing label at the bottom. "Everything," she said. "Everything in the world. *Me.*"

Michael knew she was saying this to get a reaction, but when he looked into her eyes, he saw that she believed it in her heart. "What are you talking about? You're a pretty young woman."

Falynn shook her head. "No I'm not. Not really. Sometimes I can't even look at myself."

Michael decided to go for it. He had to. "Trust me on this. Except maybe for the hair, you're very attractive."

Falynn looked sharply up at him. When she saw the smile on his face she laughed. It was a glorious sound. After a few moments — moments during which, consciously or unconsciously, Falynn Harris ran a hand through her hair — she turned silent again, but Michael knew the wall had fallen. He let her continue when she was ready.

"What's . . . what's going to happen in there?" she finally asked.

Michael's heart galloped. It always did when he made a breakthrough. "Well, I'll go into the courtroom with Mr Feretti and we will present any applications we might have – scheduling, legal, stuff like that. The judge might have an evidentiary ruling. There won't be a jury or gallery for this. After that's over, the jury will be seated and the trial will begin. After the opening statements you're going to be sworn in, and I'm going to ask you questions about what happened that day. About what you saw."

"What will I have to do?"

"All you have to do is tell the truth."

"Is he going to be there?"

The "he" of course was Patrick Ghegan. "Yes he is. But he can't hurt you. All you have to do is point him out once. After that, you don't ever have to look at him again."

The truth was, Michael would rather have Falynn look directly into the eyes of the jurors. He knew that teenagers – especially teenaged girls – could either be the greatest witnesses or an absolute nightmare. Falynn's strength was how innocent and vulnerable she looked, her soulful eyes. Michael knew that John Feretti was going to have his hands full trying to break this witness – a young girl who had seen her father murdered in cold blood.

"We're going to put him somewhere he can never hurt anyone else again," Michael added. He was, of course, hoping for more than that. The DA was going to ask for the death penalty in this case. It was not the time to bring that up, however.

Falynn stared out of the window a few moments. "Do you promise?"

There it was, Michael thought. He had faced this moment

before, specifically with the families of the employees murdered in the basement of that QuikBurger. He recalled Dennis McCaffrey standing before those men and women and making them a promise – the promise of finality, the promise of justice for their loved ones. Michael and Tommy had stood shoulder to shoulder that day and backed the DA's pledge. It was a promise that nearly cost Michael his life. It was the Patrescu brothers who ordered the car bombing, the attempt on his life he had miraculously survived. In a twisted sense, the madness of that act had brought Michael his greatest joy: Abby and Emily and Charlotte.

"Yes," he said, before he could think about it any more. "I promise."

Falynn just nodded. She worried the edge of the magazine in her hands. After a few moments, she looked up. "How long does it all take?"

"Well, that depends on a few things," Michael began, his heart beginning to soar. It was that old feeling, the feeling that the wheels of justice had just engaged, and he loved it. "The first part of the trial begins tomorrow. He has his lawyer –"

"And you're *my* lawyer."

At that moment Michael thought about trying to explain it all to her. He considered explaining how, when a person is a victim of a homicide, it is the state of New York that advocates for the victim, not a single person.

But all he could see was that face. That sad angel's face.

"Yes," Michael Roman said. "I'm your lawyer."

SEVEN

Aleks walked the city. From 38th Street and Park Avenue he headed south a few blocks and began to wind his way toward Times Square, passing many landmarks he had only read about. The vaunted Madison Avenue, the Empire State Building, Macy's, Herald Square, the stately, magnificent New York Public Library.

The city both dazzled and beguiled him. This was the center of the world. He wondered what effect a place like New York had had on his daughters, and what it would take to reverse such influence.

He knew that all he had to do in a place like New York City was walk down a street, alerting his senses to the aromas, the sounds, the sights, the rhythms. Before long he would catch the tail end of a conversation in Russian, Lithuanian, German, Romanian. He would ask after places, seeking the world beneath the world. It did not take long.

In a place called Bryant Park he found a pair of young Russian men who said they could help him find what he was looking for. For a small fee.

They played their games, took their stances, asserted their manhood. Eventually Aleks, who played the thick foreigner for them, got what he wanted.

*

The first bar was called Akatu. It was a dirty, narrow place on West End Avenue in the Sheepshead Bay section of Brooklyn, a place smelling of old grease and sour tobacco. The tavern was half-full at midday, had a parochial feel to it, as if strangers were not welcome, or at the least needed to be watched. Aleks understood. When he entered, he sensed all eyes on him. Some conversations halted.

As he made his way to the rear of the bar, there were two husky men talking softly, blocking his path. They did not move as he approached, holding their small piece of ground, as violent men will do, forcing Aleks to skirt them by, hugging the wall. One man was thick-waisted and muscular, nearly Aleks's size. He looked bloated, muscle-bound only, perhaps pumped from a just-finished workout. The other was shorter, also solid, but more likely the one to be carrying a weapon. He wore a cheap and oversized wool blazer in the too-warm bar. Aleks walked around them, giving them their territorial due. For the moment.

Aleks ordered a Russian coffee and a shot. As he put his hands on the counter, pushing forth a twenty, the barman saw his tattoo, the mark of the *vennaskond*. The man looked confused for a second – the mark was not nearly as well known as the Russian *vory* – but his face soon registered the truth. This was a man to be reckoned with. Aleks saw the bartender nod to the two men behind Aleks, and in the mirror he saw them give him some room.

Aleks asked a few questions of the bartender, letting on just enough to get the answers he sought, but give away nothing. After a few moments of conversation he discovered this man could not help him. But the bartender did have the name of a bar and another man who might be able to help.

The bartender excused himself, moved a few stools down,

poured a refill to an older, bottle-blond woman who smoked unfiltered cigarettes and read a Russian newspaper. Her lipstick was the color of dried blood.

By the time the bartender returned, Aleks's twenty had turned into a fifty, and the big man in the black leather coat was gone.

The liquor remained untouched.

The second place, a Russian restaurant on Flatbush Avenue, produced no results, other than to lead Aleks to a third place, a café in Bayview. It was a stand-alone brick building, dark and smoky, and when Aleks entered he was greeted by the hiss of the samovar, the sound of an old Journey song on the jukebox, and the shouts of men playing cards in a back room. He mind-catalogued the room: Four hard men around a pool table to the left, to the right, at the coffee bar sat a klatch of old-timers from the Ukraine. They nodded at Aleks, who returned the greeting.

He asked about Konstantine. The men claimed to not know him. They were lying. Aleks had two more places on his list to visit.

He turned, saw the REST ROOMS sign at the rear of the bar. He'd make a comfort stop first.

As he walked the length of the tavern, Aleks sensed a presence. When he turned, there was no one there, no one following him.

He continued, descending the steps. He found the men's room at the end of a short basement hallway. He opened the door partially, flipped on the light. Nothing. The room remained dark. It smelled of dried urine and disinfectant. He opened the door fully, checked for the light fixture, and in that split second a shadow stole from the darkness like a spirit, a gleam of steel catching his eye.

In the moment before the blade plunged towards his back, Aleks stepped to the side. The blade crashed into the drywall. Aleks shifted his weight, pivoted, slamming his left knee into the groin of his assailant, bringing a forearm down onto the hand holding the knife. The man grunted, buckled, but instead of hitting the floor he too shifted weight, exposing a second knife, this one a long steel filet. It was headed for Aleks's stomach. Aleks grabbed the man by his thick wrist, powering back the arm. He slipped a leg between the other man's legs and brought him to the floor. Before he could get the Barhydt out of its sheath the attacker slammed a fist into his jaw, momentarily stunning him.

In a tangle of arms and legs, the two men crashed into the walls of the dark hallway, each seeking leverage. Moments later, Aleks brought a fist to his assailant's jaw – three powerful blows that took away the fight. The man slumped to the floor.

Bleeding from both the nose and mouth, his hands sore from striking bone, Aleks stood, steadied himself against the rotted plaster wall. He turned the man over, took one of the man's arms in a scissor lock. When his eyes adjusted to the dim light, he looked at the man's face.

It was Konstantine. But it was not. The man had Konstantine's broad forehead, his deep-set eyes, but somehow had not aged a day since he and Aleks had been in the federal army together.

"Who are you?" Aleks asked.

The young man wiped the blood from his nose. "Fuck your mother."

Aleks almost laughed. If he was in Estonia, and knew that there would be no consequences to his actions, he would have drawn his blade and opened the man's throat, just for the insult. "I think you are not understanding the question." He tightened his grip on the young man's arm, exerted more downward pressure. If he wanted, he could simply apply the leverage of his full body weight, and the arm would snap. Right now, he wanted to. "Who are you?"

The young man screamed once, a sharp growl, the muscles in his neck cording, his skin a bright crimson. "Fuck . . . you."

And Aleks knew.

This was Konstantine's son.

They sat in a back room on the first floor of the tavern. With a nod of his head, the young man who had tried to kill Aleks just moments earlier had cleared the room of card players. They sat among cardboard boxes of alcohol, napkins, bar food. The young man held a bag of ice to his face.

"You look just like him," Aleks said. It was true. The young man had his father's thick shoulders, broad chest, low center of gravity. He even had the crooked smile. Although Aleks had not known Konstantine at this young man's age – perhaps twenty-two or three – the resemblance was nonetheless remarkable, almost unsettling.

"He was my father," the young man said.

"*Was*."

The young man nodded, looked away, perhaps masking his feelings. "He's dead."

Konstantine dead, Aleks thought. The man had survived the first wave in Chechnya. It was hard to believe. "How?"

"Wrong place, wrong time. He took twenty bullets from a Colombian's AK," he said. "Not for nothin', but the Colombian joined my father in hell not long after. Believe it."

Aleks remembered well Konstantine Udenko's temper. He was not surprised.

"Many times he showed me pictures of his baby son," Aleks said. "You are Nikolai?"

The kid smiled. He looked even younger, except for the pink sheen of blood coating his teeth. "They call me Kolya."

Aleks sized up the kid. He had fully expected to see Konstantine again, to depend on his devotion to him, not to mention his animal strength and fox-like cunning. His son would have to do. He hoped the young man had inherited some of his father's archness and strength.

"My name is Aleks," he said. He pulled up the sleeves of his coat, revealing his tattoos. Kolya saw the marks and went pale. It was like a cardinal realizing he was standing in front of a pope.

"You are Savisaar! My father talked about you all the time, man. You are *vennaskond*."

Aleks said nothing.

Kolya looked a little shaky for a moment, as if he might be ready to kiss Aleks's ring. Instead he opened a nearby box, and extracted a bottle of vodka.

"We'll have a drink," Kolya said. "Then I'll take you to my shop."

Kolya ran a chop shop in the Greenpoint section of Brooklyn. Two garages, side by side, fronting an alley behind a block of stores on North 10th Street. Both had steel corrugated roll doors. Two men stood at the end of the alley, smoking, watching, cellphones in hand. Inside, the smell of motor oil and Bondo permeated the air. Beneath it, the sweet smell of marijuana.

The crew inside the shop was five young men, black and Hispanic. The sound of hip hop droned from a cheap radio. Aleks saw no firearms displayed openly, but he recognized the tell-tale bulges in the waistbands of two of the men.

The garages were cluttered with half-stripped cars, engine blocks, exhaust systems, bumpers and fenders, truck caps.

Most seemed to be the low end of the high side – BMW, Lexus, Mercedes.

They gathered in the last bay, one with a broken lift. Aleks, Kolya, and a young black man named Omar. Omar was tall, powerfully built. He wore his hair in short dreads. He also sported green camouflage trousers and shirt. In a *city*. For Aleks, this defined his dubious worth as a warrior.

"So what do you think?" Kolya asked, offering a proud hand to the space.

Aleks glanced around the garages, giving the question its due. "Not bad," he replied. As much as he liked fine automobiles, he could never be involved in this end of the trade. Too dirty, too noisy, and the product took far too much space to conceal. "Do you make a living?"

Kolya mugged. "I do all right."

The words came out *a'ight*, a pronunciation Aleks was beginning to hear more and more, a rasp on his sensibilities.

"Most of the business out of here is legit," Kolya added. "Fuck, we even do work for AAA." Kolya laughed, Omar joined in. They bumped fists. It was nervous laughter. They did not know what was coming, and had to establish the illusion of a united front. Whatever Aleks was bringing them could be good or bad. Kolya decided to jump in the fire. "So, what do you need?"

Aleks glanced once at Omar, back at Kolya. "I need to talk to you alone."

Kolya nodded at Omar. Omar took a moment, sizing Aleks, as any man's second would. When Aleks did not say a word, did not avert his gaze, the kid thought better of the challenge. He got up slowly and walked to the door of the office, stepped inside, closed the door. Moments later Aleks saw him watching through the grimy shop window.

Aleks turned back to Kolya, spoke softly, even though the

sound of the radio, combined with the sounds of metal cutting metal, was loud. "I need to find someone."

Kolya nodded, said nothing.

"A man. He has an office in this place called Queens. Do you know it?"

Kolya smirked, hit his cigarette. "Fuck Queens. This is Brooklyn, yo."

Aleks ignored the territorial hubris. "The man I need to see is a lawyer. His name is Harkov."

"Harkov," Kolya said. "A Jew?"

"I don't know."

"But he is Russian."

"Yes."

"*And* a fucking lawyer."

Aleks nodded.

"*And* from Queens. Whatever you gotta do, I'll happily do it for you. Three strikes, *vend*."

Young men, Aleks thought. He thought for a moment of Villem, the young man from the village back home. At this moment Villem was probably feeding the dogs, cleaning out their cages. If he were American he would be just like Konstantine's son. Jewelry, brazen tattoos, attitude.

"I just need you to bring me to him," Aleks replied. "I'll take it from there." He took a thick roll out of his pocket. US currency. Kolya's eyes widened. "I will need a car and a driver. The car should be nothing flashy. Tinted windows."

Kolya crossed to the window, opened the blinds. He pointed to a midnight blue Ford parked near the street. The car was for sale, and had the price of $2,500 on the darkened windshield.

"This will do," Aleks said. "Do you have a driver?"

"Omar is the man."

We'll see, Aleks thought. "I also need a room at a nearby motel. Something quiet, but near an expressway. Off-brand."

"I know all the motels, yo. My cousin works at one up the way."

Aleks peeled off about ten thousand in cash, held it out to Kolya. Kolya went to take the money. Aleks pulled it back.

"Your father was a brother to me," Aleks said. "A *vennaskond*. Do you know what this means?"

Kolya nodded, but Aleks believed the young man did not fully understand the bond. Young American men like Kolya, men on the fringes of criminal society, gauged their belief of "gang" life and its fragile loyalties on what they saw in the movies and on television, on what they heard on the radio. His father and Aleks had been tested in battle. He continued.

"I am going to treat you with trust, with respect," Aleks said. "But I will not put my life in your hands. Do you understand this?"

"Yeah," he said. "I understand."

"And if you cross me, just once, you will not see me coming, nor will you see another dawn."

Kolya tried to hold his gaze, but failed. He looked away. When he looked back, Aleks had the money out.

"I need the following things," he said. "Do not write them down." He then dictated a list, a list that included a fast laptop computer, a high-megapixel DSLR camera, a portable color printer, photo-quality paper, and a half dozen prepaid cellphones.

"You can buy these things now?" Aleks asked.

"Hell yeah."

"Do you have a driving license?"

"Sure."

"May I see it?"

Kolya hesitated, apparently not used to producing ID on demand. He then took out a bulky wallet, a scuffed leather billfold attached to a chain. He extracted his license. Before leaving Tallinn, Aleks had looked up New York licenses on the Web, had studied a JPEG of the document. Kolya's permit looked genuine.

"Can you get me a license like this?"

"No problem," Kolya said. "What's the name and address?"

"I don't know yet," Aleks said. "When you come back we will take the picture. Then we will begin."

As Kolya walked across the garage, he motioned to Omar, who emerged from the office. Moments later, the two men left the shop.

One hour later Kolya returned, four large bags in hand. While Kolya was gone, Aleks looked through every drawer and file cabinet in the office. He had all the information he needed on the young man – his home address, phone numbers, cell numbers, social security number, bank accounts. He had them all memorized. Although his recall was not quite photographic, he had an eidetic talent for recollection. His greatest faculty was thoroughness. He kept both his enemies and friends at hand. In his experience, one had the potential to become the other at a moment's notice. Often, with no notice at all.

"Any problems?" Aleks asked.

Kolya shook his head. "Cash talks, bro."

After unpacking the bags and boxes inside, Aleks booted the laptop. He got through all the opening screens, launched the web browser, and began to surf the Internet for what he needed.

He soon found the official documents he needed online, hooked up the printer, and printed them.

While the laptop battery charged, he unpacked the DSLR camera, a Nikon D60. He slipped in a high-capacity SD memory card and, when the battery held sufficient charge to take a few images, he had Kolya render five close-up photographs of him standing in front of a white wall. He hooked the camera up to the laptop, launched the image program, and printed off the photographs on high-quality, semi-gloss paper.

An hour later he was ready. He gave Kolya the trimmed photographs. "At some time today I will have the name and address I need for this driving license."

Kolya nodded. "I'll have Omar take this to my man and he'll get it set up. All we have to do is call with the info and he'll get right on it. We could have it within the hour."

"Do you trust this man? This forger?"

"He did a lot of work for my father."

This was good enough for Aleks. "Do you still have enough money to cover this?"

Aleks saw the slight hesitation in Kolya's response. There was no question that there was enough money left over from what Aleks had earlier given the young man, but they were all thieves in this room. The hesitation spoke to instinct, more than reason. Perhaps involuntarily, Kolya's eyes dipped to Aleks's tattoos, and what they meant.

"I'm good," Kolya said.

"Good," Aleks replied. He slipped on his coat. "Are you ready to do this?"

Kolya shot to his feet. He held up a set of keys. "We'll take the H2. Go to Queens in *style,* yo."

Aleks unplugged the fully charged laptop, slipped it into its carrying case. "We need to make one more stop first. Are there places near here that sell hardware? Tools? We will need these things." Aleks handed Kolya a list. Kolya scanned it.

"Home Depot," Kolya said, handing it back.

Aleks took the list back, burned it in an ashtray. "Will they have all these things in one store?"

Kolya laughed. "Bro," he said. "This is *America.*"

EIGHT

The Austin Ale House was famous for many things, not the least of which was its propensity to welcome any number of members of the Queens district attorney's office in the front door, and discreetly help them out the back door a few hours later. Many times, when a major case was won, the DA's office celebrated the victory in the bar/restaurant/Off Track Betting parlor on Austin Street.

The site was also famous – or more accurately infamous – for being the site of the 1964 Kitty Genovese murder, and subsequent legend. Kitty Genovese was a young woman who was stabbed to death in the parking lot, and cried for help as she crawled across the frozen asphalt toward her apartment. According to numerous reports, neighbors who heard her pleas failed to respond, although over the years this notion has come into question. Regardless, the syndrome had become part of the justice system lexicon, dubbed the "bystander effect" or, if you lived in Queens, the Genovese Syndrome.

None of this was ever far from the minds of the prosecutors, cops, and support personnel who elbowed the mahogany at the Austin. Over the interceding years, many a glass had been raised in the name and legend and memory of Catherine Susan Genovese.

Michael had driven Falynn Harris to her foster parent's

home in Jackson Heights. They had talked for nearly two hours. During that time Michael walked her carefully through the case, twice, and she had proven herself remarkably perceptive and bright, far beyond her fourteen years. Michael knew that if she had half the poise and strength on the stand, the defense would not shake a single branch.

But it was on the drive back to her foster home that something remarkable happened. Michael told Falynn about the murder of his own parents. It just seemed to come out in one long sentence. Except for Abby, he had never told another living soul the whole story; about his fears, his unrelenting grief, his anger.

Was this wrong? Had he crossed the line? There was little doubt in his mind that he had. But he knew why he had done it. He had one chance of putting Patrick Ghegan away for life, and that chance was Falynn Harris. He needed her to be not only intellectually engaged, but emotionally engaged.

When he finished his story, Falynn just stared at him. She dabbed her eyes while he was telling the tale, but now her eyes – although a bit red – were dry. She almost looked a bit matronly.

"What does that saying mean?" she asked.

"Which one?"

"The one your mom said to you right before, you know . . ."

Michael had told her about this, then instantly regretted it. It was something planted deeply in the garden of his soul, and he did not let many people in. *"Zhivy budem, ne pomryom,"* he said. *"If we will be alive, we will not die."*

Falynn looked out the passenger window for a few moments. It had begun to rain. She looked back at Michael. "What do you think that means really?"

"I have a few ideas," Michael said. "What do *you* think it means?"

Falynn gave him a beguiling smile. "I'll tell you when this is all over."

Michael nodded. He took out his small notebook, wrote on it. "This is my e-mail address and my cellphone number. You contact me whenever you want. Don't even look at the clock."

Falynn took the piece of paper. She unbuckled her seatbelt, leaned over.

"Is it okay to hug you?" she asked.

Michael smiled. "It's okay."

They hugged, parted.

As Michael watched her climb the steps, he knew everything was in place. She was going to testify fully against Patrick Ghegan, and the man who had killed her father was, at the very least, going away for life.

Michael Roman was going to win.

Life was good.

The bar was packed. The gathering was for retiring ADA Rupert White who, it was rumored, was getting ready to join a white-shoe firm on Wall Street.

Michael looked around the room. It was a who's who of the movers and shakers in Queens politics.

For the first hour it was a standard roast – other prosecutors, defense attorneys, city councilmen, judges, all recounting stories and anecdotes, PG-rated ditties that brought casual laughter and mild reproach from the ostensibly dignified Rupert White. In the second hour, after enough Jameson had flowed under the bridge of propriety, the vulgarity was unleashed, and the stories recalled a number of less-than-public episodes, including the time Rupert White was stalked by a disturbed juror from an old case and, of course, a cache of embarrassing inter-office romantic moments.

"As I live and breathe. Tommy Jesus and The Stone Man."

The voice came from behind Tommy and Michael.

Michael's nickname, The Stone Man, grew out of two sources. He originally acquired it because he was of Estonian descent, and a lot of the street people he knew in the early years – most of whom he prosecuted – had no idea what or where Estonia was. They couldn't pronounce it. The second meaning came later, due to Michael's reputation as an ace prosecutor. As he began to try and win the bigger cases, he had to square off against more and more hardened criminals, at least those whose defense attorneys were dumb enough to put them on the stand. Michael Roman, even in those heady early days, was unflappable, solid as a rock. Thus the Stone Man.

For Tommy, the nickname also had a dual meaning. *Tommy Jesus* came first out of the obvious. Tommy's last name was Christiano. But his reputation in the office was one of a prosecutor who could take a dying or dead case, and bring it back to life, like Lazarus from the tomb.

Michael turned around. Behind him stood an inebriated Gina Torres. When Michael had started at the Felony Trial Bureau, Gina Torres had been a paralegal; a slender, leggy knockout, given to skin-tight business suits and expensive perfume. Now, a few years later, she had moved on to a private firm – they all did – and put on a few pounds, but they all landed in the right places.

"You look fucking *great*," she slurred at Michael.

"Gina," Michael said, a little taken aback. "You too." And it was true. The café au lait skin, the shiny black hair, the pastel lipstick. *That tight skirt.*

"I heard you were married," she said.

Michael and Gina had had a brief, sparking romance for a few months when he'd gotten to Kew Gardens. It ended as abruptly as it started. But Michael recalled every tryst, every coffee-room kiss, every elevator encounter. He held up his ring finger. At least he hoped it was his ring finger. He was getting hammered.

Gina leaned forward and planted one, hard and sloppy, on the mouth.

Michael almost fell off the stool.

She pulled back, ran the tip of her tongue over his lips. "You don't know what you're missing."

When Michael was able to speak, he said "I kinda do."

Gina slid her business card onto the bar in front of Michael, took one of the full shot glasses, downed it, then walked away. Every man at the bar – actually, every man at the Austin Ale House – watched the show.

Michael glanced at Tommy. For the moment, for the first time in his life, he was speechless.

"Dude," Tommy said. "You're my fucking hero."

Michael picked up a napkin, wiped the lipstick from his lips. He drank a shot, shivered. "Abby's going to know, isn't she?"

Tommy laughed, sipped his drink. "Oh yeah," he said. "They always do."

NINE

On a busy street in the Astoria section of Queens, two men sat in an SUV near the corner of Newtown Avenue and 31st Street, beneath the rumbling steel canopy of the El. They had stopped at a Home Depot on the way, paying cash for a total of twelve items. The cashier had been Pakistani. Aleksander Savisaar wondered if there were actually any Americans in America.

Aleks took what he needed from the plastic bag, and put it in his leather shoulder bag.

The address they sought was a narrow doorway lodged between a funeral parlor and a store that sold pagers. The cracked stone steps and grimy door told Aleks that this portal did not lead to a flourishing enterprise of any sort. Next to the door was a verdigris-covered bronze plaque that read:

> PEOPLE'S LEGAL SERVICES, LLC.
> VIKTOR J. HARKOV, ESQ.
> SUITE 206

They circled the block, then parked across the street. An aged sign in the window on the second floor declared *Attorney / Notary Public*. It appeared to be from the 1970s.

"Check to see if there is a back entrance," Aleks said.

Kolya slipped on his sunglasses, glanced at the side-view mirror, and stepped out of the vehicle.

Aleks reached into the box on the back seat. Inside were a half-dozen prepaid cellphones. He extracted the printout from his pocket, one he had made at the Schlössle Hotel in Tallinn, the address and phone number of Viktor Harkov. He punched in the number. After five rings there was an answer.

"People's Legal Services."

It was a man, older, Russian accent. Aleks listened to the background noise. No sounds of anyone typing, no conversation. He spoke in broken Russian. "May I speak to Viktor Harkov please?"

"I am Harkov."

Aleks noted an asthmatic wheeze in the man's breathing. He was ailing. Aleks glanced at the bank on the corner. "Mr Harkov, I am calling from First National Bank, and I would like to – "

"We do not have an account with your bank. I am not interested."

"I understand. I was just wondering if I might make an appointment to –"

The line went dead. Aleks closed the phone. The brief conversation told Aleks a few things, first and foremost was that, unless the man subscribed to call forwarding, Viktor Harkov was indeed in his office, and that he did not have a secretary or receptionist. If he did, she was not in the office, or perhaps she was in a restroom. By the looks of the building, the signs, and the fact that Harkov answered his own phone, he doubted it. Harkov may have answered the phone with a client in his office, but Aleks doubted this, too.

Kolya got back in the vehicle.

"There is a rear entrance, but you have to go by the back door of the Chinese restaurant," Kolya said. "Two of the bus boys are back there right now catching a smoke."

Aleks glanced at his watch. He opened his laptop. Within moments he got on a nearby wi-fi network. He entered the address for People's Legal Services on Google Maps and zoomed in. If the image was accurate, there was access to the target building via a fire escape from the roof to the top floor. He pointed to the image.

"Is this still there?"

Kolya squinted at the screen. He probably needed glasses but was far too vain to get them. "I didn't see it. I wasn't looking up."

Aleks had given the man a simple task, an undemanding reconnaissance of the rear of the building. He was clearly not his father.

Aleks knew he needed Kolya. But not for long.

"Wait here," he said. "And keep the engine running."

People's Legal Services was at the end of a long hallway on the second floor. Aleks entered the building next door, took the stairs to the roof. Once there, he crossed over, descended the fire escape, and entered Harkov's building on the fourth floor.

On the way down the back stairs, Aleks scanned the landings for surveillance cameras. He saw none. Still, as he entered, he put on a ball cap and pulled up the collar on his leather coat. He met no one.

When he reached the door to 206 he stopped, listened. From inside the office he heard the sound of a Russian-language radio program. He heard no other voices. He glanced both ways down the hallway. He was alone. He took a cloth from his pocket, turned the doorknob. The door opened onto a small, messy anteroom. To one side was an old pickled oak desk, covered with newspapers, magazines, and advertising flyers, all yellowed, all coated with the dust of months. Against one wall was a rusting file cabinet. The room was empty. As he had thought, there was no secretary.

Aleks closed the door gently behind him, turned the lock. When he appeared in the doorway to the inner office the man at the desk appeared startled.

"Are you Viktor Harkov?"

The old man looked at Aleks over the top of his filmy bifocals. He was lank and cadaverous, with thinning grey hair, a liver-spotted scalp. He wore a drab suit, tattered at the cuffs, a yellowed shirt and knit tie. The clothes sagged on his skeletal frame.

"The son of Jakob and Adele," the old man said. "How can I help you?"

Aleks stepped into the inner office. "I am here to enquire about your services."

The man nodded, looked Aleks up and down. "Where are you from?"

Aleks closed the door behind him. "I am from Kolossova."

Color drained from Harkov's face. "I am not familiar with this place."

The man was lying. Aleks had expected this. "It is a small village in south-eastern Estonia." He glanced toward the smudged windows. The buildings across the street had windows facing this office. He crossed the room, lowered the blinds, all the while keeping an eye on Harkov's hands. He would be surprised if a man in Harkov's world – a man with a sordid past of trafficking in human flesh – did not possess a firearm, a gun kept close at hand.

Aleks reached into his coat, removed a cheap, packable raincoat, no larger than a pack of cigarettes. "We have business, Mr Harkov."

"And what business would this be?"

Aleks slipped on the raincoat and a pair of thin latex gloves. "In spring 2005 you brokered an adoption of two little Estonian girls."

"I have been legal counsel for many adoptions. I do not remember them all."

"Of course," Aleks said. The subject was talking. This was good. If he said one thing, he may say another. He opened the shoulder bag, took out a roll of duct tape.

"How old are you?" Aleks asked. "That is, if you do not object to my asking."

The man considered him for a moment, his deeply creased brow furrowed. "I am eighty years old on my next birthday. In three weeks."

Aleks nodded. He knew this was a milestone Viktor Harkov would never reach. He did the math in his head. Viktor Harkov would have been too young to fight as a soldier in World War II. He was not too old to have been in a concentration or displaced person's camp.

"And you?" Harkov asked. "How old are you?"

Lawyers, Aleks thought. He found no reason to lie. "I am thirty-three."

Harkov took it in. "What are you going to do here today?"

"That depends," Aleks said. "Are you going to answer my question? About the two Estonian girls?"

"I cannot tell you anything. This is confidential information."

Aleks nodded. "With which hand do you write?"

Silence.

Aleks reached over to the desk, picked up a snow globe – a festive winter scene of what Aleks now knew was Times Square – and tossed it. The man raised both hands to catch it, favoring the right. He was right-handed. Aleks walked around the desk. He put his foot against the right wheel of the desk chair. Harkov tried to turn the chair, but was unable. Aleks took the snow globe from Harkov's grasp. He then took hold of the man's left arm, just below the wrist.

He wrapped duct tape around the man's chest, his left arm, his ankles, leaving the right arm free. This arm he duct-taped to the chair, leaving enough room for the forearm and wrist to move. Enough room to write. He placed a pen in the man's slack hand, a blank legal pad on the desk in front of him.

He finished by cutting off the man's trousers and stained underwear. Harkov, naked now from the waist down, trembled in fear, but said nothing.

"Do you know Radio Moscow, Mr Harkov?"

Harkov glared at him, remained silent.

Aleks would bet that the old man knew Radio Moscow to be the official international broadcast station of the former USSR, the station that ultimately became the Voice of Russia. Aleks had a different meaning.

From his shoulder bag Aleks removed a pair of electrical wires, each about six feet in length, a pair of alligator clips, and a pair of large dry cell batteries. Harkov watched his every move with his tiny hawk's eyes.

Aleks lifted the desk telephone, loosened the screws at the bottom, removed the plate, and hooked the phone up in sequence to the two large batteries.

He unspooled the wires, wrapped one wire around the man's big toe – a wire that would act as a ground – and attached the other to the end of the man's flaccid penis. Harkov winced at the pain, but made no sound.

"Some have called this the Tucker Telephone, out of respect and courtesy to its inventor, I suppose. To me it will always be Radio Moscow."

Harkov struggled feebly against his restraints. Aleks could

see bloodied spittle running from the corner of his mouth. The man had bitten his tongue.

"It really is quite ingenious," Aleks continued. "Whenever this phone rings, it will send a charge through the wires, to your genitals. I understand it is quite painful. We used it often in Grozny, but then it was only for men who had been fighting for a cause, a cause they believed in." Aleks took out one of his prepaid cellphones.

"You, on the other hand, are guilty of something far worse. You stole a child from its mother. In all of nature, this is punishable by death. I do not see why human beings should be any different."

Aleks held up the cellphone.

"You can't do this," Harkov breathed.

"Two little girls, Mr Harkov. Where did they go?"

"I . . . I help people," Harkov said. His body began to tremble even more violently. Sweat dripped from his brow.

"Have you ever thought for one moment that you might be destroying lives on the other end of your deals?" Aleks touched three numbers on his cellphone.

"These children are un*wanted*."

"Not all of them." Three more numbers.

"You don't understand. People come to me and they are desperate for children. They give them good homes. A loving environment. Many people say they will help. I take action. I make a difference"

"Two little girls from Estonia," Aleks said, ignoring him. His finger hovered over the final digit.

Harkov thrashed in his chair. "I will never tell you. *Never!*"

"Moscow calling, Mr Harkov." Aleks hit the last number. Seconds later the telephone on the desk rang, sending current along the wires.

A flash of orange sparks ignited Harkov's pubic hair. The

man screamed, but it was soon muffled by a greasy garage rag Aleks shoved into his mouth. Harkov's body shuddered for a moment, then fell limp. Aleks lifted the handset, replaced it. He snapped an ammonia capsule beneath his nose. The man came to. Aleks pulled out the rag, got close to his ear.

"Tell me where the files are located. Two little Estonian girls. Little girls you had stolen from their mother's womb. Girls you had a man named Mikko Vänskä spirit away in the night. I want to know the name and address of the people who adopted them."

Nothing. Harkov's head lolled on his shoulders.

Aleks shoved the rag back into the man's mouth, dialed again. Again the phone rang. Harkov shrieked in pain. This close, Aleks could smell the cooking flesh. He also knew that Harkov's bowels had released.

Another ammonia capsule.

Aleks walked to the window for a moment. Harkov mumbled something into his gag. Aleks returned, tapped the man's right hand. Harkov wrote a scribbled word on the pad. Unreadable. Aleks hit redial on his phone. Another jolt. This time the tail of Viktor Harkov's yellowed dress shirt caught fire. Aleks let it burn for a second, then doused the flame.

The office was becoming a landfill of offensive odors. Greasy flesh, burning hair, feces, sweat. Aleks pulled Harkov's head back. The man's face was bathed in perspiration. Aleks pinched the fleshy part of the man's nostrils until he came back to consciousness.

"Two little girls," Aleks repeated.

Nothing.

Aleks reached into the bag, pulled out a small alligator clip. He detached the clip from Harkov's genitals, and connected the wire to the smaller clip. This he attached to one of Harkov's eyelids.

On the desk was a photograph taken perhaps sometime in the 1970s, a picture of a thin, nervous looking teenaged boy.

"This is your son?" Aleks asked.

Harkov nodded slightly.

"If I do not find the people I am looking for, I will pay this man a visit. It is far too late to save yourself – indeed, the account of this day was written years ago when you crossed my path – but you have the opportunity, right now, to give me what I want. If you do, you have my word that no harm will come to him."

Aleks removed the gag from the old man's mouth, but Harkov said nothing.

Once more, Moscow called Viktor Harkov. The charge burned away the entire eyelid in a flash of bright blue flame.

Two minutes later, the old man told Aleks everything.

Aleks found the files in the bottom drawer of the steel cabinet in the corner of the outer office. Inside the cabinet he noticed the remains of a long-ago forgotten lunch, a moldy brown paper bag dotted with rodent stool. In this tableau lived the horrors of old age, Aleks thought, of its infirmities and disease and trials, in here were the whispers of these days before death, a feeling he would never know, a . . .

. . . *triumph over eternity in the moment he strides up the hill, the field of corpses thick beneath his feet, the screams of the dying a dark sonata in the distance. The stone farmhouse has taken many mortar rounds, its pitted façade now a defiant intaglio. Inside he knows he will find his answers . . .*

Aleks glanced out the window, at the street. Kolya sat in the Hummer, a pair of earphones in his ears. He smoked a cigarette. The world continued to turn. The world was not going to miss this man who traded in human flesh, who brokered children in the night.

Aleks turned back to the dead man, took out his knife, and finished his work.

Before opening the door, Aleks looked at the documents. There were two files, two families with twin girls. Both were in the right time frame from four years earlier. Both were brokered through Helsinki. There was no further detail on the children, other than their gender and their date of passage to the United States.

And, most importantly, their names and addresses.

Before he stepped into the hallway Aleks turned back to the room. He had not touched anything without his gloves on. He had worn the plastic raincoat and his ball cap nearly the entire time. Although the offices were covered in dust, the path from the door to Viktor Harkov's desk was swept clean. Aleks had not left shoeprints in the dust. Only the most sophisticated of forensic evidence gathering would reveal that he had ever been in these rooms, and even if a man like Viktor Harkov warranted such attention, Aleks would be long gone by the time he was identified.

Still, he had now committed murder in a country not his own. He could never undo this, or take it back. Everything had changed.

In Estonia he knew where all the bolt-holes were, had several identities in several safe houses along the Narva River. He knew how the police operated, how the politicians operated, who could be trusted, who could be bought. He knew the when, the where, the how and, most importantly, the how *much*. This was different. This was the United States.

He walked slowly down the hallway to the stairs. He did

not use the handrail. When he reached the back door he used his shoulder to open it. The alley behind the building was empty. Moments later he rounded the corner and put the plastic bag containing the bloody raincoat and latex gloves in a trashcan.

When he slipped into the vehicle, Kolya considered him, but did not say a word. Aleks nodded. The Hummer pulled slowly into the stream of traffic.

They idled in a parking lot of a McDonald's. Aleks scanned the files. He wrote an address on a piece of newspaper, showed it to Kolya, who entered the address into his GPS system. Aleks committed it to memory.

"This is not far," Kolya said. "Maybe one hour. Maybe less, depending on traffic."

Aleks looked at his watch. "Let's go."

They left the city and drove along a magnificent river. It reminded Alex of the Narva. He looked around, at the tidy houses, the manicured lawns, the shrubs, trees, flowers. He could settle here. If this was where his Anna and Marya had grown up, they would be happy in Kolossova.

At just after six PM they found the address. The house was set far back from the road, barely visible through the trees, approached by a long winding driveway that snaked through the woods, bordered by early spring flowers and low undergrowth. There was a single car in the driveway. According to Kolya, it was a late model compact. Aleks did not know anything about current American models. They all looked exactly alike to him.

Except for Kolya's Hummer. This was a gaudy, pretentious tank of a vehicle. It stood out.

America, Aleks thought. He lowered his window, listened.

Nearby someone was cutting their lawn. He also heard the sound of a little girl singing. His heart began to race.

Was this Anna or Marya?

Aleksander Savisaar glanced at the gloaming sky. The sun would soon set fully.

They would wait for darkness.

TEN

Abby watched the girls at the dining-room table. They had eaten dinner, just the girls, and done an assembly-line job of rinsing the dishes and putting them in the dishwasher.

When they were done they put two pots of water on the stove, hard-boiling two dozen eggs. The windows were soon covered in mist. Emily drew a smiley face on one of them.

Twenty minutes later the dining-room table was covered in newspaper, mixing bowls, wire dippers, decals, and egg cartons. The kitchen smelled of warm vinegar and chocolate. It brought Abby back to her childhood, she and Wallace coloring eggs, hand-weighing chocolate bunnies to see which ones were hollow, which ones solid, fighting over the Cadbury Cremes, spiriting away marshmallow peeps.

When Abby had learned, years earlier, that she could not have children, this was one of the scenes that flashed darkly through her mind, a scene that would never be, along with Christmas mornings, Halloween nights, birthday parties with too-sweet cakes bearing candles shaped in the forms of 2, 3, 4 . . .

It was one of the million blessings that were Charlotte and Emily.

At six-thirty the doorbell rang. Abby wasn't expecting anyone.

She crossed the kitchen, into the foyer, looked through the peephole in the front door.

It was Diane, her neighbor from across the street.

Diane Cleary was a hotshot realtor in her early forties. She was slender and toned, had collar-length dark-blond hair, and was wearing a navy blue suit that probably cost more than the left side of Abby's entire closet. Her son Mark was a junior at Princeton, her daughter Danielle was in kindergarten. Abby didn't know her well enough to ask about the disparity, but Diane and Stephen Cleary had one of those marriages that were either hell on earth, or textbook romance perfect. Regardless, Diane had the kind of metabolism that allowed her to eat anything and everything – Abby lost count at four pieces of birthday cake at the previous day's party – and not gain an ounce. She hated her.

Abby opened the door. "Hey."

"Any cake left?" Diane asked with a wink. "Kidding."

Diane stepped inside, made a beeline for the kitchen.

"Time for coffee?" Abby asked.

"No thanks. I'm showing a condo in Mahopac."

"Say hi to Mrs Cleary," Abby said to the girls.

"Hi," Charlotte and Emily said, neither looking up from their egg-decorating chores.

"You know you have the cutest girls in the world."

Now the girls looked up and smiled. Such little divas.

"You guys have to stop getting cuter every day," Diane added. "You have to save some cute for the rest of us." Diane looked at her own face in the toaster. A funhouse visage looked back. "I need all the cute I can get."

Abby could almost hear the lead sinker break the surface of the water. Diane Cleary spent half her time fishing for compliments, the other half refusing to reel them in.

"Oh, I don't think you have any problems in that department," Abby said, taking the bait.

Diane smiled. "So who was that guy who looked like a younger, taller Andy Garcia at the party?"

"That was my husband's friend Tommy. They work together."

"He's a prosecutor?"

"Yep."

"Maybe I'll get arrested."

Abby laughed. "You'll have to do it in the city."

"Speaking of which," Diane began, looking out the kitchen window, at the absolute blackness of the night, "I've never asked you this, but do you miss living in the city?"

Abby didn't have to think about it too long. "Well, except for the noise, pollution, crime, danger, and general apathy, not so much. On the other hand, I'm not *that* suburban. I haven't burned my little black dresses yet."

Diane laughed, glanced at her watch, which probably cost the entire *right* side of Abby's closet. "Anyway, I just wanted to remind you about tomorrow."

Tomorrow? Abby wondered.

"The block sale?" Diane asked.

"Oh, right, sorry." Twice a year a dozen or so of the neighborhood families pooled their junk and had a block garage sale, hosted by the luck, or misfortune, of the draw. Abby had done her time the previous sale. "I have the boxes in the garage."

"Great," Diane said. "If you have any big stuff let me know. Mark and some of his friends are coming in for Easter and they'll be happy to haul it over."

Abby desperately wanted to get rid of the old waterfall buffet they'd had since she and Michael were married, but it was one of the few things Michael had left that belonged to his parents. It was probably not the right time, or the right way, to dispose of it. "I'll let you know."

"I'll see you tomorrow."

"Okay."

"Bye, girls," Diane said.

"Bye," they said.

Abby made a note about the block sale and put it on the refrigerator with a Care Bears magnet. She was getting terribly forgetful in her old age.

Twenty minutes later, with two dozen brightly colored eggs drying on the kitchen counters, the girls turned their attention to coloring an Easter egg drawing. Or, more accurately, a portion of an egg. Emily was drawing the top half; Charlotte the bottom. Even this was not entirely accurate. They were each drawing what would turn out to be a *third* of an egg – top and bottom – leaving out the center.

Charlotte was working on the top of the egg with her usual precision and care, colors never straying over the lines. Emily was working on the egg with *her* usual flair – bright colors, bold lines, abstract images.

Abby sipped her tea, watched with amusement and no small measure of puzzlement. The girls were leaving out the middle. It was the second year running for this. To Abby's bewilderment, they'd made the same sort of drawings the previous Easter (and, now that she thought about it, the previous Halloween too, leaving out the center third of all their pumpkin drawings).

When they were done, Abby took the two drawings and taped them together. The edges didn't line up, but probably would have if there had been a center to the drawing.

Why was there always a missing third to everything the girls did? Abby wondered. Three chairs at the tea table in their room, three Peppermint Patties at the store the day before. Abby tacked the big egg on the refrigerator. The two girls stood, admiring their work.

"It's very pretty," Abby said. "Daddy is really going to like it."

The girls beamed.

Abby pointed to the odd shapes. At the top and bottom of the egg were a pair of strange looking little creatures. "What are these?"

"That's a duck and a bunny," Charlotte said, pointing to the figure at the top.

"That's a bunny and a duck," said Emily, pointing to the other.

On the top of the egg, the duck seemed to be inside the rabbit, and inside the rabbit looked to be another egg. On the bottom, it was the exact reverse.

To Abby it looked like the drawing she had seen in the Russian folk tale book at which the girls were looking in the library. Right down to the needle inside the egg.

Kids were like sponges, Abby thought. They absorb everything with which they come in contact.

She kissed the girls on top of their heads. "Okay, my little duck and bunny," she said. "Let's brush up."

The girls giggled, then took off for the stairs and the upstairs bathroom.

Abby glanced again at the drawing. An egg inside a duck inside a rabbit. Inside them all, a needle.

With the girls tucked in, Abby checked the messages on her cellphone. Nothing from Michael. She knew that he would call if he was going to be any later than midnight. He was out with Tommy, and she knew he wouldn't drink too much — he never did on the night before a case started — but if it all ran late he would call, and probably crash at Tommy's place in Littleneck.

She left a few lights on and headed upstairs.

Abby had discovered Pilates in her second year at Columbia. With all the stresses of second year she had found that she was sleeping two hours a night, eating once a day – many times while cycling across campus – and drinking a bottle of sauvignon blanc just to get sleepy enough to crash for two hours and wake up with a hangover so she could pop a fistful of Advil and start all over again. She had found a yoga center near the campus that practiced Satyananda yoga, but for some reason it did not stick. She was an A-type personality, and yoga seemed a little too passive for her. She found a speed-cycling class in the West Village, and for a while that worked.

But the problems of getting there – two trains at least – stressed her out to the point where the class was only neutralizing the excess stress.

Then she discovered Pilates. The emphasis on strengthening ligaments and joints, increasing flexibility, and lengthening muscles, combining with the quality, not quantity of workout, seemed like a perfect fit.

Now it was a natural part of her day.

She slipped in the earbuds, and began warming up. She stretched for a few minutes, and would soon move on to her pelvic tilts and abdominal exercises.

At first she had needed almost complete silence to practice, but when you have toddlers in the house, near silence, any silence at all, was a distant memory. In the past two years she found she could work out with a 747 landing in the living room. This was good news and bad news. Good news because she could grab twenty minutes when she needed it. Bad news because she, at times, seemed to block out the rest of the world. She could still hear what was going on around her, of course, but sometimes it mercifully drifted away.

Midway through her routine, she thought she heard a noise. A loud noise. In fact, she'd felt it. It was as if someone had dropped something large and heavy inside the house. She pulled out the earbuds.

Silence.

She left the bedroom, walked down the hall, looked in on the girls. Both were sleeping soundly. Emily with the covers twisted in a knot. Charlotte lying with the covers pulled up primly to her chin, like a children's bedding ad in a JC Penney's catalog.

Abby listened to her house. Other than the ticking of the grandfather clock in the foyer, the house was silent.

Had Michael come home?

"Michael?" she called out in a loud whisper. Loud enough for her husband to hear – unless he had gone down to the basement – but not loud enough to wake the girls.

Silence.

Abby moved slowly to the top of the stairs. Another glance into the girls' room. Still asleep. The Care Bears nightlight cast the room in a warm ginger glow. The house was so quiet she could now hear them breathing in tandem.

Abby half-closed the bedroom door, then gently padded down to the landing. The light was on in the kitchen, as was the light in the mud room, the small space near the back door in which they kept their boots, umbrellas, raincoats, slickers, and rain hats. In summer they usually kept that light on all night. In winter, when the snow was known to drift halfway up the back door, they kept it off.

She had imagined it. It was probably a passing car, one of the rolling boom boxes with the trunk-sized bass speakers that seemed to be passing by with more frequency of late. She hoped it wasn't becoming a trend. They'd moved to Eden Falls precisely because it was quiet, and the thought that –

A light snapped off. Abby spun around.

The mud room was now dark.

Abby's heart skipped a beat. She backed up one step. In a loud whisper: "*Michael!*"

No response. A few moments later, in the kitchen, another light snapped off.

Abby looked down the steps. She saw the alarm panel on the wall near the front door, the digital panel that armed the three doors and sixteen windows in the house. The single green light in the lower right-hand corner was aglow, meaning, of course, that the system was unarmed. If it were Michael, he would have come in through the garage door, through the kitchen, into the foyer, and armed the panel. This was his routine.

In the past year there had been two break-ins in their neighborhood. Because the houses on this block were relatively isolated, hidden by trees, there were no witnesses. Neither time were the burglars caught, nor any of the stolen items recovered. There had been no violence in either case – the owners had been out of town – but there was always a first time for everything. The burglaries were one of the reasons they had gotten an alarm system installed in the first place.

In the eight months since they had first subscribed to the security service, Michael had never failed to arm it the moment he arrived home. Not once.

If there was someone in the house – and there was no doubt in Abby's mind that there was – it was not her husband. No one else had a key.

She listened intently, searching the silence for a noise; the creak of a floorboard, the scrape of a chair, the intake or exhale of a breath.

Nothing. Just the click of the clock. Just the sound of her own heartbeat pulsing in her ears.

Abby gently leaned over the railing and glanced at the dim light spilling into the living room from the kitchen. Her cellphone was charging on the small roll-top desk, right next to the cordless phone.

Shit.

The rest of the room – the dining room and living room beyond – was consumed by darkness, a darkness that drew shapes and spirits in every corner. She knew every inch of her house, but at the moment it looked like a foreign land, an ominous, threatening landscape.

There was no phone upstairs. She and Michael either had their cellphones with them, or when the cordless wasn't charging, kept it on the nightstand.

Abby returned to the master bedroom, pulled over the short step stool, climbed on it. On the top shelf of her closet was an aluminum case. She pulled it down, spun the combination, all the while glancing toward the hallway, looking for shadows, listening for footfalls. She opened the box. Against the egg-crate foam lining was a Browning .25 semi-automatic pistol. Abby checked that the safety was on.

When she was ten, her father had taken her out to her uncle Rob's farm in Ashtabula, Ohio. There he had taught her to shoot. They hunted quail in summer, rabbits in fall. Although never a great shot, the first time she bagged a quail she felt a rush of exhilaration. Of course, when Morton, their beautiful Golden, brought the bird back, Abby cried for two straight days. After that, it was target practice, and at this she excelled. She found that shooting a target, even the silhouette of a man, was easier than shooting small game. Although she liked a good steak as much as the next person, the notion of killing a living thing was anathema to her.

But this was different. This was her family.

She slipped the pistol into her pocket, stepped down the hall. She entered the girls' room, snapped off the nightlight. She checked the windows. Everything was locked tight. Before pulling the drapes, she peeked out the window. From this vantage, at the front right side of the house, she could not see the driveway, nor the area in front of the garage. If Michael had returned, she would not have been able to see his car anyway. The yard, the street, the block was quiet, dark, serene.

Abby exited the room, closed the door, descended the stairs. Before she could turn around, she heard a noise, the unmistakable sound of someone walking across the kitchen floor. There were two boards, right next to the island, they had been meaning to shim for more than a year. Abby looked at the wedge of light spilling from the room.

There. A shadow.

Abby glanced back up the stairs. Should she try to bundle the girls up and get out of the house, or risk crossing the foyer to get to the phone and the police?

She thought about trying one last time to call her husband's name, but if it wasn't him, she would have to confront the intruder. She stepped across the foyer, and remembered. There was a panic button on the alarm panel. Press it, hit a three-number code, and the Eden Falls police would be alerted. All silently.

When she was just a foot away she heard the footsteps crossing the kitchen. The shadow on the floor grew larger, less sharply defined. Whoever was in the kitchen was coming right toward her.

She hit the panic button, drew the weapon, and put her back to the wall. The shadow grew even larger as it filled the doorway.

She smelled something in the air, something she knew. Cologne. A *familiar* cologne.

She flipped on the light. The intruder screamed.

"*Walk this waaaaay, talk this waa-aa-aay!*"

It was Michael. He was singing Aerosmith. He was listening to one of the girls' iPods and he hadn't heard her calling his name. He hadn't heard a thing.

"Hey babe!" He leaned against the counter, pulled off his headphones. His eyes focused on the .25. "Man," he said, smiling. "Am I that late?"

Abby shook. Her eyes filled with tears of relief. She let herself slide down the wall to the floor.

The girls were fine, she was fine, Michael was fine. Everything was just peachy.

"So, I guess a blow job is pretty much out of the question," Michael added.

Abby wanted to shoot her husband anyway.

ELEVEN

Aleks watched. From his vantage, in the darkness behind the house, he could see through the dining-room window, into what he imagined was the living room. Shadows danced on the walls.

He turned, and once again scanned the yard. His eyes played over the shapes. A pair of three-wheel bicycles, a swing set.

The sight filled him with a longing he had long ago relegated to that part of his heart he reserved for weakness. He tried to imagine how Anna and Marya looked when they were infants, as toddlers, taking their first, tentative steps around this yard.

He slipped to the other side of the property, assessed the structure. It was a two-story colonial, well tended, but not landscaped beyond the prestige of the neighborhood. A single pin oak graced the side yard, a tree that would one day begin to finger its massive roots into the cellar, if it had not already.

When he and Kolya had arrived there had been three lights on in the back of the house – one on the first floor, two on the second. He waited, observed. He had learned stillness in his many years in the forest, observing birds of prey eyeing their quarry. He could remain in one position for hours if needed.

He climbed the tree next to the south side of the house, and stepped onto the upstairs porch. He stepped up to the window. At first he thought the room was dark, or that heavy drapes had been pulled, but as his eyes adjusted he saw there was a dim light coming from the room.

A light snapped on in the window to the right of the bedroom. It appeared to be a bathroom. Frosted glass prevented him from seeing in. He turned back to the bedroom window.

Nothing inside the room stirred.

Within seconds, Aleks had the window raised. He slipped silently into the house. Except for the sound of the television below, the house was quiet.

He stood at the foot of the beds. The two little girls slept in the darkened room, in the hands of angels. They had not awakened, were unaware of his presence. The room was filled with plush animals – ducks, rabbits, teddy bears, turtles. On one wall was a long low table, a pair of bright plastic chairs. Above it was a large corkboard, collaged with a menagerie of Sesame Street characters.

In the dim light Aleks could only see their small forms beneath the covers.

Suddenly – noise behind him. Metal brushing metal.

The door opened. In a blur Aleks had the Barhydt out of its sheath, open, at the ready.

In front of him, in silhouette, a small figure.

Aleks flipped on the overhead light, and saw it was a woman. She was waif-like, in her late forties, south-east Asian. Aleks looked at the beds. He backed across the small room, slipped the covers down. The twins were Asian, too.

The girls were not his *tütred*.

He looked into the woman's eyes. There he saw pain, as well as fear and something that looked like understanding. She did not move. Aleks closed his knife, sheathed it. He put a finger to his lips. The woman nodded.

"This is not Anna and Marya," Aleks said softly. "I have made a mistake. If I have frightened you, you have my deepest apologies. You are in no danger."

Moments later he was out the window, down the tree, across the street, and into the waiting car.

Aleks now knew where he had to go. He knew where his daughters lived.

A town called Eden Falls.

TWELVE

Two hours later Aleks stood near the bank of the East River, in the shadow of the massive United Nations Building. A chill had fallen over the city, a wind that whispered that spring had not fully arrived.

He took out one of the disposable cellphones, tapped the number written on the cocktail napkin. After two rings, the woman answered. They chatted for a minute or two, dancing the dance. Finally, Aleks asked. Moments later, after what might have passed for coquettishness in the woman's experience, she gave Aleks her address. He committed it to memory, signed off. He then snapped the phone in half, threw both pieces into the river.

As he walked toward the avenue, and a cab stand, he felt the heft of the Barhydt on his hip.

Jilliane Murphy was the woman's name. She said she would make tapas, and open a good bottle of Barolo. She said that from the moment they met on the plane, she had known he would call.

It had been a mistake to let her see the marble eggs on the plane. This Aleks knew. What he did not know was whether or not, when she moved the papers from the seat next to his, she had seen the name Viktor Harkov, or the address of People's Legal Services. The lawyer's murder was bound to be all over the news very soon.

As Aleks slipped into a cab on First Avenue, a Yankees cap pulled low on his head, he gave the driver an address eight blocks from Jilliane Murphy's apartment.

He lay back his head thinking about the next day. His heart began to race. He was going to meet his daughters, a moment about which he had dreamed for four years.

But that was tomorrow.

Tonight he was really looking forward to the Barolo.

THIRTEEN

Whiskey dreams were the worst. In this version Michael was in his underwear, in public — so far, the standard horror show — but this dream was not about being in such a state in a junior-high classroom, locker combination unknown, surrounded by cheerleaders. It was not even the nightmare he used to have where he was in court, sans suit, standing in front of a jury populated with octogenarian garden club ladies. No such luck.

This dream had him running down the street in Astoria, chasing a scantily clad Gina Torres. Behind him was Abby who, for some reason, was carrying an AK-47.

He opened his eyes.

Gina Torres?

His heart suddenly leapt into his throat. He hadn't. He wouldn't. He *didn't*. Did he?

Pulse racing, he bolted upright, felt around the bed. Empty. He glanced around the room. His own bedroom. He had overslept, but that was the good news.

Thank you, Jesus. Put it on my tab.

Gina Torres. He *had* seen her at the bar. That much he remembered. And he remembered how good she looked, although that was a given. And that he'd kissed her.

No. She kissed *me*, your honor.

He hadn't gotten drunk, but when had he gotten home? It

was late, he knew that. It was all starting to come back to him. Especially the part where Abby had –

A gun?

He ambled into the bathroom, saw the note taped on the mirror, written in a quick script Abby saved for when she was royally pissed off:

When did you start wearing Jean Patou?

He made a mental note to buy flowers.

The girls were sitting at the table when Michael made his way downstairs. Abby was cutting fruit for the new juicer, a huge stainless-steel contraption that seemed to have more dials and settings than an MRI machine. The girls had placed a hard-boiled egg on Michael's plate. It wasn't one of the fancy eggs – they were probably saving those for his basket – but rather a solid blue egg with *Daddy* written on it in that special yellow Easter egg crayon, the kind that's invisible until you dip the egg into the vinegary bowl of mysterious dye.

Michael kissed the girls on the tops of their heads. He tried to kiss Abby, but she craftily bent away from him, a chilly, silent willow in the wind.

"So what's up for today?" Michael asked. He cracked the egg, peeled it. It was as hard as a rock, but he would happily savor it nonetheless.

"Ballet," Emily said through a mouthful of cereal.

"I *love* ballet," Michael said. The truth was, he hadn't known they were taking ballet lessons. He chided himself for this.

"Miss Wolfe is our teacher," added Charlotte. She took a spoonful of cereal, wiped her lips, then replaced her spoon on the placemat, squaring it next to the fork. Precise, geometrical Charlotte.

"Is she nice?" Michael asked.

Both girls nodded.

"She puts stars on the floor, and we have to run away from them," Charlotte said. "Then she claps her hands and we have to run back."

To Michael this sounded more like some kind of football drill. "Sounds like fun."

"Today we're going to do a dummy play," Emily said.

"A dummy play?"

"It's called a demi plié," Abby chimed in.

"Ah, okay," Michael said. "Is that like Demi Moore?"

The girls giggled, even though Michael was certain they had no idea who Demi Moore was. Abby, on the other hand, *did* know who Demi Moore was, but there would be no humor found in any of Michael Roman's terrible jokes this day.

"We do it at the barre," Emily added, matter-of-factly.

Michael recoiled in horror. He grabbed his chest. "You guys are too young to go to a bar!"

The girls rolled their eyes.

"Unlike their father," Abby said under her breath.

Michael picked up the newspaper, held it up for cover.

"Come on, girls. Let's get our dishes in the sink and get ready," Abby said.

As Abby got the girls dressed for ballet class, Michael slammed a quartet of Advil, finished his coffee, scanned the *Daily News*. There was a brief article about the trial of Patrick Ghegan, recapping the original story about the murder of Colin Harris, which had made the front page of both the *Daily News* and its bitter rival, the *New York Post*. There was even a mention of "tenacious assistant district attorney Michael Roman." It wasn't exactly front page and above the fold in the *Times*, but he'd take it.

A few minutes later Charlotte and Emily walked back into the kitchen. They were both wearing pink leotards and white quilted ski jackets, even though it was nearing fifty degrees outside. As a rule, Abby kept them bundled up until about May 1 every year. She was, after all, the one who nursed the girls through their bouts with sore throats, coughs, colds, and ear infections.

"Let me see," Michael said.

Charlotte and Emily both spun slowly around, hanging onto the edge of the table for balance, as close to being en pointe as they could get.

"My pretty ballerinas."

The girls gave Michael a hug and a kiss. Abby did not. It told Michael all he needed to know about the height, depth, and breadth of the dog house in which he was now boarding.

As he watched Abby's car pull out of the driveway he made a second mental note to get a box of Godiva chocolates in addition to the flowers.

By ten-thirty he was gaining a semblance of a day, and everything he had to do. He had to be in court at two o'clock, and after that he had to stop by and check on the progress of an office on Newark Street. A group of Queens and Brooklyn lawyer friends were opening a small legal clinic, working strictly pro bono and, as a favor – a favor he now regretted offering – Michael had taken on part of the burden of helping get the place renovated, painted, and ready for business.

He got onto his computer, logged onto the DA's office secure website. It had been a relatively slow night, it seemed. In addition to a pair of robberies in the 109, and a suspected arson in Forest Hills, there had been one homicide. A woman named Jilliane Suzanne Murphy had been stabbed to death in her apartment. She was a forty-one year old stockbroker, a divorcee, no children. There were no suspects.

New York, Michael thought, closing down the web browser. The city that never sleeps.

*

Michael was just about out the door, bagel in fist, when his cellphone rang. He looked at the LCD screen. It was a private number. It wasn't Abby, it wasn't the office, so how important could it be?

The phone rang again, loud and insistent and annoyingly cellular. Take it or leave it, he debated. His head was killing him.

Ah *shit*. He answered.

"Hello?"

"Michael?"

A familiar voice, although Michael had a hard time placing it. "It is. Who's this?"

"Michael this is Max Priest."

The name brought him back. Way back. He had not spoken to Priest in nearly five years. Priest had done some electronic and photographic surveillance work for the DA's office, had wired more than a dozen confidential informants for Michael and his team.

Back in the day Michael always considered Max Priest to be a true professional – prudent, honest, and as forthright as one can be and still maintain the anonymity needed to do the kind of work he did.

While the two men were friendly, always cordial, they were not what either of them would consider friends. Michael instantly wondered how Priest had gotten his cellphone number. On the other hand, considering Max Priest was an expert on all things electronic, it was no real surprise.

"How is suburban life treating you?" Priest asked.

It was a good question, one to which Michael still did not have an honest answer. "It took a while, but we've settled in," he said. "Suburban life is good. You should try it."

"Not me," Priest said. "If I don't hear a car horn honk every five seconds I can't sleep."

They made shop talk for another minute or so, then Michael brought the conversation back.

"So what's up?"

Michael heard Priest draw a deep breath. It sounded like a prelude to something. Something bad.

Michael had no idea.

Priest chose his words carefully, related them in a calm, reassuring manner. It didn't help. The subtext of what Priest had to say was something Michael had always feared, but never thought would actually happen.

And, for the third time in his life, the world dropped out from beneath Michael Roman's feet.

Abby said she had known the minute they stepped into the restaurant. It wasn't that she was blessed with any sort of prescience, it was just that Michael Roman – despite being one of the hottest young ADAs in New York, a job all but dependent on playing cards close to the chest – was terrible at hiding anything when it came to affairs of the heart. She saw it in the way he couldn't seem to finish a complete sentence. She saw it in the way he fawned over her, how the ice cubes rattled slightly in his glass of water, the way his leg seemed to itch every ten seconds or so. She saw it in his eyes.

As soon as they were seated, Abby told him that she knew he was going to propose. And that she had something she needed to say before he popped the question.

Michael had almost looked relieved. Almost.

Abby steeled herself, and told him that she could not have children.

For a moment, Michael said nothing. It was, Abby eventually told him, the longest moment of her life. She had prepared for it, had told herself that if there was a moment's hesitation on Michael's part, if there was any indication that he no longer wanted to spend his life with her, she would understand.

"It's okay," he said.

It really was.

Two months later they were married.

It was Abby's idea to try and adopt an Estonian child. Michael could not have been happier. At first, everything seemed to go smoothly. They contacted an agency in South Carolina, the only agency on the east coast that handled Baltic adoptions, and learned that married couples and single men and women over twenty-five years of age could adopt from Estonia. They learned that there were a number of waiting children. They were also told that before an adoption could be approved, the adopting couple needed to go to Estonia and meet the child. This was fine with Abby, and especially with Michael. He had long yearned to visit his parents' homeland.

But one day, as they got closer to the event, they got the bad news. They learned that the total process, from dossier submission until the time adoptive parents receive the child, averaged six to twelve months. And that waiting children were generally over five years old.

They agonized over the decision, but in the end they agreed that, while children five and over certainly deserved loving homes, they wanted a baby.

The process seemed hopeless, until Max Priest put Michael in touch with a lawyer, who knew a lawyer, a man who could speed up the process, and would know how they could adopt a child under the age of six months. For a price.

While the initial exit processing was done in Tallinn, the medical exam and visa preparation took place in Helsinki. Applicants with ethnic ties to Estonia were given preference.

Six weeks after their application, Michael and Abby flew to Columbia, South Carolina, and drove an hour west to a small clinic in Springdale. That afternoon, after waiting what seemed like a lifetime in a small waiting room, a nurse walked in carrying two small bundles. The girls were two months old, and they were beautiful.

Michael recalled holding them for the first time. He recalled how everything else swam away, how the sounds in the background blended together into one far off symphony. It was in that moment he knew that everything bad that had happened to him in his life was now part of the past, a dark and terrible prologue to this, the first chapter of his story. It was the happiest day of his life.

They named the girls Charlotte and Emily. Charlotte, after Abby's father Charles. Emily — and Michael would deny this under oath — because he was a slavish fan of British actress Emily Watson.

As he looked at their tiny faces, at their little fingers, he vowed that nothing bad would happen to them. He would give his own life first.

According to everyone Michael spoke to, the man to whom he had paid ten thousand dollars to broker the adoption — a Queens storefront lawyer who specialized in handling the legal affairs of people of Russian and East European ancestry — was discrete, trustworthy, and above all, appeared to be unconnected to the world of illegal adoption. Or so they had all thought.

That man's name was Viktor Harkov.

And now that man was dead.

Max Priest told him what he knew. He said that someone had tortured and murdered Viktor Harkov in his office, and had apparently stolen a number of files. If this were all true, Michael knew, investigators would begin looking into motives, into client lists, into the legality and illegality of Viktor Harkov's dealings, into his files, into his past.

Into Charlotte and Emily.

If that happened – if investigators discovered that the papers regarding the adoption of his little girls were not completely above board, that payoffs were made and documents were forged – the state could take his daughters away, and life would be over.

He could not let it happen.

Tommy answered on the first ring.

"Tommy, it's Michael."

"Hey *cugino*."

"Can you talk?"

Through the phone, Michael heard Tommy cross his office, shut the door. "What's up?"

Michael knew enough not to get too specific on an open line. "Have you heard about the homicide in the 114? The lawyer?"

"I heard something," Tommy said. "No specifics. Why?"

Michael felt as if he was about to crest the first hill of the Cyclone, the Coney Island roller coaster of his youth. He felt his stomach lift and fall. "It was Viktor Harkov."

Michael heard a short intake of breath, as well as the sounds of Tommy getting on his computer. Tommy knew Harkov professionally, had faced him in court a few times, but he also knew that Michael had had dealings with the man. "Fucking city," Tommy said. "How did you hear? It was just posted on the site maybe two minutes ago."

Michael would tell Tommy about the call from Max Priest, but not over the phone. "Who's got it?"

Michael heard the clicking of keyboard keys. "Paul Calderon."

"Do you think he'll give it up?"

Tommy took a few seconds. "Hang on."

Paul Calderon was good news. When the call had gone out at around 4 AM, it had most likely been a Group Seven notification – the ADA on call, the chief assistant, the executive staff. The ADA, in this case Paul Calderon, would have been awakened, along with a riding assistant, usually a first- or second-year lawyer. It may have been the assigned ADA who supervised everything, but it was the riding assistant who figured out the details, the legal propriety of the warrant, the probable cause, whether or not the information was timely. Staleness was always a concern.

Michael knew that Calderon was no more than a month or two from announcing his retirement, and a case like this, a brutal homicide of a well known figure, was going to take a lot of time and effort, effort Michael was hoping Calderon did not want to expend. The hope, for the moment, was that Tommy could wrest the case away.

Tommy returned a full minute later. "I'm in," he said. "We have to run it by the boss, but Calderon was happy to let it go."

"Any warrants?"

"There's one in the works. It's already with a judge."

"I want to ride on this."

Tommy fell silent. "Uh, aren't you in court at two?"

"I'll explain when I see you."

Tommy knew Michael well enough to let it go. "You know where it is?"

Michael would never forget. "Yeah. 31st and Newtown."

"That's it," Tommy said. "Meet me in front of Angelo's."

"Thanks," Michael said.

Michael clicked off the phone. He took another Advil, dressed in jeans and a T-shirt, and brought out a windbreaker with the QDA logo on the back. He scribbled a quick note on the whiteboard in the kitchen, took five hundred dollars in cash from the safe. He took his suit and shirt and new tie, grabbed his briefcase, got into the car, and headed to the train station.

FOURTEEN

Abby spent the early part of the afternoon at the block sale, haggling good-naturedly with other women from the neighborhood, bargaining over glassware, picture frames, jigsaw puzzles, flatware.

She had always thought that garage sale items were nothing more than worthless junk being sold and resold to the same people over and over again. Granted, sometimes there were pearls to be found in the suburban oyster, but rarely.

Earlier in the day she had brought over three large boxes from the house, a good deal of it things she had picked up at garage sales and flea markets over the years, proving her point. One of the boxes was full of paperbacks; yellowed mass-market copies of books she had been shelving and reshelving since college. Colleen McCollough, Harold Robbins, Stephen King. She found it terribly difficult to part with books, but she made herself a promise this time.

At just after one, while talking to Mindy Stillman, who seemed to have an immeasurable trove of anecdotes about her ex-husband's infidelities, Abby waved over Charlotte and Emily. She needed to get them fed and ready to drop off at the babysitter's house.

She did not see or hear the black SUV turn the corner, drive up her long driveway, and park behind the garage.

*

In the distance, the smoke of burning thatch writes the village's epitaph in the sky. He feels alive, connected to history by the blood beneath his boots, still electrified from the insanity of battle. He checks himself for wounds. He is unscathed. Around him is a meadow sown with the fallen.

He enters the farmhouse. He knows every stone, every timber, every sill. It has lived in his dreams for a long time.

The old woman glances up from her task. She has met Koschei before, knows the centuries of madness in his eyes. Her house is warm, heated by the burning fields, the fires that have brought Grozny to its knees. The kitchen smells of fresh bread and human flesh. The senses are ashamed of their hungers.

"You," she says softly, the tears rimming her ancient eyes. She draws the knife to her own throat. "You."

While Abby flipped through the new issue of *Architectural Digest,* the girls played in the backyard. In about an hour Abby needed to drop them off at the babysitters, before heading to the clinic. She had a twelve-hour shift coming up and, as much as she had intended to catch up on her sleep, she was tired already. On the days when she worked, and Michael was in court, there was usually a three- or four-hour window where they needed someone to watch the girls.

Regardless, she needed to give the girls a bath before they left. It was getting to be more and more of an ordeal these days, ever since Charlotte and Emily discovered the world of skincare products. She also needed to make them a snack.

As she took out the peanut butter and jelly she heard the back door open and close.

"Let's get ready for your bath, girls," Abby said.

She made the sandwiches by rote, her mind on her upcoming shift. She cut the crust off Emily's sandwich.

Charlotte liked the crust. Grape jam for Emily; strawberry for Charlotte. She bagged the half-sandwiches, listened to the house.

Had the girls come in? If so, they were a little too quiet. It could only mean one of two things. They were tired, or they were scheming.

"Come *on*, girls."

"You are even more beautiful than I imagined."

Abby dropped the jar of strawberry preserves at the sound of the man's voice. A *strange* man's voice. She spun around. In front of her, just a few feet away, stood a tall, broad-shouldered man. He wore a long black leather coat. His face was rugged, chiseled, and bore a ragged scar on his left cheek. He did not brandish a weapon of any sort. Instead, in his right hand, was a red rose.

The reality dawned. There was a stranger in the hallway.

A stranger. *In her house.*

The girls.

Abby opened her mouth to scream, but no sound emerged. It was as if her ability to make a noise was somehow stillborn within her. She darted around the man, toppling a chair in the process. Somewhere behind her another glass shattered on the floor. The man did not move in any way to stop her.

"Girls?" she yelled.

She ran into the living room. They were not there. The sense of panic soon swelled to an overwhelming feeling of terror.

"*Girls?*"

She looked in the bathroom, the downstairs bedroom. She ran to the back door, opened the sliding glass door leading to the patio, her heart racing to burst. In the backyard she saw another man sitting on the picnic table. A younger man, strong looking. Charlotte and Emily stood at the back of the property. They were holding each other, their eyes wide with fear. A few seconds later the man in the house stepped up behind Abby. He did not touch her, did not raise his voice. His voice was almost reassuring. He had an accent.

"That young man is with me. Trust me, no harm will come to you or your family if you do as I say."

Trust me. It sounded unreal, like dialogue in a movie. But Abby knew it was real. Everything she had dreaded the night before was now in front of her. Somehow, the fact that it was broad daylight did not make it any easier.

"It is important that you do exactly as I say."

Abby turned to face him. He had stepped back, into the hallway leading to the kitchen. The anger began to bloom inside her.

"Get out of my *house!*"

The man did not move.

The gun, Abby thought. Her eyes flicked to the stairs. She would never make it past him. She glanced at the kitchen counter. The scissors sat there, gleaming in the afternoon sunlight, daring her to reach for them. They looked a hundred miles away.

"You must try to remain calm," he said.

"Who the fuck are you?" Abby screamed.

The man seemed to wince at her profanity. Then his features softened. "My name is Aleksander Savisaar." He closed the sliding glass door, slid the bolt. He turned back to Abby. "Before we go any further, I would like you to do something for me."

The man spoke with a quiet authority that chilled Abby to the bottom of her soul. She did not respond.

"First, I would like you to calm down. As I said, nothing bad is going to happen to you, your husband, or your lovely home. Can you calm down for me?"

Abby tried to stop shaking. She stood staring at the man. Crazily, she thought of the time her brother Wallace fell off a jungle gym at the school playground, breaking his arm, twisting it at an unnatural angle behind his neck. Abby had been only five years old at the time, and had known that something bad had happened, but she had been immobilized by the sight of his arm doing something it could never do. He looked like a broken doll.

She felt that way now. Frozen by the idea of what was happening. In a second, it occurred to her that this man, this man who did not belong in her house, her life, her world, had asked her a question.

"What?" she asked, returning to the moment.

"Can you remain calm for me?"

Calm. Yes. She remembered helping Wallace – big, goofy, ungainly Wallace – back to the house, where her mother had called an ambulance. She had taken charge. She would take charge now.

"Yes."

The man smiled. "Good. Next I want you to go into the backyard, and tell the girls not to be afraid. Tell them that Kolya and I – Kolya is the young man – are friends of the family, and that the girls have nothing to fear from either of us. Will you do this?"

Abby just nodded.

Aleks looked out the window, nodding to the man in the backyard, then returned his attention to her. "You have nothing to fear either, Abigail."

The sound of her name was a sudden twist of the knife. "How do you know my name?"

"I know many things," he said. He held forth the rose. Abby noticed a single drop of dew on one of the petals, the way one of the thorns had broken off.

Funny that, she thought. *The things you notice.*

"And there is no need to worry." When Abby didn't take the flower from him, he put it down on the dining-room table, then slipped back into the shadows of the hallway. When he turned away from her his coat fell open. On his hip was a large knife in a leather sheath.

This was everything Abby had ever feared, and it was all happening. Right this minute.

"If you do everything I say," the man who called himself Aleksander Savisaar added, "Anna and Marya will be just fine."

FIFTEEN

People's Legal Services was on the second floor of a sooty brick building on 31st Street, near Newtown Avenue.

This day there was yellow crime-scene tape strung out onto the sidewalk, wrapped around two parking meters, and back. The sidewalk was blocked, much to the inconvenience and consternation of the people walking up 31st Street. Profanity in an assortment of languages floated just below the maddeningly enticing aroma of borscht coming from the market across the street.

Michael had driven to the Ardsley-on-Hudson station in Irvington, and taken the Metro North train. He got off at Grand Central and took the uptown 5 train to the 59th Street/Lexington station, then caught the R to Astoria. For New Yorkers, life was a series of numbers and letters, the alphabet-soup language of riding the subway. It seemed you spent half your time discussing the best and alternate routes to get where you were trying to go, and the other half stuck on trains, lamenting the fact that you didn't take another path. Today, Michael did it all by rote. He almost missed his stop.

As he walked up Ditmars Boulevard, he found that the buildings and people and pavement had melted away, replaced by a single mental image:

His father, smiling, handing a loaf of brown bread to old Mrs

Hartstein, antique even then, her rouge a deep scarlet sunburst on paper-white skin.

Ghosts walk here, Michael Roman thought. He did not glance at the building at number 64.

In the years following the murder of his parents, the bakery and the apartment above sat vacant. A few tenants tried to make a go of the downstairs space, but most prospective tenants, after learning of the horrors that had taken place at 64 Ditmars Boulevard, moved on. The upstairs apartment had never been rented again.

Four years earlier, on their first wedding anniversary, the first phase of Abby's trust fund kicked in, and at dinner that night she presented Michael with the deed to the building. If Abby's parents had not initially been enamored with Abby marrying Michael, their reaction to Abby taking the bulk of her check for $750,000 – one of two she would receive, the other to be given on her thirty-second birthday – and buying an ugly brick building on a struggling block in Astoria, had all but caused them apoplexy.

Michael had no idea if and when they would ever do anything with the property. At first he wasn't sure how he even felt about the gesture. Over time he came to understand that it somehow kept his parents closer, and for that he could never thank his wife enough. It was the most beautiful thing anyone had ever done for him.

To this day, he had not been back inside.

Tommy was waiting for him in front of Angelo's. He had on his court face.

"Hey," Tommy said.

"Hey."

"Fucking city."

"Fucking city."

Tommy told him what he knew about the case, which was not much. The 911 call had come in at 4 AM that morning.

All 911 calls for the entire city of New York were routed to a central Manhattan-based location. After the location of the call was determined, the call was routed to the local precinct and sector therein. In Astoria, it would be the 114th precinct.

The detective assigned to the case would be the one next "up" for the assignment, which was, by tradition, selected by rotation throughout the squad. Michael had never been a fan of the system, which was deeply entrenched in the NYPD, because it sometimes led to the most challenging cases being assigned to the detective with the least imagination and initiative. Detectives were 1st, 2nd and 3rd grade, with 1st being the highest. Promotion of grade was based on another tradition, a combination of time-in-grade, seniority, office politics, performance and timing. Injustice was sadly the all-too-frequent result.

When Michael saw the tall, regal figure standing in the doorway leading up to People's Legal Services, it was good news and bad news. The fact that Detective First Grade Desiree Powell was the lead investigator into the suspicious death of Viktor Harkov was good news for the friends, family, and loved ones of the deceased, among whom Michael Roman could be counted. It was bad news for anyone who had anything to hide, anyone who had even the most peripherally shady dealings with the lawyer, of whom Michael Roman might also well be grouped. If it was there, Desiree Powell would find it. She was relentless.

The scene was crawling with uniforms, suits, forensic investigators, brass. It wasn't that Viktor Harkov was a celebrity victim, or that this case was necessarily going to make headlines for more than a day, but Harkov knew a lot of people, on both sides of the law, and whenever a defense attorney was killed, the ripples went far and wide. The NYPD wanted a ring around this potential circus as soon as possible.

As Michael and Tommy crossed the street, toward the building that housed Viktor Harkov's office, Powell looked up from a report at which she was glancing. She gave a slight dip to her chin, acknowledging Michael. Michael waved back, knowing that in the next few minutes he would talk to Powell and everything he said would become part of the record, part of the maelstrom surrounding this place where evil had visited, and once again left its indelible mark.

SIXTEEN

Desiree Powell was a striking woman – soft-spoken, fastidious in her dress and speech, a legendary ballroom dancer. She was of Jamaican descent, born and raised in a small village in the Blue Mountains north of Kingston.

Powell had now been a police officer for twenty-four years, the first seven in uniform on the streets of the 103, patrolling Hollis and South Jamaica in those hard years when crack came to south-eastern Queens.

When you're a female police officer in your twenties you get it from all corners – suspects, witnesses, fellow officers, ADAs, judges, CSU techs, chiefs, captains, commanders and, providing it was not a homicide, quite often from the victims themselves. When you're just shy of six feet tall, you get even more. More than once she'd had to mix it up, and in all the years, she had not lost that edge.

These days, on the good days, when the light hit her right and she put in her forty-five minutes on the treadmill, she could pass for a decade younger than her forty-six years. Other days she looked and felt every second, plus. She knew she could still turn heads, but sometimes the effort wasn't worth the whistle.

Standing on the corner of Newtown and 31st Street, directing a perimeter, Powell knew that it may have been her gold badge that gave her access, but it was her manner that gave her authority.

What she had seen in that blood-splattered office was in every way wrong. The worse the scene, the more she wanted it.

Two men from the DA's office approached. Michael Roman and Tommy Christiano. Powell had worked with both of them. The Glimmer Twins. They were stars in the office, and, although the police and DA's office were in theory on the same side, sometimes ego trumped justice.

And, Detective Desiree Powell thought, there was definitely ego to spare on this corner, on this day.

SEVENTEEN

Powell glanced between them, back and forth. She wore an impeccably tailored black suit, lavender blouse, a simple gold chain around her slender neck. Her nails, which she had wisely cut short – a necessity for fieldwork – were highly polished, the color of her blouse. She and Michael were the same height.

"Do we have a suspect in custody I don't know about?" Powell asked.

As a rule, any number of officials could be summoned to the scene of a homicide – Squad Commander, Chief of Detectives, Crime Scene Unit, Medical Examiner. Representatives of the district attorney's office were routinely called only when the suspect was detained or arrested at the scene. There were, however, many exceptions to this.

"No," Tommy said. "I just can't resist a woman in a suit."

"Where's Paul?"

She was asking about Paul Calderon, the originally assigned ADA. "Paul needed some personal time," Tommy said. "So lucky you. You got me."

"A girl could do worse."

"I have two exes who would disagree."

Powell smiled, glanced at Michael. "And the Stone Man himself," she said. "Been a while."

She and Michael shook hands. They had not seen each other

an jargon. He had seen the woman on the stand
, and when the proceedings called for it, Powell
like a professor of linguistics. On the street though,
mes spoke in her patois. Desiree Powell could work
big or small.

onversation gave way momentarily to the traffic
the hum of the street, the apparatus of a crime scene.
glanced at Michael. "So how have you been?"

well," Michael said. He felt anything but.

u are both working this," Powell said.

ere was a direct question in that statement, a question
for Michael than Tommy. It hung in the air like smoke
darkened theater.

knew him," Michael said.

owell took a few moments, nodded. She probably knew this.
probably knew a little more about Michael and Harkov, but
t of respect for Michael's position, she didn't press it. For the
oment. "I am sorry for the loss of your friend."

Michael wanted to correct her — Viktor Harkov was by no
means his friend — but he let it drop. He knew the less he said
at this time the better.

"What did you get from the son?" Tommy asked.

"The son says he last saw his father last night. Says he brought
the old man a bowl of soup. I think he knows a little bit more
than he is saying. I'll have him in the chair later today."

"But you don't like him for this," Michael said.

Powell shook her head. "No. But I think he knows some
reason why this was done. I'll get him talking. Like they say in
Kingston, the higher the monkey climbs the more him expose,
eh?"

"Des?"

It was Desiree Powell's partner, Marco Fontova.

"Excuse me a moment," she said, stepping away.

in nearly a year. It happened [...] you been?" Michael asked.

"Better days." Powell gestur[...] crime scene. "Some fuckery this, [...]

"Bad?" Tommy asked.

"Bad."

"What happened?"

Powell teased her short hair. It was [...] but Desiree Powell was nothing if [...] appearance. Michael had not once seen h[...] ning shoes. "We don't know too much yet. [...] was tortured. Burned."

"Burned?"

Powell nodded. "This is not the worst of it e[...]

Worse than tortured, burned, and murde[...] thought. What the hell happened up there? More [...] why?

"Was it a robbery?" Tommy asked.

Powell shrugged. "Too early to say. Place was [...] sacked. There was money in his wallet. Only one d[...] the file cabinet was open. It wasn't pried."

Michael felt his heart skip a beat. The fact that a file [...] was open didn't mean anything. Yet.

"Who called it in?" Tommy asked.

"The son. He stopped by on his way home from work. H[...] a night man on the MTA. When he could not reach his fath[...] on the phone, he became concerned."

"Are we looking at the son?" Tommy asked.

Powell shook her head. "Not now. Viktor Harkov had some shady dealings, though, I believe. He knew some bad people, did some bad business. Some times these t'ings come back to haunt you, ya no see it?"

Michael had forgotten how Powell sometimes slipped into

Fontova was around thirty, disposed to striped suits a size too small and a bit too much cologne for daytime. His hair was short and spiked, a style maybe five years too young, but he pulled it off. Michael did not know him well, but knew that Marco Fontova was part of the post 9/11 class of investigators on the NYPD. And that meant, to people who didn't know better, mostly in the media, he was lacking.

Michael learned early on that detectives, good detectives, did not learn what they knew from the academy, or manuals, or the bosses. Detectives were schooled by the older cops. Techniques of interrogation and investigation were passed down from experienced detectives to rookies in a ritual as old as the department itself. But when 9/11 happened, a good bit of that changed. On that day, and for weeks and months afterward, law enforcement in the city of New York – and to a certain extent, criminal activity – shut down. Every available detective headed down to ground zero to help out.

The result was that a lot of detectives near their twenty-year mark accumulated so much overtime, that they retired that year. The further result was that the next crop of city detectives did not have rabbis from whom they could learn, and there were some who felt that many investigators on the job for the past seven or eight years were not up to the task.

Desiree Powell was not one of these detectives. She had come up on her own at a time when women, especially black women, were not welcomed into the club that was the gold shield detective. Michael could not think of anyone he would rather work with. By the same token, he could not think of anyone he would rather not go up against.

Powell stepped back over to where Michael and Tommy stood. She glanced at the window on the second floor, then at Tommy. "CSU is wrapping up. Shouldn't be too much longer."

"We'll be across the street," Tommy said, pointing at the pizza parlor.

Powell shoved her hands in her pockets, turned, and walked across the street. In that moment, a transport van from the ME's office arrived. Two weary techs stepped out, walked around back, casually slid out the gurney. They moved as if underwater, and for good reason. It was a beautiful spring day. Viktor Harkov wasn't going anywhere.

They stood at the window counter at Angelo's. Tommy worked a slice. Michael was not hungry.

Michael had related the entire story, sparing no detail, beginning with the first call made to the adoption agency in South Carolina, and ending with the moment he and Abby unlocked the door to the house and brought Charlotte and Emily into their new home.

As he was telling the tale, Michael watched Tommy's face. He knew that this would hurt Tommy – they had few secrets from each other – but Tommy just listened, implacable, not judging.

Like the savvy lawyer he was, Tommy gave it a few long moments before responding with the options. "You're saying the papers were forged?" he asked.

"Just the one document," Michael replied, matching his volume. "The adoption broker in Helsinki, the one whose job it was to approve and clear the time frame. His assistant was paid five thousand dollars to forge his name on the clearance. The man – the official – died two years ago. We always felt that, unless they began to dig deep and ask a lot of questions, it couldn't possibly come out."

Tommy folded his slice, took a bite, wiped his lips. "They're going to start digging in about an hour. You know that, right?"

Michael just nodded. He knew that, if his name was in one of Viktor Harkov's files, investigators would get around to him.

Tommy finished eating, rolled his trash and put it in the can. He carefully inspected his shirt, tie, trousers. No grease. He sipped his soda. "How did Harkov work these things Did he keep separate files?"

"I don't know," Michael said. "I met him once at his office, then a second time at a restaurant in midtown."

"Were there official documents you signed?"

"Yeah," Michael said. "The standard papers. Everything filed with the state of New York is perfectly legal."

Tommy looked across the street, at the growing official presence. He looked back at Michael. "You know if you go up there, you have to sign the log. It will all be on the record."

"I know." Michael tried to sort out all the ramifications of his presence at this scene. He couldn't think straight. All that mattered was keeping his family safe and intact.

Powell stepped out of the crime scene building, caught Tommy's eye, waved him over.

Tommy slipped on his suit coat, shot his cuffs. He handed Michael the keys to his car.

"Let me see what I can find out."

Michael watched Tommy cross the street. He looked at his watch. He was due in court in ninety minutes.

Michael stood on the street. The sun was high and warm, the sky clear. Too nice a day for dead bodies. Too nice a day for the world to end.

He recalled the first and only time he had visited Viktor Harkov in his office. He had known what he was doing was wrong, that making a covert payoff to grease the wheels of the adoption process might one day come back to haunt him, but there was a higher purpose, he had thought at the time, a nobility in his larceny.

As he stood there, watching the police do their job, getting ever closer to the truth, he asked himself if it had been worth it. In his mind, he saw his beautiful girls. The answer was yes.

He took out his phone, scrolled down to Abby's cellphone number. His finger hovered over the touch screen. He had to call her, but couldn't tell her about this. Not yet. Perhaps this had nothing to do with Viktor's side-business of adoption. Maybe this was just another robbery homicide, or some family or ethnic dispute gone terribly wrong. Maybe Viktor Harkov had gotten involved in something far more dangerous than simply circumventing adoption laws. Maybe there was nothing for them to worry about.

On the other hand, maybe there was.

EIGHTEEN

He stood about ten feet away, in the hallway leading to the first-floor office. He was half in shadow, but seemed to fill up the entire door jamb.

Abby watched him. She tried to think of how much cash she could get together. The man had said nothing yet about money, but it was coming. What else could this be about? The man who called himself Aleksander, along with his partner, had probably done this before, stalking a suburban family, holding them for ransom. She'd read about it.

How long had they been watching? How much did they want? Why had they been selected? They weren't rich. Far from it. Hell, all you had to do was check out the cars in the driveways along the street. The Murrays had a Lexus and a BMW. The Rinaldis had a Porsche Cayenne.

Abby did the math. There was less than a thousand dollars in the house. She had very little jewelry. They owned no valuable paintings or sculpture. If you added up all the gadgets – digital camera, camcorder, computers, stereo system – it didn't add up to much. Was this going to work against them?

The initial shock of seeing a stranger standing in her home had begun to fade, turning instead into something else, the slow-crawling fear one feels when things slide completely beyond one's control.

Keep it together Abby, she thought. *The girls. The girls. The —*

— cellphone rang. Abby jumped. The sound of the ringtone — a silly song she and the girls had downloaded online — sounded sardonically comic now, as if they were all in an abandoned amusement park.

The phone was on the counter, halfway across the kitchen. The man who called himself Aleksander picked up the phone, looked at it. He beckoned Abby toward him, showed her the screen.

It was Michael calling.

Abby noticed for the first time that the man was wearing latex gloves. The sight made her heart sink even lower. It added all kinds of possibilities, any number of futures to this scenario. All dark. Perhaps this was not a kidnapping after all. Perhaps this was not about money.

"I want you to speak to him," he said. "I want you to sound normal. I want you to tell him whatever it is you tell him on a beautiful day such as this. He will soon enough know his role. But not now." Aleks pointed out the window. The man he called Kolya was pushing the girls on their swings. "Do you understand this?"

"Yes."

"Please put this on speakerphone."

Abby took the phone. Despite her trembling hands, she flipped it open, pressed SPEAKER. She did her best to keep the fear from her voice. "Hey."

"Hey."

"What's up?" Abby asked. "You at the office?"

"Yeah," Michael said. "I'm going to be stuck here for a while. The *voir dire* is taking longer than I thought."

If there was one thing Abby Roman and her husband excelled at in their marriage, it was a nightly recap of their days. Abby was certain that the Colin Harris case — a case Abby knew was close to the bone for Michael – had wrapped its jury selection days earlier. The *voir dire* was complete, the panel was set, and here was her husband telling her it was not.

"You're inside your office?" Abby asked.

A pause, then: "Yeah."

Michael was lying. She heard street sounds in the background, *loud* street sounds. He was outside.

Why was he lying?

"Something wrong?" Abby asked. She looked at Aleks as she said this, feeling he knew that she was trying to communicate something. He now stood in the shadows of the hallway, listening intently to the conversation. She could not see his eyes. He was impenetrable. "Are you worried about the case?"

"Not really," Michael replied. "Just a few last-minute details. No big deal."

"The block sale went pretty well," Abby said, trying to sound chatty. "We sold the toreador painting. It went for high one-figures."

The toreador painting was a running joke. Michael, whose taste in oils and acrylics ranged from *A Bachelor's Dog* to *New Year's Eve in Dog Ville*, bought it at a flea market while he was in college. It had sat in their garage for their entire marriage – Abby refused to hang it in the house – the unsold veteran of five straight block sales, in two different counties.

"Babe?" Abby said. "The painting?"

A long pause. Abby wondered if the call had been dropped. Then: "I'm sorry," Michael said. "Let me . . . let me call you back."

"Good luck."

Another long pause. "Thanks."

Something *was* wrong. Abby glanced at Aleks. He nodded. He meant for her to hang up.

"Okay. I love you." Abby barely got the words out. She

wondered if this was the last time she'd ever speak to her husband. "And I —"

Dead air.

She pressed END CALL. The screen reverted to the photograph Abby used as wallpaper, a picture of herself, Michael, and the twins sitting on a bench near the beach in Cape May. Charlotte and Emily wore floppy straw sun hats. The sun was high, the water blue, the sand golden. Her heart ached.

Aleks held out his hands, indicating he wanted Abby to toss him the phone. She did. He caught it, put it in a pocket. "I appreciate your discretion. I am sure Anna and Marya do as well."

Anna and Marya. It was the second time he had used these names.

Abby slipped onto one of the stools at the breakfast counter. She remembered shopping for the stools in White Plains, trying to decide on color, fabric, finish. It seemed so important at the time. It seemed to matter. It seemed like a million years ago.

"What are you going to do with us?" she asked.

For a moment, the man looked amused at her choice of words. "We are going to do nothing. We are going to wait."

For how long? Abby wanted to ask. For whom? For what? She remained silent. She eyed the drawer on the kitchen island, the drawer containing the knives. Her glance was not lost on her captor.

He turned, glanced out the back window, then back to Abby.

"And now, if you would honor me with an introduction."

He crossed the kitchen, stopping just a few feet away from Abby, and for the first time she saw his face in the bright afternoon sunlight streaming through the large window overlooking the backyard, saw his pale eyes, his sharp cheekbones, the way his widow's peak met at his brow. The nausea suddenly became a violent, thrashing thing inside her. She knew this face almost as well as she knew her own. She tried to speak, but the words felt parched on her lips. "An introduction?"

Aleks smoothed his hair with his hands, straightened his clothing, as if he were a shy Victorian suitor meeting his betrothed for the first time. "Yes," he said. "It is time I met Anna and Marya."

"Why do you keep saying those names?" Abby asked, although she feared the answer. "Who are Anna and Marya?"

Aleks glanced out the window at the twins running around the yard. His profile was now unmistakable. He looked back at Abby.

His words took her legs away.

"They are my daughters."

NINETEEN

Michael sat in the passenger seat of Tommy's Lexus RR5, his mind outracing his heart. But not by much.

Abby had sounded distracted. Whenever she tried to make cocktail chatter with him, something was up. He had wanted to ask her why, but he knew he'd have to get off the phone quickly, because if he didn't, she would read *him*, and he would have been forced to tell her about Viktor Harkov. He hated to lie to her. He *didn't* lie to her. All he could hope for was that she didn't see it on the news before he could tell her. She rarely watched television news, so this was in his favor.

When he did tell her about the murder, he wanted to have a lot more information. There was only one way that was going to happen.

Tommy made his way through the traffic. He opened the driver's side door, but did not slip inside. He looked a little shaken. He took a few seconds. Tommy Christiano *never* took a few seconds. Especially with Michael.

"What's up, man?" Michael asked. "Talk to me."

Tommy looked up. "You sure you want to do this?"

Michael did not want to see it. He felt he had no choice. "Yeah. Let's do it."

*

The smell hit him first. It wasn't as bad as some of the ripe corpses he had encountered in his time in the office, but it was bad enough. Many of the crime scene personnel walking in and out of the office wore white masks.

They stood in the hallway. They were waiting for the investigating detectives to invite them in. There was a time when anyone authorized to be at a crime scene could walk onto the scene at any time. No longer. Enough contaminated crime scenes leading to forensic evidence being tossed out at trial had changed all that.

Michael could hear conversations inside the office. He strained to understand what was being said. He heard scattered words: *Telephone . . . voltage . . . serrated . . . eyelid . . . blood evidence.*

Michael did not hear anything about files, stolen or otherwise. He did not hear the word adoption. There was a glimmer of hope in this.

Five minutes later, Detective Powell waved them in.

When Michael met Viktor Harkov, nearly five years earlier, the man had walked with a limp. A long-time diabetic with a litany of other physical ailments, Harkov's body seemed frail even then. But not his mind. Although Michael had never squared off against the man in a courtroom, he knew a few lawyers who had, including Tommy, and they all agreed that Viktor Harkov never walked into Kew Gardens unprepared. He was much sharper than he looked. It was all part of the act.

Now Viktor Harkov looked hardly human.

The dead man slumped in his chair behind the desk. The sight was horrific. Harkov's skin was paper white, leached of all color. His mouth was open in a slash of terror, baring yellowed teeth, gums thick with dried blood and saliva. Where his left eye had been was now a charred bubble of flesh, a red bull's-eye at the center. A thin column of phlegm leaked from one of his nostrils.

As Michael passed to the left of Harkov's desk, he had to look twice to be certain what he was seeing was true. It appeared as if Harkov's trousers had been ripped or torn away. The area surrounding his genitals too had been burned, the flesh there blackened and spilt. Michael had seen many indignities in homicide victims – from the targets of sexual predators, to gang hits that left little to identify, to the nearly superhuman violence of murder done in a jealous rage – and in each there was a mortification to the way these people were seen in death. Perhaps a violent demise was in and of itself the final humiliation, one the victim could not avenge. Michael had always thought that this was part of his job as a prosecutor. Not to necessarily exact revenge – although anyone on the state side of the aisle who denied vengeance was part of their motivation would be lying – but rather to stand up in a court of law and restore some measure of dignity to those who could not rise.

What was done to Viktor Harkov was as brutal a humiliation as Michael had ever seen.

On the desk was a desk phone, an older touch-tone model, a nicotine-stained avocado green popular in the Seventies. From beneath the phone extended a pair of long electrical wires; one snaking across the desk and attached to one of Harkov's toes. The other wire, ending in an alligator clip, lay along Harkov's left leg. The alligator clip was scorched black.

But that was not the worst of it. The reason that the desk was covered in dark, drying blood, was that whoever had tortured this old man, whoever had killed this man, had thought the act of murder was not enough.

He had cut off the old man's hands.

Michael looked up from the mutilated corpse, his eyes

roaming the scene, for what? Perhaps some respite from the horror. Perhaps for some justification to why this man had been so destroyed in his place of business. Then it hit him. He was looking for something that would tell him to what degree to be worried. For a moment he felt deep shame, realizing he was leaping over the horror of what had happened to Viktor Harkov, and thinking about himself. As he glanced around the room, his gaze landed on Desiree Powell. His heart skipped.

Powell was watching *him*.

They stood in the outer office. Michael looked at the file cabinet. It was a five-drawer steel model. The bottom drawer was slightly open. A crime scene technician was dusting the file cabinet for prints.

"Is that how they found it?" Michael asked. "With only one drawer open?"

Tommy nodded.

Michael glanced below the desk. There he saw an old Dell tower computer, perhaps a Pentium II model from the Eighties or Nineties. It too was covered in black fingerprint powder. Michael knew they would take the entire computer system back to the lab for more controlled tests – including an examination of the data on the hard drive – but with a vicious murder like this, they did field tests to get prints up and into the system as soon as possible. The old adage about the first forty-eight hours of a homicide investigation being critical was not just an adage, it was true.

Whenever Michael rode to homicide scenes, he always stood on the sidelines, confident and somewhat in awe of the job that the criminalists did. He watched how they addressed the scene, always mindful of every aspect and department of the forensic team – fingerprints, hair and fiber, blood evidence, documents.

He had never wanted to jump in and help. Everyone had their job, and in Queens County those people were among the best in the city. But now, watching the glacial pace of the physical investigation, he felt helpless and increasingly hopeless. He wanted to tear through the file cabinets and see which files were missing. He wanted to go through the disks and CDs in Viktor Harkov's desk and delete any mention of the names Michael and Abby Roman. He wanted to drop a match in the middle of this dusty, ugly office, and destroy the essence of the practice. He wanted to do all these things because, if there was any possibility that his relationship with Viktor Harkov became known, there was a *real* possibility that Charlotte and Emily could be taken away. And that would be the end of his life.

All he could do, for the moment, was stand on the sidelines. And watch.

Fifteen minutes later, after the body had been moved to the morgue, which was located in South Queens, Michael and Tommy stood next to Tommy's car. Every other car on the block had gotten a ticket. Tommy had his Queens County DA's placard on the dashboard.

Neither man spoke for a long minute.

"Go to work," Tommy finally said. "You have a case to try."

Before Michael could respond, Tommy's cellphone rang. He stepped away, answered. While he talked, Michael looked down the street, toward Astoria Park. He watched them working on the huge pool in the park, getting it ready for the summer season. He recalled many a hot July or August day when he was small, jumping into the clear blue water, not a care in the world.

Tommy closed his phone. "We don't know too much yet," Tommy said. "First, they lifted a dozen prints off the file cabinet. They're running them now. Second, it looks like there were no backup files in the office. They took a quick look at the hard drive of the computer, and it was wiped clean."

"Do you think they'll be able to salvage anything from it?"

"They've done it before."

"So this *was* about Viktor's business."

"We don't know that yet," Tommy said. "But get this. They're pretty sure that the telephone and the wires were set up as some sort of torture device."

"The phone?"

"Yeah. I heard that the way it was hooked up was that if the phone rang, it would send a charge through the wires. They think whoever did this had it hooked up to the old guy's genitals, and his left eye."

"Christ."

"Sick bastard. They dumped the phone records from the office, and they found out that Harkov's office phone got sixteen calls in a ten-minute period, all from a disposable cell."

"My God."

"Whatever this guy wanted out of Harkov, the old fucker didn't give it up easily."

"What about his hands?"

"They figure it was post-mortem. But just."

"And this is how Harkov's son found him."

"Can you imagine?" Tommy said. "Turns out Viktor moved in with his son Joseph a year ago," he continued. "I guess they were pretty close."

"Did Powell get a statement from him yet?"

"Just a preliminary statement. And dig this. Joseph Harkov told Powell the police could *not* go through the old man's effects."

Because Viktor Harkov had something to hide, Michael thought. He felt his stomach churn with every breath.

"As you might expect, Powell is none too happy about this," Tommy added.

"Where is that warrant?"

"Calderon started working it around eight this morning. It was in the pipe before you called me."

Michael knew the process. A fresh homicide warrant would be expedited, as time was of the essence. It could come through any minute, or it might still be a few hours.

"Does anyone else live in the Harkovs' apartment?" Michael asked.

"I don't think so," Tommy said.

"Do you think the old man may have kept something at the apartment? Backup files, duplicate files?"

Silence from Tommy. He knew what Michael meant. He glanced at his watch.

"Let's go."

TWENTY

Aleks stood in the hallway on the second floor. On the walls were enlarged photographs of Michael and Abigail Roman and their two adopted daughters. One had them standing on a beach somewhere, tall sawgrass tufting through the sand all around them. Another had them all looking down into the lens, as if the photographer was in a hole of some sort. Yet another, when the girls were quite small, showed them standing between Abigail and Michael, against a brick wall. The girls barely came up to the adults' knees, and the photo was cut off at the parents' waists. It was clearly meant to be amusing, to show scale. The girls were much taller now. It made Aleks consider how much time had passed since he had ridden down to the Keskkülas' farm that dark night, how much time had passed since the midwife had found him and told him that Elena had gone into labor early.

He stood in the doorway to their room. There were two beds. The walls were pastel pink; the windows and doors had white trim. The furniture in the room – a nightstand between the beds, a low dresser, a pair of desks – were all white as well. The room was tidy, considering the occupants were four-year-old girls. There was the odd toy on the bed, a sweater folded on one of the desks. Beyond these things, the room was arranged with a casual precision.

In the far corner was a table with four little chairs, a table bearing place settings for three.

The room smelled of powders and fruity shampoo. On the walls were posters and drawings. The posters were of someone called Dora the Explorer. The drawings were of Valentines and shamrocks and Easter eggs.

He crossed the room, opened one of the drawers in the dresser. In it were neatly folded little T-shirts, rolled socks in shockingly bright colors. The second drawer held small plastic purses, folded nylon knapsacks, and two pairs of white gloves.

Aleks reached into the drawer, held the gloves in his hand, closed his eyes, felt their presence within him, saw the women . . .

. . . standing by the river, eternal, caught in that ephemeral beauty that knew neither youth nor age . . . at their feet the clear water runs . . . the ceaseless cycles of life. He sits on the nearby hill, flute in hand, his pride boundless. As everything around them is birthed and dies, generations flitting by in seconds, they remain the same. Above them, a light in the deep violet sky. Olga, never seen, always present . . .

The master bedroom on the second floor overlooked the front of the house. It was tastefully, if not expensively decorated. A four-poster bed, a dresser with an LCD flat-screen TV on it, an exercise bike in the corner. This room was not quite as tidy as the girls' room. It had the look and feel of people who lived their lives in a hurry.

Aleks went through the drawers. It seemed Abigail had control of the top three drawers in the dresser; Michael the bottom two.

The closet was packed with suits, shirts, skirts, dresses on wooden hangers. The shelves were crowded with boxes containing folded sweaters and vests. The top shelf held a box full of photos and memorabilia. Aleks removed the box, placed it on the bed.

He flipped through a pair of photo albums – Michael and Abigail at their wedding, their honeymoon, at Christmas and birthday parties. The second photo album was dedicated to the girls. On the first page was a large photo of Anna and Marya in a crib, in what looked like a doctor's office. They were no more than a few months old. Aleks tried to recall this time in his life, the first year or so after the girls had been stolen from him. The fury he felt was never far from the surface. The rest of the album was of the girls on the beach, the girls in the backyard, the girls on their tricycles.

At the bottom of the box was a scrapbook of sorts. Near the back of the book he found a series of articles about Michael. The longest article – indeed a cover story – was from *New York* magazine, dated five years earlier. The title on the front:

A QUEENS PROSECUTOR ESCAPES DEATH TO PUT
GANGSTERS AWAY

Aleks flipped to the table of contents, scanned it, then turned to the article. On the left-hand page was another photograph of Michael Roman, this time leaning against a car on a New York side street. Aleks began to read. The lead was typical fluff, but it was in the fifth paragraph that Aleks found something that fascinated him, something he had never expected.

Mr Roman, 30, has served as an assistant district attorney in Queens County for five years. Born in Astoria, he is no stranger to the world of street violence. When Roman was just nine years old, his parents, Peeter and Johanna, were murdered in a botched robbery of their shop, a specialty bakery called Pikk Street on Ditmars Boulevard.

A graduate of St John's Law School, Roman came to work for the Queens County DA's office in 1999, and since that time has prosecuted a number of high-profile cases.

Aleks's eyes skimmed down the page.

Investigators believe the car bombing was the work of the Patrescu brothers in an attempt to delay the trial. Incredibly, in the blast that destroyed half a city block, Mr Roman received just a few minor wounds.

Aleks looked at the photograph of the bombing. The car was a charred shell; the building behind it was all but rubble. It reminded him of many of the city streets in Grozny. It was truly stunning that the man had not been killed. A miracle.

And that's when it occurred to him. The man who had taken care of Anna and Marya all these years, the man whom his daughters called Daddy, was just like him. Michael Roman had faced the devil and walked away unharmed.

Michael Roman, too, was deathless.

TWENTY-ONE

In the backyard, Abby talked to the girls. She saw the fear in their eyes, but she did her best to allay it. The young man stood at the back of the property, smoking a cigarette. The one who called himself Aleks — the one who claimed to be Charlotte and Emily's biological father — was still in the house. Abby could not see him, but she could all but feel his predator's cold eyes on her.

For the moment, the girls still looked concerned, but not nearly as frightened as they had before. "Everything is okay, guys. There's no reason to be scared." Abby wished she knew this to be true. "Okay?"

The girls nodded.

"Are we going to Brittany's house?" Emily asked.

Brittany Salcer was a babysitter two streets over. She also babysat for her own sister's twin boys, who were just over three years old. "Not today honey."

"But why?"

"The boys have a cold. Brittany doesn't want you guys getting sick."

"Are you going to the hospital?"

The hospital was in fact the Hudson Medical Clinic, an urgent-care facility on Dowling Street. When they had moved from the city Abby had tried to hang onto her job as an ER nurse at Downtown Hospital, but the commute – an hour each way, not to mention the expense – was killing them. Her work at the clinic was not nearly as challenging, but she had fallen into a rhythm there. Throat cultures, lacerations, flu shots, skinned knees – what the job lacked in challenge it more than made up for in satisfaction.

"No," she said. "Not today."

Abby suddenly saw movement to her left. She noticed that the young man at the back of the yard noticed as well. A flash of bright red in the woods behind the house.

Abby glanced over. Zoe Meisner was walking through the woods, down by the creek. Her golden Lab Shasta was following a scent. Abby saw the dog stop, glance up the hill, nose high in the air. Was he picking up the scent of the young man? Of Kolya? In a flash the dog came bounding up the hill, churning leaves, kicking dirt, vaulting over logs. Zoe called to Shasta, but the dog did not heed her.

Zoe – she of the outrageously bright floral gardening smocks and even more outrageous floral perfume – noticed Abby and the girls and waved. Abby lifted a hand to wave back, but stopped herself. If she acknowledged Zoe, maybe the woman would take it as a reason to walk up the hill for an over-the-fence hen session. On the other hand, if Abby didn't acknowledge her, she might come over to see why. Abby waved back.

A few seconds later Zoe started to walk through the woods, up the hill, to the Roman house.

Shasta was already romping with the girls.

Abby saw the young man at the back of the yard toss his cigarette, stand a little straighter. His eyes flicked from the big dog, to the woman walking up the hill, back. He unbuttoned his jacket.

Inside the house, the curtains parted.

No, Abby thought.

No.

TWENTY-TWO

Joseph Harkov's apartment was a third floor walk-up on Twenty-First Avenue, near Steinway. According to the report, Joseph Harkov worked night shift at the MTA station at Broadway and 46th Street.

Michael and Tommy stood across the street in a Super Deli, watching the entrance. Michael had met Joseph Harkov twice, but that had been a few years ago, and only in passing. He wasn't sure he would remember the man if he saw him.

At just after one, Joseph Harkov walked out of the front door. Michael pegged him instantly. He looked like a younger version of his father and had already taken on the old man's bent posture, although he was probably only in his forties. He waited at a bus stop on the corner for fifteen minutes or so, every so often dabbing his eyes with a tissue, then boarded a bus.

Michael and Tommy waited five minutes. Joseph Harkov did not return. They crossed the street, and entered the building.

The hallways smelled of frying foods, disinfectant, room deodorizers. The sound of soap operas poured out of more than one room.

Tommy Christiano had developed his techniques of

breaking and entering as a street kid in Brooklyn. He perfected them as an undercover officer in the 84th Precinct before taking night law classes at CUNY.

Within seconds, they were inside.

Viktor Harkov's bedroom spoke of age and despair and loneliness. It contained a chipped mahogany dresser and a single bed with rumpled, soiled sheets. On top of the dresser were a pair of framed photographs, nail clippers, a pair of uncancelled postage stamps, cut from envelopes. The closet contained three suits, all an identical featureless grey. There was one pair of shoes, recently resoled. On the floor were a stack of folded, plastic dry-cleaning bags. Viktor was a saver. Michael's mother had been the same way. Even something like a dry-cleaner bag had some worth.

"Mickey."

Tommy Christiano was the only person who called him Mickey, the only person allowed. And he only called him that when something was important.

Michael went out into the living room. Tommy had the bottom drawer in the kitchen open. In it was a rubber-banded stack of 3.5 inch floppy disks, and a small stack of what were either CDs, or DVDs.

"Look." Tommy held up three of the floppies. They were coded by year. The third disk was labeled TAYEMNYY 2005. "Any idea what this means?"

"I think it means 'private' in Russian. Maybe Ukrainian."

"Private files?"

"I don't know."

Tommy looked at his watch. Michael followed suit. They'd been in the apartment more than ten minutes. Every minute they lingered put them in jeopardy of getting caught.

Tommy glanced at the old computer in the corner of the living room. "You know how to make a copy of one of these?" he asked.

Michael hadn't worked with floppy disks for a few years, but he figured it would come back to him once he got in front of the computer. "Yeah."

Tommy handed him the 2005 disk, and a blank. Michael crossed the living room, sat down in the old desk chair in front of the computer. A puff of dust rose into the air as he sat down. He turned on the monitor, pressed the ON button on the old Gateway desktop. The boot-up process seemed to take forever. As the screens scrolled by, Michael realized he had not seen DOS prompts in a long time.

As he waited, Tommy walked over to the window overlooking 21st Avenue. He parted the curtains an inch or so.

When the screen finally reached the desktop, Michael inserted the disk. Moments later, he clicked on the file that read *TAYEMNYY*. The file opened – launching a Microsoft Excel spreadsheet program. Michael's eye scanned the data. His heart began to race. It was a list of adoptions from 2005. The list was only six entries long. Michael knew that Viktor Harkov brokered dozens of adoptions each year. This was a separate list. A private list. This was a list of people who had adopted illegally. He scrolled down.

There. He saw it. *Michael and Abigail Roman*. So there *was* a record, a record separate from the legal record.

"*Mickey*," Tommy said.

Michael looked up. "What?"

"Powell just pulled up across the street."

Michael pushed the blank floppy into the 3.5 drive. He heard the hard drive turn, heard the disk click into place. Each click was a beat of his heart.

"She just got out of the car," Tommy said. "She's headed this way. Fontova's with her."

Michael watched the progress bar move glacially to the right. It seemed to take forever.

Tommy tiptoed across the room, put his ear to the door.

"Let's go," he whispered.

"It's not done yet."

"Just take it then," Tommy said. "Let's *go*."

Michael looked at the remaining disks in the drawer. He wondered what data was contained on them. Were there back-up files of the disk he was trying to copy? This was more than simple breaking and entering, he thought. Making a copy was one thing – no one would ever know – but taking the actual disk was a felony. They were stealing someone's personal data.

There was no time for debate. He popped the disk from the drive, then unplugged the computer. It shut down with a loud whirring sound, one Michael was sure could be heard from the hallway.

There was suddenly a loud knock on the door.

"New York Police Department," Fontova said. "We have a search warrant."

Michael and Tommy crossed the living room, into the small bedroom. They looked onto the alley behind the building. There were no policemen. None that they could see.

A second knock. Louder. It seemed to shake the entire apartment.

"*Police! Search warrant! Open the door!*"

Michael tried to open the window, but it was painted shut. Tommy took out his pen knife and began to cut away the dried paint, but Michael stopped him. If they cut away the paint, then closed the window behind them, police would know what happened. There would be paint slivers all over the sill, the floor.

Behind them, Michael heard a key enter a lock.

The two men slipped out of the bedroom, into the bathroom. There it was clear that the window had been opened and closed many times. Michael reached over, slipped it open. The window was small, but it looked big enough for them to fit through.

A second key turned in a second lock and the front door opened just as Tommy crawled out of the window behind Michael.

"*NYPD!*" Michael heard as he and Tommy made their way down the fire escape. They'd had to leave the window open, but there was nothing to be done about that.

Moments later they were in the alley behind the apartment. Shortly after that they were out on the busy street.

They circled the block to Tommy's car.

Michael arrived at Kew Gardens at one forty-five. He had fifteen minutes to get changed and get to the courtroom. He had no fewer than twenty phone messages on his desk. He stepped into his office, closed and locked the door.

There was something he had to do first.

He sat at his desk, opened his laptop. He did not have a built-in floppy drive, but he had an external USB 3.5 floppy drive. Somewhere. He did not use it often and had stuffed it somewhere in his office. After a few minutes he found it, jammed behind a box of old files in the closet.

It was 1:46.

He connected the floppy drive, slipped in the disk. The screen came up much more quickly than it had on Viktor Harkov's PC. In seconds he was looking at the spreadsheet. There were six rows, eight columns. Across the top were the expected entries – *First Name H*, *First name W*, *Last name*, *Address*, etc. The final entry was *A*. Michael figured this to mean "Adoptee," for when his eye ran down the column, the entries were *F* and *M*. Two entries leapt out. One entry for a couple in Putnam County and the entry for Michael and Abigail Roman. Both had an entry for *2F* in the last column.

Two females. Twins.

One other couple had adopted twins through Viktor's office in 2005. Michael clicked on the printer icon. Seconds later he had a hard copy of the file.

At 1:49 there was knock on the door, followed by someone jiggling the doorknob. Michael instantly hit the eject button, removed the floppy. He then held the floppy, slid over the protective window on the diskette, took out a pair of scissors, and snipped the plastic disk inside, cutting it into three pieces, irretrievably destroying the data. He tossed it all into the wastebasket. Another knock.

"Hang on," Michael said.

He put the scissors in the drawer, turned off the computer, rose, opened the door.

It was Nicole Lanier, his tireless and overworked paralegal. Nicole was a petite and trim forty, a veteran of the office, birdlike in her movements, ursine in her protective nature. If you weren't expected, you did not run the gauntlet that was Nicole Lanier. She looked at Michael, at the casual way he was dressed. "Okay. Why was the door locked?"

"Where am I supposed to smoke my crack, in the hall?"

"Why not?" Nicole said. "The rest of us do." She looked at the clock. "Um, aren't you supposed to be in court?"

"I'm on it." He pulled off his QDA windbreaker, took his suit out of the dry cleaner's plastic bag. "Running late."

"Want me to call over there?"

"No, I'm good."

"You don't look good."

"Sweet talker." He handed Nicole his briefcase. "Just get

this in some kind of order for me. Outline on top. I'm going to change and be out of here in two minutes."

Nicole took the briefcase, but didn't move. "You sure you're okay?"

"Nicole."

"Okay, okay, boss." She took the briefcase from him, but still didn't leave.

"You know, if you don't leave right now you're going to see me naked."

"Beats looking through the keyhole."

Michael shooed her away. Nicole winked, spun on her sensible heels, closed the door.

Michael took a deep breath, looked around his office. Everything was where it was supposed to be: his desk, his bookcases, his apartment-sized fridge, the framed articles on the wall, even the 8 × 10 photograph of him and Tommy at ground zero, a picture taken on September 13, 2001. Everything was the same, but suddenly looked completely different, as if he were a stranger in this place he knew so well, as if the comfortable, well-worn things that made up his life had now been replaced by duplicates.

Focus, Michael.

Yes, Viktor Harkov's murder changed everything. And yes it was entirely possible that the state of New York might discover the illegalities surrounding the adoption, and start proceedings to take his daughters away. But that did not change the fact that the state of New York – and more importantly, a girl named Falynn Harris – was depending on him today.

He stripped off his T-shirt, jeans and sneakers, slipped on his suit pants, dress shirt. He tied his new tie – the one Abby had given him in a ritual that suddenly felt as if it had taken place weeks earlier – then put on his suit coat. He gave his hair a quick brush, checked himself in the mirror. It was as good as it was going to get. He opened the door, grabbed his briefcase, bumped a quick fist with Nicole for luck, and headed down the hall. He was already five minutes late.

TWENTY-THREE

Sitting at the dining-room table, Abby felt as if she were going to throw up. The words Aleks had spoken still seemed to be ringing in her ears.

They are my daughters.

When Zoe Meisner had come over, Abby met her at the edge of the property. Abby explained away the man named Kolya as a man who was there to give them a price on some landscaping. Zoe had given Abby a sly smile – Eden Falls was nothing if not discreet about its various trysts and daytime assignations – and it was probably due to her salacious suspicions that Zoe had scurried away rather quickly, only to observe Abby and Kolya from the alleged cover of the small greenhouse at the rear of the Meisner property.

They are my daughters.

As much as Abby wanted to believe it was all a bad dream, as much as she wanted to believe this man was lying to her, that it was some sort of ploy to extort money out of them, one look at Aleks's face told her it was none of the above. There was no mistaking the resemblance. He looked like the girls.

But why, after all this time, had he shown up now? What did he want?

Abby watched the girls playing tag, each taking turns being 'it'. They never seemed to let each other take the role of seeker or sought too long. Abby wondered what it would be like to be that selfless. She loved Michael with all her heart, but she had to admit to a certain dark glee at besting him at backgammon or chess or even gin rummy. Not so for the twins.

Abby looked at the corner of the lot. She noticed a small shiny object. When she focused she realized it was a bow, a shiny pink bow. A breeze soon gathered it up and tumbled it across the yard.

It's from the party, Abby thought. The party that now seemed to be a hundred years ago, a time when her family was intact, and there were no monsters in a place called Eden Falls, New York.

While Kolya watched her from the backyard, Abby turned her head to the sounds of the house. She heard footsteps above her – barely, Aleks seemed to be extremely light on his feet. She heard a closet door open and close. She tried to think of what he might find. There wasn't much. Most of their important papers – the deed to the house, insurance, passports – were in the file cabinet in the office on the first floor. There was a jewelry box on the nightstand, but nothing in it of value. She and Michael used to joke that if the jewelry box cost more than the jewelry, you don't need a jewelry box.

Then there was the gun. The gun was usually kept in a foam-lined aluminum case on the top shelf of the bedroom closet, beneath a box of old greeting cards. Had she locked it? Of course she had. She always locked it.

Then it hit her. The alarm system. The panic button. It was across the living room, three steps to the right, next to the front door. If she could just get there without Aleks or Kolya noticing, she could have the police on the way in minutes.

Was this the right thing to do? Would these men hurt her or

the girls if the police just showed up at the door? What would Michael do? What would Michael want *her* to do?

She tried to put all these questions out of her mind as she slowly rose to her feet and, before she could think of a reason to stop herself, ran to the foyer.

TWENTY-FOUR

The window, Powell thought. *Why was the bathroom window open?*

Standing in the middle of Joseph Harkov's shabby apartment, Powell tried to put Viktor Harkov's last few hours together. It was something at which she was very good. She didn't always understand the finer points of forensic detail, but she was quite skilled at divining the motives and movements of people.

In her years on the force, she had faced a number of obstacles, each one of them cleared with her fierce determination to succeed and advance, her unyielding belief in the power of logic.

She had grown up in Kingston, Jamaica, a shy, serious girl, one of five daughters born to Edward and Destiny Whitehall. They were poor, but they never went hungry, and until her death from cancer at the age of thirty-one, Destiny, who took in washing and sewing for the smaller hotels along the bay, saw to it her children's clothes were always clean and pressed.

Desiree had married Lucien Powell when she was just fifteen, a gangly *dawta* sketched of skinny arms and legs, topped with a seemingly constant blush, an embarrassment given rise with each of Lucien's sweet proposals, beginning when she was only fourteen. Day after day Lucien would follow, always at a respectable distance, preaching Desiree's not-quite blossomed loveliness to the hills, to all who would listen. Once he presented her with a basket of lilies. She kept the flowers alive as long as she could, then ultimately pressed them into a dog-eared copy of *The White Witch of Rose Hall* by H. G. de Lisser, her favorite book.

Then, after more than six months of this gavotte, Lucien walked her home. Standing on her mother's porch, with a simple kiss on the cheek from Lucien Powell, Desiree's heart was forever detained. Seven months later, with the blessing of their families, they married.

When Desiree was just three days shy of her sixteenth birthday, Lucien was gunned down in a Kingston back alley, the victim of a police vendetta. The Acid, they were called, the brutal arm of the police force. Lucien was shot four times – one in the throat, one in the stomach, one in each shoulder. The sign of the cross.

Lucien had been a hard-working young man, a brick mason by trade, but he had flirted with the fringes of the *bandulu* life, the criminal existence so common to the Jamaican way. They say the last thing Lucien said was "Tell Des I did not hear the bullet coming."

Six months later, Desiree's father moved the family to New York. Her father, already widowed himself, brought them to the Jamaica section of Queens, having no idea the area had nothing to do with the Caribbean island of his birth. Instead, her father would one day learn, the neighborhood acquired its name in 1666 or so by the British, taken from *jameco*, the Algonquian Indian word for beaver. The locale, although now home to many Jamaicans, was a diverse, struggling section of the borough, just a mile or so from JFK Airport.

In her shearing grief, Desiree thrust herself into study, and in just over three years earned her BA in criminal justice from CUNY.

She'd taken her share of lovers over the years, always on her timetable and terms, made the mistake of seeing a married lieutenant from Brooklyn South in her mid-thirties, her loneliness overruling her good sense. But that was a long time ago. These days she had the job, her two alley cats Luther and Vandross, her three inches of Wild Turkey – no more, certainly no less – every night before Tivo and bed. But mostly she had the job.

The front door of Harkov's apartment had a recently installed deadbolt, the windows were all closed and latched with clasp-locks, and were also fitted with a vertical steel window bar, which prevented the double-hung-style windows from being lifted. The door and windows were all secure, except for one. The window in the bathroom.

Why?

Powell instructed the CSU team to print the bathroom window sill and glass, paying particular attention to the locking clasp and hardware. As the two CSU officers went about their business, processing Viktor Harkov's apartment for trace evidence, and Marco Fontova did a canvass of the other tenants in the building, Desiree Powell examined the area around the window. There was no broken glass, no fresh chips out of the enamel-painted casing, which might have indicated a forced entry.

So why was the window wide open? There was no screen on it, and a fire escape just beyond. Anyone could easily break into the apartment. It wasn't as if there were a lot of high-ticket items in the apartment, but still. Nobody left their windows open in Queens.

Had someone been in the apartment and gone *out* the window?

And why was the computer unplugged?

Powell returned to the desk in the living room. She had put her hand on the monitor, and found it still warm. Which meant that it was probably only recently unplugged. Powell had plugged the computer and the monitor back in, and watched as the computer went through its cycle, informing the user that it had been improperly shut down. If Joseph Harkov was some kind of paranoid regarding fire, or figured on saving a few pennies on electricity when the computer was not in use, why not shut it down properly? Powell wondered.

Fontova returned, gloved up, and began to poke unenthusiastically around Harkov's bedroom. "Remind me never to go to law school," he said. "This place is wicked fucking bad."

Fontova rolled his eyes, pulled a thin roll of bills out of his pants pocket, peeled a dollar, handed it to Powell. She took it without a word. They had a running contest during Lent. Whoever said the f-word owed the other a dollar. After about a month they were about even.

"This guy was a street lawyer," Powell said. "And probably not a good one. It's almost impossible to make this little money."

Fontova grunted, continued opening drawers, closets, lifting sheets and emptying pockets, as anxious as Powell was to get in and out of this grim place.

They would take Harkov's old computer, as well as any files, documents, and paperwork. Whoever did this had a vendetta, a deeply planted hatred, and that doesn't just happen overnight. There was a connection here somewhere. They would find it.

TWENTY-FIVE

Something was wrong. The two green lights on the right side were dark. Abby tapped out the panic code anyway. Twice. Nothing happened. She banged on the panel. The sound seemed to resonate throughout the house.

Nothing. No flashing lights. No response of any kind.

"I am disappointed," came the voice from behind her. She spun around. Aleks was standing just a few feet away. She had not heard him come down the stairs.

Aleks descended fully into the foyer. He opened his shoulder bag, pulled out rope and duct tape.

"Unfortunately," Aleks said, "many of the American home-security systems run on telephone lines. If there is a large storm, or for any other reason the telephone service is interrupted, so too is the connection to the security firm's center." He held up a pair of clippers. It seems he had cut the phone line before they had entered. "I told you no harm would come to you or your family if you did exactly what I said. I am a man who does not like to repeat himself."

He crossed the foyer in a blur, lifted Abby in the air, as if she were weightless. He carried her across the foyer, down the stairs, into the basement. He placed her onto an old metal folding chair. His physical strength was terrifying.

"No," Abby said. She did not fight him. "You don't have to do this. I'm sorry."

In moments Aleks had her arms and legs bound to the chair. Abby did not struggle. She tried to fight the tears.

She lost.

Aleks watched the girls through the basement window. His face was unreadable, but Abby scanned his pale-blue eyes as he followed Charlotte and Emily swing on the swing set. His expression seemed to be one of deep longing.

His friend – his accomplice, Abby reminded herself – had left. The girls seemed to be okay, but every so often they would glance at the house. They were bright, intuitive children, wise far beyond their years, and Abby was certain that they knew something was wrong, despite her assurances that the men called Aleks and Kolya were friends of the family.

They are my daughters.

Abby's stomach turned at the thought. As she stared at the man's profile, there was no doubt in her mind that it was true. This man was Charlotte and Emily's biological father.

She found herself wishing it was all about something else, that it was some sort of a home-invasion robbery, and that these men were there seeking ransom, or jewels, or cash. These things she understood, and was willing to relinquish in a second if it meant keeping her family safe.

But one question loomed large. How did this man know where they lived and who they were? How had he found them?

Abby's worst nightmare was rapidly becoming a reality. He wasn't here to see his daughters. He wasn't here to merely establish contact, or a bond.

He was here to take them back.

Aleks leaned close to her ear. When he leaned over, Abby

saw something sparkle, catching the light, something hanging on a chain around his neck. On the chain were three small crystal vials. One of them held what appeared to be blood, with small bits of what might be flesh suspended in the deep-red liquid. The other two were empty. The dark possibilities made Abby sick.

Aleks whispered: "If you disobey me one more time, I will kill you in front of the girls."

Abby struggled against the ropes and duct tape. She could not move. Her tears coursed down her cheeks.

Without another word Aleks climbed the steps, opened the door, and closed it behind him.

TWENTY-SIX

The courtroom on the first floor was ornate and ceremonial, frequently used in high-profile, media-intense cases. In contrast to the courtrooms on the third floor – four courts reserved for a "Murderer's Row" of judges, senior, well-regarded justices who treated the spaces as something of a judicial status symbol – courtroom 109 seated more than 150 people in its gallery, and was used when press and security demanded it, when the system needed to flex.

There were two judges who presided over homicide cases in the division, each called a "part." There was Judge Margaret Allingham's part. Judge Allingham was a hardliner, born and raised in the South Bronx, the daughter of a former FBI agent. It was rumored that Iron Meg Allingham kept a six-inch sap under her robe. The other was Judge Martin Gregg's part. If you were unprepared or unfamiliar in any way with the incredibly complex details of criminal court procedure, you did not want to be up before Judge Martin Gregg, especially on a nice day, a day when he could be out golfing.

God help you if you showed up late in courtroom 109.

Michael Roman was late. He was about to be even later.

As he approached the door to the courtroom he took out his cellphone to turn it off. It beeped in his hand. There was only one message, a text from Falynn Harris. The time code on it was five minutes earlier. All it said was:

I can't do it. I'm sorry.

"Oh, Christ," Michael said. "Oh no no no."

Michael stepped into the small vestibule, scrolled through the phone numbers on his phone, dialed Falynn's cellphone, got her voicemail. He then called her foster home. After two rings, a woman answered. It was Deena Trent, Falynn's foster mother.

"Mrs Trent, this is Michael Roman. May I speak to Falynn?"

Michael heard a quick intake of breath. Then, "You're the lawyer."

It was not a question. "Yes," Michael said. "And if I could just speak —"

"She's gone."

Michael was certain he misunderstood. "Gone? What do you mean she's gone?"

"I mean she's gone. She took her suitcase and she's gone."

"She didn't say anything?"

"Just a note telling me she was never coming back."

"Where did she go?"

"I don't know. She's scared maybe. Those boys — the ones responsible for killing her father — maybe she's scared of them."

Michael was incredulous. "Nothing is going to happen to her, Mrs Trent. I could have the police there in two minutes. You have to tell me where she went. She'll be safe."

"I don't think you heard me. I don't *know* where she went."

"What about her friends? Can you call one of her friends?"

Deena Trent laughed, but there was no mirth in it. "Her *friends*? You've met her. You think she has any friends? This is the fourth time she's up and gone, you know."

"Mrs Trent I'm sure she's —"

"And to tell you the truth, this is a lot more than I bargained for when I signed on for this. I thought I was just taking in a teenage girl who needed a home. I don't need this. She's not my kin. And, between you and me, the money isn't all that good."

What a delightful woman, Michael thought. He made a mental note to look into her qualifications as a state-subsidized foster home. "Look," he began, his head spinning with the afternoon's ramifications from this, "if you hear from her –"

But the line was already dead. Michael stared at the phone for a long time. He tried to remember what his life was like just a few hours earlier, just that morning before the phone rang and it was Max Priest on the other end, Max Priest calling to tell him that Viktor Harkov had been murdered.

Now his one and only witness was missing.

Do you promise? Falynn had asked.

Yes, he had replied.

He had to plow ahead. He would find her, change her mind. He could not let the court know the state no longer had a witness. He was afraid that without Falynn, there was too much of a chance that Ghegan would walk. No one on the jury had to know.

Not yet.

As Michael walked to the prosecutor's table, he tried to keep the news off his face.

"Mr Roman," Judge Gregg said. "Nice to see you. Problems?"

Michael walked around the table. He set down his briefcase. "No your honor. I'm sorry I'm late."

Michael had never been late to Judge Gregg's courtroom. He had never been late to *any* courtroom.

"Is the state ready to begin, Mr Roman?"

The state is not ready, Michael wanted to say. *The state is worried. Not about the case, your honor, but about the fact that Michael Roman, Esquire, defender of the rights of the citizens of this fair state, champion of the downtrodden, speaker for the voiceless victim, has broken the law. Now a man is dead and the proverbial chickens are coming home to roost. What's worse is that the state itself may soon be coming after the upstanding Mr Roman, pillar of the aforementioned community. Add to that the fact that the lead witness in the current matter before the court has just taken a powder. Oh, yeah. We're in fighting shape. Never better.*

"We are, your honor "

Judge Gregg nodded to his bailiff, who opened the door leading to the jury room. One by one, the twelve jurors filed through the door, followed by the four alternates.

Michael glanced first at John Feretti, who was resplendent in a bespoke navy-blue three-piece suit. The two men nodded at each other. Michael then glanced at Patrick Ghegan, the defendant. Ghegan wore a long-sleeve white shirt. Michael noticed that the creases from where the shirt had been folded were still in the arms. Ghegan was clean-shaven, combed, angelic, with his hands folded on the table. He did not look at Michael.

Once the jury was seated, Judge Gregg began to speak.

"Good afternoon, ladies and gentlemen."

Gregg then proceeded to give the jury their instructions, reminding them of their basic function, duties and expected conduct, and about how they were not permitted to read or view any accounts or discussions of the case reported by the newspapers or other media, including radio and television. When Gregg was satisfied he had communicated the instructions, he turned to Michael.

"Okay," Gregg said. "Mr Roman, on behalf of the people."

"Thank you, your honor." Michael rose from his table,

crossed the courtroom, stood in front of the jury. "Good afternoon ladies and gentlemen."

All twelve jurors and four alternates mumbled some version of an answer.

"Welcome back," Michael added. He took a moment, running his gaze across the men and women before him. This was one of the most important moments in a trial, especially a homicide trial. Michael often viewed it as the first image in a film. It set the tone and tenor for everything that followed. A weak opening could usually not be overcome. "This trial is about two men. Patrick Sean Ghegan, and Colin Francis Harris. More specifically, about what Patrick Ghegan did to Colin Harris on April 24, 2007."

Michael continued, walking the jury through the events of the crime, slowly building to the moment when Patrick Ghegan pointed his handgun – a large-caliber Colt – at Colin Harris's head, and pulled the trigger.

As he began his summation, he walked over to the easel sitting to the left of the witness stand. On the easel was a large blow-up of a photograph of Colin and Falynn Harris, a picture taken just a few months before the murder.

As Michael turned the large photograph on the easel, he felt a slight shift in the atmosphere in the room behind him. It wasn't anything specific, not at that moment, just a transfer of energy.

"Fuck you!" a voice yelled.

Michael spun around. The entire courtroom was looking at the back of the room. There, a red-faced young man – a man Michael knew to be Patrick Ghegan's younger brother Liam – was being restrained by a court officer.

"Rot in hell you fucking cocksuckers!" Liam screamed. "All of you!"

As jurors and gallery members scattered, two more officers rushed forward and took Liam Ghegan to the floor. In seconds they had him cuffed. At the door he turned and yelled. "And that bitch? That little bitch? She's fucking *dead*."

That little bitch, Michael thought. He was talking about Falynn Harris. He looked around the courtroom, especially at the jury. They were, to a last person, shaken. Granted, they were all New Yorkers, and used to incidents of all kinds. But in this post-9/11 world, especially in a municipal building, nerves were constantly on edge. Michael wondered if he could get them back.

In the movies, this would be where the judge pounded his gavel, calling for order in the court. This was not the movies, and Martin Gregg was not a cinematic judge.

"Is everyone all right?" Gregg asked.

Slowly, everyone in the courtroom shook it out, returned to their seats, offered nervous conversation with their neighbors. A minute or two later, it was as if nothing had happened. But it had.

"In light of this little unscheduled Broadway matinee performance," Judge Gregg continued. "We will recess for one hour to consider our reviews."

Good, Michael thought. A break was what he needed. Maybe he could get them back after all. Maybe he could find Falynn.

Michael got back into his office just before three o'clock. The court usually recessed for the day at around 4:30, and Michael still had hopes of completing his opening statement. Still, if Liam Ghegan had wanted to disrupt the trial, and especially the jury's train of thought, he had certainly accomplished that mission. Bringing the jury back into the rhythm of the state's case was not going to be easy.

Michael began to make new notes on his statement when a shadow crossed his doorway. It was Tommy.

"You hear what happened?" Michael asked.

"I heard," Tommy said. "Maybe in two or three more generations the Ghegans will finally be able to walk on their hind legs."

"Was there media outside?"

"Oh yeah. Cameras got them hauling Ghegan away, screaming his ass off."

Michael thought about this. It was never good. Even worse in this case. If Falynn saw the footage, she might disappear forever. "Can you do me a favor?"

"Sure."

He told Tommy about the text message from Falynn, as well as the conversation with Deena Trent. "See if you can find out where she might have gone."

With any luck, Michael would complete his opening statement today, Feretti would open in the morning – and, if they found Falynn, and Michael could talk her into it – she would be on the stand by eleven o'clock.

"You got it," Tommy said.

"Thanks, man."

When Tommy left, Michael stood, closed the door, took off his suit coat. He found that the tension of the day had settled into his shoulders. He did some of his stretching exercises, soon felt a little better.

He poured himself some coffee, paced his small office, trying to re-engage the mindset. He had only been interrupted during an opening statement once in his career, and that had been in law school, as an exercise. He had not done well that time, but that was a long time ago. Before he was a prince at the Palace.

A few minutes later his cellphone rang. He looked at the screen. Private number. He had to take it. It might have been Judge Gregg's clerk telling him there was a delay, which would be the first good news he'd had all day. He flipped open the phone.

"This is Michael."

"Mr Roman."

A statement, not a question. It was a man's voice. Foreign.

"Who is this?" Michael asked.

"I will tell you this soon. But first I want you to promise me that you will remain calm, no matter what occurs in the next few moments."

Michael stood up. Something turned in his stomach, the way it used to when he had a witness on the stand, and the person's story began to crack. Except at this moment he knew this was wrong, but he wasn't sure *how* he knew.

"Who is this? What are you talking about?"

"Before I begin, I want your assurance that you will listen to what I have to say in its entirety."

Michael would make no promises. "I'm listening."

"My name is Aleksander," the man said. "May I call you Michael?"

Michael remained silent.

"I will take that as a yes," the man continued. He spoke with an accent, the unmistakable Estonian inflection Michael knew very well.

"By now I believe you have heard about the tragic murder of a man named Harkov. A lawyer like yourself."

Michael's stomach fell. This man was calling about Harkov. Was this a detective? No. A cop wouldn't be playing games. A cop would be standing in this office with his handcuffs ready. Maybe this was a fed. No. Feds had an even lower tolerance for bullshit. "I heard."

"I believe that at one time you retained his services. Am I correct in this knowledge?"

"What do you want?"

"I want you to answer my question. It is in your best interest to do so."

Michael felt the old anger begin to boil. "What the fuck do you know about my best interest? Tell me what this is all about or I hang up the phone."

"Ah," the man said. "The temper."

"The *temper*? What the fuck is this? Have we met?"

The man hesitated for a moment. "No, we have never met, but in the past few hours or so, I have learned a great deal about you."

"What are you talking about?"

"You have faced death," the man said. "You have looked into Satan's face and lived to tell. As have I."

The man continued, but the sounds seemed to drift away. Michael didn't hear what the man was saying, until he said:

"I am in your home. Abigail and the girls are just fine, and they will remain so, as long as you follow my instructions."

A deadening cold radiated through Michael's limbs, as if he had suddenly been anesthetized. What had moments ago been a dark possibility – that this man somehow knew about the illegalities of the girls' adoption – had now blossomed into a different, more terrifying reality.

The man continued. "Do not call the police, do not call the FBI, do not contact anyone," he said. "If you do, it will be the mistake by which all other mistakes will be measured until your last breath. Do I have your attention and your belief?"

Michael began to pace again. "Yes."

"Good. I want you to listen to me," the man said. "My full name is Aleksander Savisaar. I want you to call me Aleks. I am telling you this because I know you are not going to contact the authorities."

Up came the prosecutor in Michael. Up came the heat. Before he could stop himself he said, "How do you know what I will or won't do?"

A moment. "I know."

Michael stopped pacing, every muscle tightening. Every instinct within him told him to go to the police. This was his training, this was his belief, this was consistent with every case he had ever tried, everything he had come to believe. If this were happening to a friend or colleague, it would be the advice he would give them.

But now it was *his* life, *his* wife, *his* children.

Michael picked up his office phone. He dialed his home number. There were two house phones in the Eden Falls house, two extensions of the land line. One in the kitchen, one in the bedroom. For some reason he got a disconnect recording. The sound of the disembodied voice chilled him. He dialed Abby's cellphone. After a second, he heard it ring in the background. It was Abby's special ringtone. His heart froze. The man *was* in his house.

"And now you have proof," Aleks said.

"Look" Michael began, his rage a gathering gale. "If anything happens to my family there is nowhere on earth you will able to hide. Nowhere. Do you hear me?"

For a moment Michael thought, and feared, that the man had hung up.

"There is no need for anyone to be hurt," Aleks said. His calmness was as infuriating as it was chilling. "But this is entirely up to you."

Michael remained silent as the clock passed four o'clock. Any second now his office phone would ring. They would be looking for him.

"I am looking at your schedule," Aleks said. "You should be in court. Are there problems?"

"No."

"Good. And I see that later today you are due to meet some tradesman on Newark Street."

The cold began to spread. Michael found that he had not

moved a muscle in minutes. This man knew his whole life.

"You are to go about the rest of your day as if everything were normal," Aleks continued. "You will keep all of your appointments. You will not contact anyone about this, or send anyone to this house. You will not call this house for any reason. You will not come home."

"Let me talk to my wife."

The man ignored him, continued. "You are being watched, Michael Roman. If you do anything out of the ordinary, if you are seen talking to anyone in law enforcement, you will regret it."

My God, Michael thought. It was all connected. The brutal murder of Viktor Harkov, the stealing of confidential files. And now a madman had his family.

But why? What did he want?

"When you step out of the office, one of the people you encounter will hold the lives of your wife and these little girls in their hands. You will not know who it is. Be wise, Michael. I will contact you soon."

"You don't understand. When I go into the courtroom there will be all kinds of police officers, detectives, marshals. I can't —"

"No one."

The line went dead.

What Michael had feared, just a few short moments ago — the possibility he might lose his daughters in a long, protracted legal battle — was nothing.

Now he was fighting for their lives.

TWENTY-SEVEN

The Queens Homicide Squad was located on the second floor of the 112th Precinct headquarters in Forest Hills, a square, nondescript building with mint-green panels below the windows, and a black marble entrance.

Of the twelve full-time homicide detectives, only two were women, and that was just the way Desiree Powell liked it. Although she had many female friends on the job, most of them were drawn to other squads as a career — vice, narcotics, forensic investigation. Powell knew she had a knack for this work, always had, even as a child. There was logic to it all, but it was more than that. As a student she had been far better at algebra than geometry. A always led to B then to C. Always. If it didn't, you had the wrong A to begin with. She did not consider that she had a gift — few investigators were gifted at detection. She believed it was something that came from instinct; you either had the nose, and the gut, or you didn't.

She had recently investigated a case in North Corona where the victim, a forty-nine-year-old white male, a family man with a wife and three children, was found lying in his backyard, middle of a nice summer day, his head bashed in. There was no weapon found, no witnesses, no suspects. There was, however, a ladder leaning up against the back of his house. The man's wife said when she left for work that day, her husband told her he was going to replace a few shingles. CSU found blood on the roof, in the gutter as well, which led them to conclude that the man had been bludgeoned on the roof, and not in the backyard as they had originally thought.

Desiree Powell mused: Who climbs a ladder, bludgeons a man, watches the victim roll off, then climbs back down? Why risk being seen by the entire neighborhood? Why not wait until the guy was on the ground, or in the house?

Three times during the neighborhood canvass Powell found she'd had to stop for a moment and wait for the jets overhead to pass. The neighborhood was directly in the flight path of LaGuardia airport.

When the case stalled, Powell reached out to an old friend in TSA, who in turn called a few of the airlines and discovered that, on the day the man died, a cargo plane had reported some engine trouble on take-off from LaGuardia. Powell visited the hangar and discovered that a piece of metal had come off the engine housing, a piece never recovered by investigators. She also discovered that the plane had passed directly over the community of North Corona. She brought back CSU, and they did a search of the chimney. Inside, they found a chunk of metal near the flue, a ragged piece that fit the engine's housing perfectly. It was caked with the dead man's blood.

Airplane, Body, Chimney.

ABC.

Sometimes Powell scared herself.

Marco Fontova walked into the duty room, dropped into his chair on the opposite side of the desk, one of nine or so desks in the small, paper-clogged office. He glanced once at the whiteboards on the wall, the board displaying who was in court that day, who was on the range. He checked his box for mail.

"Nice suit, by the way," Powell said. She didn't really mean it, but the kid was a peacock, and she liked to keep him happy. "New?"

Fontova smiled, opened up the jacket. The lining was mauve paisley. "Like it?"

It was a special brand of ugly. "Very becoming. What do we have?"

Fontova had a thick sheaf of paper in his hand, as well as a CD in a clear crystal case. "We have a printout of some of the files on Harkov's computer, along with a copy of the original data files."

"That was fast."

"You want the big half or the small half?"

"I'll take it all. You know I love this stuff."

Fontova gave it to her.

Powell looked at the files. It was a database, a listing of Harkov's clients. The dates went back ten years, and had to contain three hundred names. There were brief notations regarding the nature of the work Harkov had done for these people. Most were civil matters, but there were a number of criminal matters.

Was their killer in here somewhere?

The brutality of the murder suggested something other than a robbery. This was revenge. No one took the time to do what was done to Viktor Harkov just because they had a few hours to spare.

There were really only a few reasons to torture someone. Two, actually, that Powell could think of. One, the hatred for the victim ran so deep, the sense of vengeance was so strong, that nothing less than a slow, painful death would salve the loathing. The other reason was that you wanted information from that person, information the person was not ready to give up. That was pretty much it. Unless you just happened to have a taste for it, which, even for New York City, was fairly uncommon.

According to the database, Viktor Harkov was only a mediocre criminal defense attorney. He had won only half the criminal trials in which he was involved. Of the cases he had lost, the longest prison term imposed on one of his clients was a five-year stretch at Dannemora.

Was that a long enough sentence for someone to want to extract this depth of revenge upon release? Powell imagined it was possible, depending on the person.

Their initial canvass of the scene and the neighborhood had produced nothing. Once again, a ghost had floated through the crowded streets of New York City, committed murder, and floated out.

"Let's run the people whose cases he lost," Powell said. "Maybe someone thought he didn't provide a vigorous enough defense and had it in for him."

"You mean like in *Cape Fear?*"

Powell just stared at him.

"*Cape Fear?* The movie?"

The last movie Desiree Powell had seen was *Jaws.* She hadn't been to the movies, or Rockaway Beach, since. "Right," she said. "Exactly. Just like *Cape Fear.*"

Powell glanced at the crime-scene photos. This was a monster, this guy. A real boogeyman. And he was currently walking the streets of her city, breathing her air, which was just unacceptable.

Not for long, she thought.

Not for long.

*

The courtroom seemed dreamlike, an alien landscape populated with strange apparitions. Yes, the bench was where it always was. The defense and prosecution tables were just about where they always had been. The court reporter sat at her station, machine on its tripod, her nimble fingers at the ready.

Michael had entered this room hundreds of times, had held the lives of both victims and defendants in the balance, had navigated the rocky shoals of justice with skill and precision and no small measure of luck. But each of those times he had been in control.

Be wise, Michael. I will contact you soon.

Michael ransacked his memory, trying to place the voice he had heard on the phone. He could not.

My full name is Aleksander Savisaar. I want you to call me Aleks. I am telling you this because I know you are not going to contact the authorities.

He did not recognize the man's name, either. Was it someone he had once prosecuted? Was it a relative of someone he had put in prison, or upon whom the state of New York had imposed the death penalty? Was this about vengeance? Money? Was this someone with a grievance against the legal system taking it out on him?

The lot of anyone in a district attorney's office, or anyone in any branch of law enforcement, was to be ever vigilant. You spend your working life locking up criminals, only to have these people one day get out, many times holding you responsible for their miserable lives.

Had he neglected or failed to see this coming, and now his family was going to pay for it?

With all these questions unanswered, Michael was certain of one thing. The man who had called him was responsible for the atrocity of Viktor Harkov's brutal murder.

Michael glanced into the gallery. At the back of the courtroom he saw the two detectives from the 114 who had initially been given the task of investigating the murder of Colin Harris. It would be so easy to cross the room, lean over, and tell them what was happening.

Be wise, Michael. I will contact you soon.

A few moments later, the jury was led back into the courtroom. Judge Gregg summarized what he had said earlier.

Normally, Michael would watch the defendant at a moment such as this. Instead, he looked at the faces of the jurors, the faces of the gallery, the faces of the police officers and officers of the court scattered around the room. He even watched the court reporter.

Was one of these people watching *him*?

"Mr Roman," Judge Gregg said. "You may continue."

Michael Roman stood, walked around the table, and began to speak. He was certain he apologized to the jury for the interruption. There was no doubt he gave a brief recap to where he had been. Unquestioningly, he picked up essentially where he had left off.

He just didn't hear any of it. Not a word. Instead, his focus was on the people around him. Faces, eyes, hands, body language.

There was a man, perhaps fifty, sitting in the front row of the gallery. He had a scar on his neck, a military buzz cut, thick arms.

There was a woman, two rows back. Forties, too much make-up, too much jewelry. She wore long fake red fingernails. One nail was missing on her left hand.

There was a young man at the back of the gallery, a stocky kid in his twenties with an earring in his left ear. He seemed to be tracking Michael's movement across the courtroom with a particularly close scrutiny.

Michael looked at the faces of the people in the jury. He had an ideal juror – all lawyers did, both defense and prosecutors. You always wanted to go with a juror who would be sympathetic to your case. Contrary to popular belief, lawyers did not want anyone on the jury who was free from bias or prejudice. Just the opposite. You wanted someone who held the *right* bias and prejudice. As a prosecutor, Michael wanted the Con Ed worker, the bus driver, the tax-paying citizen over forty. He wanted the person old enough to have grown weary of crime and criminals and excuses. The last person he wanted was the twenty-three-year-old inner-city school teacher, ever the true believer. For Michael, the less idealistic the juror, the better.

As he scanned the jury, he tried to remember what they had discussed during the *voir dire*. What a lot of people didn't know was that the seemingly extemporaneous banter with a prosecutor or defense attorney was as telling, or more telling, than the direct questions. As a rule, this all came to Michael in toto during a trial. But today was a little different, wasn't it? He couldn't remember a thing.

Had Aleks, the man on the phone, the man who had kidnapped his family, gotten to someone on the jury? One of the alternates? One of the gallery? Had he gotten to one of the officers of the court?

Who was watching him?

"Mr Roman?"

Michael turned. The judge was talking to him. He had no idea what he was saying, what he had said. Moreover, he had no idea how long he had been gone. He turned and glanced at the jury. They were all staring at him, fidgeting, waiting, anticipating his next word. What had his *last* word been? It was every lawyer's nightmare. Except today, it was nothing compared to Michael Roman's real nightmare.

"Your honor?"

Judge Gregg motioned him to the bench. Michael turned, looked at the defendant.

Patrick Ghegan was smiling.

TWENTY-EIGHT

In his mind, in the realm of both near and distant future, often-
times *centuries* into the future, he could not see himself. Not in
the sense in which one sees oneself in a mirror or a store
window, or even the slightly ethereal vision of one's face in a
body of still water, looking back in a dream, only to be
disturbed by a breeze, rippling away.

No, his vision of himself as the deathless one was more in
the realm of a god. He had no physical presence, no matter
composed of flesh and blood and sinew, no muscle, no bone.
These were things organic, things of the earth. He was of the
ether.

They say that he was found, swaddled in a white altar cloth,
lying in the cemetery next to a crumbling Lutheran church in
south-eastern Estonia, thirty-three years ago. They say one
winter morning, a grey wolf scratched the rector's door, and
led the man to the baby in the graveyard. The elderly priest
took the baby six miles to the Russian orphanage at Treski.
They say the wolf sat outside the gate of the home, day and
night, for days, perhaps weeks. One day, one of the Russian
workers brought the boy, who had begun to regain his
strength, to the gate. The say the wolf licked the boy's face,
just once, and disappeared into the forest.

They say that, pinned to the brilliant white cloth had been a piece of yellow paper, a note card with a single word written out in a young girl's loopy scrawl. *Aleksander*.

As a child, as he moved like a ghost through the Soviet-run orphanages, he was considered unmanageable, and therefore passed from one home to another. He learned many things. He learned how to hoard and ration his food. He learned how to lie, to steal. He learned to fight.

Often he was discovered in the small schoolrooms, the sparse libraries, reading the books of older children by candlelight. He was beaten many times for this, deprived of supper, but he never learned the lesson. He did not *want* to learn the lesson. For it was in these worn, leather-bound volumes that he found the world outside the stone walls, where he learned the history of his country, his people, where he learned of Estonia's much conquered shores by the Danes, the Norse, the Russians. He would study the photographs of these men, then study his own in the mirror. From whom had he descended? What blood coursed through his veins? He did not know. At the age of eight he decided it did not matter, he would learn to be unconquerable, a nation of one.

At ten, a visiting teacher named Mr Oskar showed him how to play the flute. It was the first kindness ever shown him. He taught Aleks the basics, and every Sunday afternoon for two years gave him lessons. Aleks learned not only the Estonian composers – Eller, Oja, Pärt, Mägi – but many of the Russian and German composers as well. When Mr Oskar died from a massive stroke, the elders saw no worth in the battered old flute. They let Aleks keep it. He had never been given anything.

At eighteen, Aleks joined the federal army. Over six-feet tall and powerfully built, he was immediately deployed to Chechnya.

Soon after completing his basic training he was recruited

and trained by the FSK in interrogation techniques. He did not take the lead so much as provide a presence, a phantom that haunted prisoners by night, and shadowed them by day. He learned to sleep soundly as men around him pierced the night with their screams.

Within six months he was deemed ready for the front. They sent him first to the border city of Molkov, but that would prove to be only a stopover. Three weeks later they sent him to a place called Grozny.

They sent him to Hell.

The siege of Grozny began on New Year's Eve 1994, and was a disaster for the Russian forces. At first, the one thousand men of the mighty Maikop 131st Battalion, amassed just north of the city, met with little resistance. They took the airport north of Grozny with few casualties.

But their gains were short-lived. Ill-trained, poorly supplied, the Russian soldiers were not ready for what awaited them in the city. Some commanders were as young as nineteen.

The Chechens, in contrast, were fierce and determined warriors. They were, by and large, trained and highly experienced marksmen, having learned to shoot and handle weapons since they were children. After picking off fleeing and confused soldiers, they would come down from the hills and grab weapons from the dead Russians, bolstering their meager armories. Some managed to steal machine guns from the armored vehicles, turning them on the doomed men inside.

As the day wore on, the Chechen separatists fought back, using everything they could: Russian-made, rocket-propelled grenades, fired from rooftops; Russian grenades thrown into tanks; even the deadly *kinzbal*, the prized Caucasian heirloom daggers. The number of dismembered and decapitated Russian soldiers all over the city were testament to the effectiveness of these comparatively primitive weapons. It was estimated that in the Battle of Grozny, Russians lost more tanks then they did in the battle for Berlin in 1945.

Over the month of January, federal forces would suffer even greater humiliations and defeat.

In each ill-conceived and executed battle, against clearly under-estimated Chechen separatist forces, the bodies fell. All around Aleks, Russian soldiers and Chechen rebels were dead or dying. Yet, many times, while the blood of his fellow soldiers, his enemies, drained into the fields, mingling with the bones of centuries below, only Aleks was left standing.

Three times that January, in three fierce firefights, he emerged with little more than a scratch. His legend began to grow. The Estonian who could not be killed.

Then came January 15, 1995. One hundred and twenty federal soldiers were hunkered down in the marshes, outlying buildings, and silos just south of the Sunzha River. Intel, or what little they could gather with their primitive radios, told them that there were one hundred rebels holed up in the village. Their orders were to wait them out. For three days, with few rations, and even less sleep, they waited. Then the order came to advance.

At just before dawn Aleks's unit of twenty began to make their way slowly across the frozen marsh. Some marched with newspaper stuffed into their boots for warmth. They did not make it far.

First came the mortar fire, huge 150-millimeter shells. The outbuildings and silos exploded on impact, killing all inside. Red rain fell. The shelling went on for more than six hours, the incessant roar of the explosions was deafening.

When the quiet came, Aleks dared to take a look. Body parts were scattered up the hillside. The armored cars were destroyed. The sounds of moaning could be heard beneath the staccato of automatic-weapons fire near the river.

Nothing stirred.

Then came the helicopters and their NURS mini-rockets.

In all, one hundred and nineteen Russian soldiers were killed. Most of the village was burned to the ground. Livestock were slaughtered and the streets ran crimson.

Only Aleks lived.

When the smoke cleared, and the screaming stopped, Aleks prepared to return to his base. He walked through the deserted village, now little more than blackened rubble. The smell of death was overpowering. At the end of the main street was a rise. In the near distance was a farmhouse, mostly intact.

As he strode up the hill, on alert, he began to feel something, something that had been growing within him for years. He stood tall, threw his rifle sling over his shoulder. He felt strong, the numbing fatigue and fear sliding away.

He looked through the doorway of the farmhouse, saw a Chechen woman, perhaps in her seventies, standing at her small kitchen table. On the table was an old leather-bound book. The walls were pitted clay, the floor dirt.

It was clear that the woman had seen the firefight, the grenades, the torn flesh and rivers of blood. She had seen it all. When it was over, she was not afraid of the Chechen rebels, or the Russian soldiers. She was not afraid of the war itself, or even of dying. She had met many devils.

She was afraid of Aleks.

He put down his weapon, and approached her, hands out to his sides. He was starving, and preferred to sit at a table. He meant her no harm. As he neared the woman, her eyes grew wide with horror.

"You," she said, her hands beginning to tremble. "*You!*"

Aleks stepped into the house. It smelled of fresh bread. His stomach lurched in hunger.

"You know me?" he asked in halting Chechen.

The woman nodded. She touched the weathered book on the table. Next to the book was a loaf of black bread, a stone-sharpened carving knife.

"*Koschei*," she said, her voice quivering. "*Koschei Bessmertny!*"

Aleks did not know these words. He asked her to repeat them. She did, then crossed herself three times.

In a flash she lifted the razor-sharp knife from the table, brought it to her throat, and slashed her jugular vein. Bright blood burst across the room. Her body slumped to the cold floor, quaking in its death throes. Aleks looked at the table. The loaf of bread was splattered with deep carmine.

Aleks fell upon the blood-soaked bread, wolfing it down, the taste of the old woman's blood, along with the yeast and flour, an intoxicating mixture that both sickened and exhilarated him.

It was not the last time he would taste it.

In the dying light he read the book, a book of folk legends. He read the fable of Koschei the Deathless. There were many tales, but the one that moved him was the tale of the immortal Koschei – a man who could not die because his soul was kept elsewhere – and Prince Ivan's sisters: Anna, Marya, and Olga.

He wept.

After his discharge, Aleks returned to Estonia, where he took odd jobs – carpentry, plumbing, fixing fifty years of shoddy Russian construction. He worked the slaughterhouses in the south, the mines in central Estonia, anything to get by. But he always knew he was destined for something else, something greater.

Aleks befriended the mayor of the town, a man who also owned just about every business within fifty kilometers.

The man brought him along on a job, a job robbing an old Russian of his wealth accumulated on the backs of Estonians. Aleks had no loyalties, no God. He went. And found that the violence was still deep within him. It came easy.

Over the next few years, from the Gulf of Finland to the Latvian border to the south, and sometimes beyond, there was not a shop owner, business man, farmer, politician, or criminal enterprise, large or small, that did not pay Aleksander Savisaar tribute. He always worked alone, his threats and assurances couched in his ability to make believers of those who doubted his sincerity with torture and cruelty of such intensity, such speed, that his actions never had to be repeated.

By the age of twenty-seven his legend was widely known. In his pocket were politicians, law-enforcement agents, legislators. He had bank accounts and property in six countries. A fortune he never dreamed of.

It was time to turn his attention to his legacy but, with all his wealth and power, he did not know where or how to begin.

He began by building a house, a large A-frame set among tall standing pines atop a hill in Kolossova. Isolated, secure, and tranquil, he began to fell the logs he needed. By fall he had all the lumber milled, and had the structure fully framed.

He returned to the long-abandoned Treski orphanage, the place where he had been left. At great expense, he had locals tear it down stone by stone. Back in Kolossova he hired stonemasons to build a wall around his house.

Hurrying to close in the roof before the winter snows came, Aleks worked well into the evenings. One night, just as dusk claimed the day, he sat on the second floor, looking out over the valley as it began to snow in earnest.

He was just about to gather his tools when he thought he saw movement amid the stand of blue spruce to the west. He waited, stilling his movements, his breathing, dissolving into his surroundings, becoming invisible. He fingered the rifle at his side, shifted his eyes back and forth, scanned the clearing, but there was no movement. Yet there *was* something. A pair of shining pearls, seemingly suspended on the snow. He looked more closely, and a form began to take shape, seeming to grow around the glistening orbs. The high dome, the pointed ears, the dusty rose of a lolling tongue.

It was a grey wolf.

No, he thought. It cannot possibly be. The wolf who had discovered him in the cemetery, by all accounts, was full grown at *that* time.

When he saw the old wolf slowly rise, on its terribly gnarled forelegs, and begin to move with an arthritic sluggishness, Aleks believed. The ancient wolf had come to see him before he died.

But what was the message?

Days later, when he saw the young girl, the soothsayer named Elena Keskküla, standing on the same spot, observing him, it was an epiphany.

He watched many times over the next few years, even after her family moved north, observed the people coming to her farmhouse, their tributes in tow – money, food, livestock.

In these days he often envisioned himself on a hillside, the days speeding by, spring given unto winter in seconds, decade born of decade. He watched the fields grow ripe with fruit, fall fallow. He watched cities grow from timberland, only to flourish, expand, reach for heights of glory, then decay, and crumble into ash and dust. He watched saplings reach to the sky, then yield to farmland. He watched animals grow fatted, calve, nurse their young, only to see their offspring seconds later begin the wondrous cycle again. Skies blacken, seas churn and calm, the earth opens and closes in massive quakes, pines grow down the mountains to the valleys, only to farther lakes and rivers, which in turn gave life to the gardens and farms.

Through all of it, through eons of war and pestilence and greed, generations of lawlessness and avarice, there would be his daughters at his side. Marya, the pragmatist, the keeper of his mind. Anna, the artist of his heart. Olga, never seen, but always felt, his anchor.

He fingered the three vials around his neck. Together, one way or another, they would live forever.

He watched them play their games in the backyard, their gossamer blond hair lifting and falling in the breeze. They had Elena's air about them, an aura of prudence and insight.

He crouched down to their level. They approached him, showing no fear or apprehension. Perhaps they saw in his eyes their own eyes. Perhaps they saw in him their destiny. They were so beautiful his heart ached. He had waited so long for this moment. All the while he had feared it would never happen, that his immortality had been something of fairy tale.

Without a word he reached into his pocket, produced the two marble eggs. He handed them to the girls.

The girls studied the eggs closely, running their small fingers over the intricate carving. Aleks had seen the drawing they had made on the refrigerator. He saw that one section of the drawing was missing.

Anna, the one they called Emily, beckoned him close. Aleks got down on one knee. The little girl leaned even closer, whispered: "We knew you would be tall."

TWENTY-NINE

The white van parked in front of the townhouse had *Edgar Rollins & Son Painting and Decorating* on its side. Michael pulled up behind it, cut the engine. Nothing seemed real. This was the last place he wanted to be, but he could not take the chance of breaking with his schedule. He checked his cellphone for the five hundredth time. Nothing.

When Judge Gregg had called him and John Feretti to the bench, he had seen something in the man's eyes that looked like compassion. Rare for a sitting homicide judge. He had asked both lawyers if they wanted to break for the day, seeing as it was getting close to 4:30. As expected, John Feretti wanted to continue. Any time your opponent is melting down, the last thing you want to do is stop him.

Michael took Judge Gregg up on his offer, and the session was adjourned.

As the jury was filing out, Michael looked into the eyes of every single person in the gallery. If there was a kidnapper among them, he did not see it. What he had seen was confusion and no small measure of distrust. Michael would have to see the daily transcript from the court reporter to know precisely what he had said.

He knew enough to know that a lawyer rarely recovered from a bad opening statement. It set the groundwork for the entire case. A bad opening meant playing catch-up the rest of the trial.

None of that mattered now.

Tommy had not been able to locate Falynn.

On the way to Newark Street he looked at every car that pulled up next to him, at every cab driver, at any car that seemed to follow him for more than a block. No one stood out. His phone had not rung again. Nor had he called. His finger had hovered over the speed dial ever since leaving the office, but he had not pressed it.

You will not call this house for any reason.

The noxious smell of latex paint greeted him at the door. It filled his head, dizzying him for a moment. He checked his cellphone again.

The painter stood on the second floor landing, smoking a cigarette. He wore a pair of white overalls and cap, a latex glove on his left hand. He smoked with his right.

When he saw Michael he flicked his cigarette out the window, a look of guilt on his face for smoking inside a building. It was almost a capital crime in New York these days. "Are you Mr Roman?" the painter asked.

Michael nodded his head. The painter checked his hand for wet paint, found it dry. "Nice to meet you. I'm Bobby Rollins. Edgar is my dad."

They shook hands. Michael noticed the flecks of drying paint on the man's hands and arms.

"That's the cranberry." The young man laughed. "It dries a little darker."

"Thank God." Michael peeked inside the door to the second-floor offices. His heart was racing to burst. He had to get rid of this man. He had to think straight. "How's it going in there?"

"Good. Whoever did your plaster work was pretty good."

Michael stepped back, took a moment. "Look, something's come up. I'm afraid I'm going to have to ask you to come back another time."

The young man stared at the second-floor office for a moment, glanced back at Michael, then at his watch. It looked like Miller Time was coming a bit early. "Sure. No problem. It's going to take me a few minutes to close the cans and clean the brushes and rollers."

"I appreciate it," Michael said. His own voice sounded distant, like he was hearing himself talk through a long tunnel.

Bobby Rollins walked down the stairs, said over his shoulder, "I'll be out of here in ten minutes."

Michael stepped back into the second-floor office. There was little furniture, just a desk and a pair of plastic chairs. He paced the room, his mind and heart ablaze with fear. He had to make a move, to do something. But what?

He looked over at the long bookcase against the wall, at the leather-clad books of legal doctrine and opinions. What had always seemed like the solution to everything, things he believed in with all his heart, were now merely paper and ink. There was nothing in any of those books that could help him now.

Before he could decide what to do his cellphone rang. He almost jumped out of his skin. He picked up the phone, looked at the screen.

Private number.

Pulse racing, he flipped open the phone. "This is Michael Roman."

"How did it go in court?"

It was the man who had his family. The man called Aleks.

"Let me talk to my wife, please."

"In time. You are at the new office? The office for the

planned legal clinic?"

It was a question, Michael thought. Maybe he wasn't being watched. He peeked out the window. There were cars parked all along Newark Street. All appeared empty.

"Look, I don't know what you want, or what this is all about," Michael began, knowing he had to talk. He didn't know what he was going to say, but he knew he had to try and engage this man on some level. "But you obviously know a lot about me. You know I am an officer of the court. I am friends with the chief of police, the commissioner, many people in the mayor's office. If this is just about money, tell me. We'll work this out."

Michael heard the man take a deep, slow breath. "This is not about money."

Somehow, the words were even more chilling than Michael expected. "Then what is this about?"

More silence. Then, "You will know very soon."

Something inside Michael flared red. Before he could stop himself he said, "Not good enough."

He jammed shut the phone, instantly regretting what he had done. He opened it a second later, but the connection had been broken. It took every ounce of restraint within him not to smash the phone against the wall. He scanned the office frantically, trying to think of what to do, how to act at such a moment. He knew that he would never get this minute back, and every wrong move he made at this moment could mean disaster, could mean the lives of his wife and daughters.

Go to the police, Michael.

Just go.

He grabbed his keys, headed for the door.

As he rounded the platform he saw a shadow cross the stairs below. Someone was blocking his way.

It all fell into place. It had been nagging his conscious thought for the past few minutes. Nick St Cyr had told him that Edgar Rollins & Son was really only one man, that Edgar Rollins's son had been killed by a drunk driver in 2007, and the old man didn't have the heart to take the name off the business. St Cyr had represented the old man in a lawsuit against the drunk driver.

The man who called himself "Bobby Rollins" was not a painter at all. He now stood in front of the door leading to the street. He had shed the painter's overalls, removed his painter's cap. He had also removed his latex glove.

He was now pointing a weapon at Michael's head.

In his other hand was a cellphone. He handed the phone to Michael. For a moment, Michael couldn't move. But the insanity of the moment soon propelled him forward. He took the phone from the young man, put it to his ear.

"His name is Kolya," Aleks said. "He does not want to harm you, but will if I give him the order. His father was a corporal in the federal army, and a vicious man. A sociopath by all accounts. I have no reason to believe that the apple has fallen far from the tree. Do you understand this?"

Michael glanced at Kolya. The young man lowered the gun slightly, leaned against the door jamb. Michael took a deep breath. "Yes."

"I am most pleased to hear this. And, if it puts to bed your fears for the moment, let me say that your wife and your adopted daughters are just fine, and they will remain that way, as long as you do what I say."

Your adopted daughters, Michael thought.

"May I please speak to my wife?"

"No."

Michael wondered what had happened to the real painter. He shuddered at the possibilities. He tried to calm himself, to tell himself that there was only one job: getting his family back.

"Are you ready to listen?" Aleksander Savisaar asked.

"Yes," Michael said. "What do you want me to do?"

THIRTY

Sondra Arsenault stared at the television, an icy hand squeezing her heart. In the past twenty-four hours she had not eaten, had not left the house, except to get the mail, and even then she had all but run back to the front porch and slammed and locked the door, as if being chased by invisible demons. She had not slept a single minute. She had alternated between pots of black coffee, vitamins, scalding showers, and runs on the treadmill. She had taken her blood pressure a dozen times, each time registering a higher reading. She had cleaned the refrigerator. Twice.

Now, watching this news report, she realized her fears had not only been justified, but horribly understated. There was a good chance that, before the day was over, her world would end.

At six o'clock James walked through the door, his briefcase bulging at the seams, a pile of papers under his arm. As one of the newer teachers at Franklin Middle School he not only taught English but also a fourth-grade civics class, and served as the school's soccer coach. In the past three months he had lost fifteen pounds from his already tall and lanky frame. At fifty-one, he was beginning to walk with an old man's slouch.

James kissed Sondra on the top of her head – Sondra was nearly a foot shorter, and they had fallen into this routine years earlier – put his case and papers on the dining-room table, and crossed into the kitchen.

The kids were staying with Sondra's mother in Mamaroneck for a few days, and the house was preternaturally quiet, a state made even more pronounced to Sondra by the savage beating of her heart. She could swear she heard her diastolic pressure rise and fall.

James reached into the cupboard over the stove, took down a bottle of Maker's Mark. It had become a ritual for him. One drink before retiring to what passed for a den in their three-bedroom colonial. He would mark papers for an hour before dinner, catch up on his e-mail. If something unusual happened at school that day, this would be the ten-minute window in which he told his wife.

This was one of those days.

"You're not going to believe what happened today," James began. "One of the kids in my civics class, this big fourth-grader who thought it would be a good idea to bring a pair of chameleons to school –"

"I have something to tell you."

James stopped pouring his drink, his shoulders sagging. All the dark possibilities of what might be coming his way danced across his face – *an affair, a disease, a divorce, something happened to the kids.* As long as Sondra had known him, he had never faced adversity well. He was a good husband, a great father, but a warrior he was not. It was Sondra who was always on point in every conflict they had faced as a couple, as a family. It was Sondra who stared down the dangers and misfortunes of their lives.

This was one of the reasons she had not said anything about what had happened. Now she had no choice.

"Is everything okay?" James asked, his voice trembling. "I mean, the *kids* . . . are the kids – ?"

"They're fine, James," she said. "I'm fine."

"Your mom?"

"She's good. Everybody's good."

Sondra walked over to the sink, eyed the coffeemaker. She couldn't have another cup. Her nerves were frayed as it was. Her veins felt like electrified copper wire. She began to make a pot anyway. She needed to do something with her hands.

As she circled an entry point to the story she had to tell her husband – a challenge that had run through her mind constantly for the past twenty-four hours – she considered how she had gotten to this moment.

The only child of Laotian immigrants, the cherished daughter of a celebrated mathematician and a forensic anthropologist, Sondra had grown up in the rarefied world of academia and applied science. Fall in New England, summer in North Carolina, at least three birthdays spent in Washington DC.

She met James at an all-nighter on the campus of Smith College, where he was one of the younger teaching assistants, and she was a grad student coasting to her MISW. At first she found him bookish and a little too passive, but after their third date she rooted out his charm, and found herself falling for this quiet young man from Wooster, Ohio. They married a year later, and although both would admit privately that their courtship and marriage did not burn with the heat of any grand passion, and that their inability to conceive was a source of sadness and disappointment, they both staked out, and claimed, contentment.

In the eighteenth year of their marriage, when they decided to adopt, the two little girls from Uzbekistan who bubbled into their lives caused a reaffirmation – perhaps even a true discovery – of love for each other. Life was good.

Until this moment.

James floated slowly over to the dinette table, pulled out a chair, drifted down to the seat, as if he were weightless. He had not yet taken a sip of his bourbon.

Sondra sat across from her husband. Her hands began to shake. She put them in her lap. "Something happened last night," she said.

James just stared at her. For some odd reason Sondra noticed that he had missed a large spot on his neck when he shaved that morning.

Despite all her careful preparation, she just told him what had happened in one long sentence. She told him how she had been doing the laundry, how she had just put the towels in the linen closet on the second-floor landing. She told him how, at that moment, she had been thinking about their upcoming trip to Colonial Williamsburg, and whether or not the girls would like it. They were bright, inquisitive children. When it came down to a trip to Disney World, or a trip to a place with real history attached to it, it hadn't taken long for them to decide.

When she opened the door to the girls' room, it suddenly seemed as if all the air in the world had changed, had become red and overheated. The girls were sleeping, the nightlight was on, and everything was where it was supposed to be. Except for one thing.

"There was a man standing in their room," Sondra said.

James looked gut-punched. "My God!" he said. He began to rise to his feet, but it seemed his legs would not support him. He eased back down to the chair. His skin turned the color of dried bones. "He didn't . . ."

"No. I told you. The girls are fine. I'm fine."

She told him what the man said, and how he had slipped out of the window like a wraith in the night. One moment there, the next moment gone. She went on to tell James what she had seen on the news. The Russian lawyer was dead. *Their* Russian lawyer. Murdered in his office. And it looked like files had been stolen.

For what seemed like hours, but was in reality only a minute or so, James Arsenault did not say a word. Then: "Oh no."

"I'm going to call the police," Sondra said. She had rehearsed these six words all day, concocting what seemed like an infinite variety of phrases, and now that she'd said them she felt an enormous sense of relief. Although, as soon as the words crossed her lips, she wondered if she had spoken them in English or Laotian.

A few moments later, when Sondra Savang Arsenault picked up the phone, her husband was still sitting at the table, his drink untouched.

In the background, the coffeemaker began to brew.

THIRTY-ONE

Michael figured Kolya to be around twenty-three. He was short and solid, powerfully built, definitely a weight trainer. Michael had about six inches in height on him, and they probably weighed the same, but that was where any similarities ended.

Then there was the gun.

They were driving east on the Long Island Expressway, Michael at the wheel, Kolya next to him.

Michael thought about Viktor Harkov's body. He had seen his share of carnage over the last decade. He had gotten a brutal introduction of his own that horrible day at the Pikk Street Bakery.

Michael considered what a physical confrontation might be like. It had been many years since he'd had to fight anyone. Growing up ethnic in Queens, it was a weekly occurrence; everyone had their corner, their block. He'd had his share of scuffles in and around courtrooms over the years, of course, but nothing that progressed much beyond the shoving or shirt-bunching stage.

The truth was, he had been hitting the gym with regularity. On a good day, he could put in an hour on the treadmill, lift free weights for another thirty minutes, and work the heavy bag for three full rounds. He was in the best physical condition of his life. But that was a long way from physical violence. Could he handle himself? He didn't know, but he had the dark feeling that his condition was going to be tested, and soon.

As they passed through Flushing Meadows, Queensboro, and Corona Park, Michael thought about the man who called himself Aleksander Savisaar. How did the man know so much about him? Would he really hurt Abby and the girls? Michael had no choice but to believe him.

In the meantime, he knew he had to remain calm, play this cool. He would find an opening. Until then, the lives of his wife and daughters depended on it.

"Look, you look like a smart young man," he began, trying to keep the fear out of his tone. "You're name is Kolya? Short for Nikolai?"

The kid remained silent. Michael continued.

"You've got to know that this is going to jam you up for the rest of your life."

The kid still didn't say a word. He'd probably heard the routine before. After what seemed like a full minute of silence, Kolya responded. "What do you know about it?"

Here it was. As much as Michael wanted to drive the SUV into a guardrail, take the gun from the kid's belt and put it to his head, he had to take another tack. For now. He took a deep breath.

"You know I'm a prosecutor, right?"

The kid snorted laughter. So he hadn't known.

Even before he said it, Michael knew it might be a mistake. Telling a criminal you were an ADA could open a lot of possibilities, most of them bad. If this kid had been to jail – and Michael was fairly certain he had – a prosecutor had put him there. Michael had gotten his share of jailhouse threats over the years.

The kid mugged. "A prosecutor."

"Yeah."

"Un-fucking-real. Where at?"

"Queens."

The kid snorted another laugh. He was clearly from another borough. Michael would bet Brooklyn. He had to keep him talking. "Where are you from?"

The kid lit a cigarette. For a few long seconds it appeared he wasn't going answer. Then on a trail of smoke, he said: "Brooklyn."

"What part?"

Another long pause. "So, what, is this where we have a heart-to-heart? The part where you tell me that I really don't want to hurt anybody, or that if only my mother could see me now she would be ashamed of me?" The kid looked out the window for a moment, back. "My mother was a fucking whore. My old man was a sadist."

Michael had to get off this subject. "This is my family. Do you have family of your own?"

Kolya didn't answer. Michael stole a glance at the kid's left hand. No ring.

"Why are you doing this?" Michael asked.

The kid shrugged. "Everybody's got to have a hobby."

"Look, I can get my hands on some money," Michael said, his stomach turning at the thought of ransoming his family. "Serious money."

"Don't talk."

"Whatever he is paying you, it's not enough."

The kid looked over at him. Michael could not see his eyes. All he saw was his own face reflected in a fish eye view in the kid's wraparound sunglasses. "What he's paying *me*? What the fuck makes you think this isn't *my* idea? *My* play."

It hadn't occurred to Michael, and with good reason. It seemed impossible. When he first looked the kid over —

something at which he was skilled, an ability he developed in his first years in the DA's office on those days when he had to chair three dozen preliminary hearings in a single day and had to read a defendant in ten seconds flat — he noticed the dirt under the kid's nails, the smell of axle grease and motor oil in his clothes. This kid worked in or around a garage, and Michael was willing to bet he was not servicing his own fleet of classic sports cars.

"You're right," Michael began, hoping to placate the kid. "I didn't mean any disrespect by that. All I'm saying is that, whatever this is paying, I'm hoping it's enough."

The kid lowered his window, flicked the cigarette out. "I'm touched by your concern." He raised the window. "Now drive the fucking car, and shut the fuck up."

The kid pulled back the corner of his jacket. The butt of the automatic weapon emerged from the waistband of his jeans. It was on the kid's right side, furthest from Michael's reach. The kid might have been a thug, but he wasn't stupid. The gun was all he had to say.

Ten minutes later they pulled off the road on Hempstead Avenue, near Belmont Racetrack, just east of Hollis, into the parking lot of a somewhat isolated off-brand motel called the Squires Inn.

The motel was L-shaped, tired, with a broken asphalt parking lot, missing shingles. It may have at one time been part of a chain, but had long since fallen into disrepair. They pulled into the lot. Kolya pointed to a space. Michael put the car in park, cut the engine. Kolya reached over, took the keys from the ignition.

"Do not get out of the car," Kolya said. "Do not do a fucking thing. You move, I make a call, and it starts raining shit."

Kolya reached into the back seat, grabbed two large grocery

bags, exited the car, crossed the walkway. He reached into his pocket, fished out a key, opened the door to room 118. Michael checked his coat pockets, even though he knew that Kolya had frisked him before leaving the office, taking his house keys, car keys, cellphone, and wallet. All he had left was his watch and his wedding ring. He reached over, tried to open the glove compartment. It was locked. He checked the back seats, the console, the pockets on the doors. Nothing. He needed something, something he could use as a weapon, something with which he could get the upper hand. There was nothing.

A minute later Kolya emerged from the room, looked left and right, scanning the parking lot. It was all but empty. He motioned to Michael to get out of the car. Michael emerged, crossed the sidewalk, and entered the room. Kolya closed the door.

The room was standard issue for an off-brand motel – worn teal green carpeting, floral bedspread with matching drapes, laminate writing desk, a nineteen-inch television on a swivel stand. Michael noticed a rusty ring on the ceiling over the bed. He heard the pipes rattle inside the walls. The room smelled of mildew and cigarettes.

Kolya locked the door. He pointed to the chair by the desk. "Sit there."

Michael hesitated for a moment. He was not used to being given orders, especially by someone the likes of which he put in jail for a living. The fact that this man had both a 9 mm weapon and his family got him moving. He eased himself onto the chair.

Kolya parted the drapes slightly, looked out into the parking lot. He took out his cellphone, punched in a number. After a few moments he spoke into the phone. He closed the phone. He then extracted the weapon from his waistband, held it at his side. He turned to Michael. "Come here."

Michael stood, walked over to the window. Kolya opened the drapes further, pointed. "You see that car over there? The one parked underneath the sign?"

Michael looked out the window. Under the sign for the motel was a ten-year-old Ford Contour, dark blue, tinted windows. He could not see inside. "Yes."

"Go back and sit down."

Michael did as he was told.

"I am going to leave now," Kolya said. "I want you to listen to me carefully. Are you listening?"

"Yes."

"You don't leave this room. You don't make any phone calls. There's a man sitting in that Ford over there. He works for me. If you so much as open the door to this room, he will call me, and your family is dead. Do you understand this?"

The words sliced through Michael's heart. "Yes."

"I'm going to call you on this room phone every thirty minutes. If you don't answer within two rings, your family is dead." Kolya pointed to the wall. "The girl working the front desk here is my cousin. In front of her is a switchboard. If you make an outgoing call, she'll know. If you even pick up the phone without receiving an incoming call, she'll know. Do either of these things and I will light up your family. Do you understand this?"

The fear began to crawl around Michael's stomach. The possibility that he may never see Abby and the girls was real. "Yes."

"Good."

Kolya pointed to the two large grocery bags he had brought in with him. "There's food in there. You're gonna be here awhile. Eat healthy, counselor."

Kolya laughed at his joke, then held Michael's stare for an

uncomfortable amount of time, asserting his authority. Michael had met so many men like Kolya over the years. He could not look away. He *would* not.

Finally Kolya backed off. He crossed the room, gave everything one more look, opened the door, and left. Michael slipped up to the window, peered through the curtains. He saw Kolya walk up to the blue Ford. Whoever was inside the Ford rolled down the window. Kolya pointed to the room, to his watch. A few seconds later he slipped into his own car, pulled out of the parking lot and soon disappeared into the traffic on Hempstead Avenue.

Michael paced around the room.

He had never felt more helpless in his life.

THIRTY-TWO

Aleks looked through the two-drawer file cabinet in the small bedroom Michael and Abigail Roman used for a home office. He scanned the history of their lives, taking in the milestones, the events. He learned many things. He learned that they owned their own home, having paid cash for it. They also owned a commercial space on Ditmars Boulevard. Aleks perused the photographs of the boarded-up building. He recalled it from the story he'd read about Michael. It was the place in which Michael's parents were killed. The Pikk Street Bakery. Inside the envelope were a pair of keys.

Marriage license, deeds, tax returns, warranties — the residue of modern American life. He soon found the documents he sought. The girls' adoption decree, forms which would serve as their birth certificates.

Aleks sat down at the computer, conducted a search for the government agency he needed. He soon heard a car door slam. He glanced out the window.

Kolya had returned.

They stood in the kitchen. Aleks smelled the marijuana on Kolya. He decided to say nothing for the moment.

"Any problems?" Aleks asked.

"None."

"Do you have the license?"

Kolya reached into his pocket, removed an envelope, handed it to Aleks.

Aleks opened the envelope, slid out the plastic laminated license. He held it up to the light, caught the shimmer of the holographic image. It was good work. He put the license in his wallet.

"Where do you have him?"

Kolya told him the name and address of the motel, along with the room number and phone number. Aleks wrote nothing down. He did not need to.

Aleks glanced at his watch. "I will return within one hour's time. When I come back you will return to the motel and make sure Michael Roman does not leave. Are we clear on this?"

Kolya mugged. "It's not that complicated."

Aleks held the young man's stare for a few moments. Kolya glanced away.

"You may be there for a while," Aleks said. "You will need to guard him until I am out of the country."

"The money is right, bro. No worries."

Bro, Aleks thought. The sooner he left this place, the better. "Good."

"What do you want me to do with him then?" Kolya asked.

Aleks glanced down at the butt of the pistol in Kolya's waistband. Kolya saw the look. Neither man said a word.

Aleks looked at the photos of the girls. He had taken them against the wall in the kitchen, an off-white background that could have been anywhere. He took a pair of scissors out of the drawer and cut the photographs into 2 × 2-inch squares. He needed two photographs of Anna, and two of Marya. For their passports.

*

The girls sat on the couch in front of the television. They were watching an animated film, something about talking fish.

He got down to the girls' level. "We're going to go to the post office," he said. "Is that all right?"

"Is Mommy coming with us?" Marya asked.

"No," Aleks said. "She has some work to do."

"At the hospital?"

"Yes, at the hospital. But on the way back we can stop and get something for dinner. Are you hungry?"

Anna and Marya looked apprehensive for a few moments, but then they both nodded.

"What would you like for dinner?"

The girls exchanged a guilty glance, looked back. "McNuggets," they said.

Abby watched the door at the top of the stairs, and waited. She had always feared for her daughters, as any mother would. The stranger in the car, the terminal childhood disease. She had also feared the legal ramifications of what they had done. She had even rehearsed what she might say if ever called before a judge or a magistrate, the pleadings of a woman desperate for a child.

But never this.

A few minutes later Aleks came downstairs. Abby had long ago stopped struggling against her restraints. Her limbs had fallen numb.

"Do you need anything?" he asked.

Abby Roman just glared at him.

"We are going to leave for a while. We will not be long." He crossed the room, sat on the edge of the workbench. Abby noticed that he had gelled his hair. What was he getting ready to do?

"Kolya will remain here. You will obey him as you obey me."

Abby noticed he was carrying a manila envelope. She saw her own handwriting on the front. It was the envelope that had Charlotte and Emily's adoption papers in them.

Her blood turned to ice water. "You can't do this."

"Anna and Marya were stolen from their mother's bed in the middle of the night. They are mine."

Abby had to ask. Perhaps, in the answer, she would find something she needed. "Why do you call them Anna and Marya?"

Aleks considered her for a few long moments. "Do you really want to know the answer to this question?"

Abby wasn't sure. But she knew she needed to keep him talking. If he left an opening, any opening, she would take it. She tried to keep the fear from her voice. "Yes."

Aleks looked away, then back.

"It is the story of a prince and his three sisters . . ."

Over the next five minutes Aleks told her a story. What Abby had feared – that she was dealing with a dangerous but rational individual – was not true. This man was insane. He believed he was this Koschei. He believed that, with his daughters, he would be immortal. He believed that his soul was in the girls.

The part that stole Abby's breath, the part that frightened her to the limits of her being, was that the girls *knew*. They had been looking at pictures from the same story in the library.

When he finished telling her the story Aleks stood, watched her for the longest time, perhaps waiting for some sort of reaction. Abby was speechless for a moment. Then:

"You'll never get them out of the country. Someone is going to catch you."

"If I cannot have them I will take their essence," Aleks said.

"What are you talking about?"

Aleks touched the vials around his neck.

My God, Abby thought. The vial filled with blood. The two empties. He was going to kill the girls if he had to.

As Aleks climbed the stairs, Abby felt her heart break.

She would never see Charlotte and Emily again.

THIRTY-THREE

Desiree Powell was hungry. Whatever was cooking in the kitchen – it smelled like a pork roast with rosemary and garlic, three of her favorite things – was making her salivate. She'd forgotten to eat lunch. It often happened in the tornado of the first twenty-four hours of a homicide investigation.

The ride up to Putnam County had been stop and start, due to construction. Fontova had taken a nap, a skill Powell had never been able to cultivate. She barely slept in her own bed, at night, with a righteous snort and 5 mg of Ambien as a chaser.

But now a question hung in the air.

Powell stared at the woman, tapping her pen on her notebook, waiting for an answer. With her hooded eyes and unwavering gaze, Detective Desiree Powell knew she was all but impossible to read.

Powell had dealt with many social workers and behavioral therapists in her career. She knew the mindset. She knew that Sondra Arsenault had spent most of her adult life exploring people's motives, ferreting out their agendas, divining their purpose. She was probably good at these things. Powell knew that she presented Sondra Arsenault with a cipher. By nature, social workers asked the questions. Today, it was Powell's job.

When Sondra had called the local police department they had sent around a pair of uniformed officers to take down a report regarding the man who had broken into her home. When she told the uniformed officers that there might be a connection between the break-in at her house and the murder of a New York City lawyer named Viktor Harkov, they had wrapped things up quickly. They told her that someone would be contacting them soon.

Powell asked again. "So, the only people in the house were your daughters and yourself."

"Yes."

"And you didn't hear anything? No breaking glass, no door being kicked in?"

Powell knew that the uniformed officers had looked at all the doors and windows, and written down that there had been no forced entry. It never hurt to cover it again.

"No."

"You walked into you daughters' room, and there he was."

"Yes."

"What was the man doing?"

"He was just standing there, at the foot of the bed," Sondra said. "He was . . . he was watching them."

"Watching them?"

"Watching them sleep."

Powell made a note. "Was the light on in the bedroom?"

"No. Just a night light."

"I know you described this man to the officers, but I need you to tell me. Once again, I'm sorry to put you through this. It's just routine."

Sondra didn't hesitate. "He was tall, Caucasian, broad shouldered. He had close-cropped sandy hair, almost blond. He wore a black leather coat, dark jeans, white shirt, black vest. He had a small scar under his left cheekbone, a few days of stubble, light-blue eyes. He was in his thirties."

Powell stared at her again, unblinking. "This is a remarkably precise description, Mrs Arsenault."

Sondra remained silent.

"And you saw all this with just a night light?"

"No," Sondra replied. "After I entered the room he turned on the overhead light."

Powell scribbled another note, asked another question, one to which she already had the answer. "May I ask if you work outside the home?"

"Yes. I am a social worker. Part of my job is to observe people."

Powell nodded. "Here in Putnam County?"

"Yes," the woman said. "It's not only people in the city who need counseling."

Attitude, Powell thought. She left it unchallenged. "You said he spoke to you?"

"Yes."

"What did he say?"

"He said: *This is not Anna and Marya. I have made a mistake. If I have frightened you, you have my deepest apologies. You are in no danger.*"

She pronounced the name *Ma-RYE-a*. Powell glanced at the photograph of the twins on the mantel, back. "Your daughter's names are Lisa and Katherine?"

"Yes."

"Who are Anna and Marya?"

Sondra said she had no idea. The look on her face, along with the way she worried one finger around another, told Powell that deep inside, where fear makes its nest, she probably had the feeling she was going to find out.

"After this you say he slipped out the window, and you never saw him again."

"That's correct."

"Did you watch where he went? Did you see if he got into a car?"

"No," Sondra said. "I did not."

"What did you do?"

"I closed the window, drew the blinds, and turned off the light. Then I held my daughters."

"Of course." She made another note, took a few moments, then glanced at James. "May I ask where you were when this happened, sir?"

James cleared his throat. It sounded like a stall. Powell knew all the delay tactics – clearing the throat, scratching the lower leg, asking for a simple question to be repeated.

"I was at the school where I teach. Franklin Middle school on Sussex Avenue."

Powell flipped a few pages back. "You were there at nine o'clock at night?"

"We had a parent-teacher meeting that night. I was helping clean up."

Powell wrote this down. She would contact the school to see if James was telling the truth, as well as plug this information into the timeline surrounding the murder of Viktor Harkov.

"And what time did you get home?"

"I think it was just before ten."

"The school is an hour away?"

"No," James said. "We stopped for coffee."

"We?"

James gave Powell the names of two of his colleagues.

"And your wife said nothing about this incident when you got home?"

"No."

"Does this person she described sound familiar to you?"

"No."

Powell turned back to Sondra. "Have you cleaned the bedroom since the incident, Mrs Arsenault?"

"No," Sondra said. She looked slightly embarrassed by this, as if by implication it made her a bad housekeeper.

"I have a forensic team standing by," Powell said. "Would it be okay if they processed the room for DNA and fingerprints?"

"Yes," Sondra said.

Powell took out her cellphone, dialed the weather, listened. She would not be able to get her own CSU team out here for at least two hours, but the Arsenaults did not need to know that. When she got the forecast, she said a few perfunctory, official sounding phrases. She clicked off, took a sip of her coffee, which had grown cold. She leaned forward in her chair, a sure sign of intimate friendship, and continued.

"You both strike me as decent, intelligent people, so I think you know what I have to ask you next."

Here it comes, Sondra's face said.

"A man breaks into your house," Powell continued. "It appears he does not steal anything, or harm anyone. It appears he thought your daughters were little girls named Anna and Marya. Have I gotten this right so far?"

Sondra nodded.

"So why do you think this has anything to do with the murder of a lawyer in Queens?"

Sondra took her time answering. "The newspaper account said that the lawyer handled foreign adoptions."

"Yes," Powell said. "He did."

"And when the man – this intruder – spoke, he had an accent. Eastern European, Russian, perhaps Baltic."

Powell pretended to consider this for a moment. "Mrs Arsenault, with all due respect, there are a lot of Russian people in New York. A lot of people from Romania, Poland,

Lithuania. You'll forgive me if I don't see the immediate connection."

Sondra tried to hold Powell's gaze. She withered. "We . . . we knew Mr Harkov."

Powell felt her pulse kick up a notch. "You mean professionally?"

"Yes."

"He did some legal work for you and your husband?"

Sondra took James's hand in hers. "You could say that."

"What would *you* say, Mrs Arsenault?"

Tears began to gather in Sondra's eyes. "Yes. He did some work for us."

"I have to tell you that when we got the call from your local police department, we looked through Mr Harkov's files, going back twelve years. We didn't see your name."

Powell did not wait for her to respond.

"Tell me how you came to meet Mr Harkov."

Sondra told him about the process. How they had tried to adopt, three different times, and been rejected. How Sondra had heard about Harkov from a woman she had befriended at a medical conference in Manhattan. She recalled how Harkov said that he could get around certain things, that being their ages, and how they wanted a baby, not a child of five years. For a fee.

"Are you saying that Mr Harkov may have done something off the books? Something illegal regarding the adoption of Lisa and Katherine?"

It appeared that Sondra Arsenault might have had a million words to say, but in the end only three words found her lips.

"Yes," she said. "He did."

Powell looked at the woman. It was the break she had been waiting for. She glanced at Fontova, who had been sitting quietly on a rather severe-looking Danish modern dining-room chair. He moved his head an inch to one side, then back. No questions.

Powell stood, walked to the front window. *A* had just led to *B*. It was on. She had never gotten past *C* in her career, had never needed to. When she got to *C* she had her killer.

There was a good chance that the man who had destroyed Viktor Harkov had broken into this house. Maybe he had left a fingerprint. Maybe an eyelash or a drop of saliva. Maybe he had been seen by one of the neighbors. They would begin a canvass.

But who were Anna and Marya? Was there another couple out there in jeopardy?

And if so, why? Why was a killer looking for two little girls?

Powell had one more question for the moment.

"Mrs Arsenault, this woman, the one you met at the medical conference, what was her name?"

Sondra Arsenault looked at her hands. "I never got her last name, but I remember she was a nurse," she said. "An ER nurse. Her name was Abby."

THIRTY-FOUR

Michael put his ear to the motel wall, listened. He could hear a muffled voice coming from the room next door.

He picked up the remote, turned on the television, all the while holding the volume down button. In seconds the picture came on. Ear still tight to the wall, Michael flipped through the channels. The service was basic cable, and soon he returned to the channel where he began. The sound from the other room did not sync with any of the TV channels. The sound was either a radio talk show or another motel patron talking on the phone.

He turned off the TV, cupped his ear to the wall once more, concentrated. The rhythm sounded like a man having a telephone conversation, like the man was agreeing with someone. A yes-man talking to his boss. Or his wife.

After five minutes or so, there was silence. Michael heard the water flowing through the pipe, but he could not be sure it was coming from the next room. He then heard the television click on, a few ads, then the unmistakable rhythms of a game show. After another five minutes the television was turned off.

Michael heard a door open then close. He stepped quickly to the window, inched over the vertical blind. He saw a middle-aged man in a wrinkled grey suit exit the room next to his, walk over to a red Saturn. He fumbled with keys for a moment, then opened the car door, slipped inside. Michael saw the man unfold a map, study it for a full minute. Soon the car backed up, drove out of the parking lot, pulled onto the marginal road, and head toward the avenue.

Michael glanced over at the motel sign. The blue Ford with the tinted windows was still in position.

He crossed the room, put his ear to the wall again. Silence. He held this position for a few minutes, listening. No sounds came from the room next door. He knocked on the wall. Nothing. He knocked louder. Silence. The third time he pounded on the wall, hard enough to dislodge the cheap framed print above the bed in his own room and send it crashing to the floor.

He listened again. Unless the world's soundest sleeper was in the next room, it was empty.

He ran his hands along the wall. It felt like drywall beneath the cheap wallpaper, perhaps half-inch gypsum. There was vinyl cove base at the floor, no crown molding at the ceiling. He wondered if –

The phone rang. Michael nearly jumped out of his skin. He ran across the room, stumbling over the desk chair, and picked up the receiver before the phone could ring a second time.

"Yes."

"Just checking in, counselor."

It was the one called Kolya. Michael knew enough about the world to know Kolya was the accomplice, a lackey, despite his claims to be the mastermind. "I'm here."

"Smart man."

"I need to talk to my wife."

"Not gonna happen, boss."

Boss. Prison.

"I need to know she is all right."

No response. Michael listened closely to the receiver. There was no background noise. It was impossible to tell where Kolya was calling from. After a few moments pause, Kolya said:

"She's a good-looking woman."

A sick feeling washed over Michael. He had not considered for a moment that this could get worse. It just did. He battled back his rage. He lost the fight.

"I swear to Christ if you fucking touch – !"

"Thirty minutes."

The line went dead.

It took every ounce of discipline within him not to slam down the receiver. He did not need a broken phone on top of everything. He took a few deep breaths, then calmly set the phone in its cradle.

He set the timer on his chronograph watch. He started it. In an instant the readout went from 30:00 to 29:59. He did not have much time to do what he needed to do.

He looked around the room for something to use. Something sharp. He opened the drawers in the dresser. Inside one was a yellowed cash-registry receipt, a glossy slip for three pairs of men's support hose from Macy's. The other held only the fading scent of a lavender sachet.

The two nightstands were empty, as were the closets, save for a pair of wire coat hangers. He took them off the rod, then stepped into the bathroom.

He tried to pull the mirror off the wall. It didn't budge.

He wrapped his arm in his coat, turned away his head, and slammed his elbow into the mirror as hard as he could. Nothing. He planted his feet, tried again. This time the mirror cracked. He wrapped his hand in a towel, and pulled off the largest piece.

*

On the wall facing the adjoining room there were two electrical outlets, spaced about six feet apart. When Michael was in high school he had worked three summers for a leasing company that owned three apartment buildings in Queens. He picked up a few skills, one of which was hanging drywall in newly renovated apartments. As a rule of thumb, the studs in the wall were sixteen inches on center. If a contractor wanted to skimp, he sometimes placed them twenty-four inches apart. In most residential structures waterlines ran through the basement or crawlspace, coming up through the floor plates to the sinks, tubs, and toilets, leaving only electrical wire or conduit to run behind the plaster or drywall.

Michael stood in front of one of the electrical outlets, and began to tap along the wall with the middle knuckle on his right hand. Outlets were always attached to a vertical stud, on one side or the other. Directly above the outlet it sounded solid. As he moved left a few inches, it sounded hollow. When he reached what seemed like sixteen or so inches, it sounded solid again. He thudded the heel of his hand eight or so inches to the right. Hollow.

The bathroom was on the other side of the bedroom, so the chances of there being a sanitary stack or waterlines on this side were unlikely.

He dug the sharp shard of mirror into the wall. He peeled back the wallpaper. Beneath the wallpaper, as he had thought, was drywall, not plaster and wood lath. He pushed on it. It felt thin. He set himself, reared back, lifted his leg at the knee, and kicked the wall. The drywall cracked, but did not buckle.

He checked his watch. The readout said 12:50.

He picked up the shard of silvered glass, and began to cut into the drywall. Because he could not get a firm grip on the sharp glass, it was slow going, but after five minutes or so he cut all the way through to the other side. After three more kicks he had a hole large enough to crawl through.

His watch read 3:50.

He walked back to the window, inched aside the blind. The blue Ford had not moved, nor had the red Saturn returned. He went back to the hole in the wall, looked through. The room was identical to his, save for the rollaway suitcase on the bed, opened.

He stood, turned, picked up the motel phone, being careful not to dislodge the handset. The cord barely reached the opening.

He kicked the rest of the drywall in, squeezed himself through the opening. He walked across the room to the closet, opened the door. Inside was a black raincoat, along with a pair of maroon golf slacks and a white Polo shirt. On the shelf was a tweed cap, a pair of sunglasses.

Before Michael could get the clothes off the hanger, the phone rang. His phone. He dashed across the room, reached through the hole in the wall. He barely got there before the third ring.

"Yes."

Silence. He had gotten to the phone too late.

"Hello!" Michael shouted. "I'm here. I'm *here!*"

"You're cutting it close, counselor," Kolya said. "Where were you?"

"I was in the bathroom. I'm sorry."

A long pause. "You're gonna be a lot fuckin' sorrier, you know that?"

"I know. I didn't —"

"You get one ring next time, Mr ADA. One. Don't fuck with me."

Dial tone.

Michael reached through the wall, put the phone back in its

cradle. He set his watch again. This time for twenty-eight minutes. He changed his clothes, putting on the golf slacks and the raincoat. They were both two sizes too large, but they would have to do. He put on the tweed cap and the sunglasses, checked himself in the mirror. He did not look anything like the man who Kolya had brought to the motel, the man being held prisoner in Room 118.

At the door, he made sure he turned the knob, unlocking it. He had no idea what he was going to do, but whatever it was, he needed to be back in this room in twenty-six minutes and six seconds.

THIRTY-FIVE

Kolya came down the stairs, closing his phone, a smug smile on his face. He had in his hand a sandwich. Abby could smell the hard salami from across the room. The smell nearly made her gag.

Kolya poked around the basement room, feeling the couch cushions, opening and closing the drawers on the old buffet. He flipped on the small television, ran through the channels, flipped it off. To Abby he looked like someone at a house sale, browsing the contents, seeing if things worked. Except, people like Kolya didn't go to house sales.

He leaned against the washer, studied her, took another bite of the sandwich. His gaze made Abby want a shower.

"Your husband said something about money," he finally said.

The words sounded strange. Money, after all this. "What are you talking about?"

He picked up a pair of crystal candlesticks Abby had been meaning to polish, looked underneath. He looked like a gorilla in a Waterford boutique. "He said he could get his hands on some serious money. You know anything about that?"

"No."

He glanced around the basement again. "Now, not for nothin', I mean, this *is* a nice house and all. More than I got. But you don't look rich. Is there a safe in this place?"

Abby thought about the safe in the office. There was never more than two thousand dollars or so in there at any given time. Emergency cash. Abby could not imagine that such a small sum would be enough to make this all go away. Still, she had to try.

"Yes."

"No shit. How much is in it?"

"I . . . I'm not sure. Maybe two thousand dollars."

Kolya mugged, as if two thousand was beneath him. On the other hand, he didn't turn it down. He turned to the corkboard next to the workbench. On it were calendars, greeting cards, family photographs. Kolya pulled out a push pin, studied a picture of Charlotte and Emily from the previous Halloween.

"So, the little girls are adopted, right?"

"Yes."

He considered the photo for a while, push-pinned it back. "What, you couldn't have kids?"

Abby didn't say a word. Kolya continued.

"How old are you? I mean, I don't mean to be rude or anything. I know you're not supposed to ask a woman's age. I was just wondering."

"I'm thirty-one."

"Yeah? Thirty-one? You don't look it."

Abby almost said thank you, but she soon realized who she was talking to, and what this might be leading up to. She remained silent.

"See, most women your age, they've got two or three kids. I mean, kids they actually *had*. Their bodies are a fucking mess. Stretch marks, saggy boobs. A woman your age, in pretty good shape, no stretch marks. You may not believe me, but that's my thing."

He smiled again and it made Abby sick. Kolya crossed the room, peeked out the basement window, returned, took out a pocket knife. Abby struggled to move the chair away from him. She nearly toppled over. He put a hand on her shoulder.

"Relax."

He cut her loose.

Abby rubbed her wrists. The ropes had made a deep red welt. After a few seconds, she began to get the feeling back in her arms.

"Thank you," she said.

Kolya sat on a bar stool. "What can I say? I hate to see a pretty woman suffer. I'm sensitive that way."

Abby just stared. *A pretty woman.*

"Now take off your clothes."

Abby felt punched, as if all the air had been sucked out of her lungs. "*What?*"

"I think you heard me."

Abby wrapped her arms across her chest, as if she was suddenly freezing. She glanced out the high basement window. From this vantage she could see part of the driveway. "He's going to be back soon."

"He?"

"Yes. Aleks."

"*Aleks?* You guys friends now?" Kolya laughed. "Don't worry. It ain't gonna take that long."

Abby thought about making a break for the stairs. She shifted her weight in the chair. "Is that what this is all about?"

"Shit. For me it is. I'm just an employee. You know how it is. You take what you can get. You know what I'm talking about, don't you?" He pulled back the hem of his jacket. Abby's eyes were drawn to the butt of the large pistol in his waistband. "Besides, I just *met* this guy. He's a fucking dinosaur. Old country, old school. I hate that shit. Reminds me of my old man, who was so fucking stupid he trusted a Colombian."

Abby glanced again at the steps, her mind reeling. "You don't have to do this."

Kolya killed a few moments, rearranging some jars of nails and screws on the metal shelf next to him. "You work outside the home?"

"Yes."

"What do you do?"

The last thing Abby wanted to do was let this animal even further into her life. But she knew she had to keep him talking. The longer she kept him talking, the sooner it would be that Aleks got back. "I'm a nurse."

"A nurse! *Oh*! Jackpot," he said, sounding like a little kid. "You wear the whites and everything?"

Abby knew he was talking about the dress-style uniform. Nobody wore them anymore. At the clinic, she spent most of her time in solid-color scrubs. But she would say or do anything to get out of this basement. "Yes."

Kolya rubbed himself. Abby wanted to be sick.

"So, what, you're saying you have your nurse's uniform here?"

The truth was, she did not. Her three sets of scrubs were at the cleaners. It was going to be one of her stops on the way to the clinic. She glanced at the clock on the workbench. She was to start her shift soon. When she did not show up, they would call. "Yes," she said.

"Where is it?"

"Upstairs," Abby said. Her face burned with the lie. She was sure he could read it. But she had to buy time.

Kolya glanced at his watch. "So let's go upstairs."

They walked up the steps, across the kitchen, into the foyer. Kolya motioned to the stairs. Abby hesitated, then started up. She had no choice.

Kolya smiled. "You've done this before, haven't you? You bad girl."

As they went up the stairs she could feel his eyes on her. She was certain that, if she wasn't a Pilates-freak, her legs would be giving out on her.

"Damn, girl. For a skinny little thing you got back."

Get me to the bedroom, God.

"Most women your size have no fuckin' hips at all. You know what I mean? Built like boys."

Just get me near that closet.

They stepped into the bedroom. Kolya directed Abby to sit on the bed. He opened the closet door, rummaged through the suits, the shirts, the sweaters, the slacks. "There's no fuckin' uniforms in here."

Abby stood, backed to the wall. "I forgot. They're at the cleaners."

"Where's the ticket?"

Abby pointed to the small wicker tray on top of the dresser, the catch-all for parking stubs, receipts, claim checks. Kolya found the dry-cleaning ticket, read it, put it back. He then started looking through the dresser, tossing out underwear, socks, sweats. He reached the third drawer from the bottom. In it were neatly folded camisoles and teddies. He pulled a few out, examined them. He arrived at a scarlet red slip, one Abby had not worn in a few years, one of Michael's favorites. Crazily, she tried to remember the last time she had worn it for her husband.

"Nice." Kolya threw it across the room. "Put it on."

Abby glanced at the closet. She remembered. The previous night she had not locked the gun back into the case. It was underneath her sweaters on the bottom shelf. It was less than five feet away.

"I've got something better than this," Abby said.

"Oh yeah?"

Abby made no moves. She raised an eyebrow, as if to ask permission. Kolya seemed to like this. "Yeah," she said. "A new cocktail dress. Short. High heels to match."

"Sweet," Kolya said. "Let's see."

Abby turned, slowly, walked to the closet.

She slid open the door, and reached inside.

THIRTY-SIX

The Millerville post office was a quaint standalone building with a mansard roof, multi-paned windows, two chimneys. The walkway was lined with driftwood posts connected with white chain. On the sculpted lawn was what looked like a Revolutionary War-era cannon. Two large evergreens flanked the double main doors.

Aleks had located three other post offices that were closer to Eden Falls, but he could not take the chance that the girls would be recognized. Or, for that matter, his new name and identity. According to his driver's license he was now a thirty-five-year-old New Yorker named Michael Roman. He walked into the post office, both girls clutching his hand. How many times had he thought about scenes like this? How many times had he envisioned taking Anna and Marya somewhere?

There were eight or nine people waiting in line, another half-dozen people tending to their post office boxes or glancing at the racks of commemorative stamps and mailing supplies.

Aleks glanced around the ceiling. There were three surveillance cameras.

They inched their way to the head of the line. The girls were very well behaved.

"May I help you?"

The woman was black, in her forties. She wore silver eye shadow. Aleks approached with Anna and Marya. "Hi. I need to apply for a passport."

"For yourself?"

"No, for my daughters."

The woman leaned slightly over the counter. She waved at the girls. "Hi."

"Hi," the girls replied.

"*It's double the giggles and double the grins, and double the trouble if you're blessed with twins.*"

Anna and Marya giggled.

"How old are you?" the woman asked.

The girls held up four fingers each.

"Four years old," the woman said. "My, my." She smiled, leaned back, looked at Aleks. "My sister has twins. They're grown now, of course."

A man standing behind Aleks – the next person in line – cleared his throat, perhaps indicating that Aleks's small talk was wasting his time. Aleks turned and stared at the man until he looked away. Aleks turned back. The woman behind the counter smiled, rolled her eyes.

"I'll need to get the applications," she said. "I'll be right back."

The woman disappeared into the back room for a few moments. She returned with a pair of forms. "Do you have photographs of the girls?"

Aleks held up the manila envelope. "I have them right here."

The woman opened the envelope, took out the photographs. "They're so adorable."

"Thank you," Aleks said.

"They look just like you."

"And now you flatter me."

The woman laughed. "Okay. First off I'll need to see some identification."

Aleks reached for his wallet. He handed the woman his newly minted driver's license. It had Aleks's photograph, and Michael Roman's name.

This was the first test. Aleks watched the woman's eyes as she scanned the license. She handed it back. Hurdle cleared.

"Next you'll need to fill these out, and I need you to both sign at the bottom of each form." She handed Aleks a pair of application forms for the issuance of a passport to a minor under the age of sixteen.

"Both?" Aleks asked.

"Yes," the woman said. She glanced around the crowded room. "Isn't the girls' mother here?"

"No," Aleks said. "She had to work today."

"Oh, I'm sorry," the woman replied. "You seemed so organized, I thought you knew."

"Knew what?"

"Your wife needs to be present."

"We both need to be here at the same time?"

"Yes, I'm afraid so. Either that, or she needs to fill out form DS-3053."

"What is that?"

"That is a statement of consent form. It needs to be filled out, signed, and notarized. Would you like to take one with you?"

"Yes," Aleks said. "That would be most helpful."

The American bureaucracy, Aleks thought. It was at least as wearying as the Soviet edition. He now knew that everything had changed. He would not be able to get the girls out of the country legally. He also knew that the girls would not need a passport to get over the border into Canada, only the equivalent of their birth certificates, which he already had. The Canadian border was not that far away.

The woman returned in a moment with the form, handed it to Aleks.

"I'll be back tomorrow," he said.

"That will be fine." The woman stole another glance at the girls, smiled at them. "Where are you headed?"

Aleks tensed at the question. "I'm sorry?"

"On your trip. Where are you headed?"

"We are going to Norway," Aleks said. "We have family there."

"How nice."

"Have you ever been to Norway?"

The woman looked up. "Gosh, no," she said. "I've only been out of the country once, and that was on my honeymoon. We went to Puerto Rico. But that was a few years ago." She winked at him. "I was a bit younger then."

"Weren't we all?" The woman smiled. Aleks looked at her nametag. Bettina.

He extended his hand. "You've been most kind and helpful, Bettina."

"My pleasure, Mr Roman."

Aleks took the girls by the hands and, noticing the security camera over the door, lowered his head. Once out in the parking lot, Aleks put the girls in the back seat, fastened their safety belts. He got back into the car.

"Ready?"

The girls nodded.

Aleks turned the key, started the car. And it came to him.

He would take Abby with them. As long as he had her husband, and she could see that the girls were safe, she would go along. It would make crossing the border that much easier.

Canada, he thought. Once they were safely over the border, he would cut the woman's throat, bury her, and he and the girls would disappear for as long as it took. He would be one step closer to his destiny.

They would leave tonight.

PART THREE

THIRTY-SEVEN

Abby stood at the foot of the bed. The dress was laid out in front of her, along with a pair of black stiletto heels. Kolya sat on a chair at the other side of the room, next to the windows that looked onto the street. Every so often he would part the curtains.

Abby turned to face Kolya, held the black dress in front of her. Vera Wang. She'd only worn it once.

"Oh, *yeah*. That's the one," Kolya said. "Put it on."

When she had taken the shoebox from the shelf she had slipped the .25 inside. The box now sat on the bed.

Abby turned away from Kolya, slipped out of her sweats and fleece top. She was grateful she was wearing a bra.

"Don't get all shy on me now," Kolya said.

Abby stole a glance at Kolya in the dresser mirror. He parted the curtains for what seemed like the tenth time, glancing down at the driveway. He *was* worried about Aleks returning.

"I'll do anything I have to do for my daughters, you know," Abby said.

"Yeah?" Kolya asked. "Anything?"

She slipped the dress over her head, moved the shoebox closer to the edge of the bed. "Anything."

"I've got a few ideas."

Abby backed up a few inches, pulled her hair out of the way. "I need you to zip me up."

Kolya laughed. "Why? You're just going to take it off in a minute."

Abby shifted the top of the shoe box, but didn't open it fully. "Please," she said. "This is how it has to be."

She sensed him getting up behind her. He ran his hands along her hips. The revulsion she felt was complete.

"God*damn* you are one fine looking woman," he said. "This is even better than the nurse uniform." He reached over, zipped up the back of her dress. She slipped on her high heels.

When Abby turned around to face him, she picked up a small atomizer of perfume, spritzed twice. She put the atomizer down, slipped her arms around his neck. "I don't like it rough, okay?"

"You can have it any way you want it."

Abby glanced down at Kolya's waist, back up. "I don't think I can relax if you have that gun on you. Guns scare me."

"Forget it."

Abby ran a hand through his hair. "Look. *Kolya*. What am I going to do? Aleks has my girls. You have me. I'm not going to do anything stupid." Abby ran a finger over his lips. "If I'm nice to you, maybe you'll be nice to me. Maybe we can work something out." She moved even closer. She could see Kolya's nostrils widen slightly, taking in her perfume. "You said yourself that you just met Aleks. Maybe you don't have any loyalty to him. Maybe you could be loyal to me."

Kolya studied her for a few moments. He wasn't buying all of this, but other engines within him had been engaged. He peeked out the window one more time, turned back to Abby. "You try something, I'm gonna get really fuckin' mad."

"I know," Abby said. "I won't."

Kolya, took the pistol from his waistband, ejected the magazine. He flipped on the safety, racked the slide, checked the chamber. Seeing it empty, he put the magazine in his jeans pocket, the pistol on top of the dresser. He turned back to Abby, sliding his hands around her hips. He squeezed her hard, pulled her into him. Abby could feel his thickening erection. "That's not a full clip in my pocket, lady. I'm just happy to see you." He laughed at his own joke.

Abby leaned in, kissed him gently on the lips. When she pulled back, Kolya's eyes glazed for a moment, and Abby Roman knew she had him. She shifted her weight onto her left foot, centered herself, and brought her right knee up as hard as she could, slamming it into Kolya's groin.

Kolya barked in pain, releasing a lungful of sour breath, doubling over. Abby stepped back, grabbed Kolya's weapon from the dresser, flung it into the hallway. While Kolya's hands covered his damaged testicles, Abby pivoted and delivered a second blow, this time with her right foot, delivered full force to the center of his face. With her years of Pilates training she knew her legs were toned and strong, and when the pointed toe of her high heel caught Kolya square in the jaw, she could hear bone break. A spurt of blood shot onto the bedspread. Kolya folded to the floor.

Abby spun around, knocked off the top of the shoebox and took out the .25. When Kolya rolled onto his back, clutching his stomach, his eyes widened at the sight of the pistol.

"You . . . fucking . . . *cunt!*"

Abby stomped on his crotch, driving in her spiked heel. Kolya screamed, rolled onto his side, a fat cord of foamy pink-and-green bile leaking out of his mouth. Muscles corded in his neck. His face was bright scarlet, raked with blood.

Abby kicked off her shoes, leaned over. She put the barrel of the gun to Kolya's head.

"Say that word again."

THIRTY-EIGHT

While the forensic team processed the Arsenault house, Powell and Fontova returned to the office. Sondra and James Arsenault had followed them into the city, and would be looking at mugshots in hope of identifying the man who had broken into their home.

Back in the office, Powell and Fontova had run thirty-five names, and found that many of the people whose cases Harkov had lost no longer lived in New York. Of the seven who did, two were currently in jail, five were gainfully employed, more or less, and had, since their incarceration, kept their noses clean.

None had records that would suggest anything near the propensity for extreme violence seen in that room. This was not an ag assault that had gone too far, or an accidental death that occurred as the result of some pushing match that went terribly wrong. This was the work of a bona fide psychopath.

Things were not always so straightforward. There was recently a case where an employee of a gas station was robbed at gunpoint. Thirty minutes later, while being interviewed by detectives, the man had a heart attack, collapsed and died at the scene. In another instance, one that occurred before Powell became a homicide detective, a man was attacked on a Forest Hills playground, wounded with a knife. The man slipped into a coma, where he remained for years. In the meantime, the attacker was arrested, prosecuted, and convicted of aggravated assault, for which he served eight years on a fifteen year sentence. Three weeks after the attacker's release the man in the coma died.

Were these homicides? There was no question in Desiree Powell's mind – or indeed the mind of any detective Powell had ever worked with – that they were. The decision, however, was not up to the police. It was up to the district attorney. Plus, it was one thing for a police officer to be certain of someone's guilt or culpability in a crime. It was another matter to be able to prove it.

Powell studied the possibilities. Nobody jumped out.

She handed the list to Marco Fontova. The addresses were spread out over Jackson Heights, Elmhurst, Briarwood, Cypress Hills. In other words, all the way across Queens County, and halfway across Brooklyn.

Fontova reached into his pocket, handed Powell a dollar.

"What's this for?" she asked.

"I have to go to fucking Cypress Hills?"

Powell nodded, took the bill. "Reach out to Brooklyn Homicide if you have to."

Fontova pulled a face. There was no love lost between Brooklyn detectives and Queens detectives. Sometimes they had to work together, but they didn't have to like it.

Grumbling under his breath, Fontova grabbed his coat and left the office.

Powell sank back in her chair. Seniority had its perks, she thought, one of which was certainly not the part where she was older than half the people she worked with.

She checked off a list of people she would be interviewing, then poured herself some coffee. Contrary to popular belief, the cop-shop coffee at Queens Homicide was good. Somebody's wife or girlfriend – Powell could never keep the rosters straight –

had signed somebody up for a Coffee of the Month-type club and either on a lost bet, or under threat of exposure for some office indiscretion, the coffee ended up in the small fridge they kept. Today it was a Kona blend.

Powell sat down at the computer.

She popped in the CD that had been duped from Viktor Harkov's hard drive. It seemed the man saved everything, including JPEGS of menus from all the takeout restaurants near his office. Powell waded through the first half. Nothing.

She was just about to get on the street when she saw that hidden in one of the folders was a database with only a handful of names and addresses. It was separate from the others. It was mixed in with the files of letters and correspondence. The file was called NYPL 15.25 EFFECT OF INTOXICATION UPON LIABILITY. But that's not what it was at all. Instead, it was a short list of names, addresses, and other data, with the subhead of ADOPTIONS 2005 (2).

What have we here? Powell thought.

In April 2005 Viktor Harkov brokered the adoption of two sets of twins. One, as Powell already knew, went to Sondra and James Arsenault. In addition to the two little girls adopted by Sondra and James Arsenault, a pair of twin girls, born in Estonia, processed in Helsinki, were adopted by a couple then living in the Whitestone section of Queens. A shiver went up and down Powell's back when she saw the names. It was one of her favorite feelings.

She picked up her phone, dialed.

"Tommy, Desiree Powell."

"Hey," Tommy Christiano said. "You ready for us already?"

"From your mouth to Jah's ear, eh?"

"What's up?"

"Do you know Michael Roman's wife?"

There was a slight hesitation on the other end. Powell waited it out.

"Sure. She's great. Michael married up, big time."

"What does she do?"

"She works at a clinic up in Crane County."

"That's where they're living now?"

"Yeah."

"Must be nice," Powell said. "She's a doctor?"

"No," Tommy said. "She's an RN. Why do you ask?"

"Do you know where she worked before that?" Powell continued, steamrolling over Tommy's question. She knew that this tactic would not be lost on a prosecutor.

"She was an ER nurse at Downtown Hospital."

B just rounded the corner, sliding into *C*, Powell thought. She was not quite there, but she could smell it. She felt the rush. She made her notes, kicked the small talk down the alley as far as it would go. She wanted to ask Tommy a bit more about Michael Roman's wife and children, but it made more sense to be coy at this moment. Tommy Christiano and Michael Roman were close.

"Is Michael still in the office by any chance?"

"No he's gone for the day."

"Ah, okay," Powell said. "Well, Tommy. Thanks a lot."

"No problem. Let me know if —"

"I sure will," Powell interrupted. "I'll keep you posted."

Before Tommy said anything else, Powell clicked off. She turned her attention back to the computer monitor. She recalled Sondra Arsenault's words.

I never got her last name, but I remember she was a nurse. An ER nurse. Her name was Abby.

Powell tapped her pen on the desk. She got back on the Internet, did a search for Michael Roman. In a few seconds she got a hit on an article that had been written in *New York Magazine* a few years ago, a cover story about how Roman had survived an attempted car bombing. Powell remembered the incident well. She had never seen the article.

She began to skim the piece of writing for details. It was lengthy, so she decided to just do a Find search on the page. She got a hit immediately.

"Interesting," she said to no one in particular.

Michael Roman's wife was named Abigail.

Sondra and James Arsenault sat in the squad room of the 112th Precinct. Sondra had never been in a police station before, and she had no idea how unrelentingly grim they could be.

In her time as a social worker she had met many types of people. Granted, the nature of her work meant that many of the people with whom she came in contact were in some way troubled but, for Sondra Arsenault, this was both the joy and the challenge. While it was true that some people entered the mental health field with a god complex – an exaggerated sense of hubris in which a patient is formed and molded by the therapist into a vision of normalcy – most of Sondra's colleagues in the field were dedicated people to whom a person entering into therapy was not a blank slate to be recreated in some sense of normalcy, but rather that few behaviors are hardwired, and that adjustment could be made.

Until today. As she scrolled through computer screen after computer screen of mugshots she realized she had seen more evil in an hour than she had seen in her previous eighteen years in the field of mental health.

Looking at these faces she was reminded of the difference between working the city and working the suburbs. Perhaps Detective Powell had been right when she asked her about where she applied her science, and whether there might be a difference in what happened in a city, as opposed to the comfort and safety of the suburbs.

The detective was right. There was a difference.

Powell stepped into the cramped, windowless room. "How are you guys doing?"

Sondra looked up. "All of these men have broken the law?"

Powell cleared a chair of papers, sat down. "Some more than once," she said with an understanding smile. "Some more than ten times. Some are working their way through the alphabet — assault, burglary, car theft, driving without a permit." She winced at her reach on that one, but no one seemed to notice. "Have you seen anyone who looks familiar?"

"This is what frightens me," Sondra said. "I have seen a *few* people who look familiar. Or maybe I'm just projecting."

"Don't worry if you don't find the man who broke into your house among these photographs. He may not be in the system. It's always worth a shot, though."

Powell opened up a 9 × 12 envelope. She had printed off two pictures from the *New York Magazine* article. "If you don't mind, I'd like to show you a couple of other photographs."

"Sure," Sondra said.

Powell held forth the first one. It was a picture of Michael Roman, taken from the cover of the magazine. He was leaning against a BMW convertible coupe, black trousers and open white shirt, his suit coat over his shoulder, looking pretty *GQ*, if Powell had to say so herself. Powell had cropped out the magazine's logo, and everything else that might indicate it came from a magazine. She didn't want to give the woman the impression this was some kind of celebrity, even though he probably was in certain New York legal circles. It might taint the woman's identification, although Powell found Sondra Arsenault to be a careful, meticulous professional, and didn't think she'd fall for the hype. "Do you know this man?"

Sondra took it from her, looked at it closely. She shook her head. "No."

"This was taken five years ago. Are you sure?"

"Yes. I'm quite sure."

"He doesn't look at all familiar to you?"

More scrutiny, probably just to be polite. "I've never seen this man before in my life."

"Okay," Powell said. "Thanks. Mr Arsenault?"

James Arsenault shook his head immediately. Powell noticed that his lips were chapped and cracked and white. In his hand was a small bottle of Tylenol. He was probably taking one every twenty minutes, without water. This guy was a wreck.

Powell put the first picture back in the envelope, handed the woman the second photograph. This one too had been cropped. "What about her?" she asked. "Does this woman look familiar?"

Sondra took the color copy of the magazine page. "That's her!" she said. "That's the woman who gave me Viktor Harkov's phone number."

"This is Abby?"

"Yes. No question."

"And you don't know her last name, where she lives, where she works, anything else about her?"

"No," Sondra said. "Sorry. I met her at the conference, we talked about adopting, and she told me that she and her husband had just adopted, and that she knew a lawyer who did a really good job. She gave me Viktor Harkov's phone number, and that was about it."

"Did she say anything to you about his methods, the way he worked?"

"No," Sondra said, perhaps more forcefully than she would

have liked. "I mean, I later got the impression that Abby may not have known that the guy was a little . . ."

"I know what you mean," Powell said, finding no reason to supply Sondra Arsenault with a pejorative term for a man who was at that moment being dissected on a cold steel table in South Jamaica. They all knew who he was and what he did. The question, if there would *be* a question, was what did Abby Roman know about the man, and when did she know it? Before she recommended Harkov to the Arsenaults, or after.

There had been two sets of twins illegally brokered by Viktor Harkov in 2005. Two sets of girls. If Harkov's killer had visited the Arsenault house perhaps he was now in search of the other pair of twins. Perhaps he had already found them. Perhaps there *was* another family in jeopardy.

Like *Cape Fear*, Powell thought.

She had to get that movie, check it out.

While the Arsenaults spoke to a police artist, and created a composite of the man who had broken into their house, Detective Desiree Powell left the Homicide Squad, stopped at the Homestead on Lefferts Boulevard for a cherry strudel and a coffee.

Within twenty minutes she was on the Van Wyck, heading toward a small town in Crane County called Eden Falls.

THIRTY-NINE

There were four vehicles in the parking lot. A pair of Fiestas that looked like rental cars, a ten-year-old van, and the blue Ford.

Michael walked slowly over to one of the Fiestas. It was parked three spaces away from the Ford. He glanced quickly at the Ford and saw that the man sitting in the driver's seat was black, perhaps in his twenties, earbuds in his ears. He had most likely seen Michael emerge from Room 119, but had paid no attention to the man in the baggy raincoat, tweed hat, and sunglasses. He had his eyes closed, his head bobbing to the music.

Michael stepped over the low guard-rail fence behind the cars. He searched the area near the expressway for something, anything. He found a short length of steel rebar, the material used to strengthen concrete. He picked up the pipe, slid it into his waistband in the back, then dropped to the ground behind the Ford. He waited a full minute. The man in the car had not seen him in the rear-view or side mirrors. Michael crawled along the ground, along the right side of the Ford, then circled in front of the car. When he reached the left front tire, he took out a small piece of the broken mirror. He had wrapped it in a washcloth, but it had cut through the fabric. His hand was bleeding. He began to cut along the tire, right at the rim. After a minute or so, he heard the air begin to leak out.

Two minutes later, with the tire almost flat, Michael crawled to the back of the car, stood up, and made his way back over to the Fiesta.

When he reached the car, he dug into his pocket as if he was fishing around for car keys. He glanced over at the driver of the Ford. The man looked over. Michael pointed to the front tire on the Ford, mouthed a few words. The man just stared at him for a few moments, then rolled down the window.

"You've got a flat tire." Michael said. He knew the man could not hear him.

The man opened the door. He was about Michael's size, but younger. He was dressed in green camouflage pants and a black hoodie. Michael knew that once the man got out, he would only have a few seconds to act.

The man stepped out of the car, pulled the headphones out of his ears. He regarded Michael with suspicion. "What?"

"Your front tire," Michael said, doing his best southern accent, the word *tire* coming out *tar*. "It looks like you've got a flat."

The man considered Michael for a few more moments, then walked around the open car door. "God*damn* it." He stood for a few seconds, hands on hips, as if willing the tire to inflate. He then reached into the car, extracted the keys from the ignition. He walked to the rear, opened the trunk. Michael sidled up.

"You want me to call Triple A or something?" Michael asked. "I got the Triple A."

"I'm good," he said, with a look that said *back the fuck off*.

At the moment the man turned his back on Michael, Michael slipped the pipe out of his waistband, and brought it down on the back of the man's neck, pulling back at the last second. This was far from his area of expertise, and he didn't want to kill the man. It was a mistake. The man grunted on the impact, and staggered away a few steps, but didn't go down. He was strong.

"Mother*fucker*." The man reached behind his head, saw the blood on his fingers.

Before he could turn around to face him fully, Michael stepped in, raised the pipe again, preparing to deliver a second blow, but when he brought his arm down, the man raised an arm to block it. He was fast. The man then wheeled around, shifting his weight, and caught Michael on the side of the face with a glancing blow. Michael saw stars for a moment. His legs buckled, but he maintained his balance.

When he recovered he saw the man reaching into the trunk, coming back with a handgun.

There was no time to react. Michael brought the pipe up and around as hard as he could. He caught the man on the bridge of his nose, exploding it into a thick mist of blood and cartilage. Michael saw the man's eyes roll into his head. His legs sagged, gave out. He fell backwards, half-in and half-out of the trunk. The gun, a small-caliber revolver, fell from his hand onto the pitted asphalt of the parking lot.

And it was over. The man did not move.

For some reason, Michael was frozen with inaction. He was afraid he had killed the man, but soon got over it. He realized that he was standing in a motel parking lot, within sight of the avenue with a bloodied steel pipe in his hand, and a man's body laying in the trunk of a car in front of him. He gathered his wits, his strength. He threw the pipe in the trunk, picked up the gun, stuffed it into his pocket. He glanced around, turning 360 degrees. Seeing no one watching him, he pulled the spare tire and the jack out of the trunk. He then lifted the man's legs, and maneuvered the body fully

into the trunk. He closed the lid, grabbed the keys out of the
lock.

Ten minutes later, with the tire changed, he got into the
car. He found that he could not catch his breath. He glanced
around the front seat. An MP3 player, a half-eaten Whopper,
an unopened forty-ounce. The smell of cooked meat and
blood made his stomach churn.

He opened the glove compartment. A pair of maps, a pack
of Salems, a small Maglite. Nothing he could use. What he
needed was a cellphone. He looked in the back seat, in the
console. No phone.

He grabbed the keys out of the ignition, got out of the car.
He walked around to the back of the car, opened the trunk.
The man had not regained consciousness, but his face looked
all but destroyed. Michael reached in, touched the side of his
neck. He found a pulse. He began to pat the man down,
searching his side pockets, his back pockets. He found a small
roll of cash, a small bag of marijuana, another set of keys. But
no phone. He tried to turn the man onto his side, but he was
heavy, and a dead weight. He tried again. He couldn't budge
him.

Suddenly, the man began to moan. Michael reached further
into the trunk, retrieved a long steel crowbar. He slipped it
beneath the man, began to roll him over. The man coughed,
spitting blood into the air.

"The *fuck*, man . . ." the man managed. He was coming to.
And getting louder. Michael reached into the pocket of his
raincoat, got out the now bloodied washcloth. He rolled it
into a ball, stuffed into the man's mouth.

Michael then went back to his task of prying the man's body
onto its side. After a few more tries the man rolled over.
Michael reached into the pocket of his fleece hoodie, and
found a cellphone, along with a few hundred in cash, and an

ID that identified the man in the trunk as Omar Cantwell. Michael took the phone and cash, slammed shut the trunk, got back in the car.

With his hands surprisingly steady, considering what he had just done, what he was *about* to do, he opened the phone, punched in the numbers, and called Tommy Christiano.

Tommy fell silent. Michael knew enough to wait it out. His head throbbed, his eyes burned.

"Is he dead?" Tommy asked.

The truth was, Michael had no idea. "I don't know. I don't think so."

He had told Tommy everything, beginning with the phone call from the man called Aleksander Savisaar.

"You've got to come in, man."

"I can't, Tommy."

"You have to. This is getting worse and worse. How long do you think it will be before Powell adds it up?"

"This is my family, man. We can't call in the cavalry. Not until I know the play."

"You can't do this alone."

"It's the only way."

Tommy quieted again. Michael glanced at his watch. He had three minutes to get back inside the motel room.

"Powell just called here," Tommy said. "She was asking about Abby."

"*What*? Abby? Why?"

"She wouldn't say."

Michael tried to anticipate the course of the investigation. "What did she ask?"

"She asked about where Abby worked. About where she *used* to work."

"What did you tell her?"

"I told her the truth," Tommy said. "It's not like she couldn't get the information elsewhere."

Michael tried to process it all, but everything seemed to bottleneck.

"What are you going to do?" Tommy asked.

Good question, Michael thought. "I'm going to go back into the room and wait for the call. Then I'm going to my house."

"You'll never get there in thirty minutes."

"I'm going to try," Michael said. "And Tommy?"

"What?"

"Promise me you're not going to make a move."

Tommy took a moment, perhaps weighing all the odds. "I'll meet you."

"No," Michael said. "Look. I've got this phone. Have you got the number on that end?"

Michael could hear Tommy scribbling on a pad. "Yeah," he said. "I've got it."

"Okay. Just put your ear to the rail and call me the second you know something. If Powell gets any closer, you call."

"Mickey," he said. "You've got to —"

"I know, man. I know."

Michael closed the phone, put it on vibrate, slipped it into his pocket. He listened. There were no sounds coming from the trunk of the car.

He looked into the rear-view mirror. The sight he saw there unnerved him. His face was dotted and streaked with blood, slightly swollen and bruised. He reached into the Burger King bag, pulled out a handful of napkins. He opened the forty-ounce, dampened the napkins, and did his best to clean his face.

He looked again. Clean enough. His ears were still ringing from the blow he had taken to the side of his face, his heart was pounding, his head ached. He said a silent prayer, put his hand on the door. He had sixty seconds to get into the room. He prayed his watch was accurate – that Kolya's watch was accurate – and that he had not missed the call. He opened the car door, got out.

"Put your hands where I can see them!" the voice behind him shouted.

Michael spun around. Flashing lights dazzled his eyes.

He was surrounded by police cars.

FORTY

Abby could not wait any longer. Every second the girls were
gone, every second she did not know Michael's whereabouts, was another arrow in her heart. Keeping the gun on
Kolya, she had made a number of phone calls. She had called
the office and was told Michael had left for the day. She had
called his cellphone and gotten voicemail. She had called a
few of his haunts – the Austin Ale House, the Sly Fox. No
one had seen him. She almost called Tommy, but Tommy
would see right through her. Tommy would know something was terribly wrong.

She wanted to put an end to this, to see the reassuring
presence of a police car in her drive, the calm, assured manner
of detectives and FBI agents, authority figures who could take
this out of her trembling hands. She wanted to hold her
husband, her girls.

But unless she knew her daughters would be safe, she could
not take that chance. She looked out the window for what was
probably the fiftieth time in the past ten minutes.

"You know, he's probably not coming back," Kolya said. He
was slumped in the upholstered chair in the corner, a chair that
until recently had been a putty velvet. Now it was caked and
streaked with deep brown blood. He was breathing through his

mouth, which for him, Abby thought, was probably business as usual.

"Shut up."

"You know what I think, Mrs ADA? I think he took your precious little girls and he hit the road. God only knows what he's doing with them right this second. He's probably –"

"I said shut the fuck *up!*" Abby pointed the .25 at him. Kolya didn't react. Abby wondered just how many times this man had had a weapon shoved in his face over the years. "I don't want to hear another word. You don't get to talk."

Kolya acquiesced. For the moment. He shifted his weight in the chair, trying to find a comfortable position. Abby hoped he was never going to be comfortable for the rest of his life. Hopefully he would spend it in a prison cell.

Kolya looked at his watch. "Fuck this. I'm outta here." He struggled to his feet.

"What are you doing?"

"I'm leaving."

Abby tensed. "Sit down."

Kolya stood, facing her, not ten feet away, his hands behind his back. "No."

This isn't happening, Abby thought. "I swear to God I will put a bullet in your head. Now sit down."

Kolya smirked. "You a killer now? That what you are? A killer nurse?" He edged a few inches toward her. "I don't think so."

Abby backed up. She cocked the weapon. "Sit down. Don't make me do this."

Kolya looked around. "So, what's stopping you? There's no one here. Who's gonna know it was cold-blooded murder?" He took another step. He was five feet away now. "All you gotta do is tell them I tried to jump your bones. They'll believe you. You being a citizen and all."

Abby backed up another inch. She was almost against the closet now. "Stop."

Kolya stopped moving forward, his hands still behind his back. "You know what? I don't think you can do it, Mrs ADA. I think you're all talk. Just like your husband."

"Shut up," Abby said, her voice cracking. "Just shut up!"

Kolya took another small step forward, and suddenly there was another voice in the room. Somebody talking about how the lottery jackpot was up to $245 million, and how you too could be a winner. Somehow the flat-screen television on the dresser had clicked to life. Instinctively, Abby glanced at it. And understood. This was why Kolya had his hands behind his back. He had the remote. He was trying to distract her, and it worked. She only looked away for a second, but it was long enough for Kolya. He lunged across the room. For a short, stocky man he was incredibly fast.

Abby fell back against the wall, raised the gun, and pulled the trigger. Twice.

Nothing. The weapon didn't fire. It was empty.

Once Kolya realized he was not going to be shot and killed in this suburban house in Eden Falls, New York, Abby saw the full animal emerge.

In a second he was on top of her. "You fuckin' cunt! I'm gonna fuckin' *kill* you!"

Kolya lashed out with his right hand, catching her high on her forehead. The blow knocked her back to the dresser, shattering perfume bottles, toppling pictures, dumping the television onto the floor. Before she could recover her balance Kolya grabbed her by the hair and dragged her to the bed. Abby kicked her feet, flailed her arms, trying to connect, but he was too strong.

"But first I'm gonna fuck your brains out."

He threw her to the bed, slapped her a second time. This time the blow was more powerful, more expertly leveraged. Abby felt herself fall to the edge of consciousness. Still she fought. Kolya pulled out his small pocket knife. He cut her dress away from her body, tearing it off, flinging it across the room.

Abby, nearly insensible, tried to bring her knee into his crotch again, but this time he was prepared. Stars danced at the edges of her eyes, and she felt for a moment as if she was going to pass out. She tasted blood in her mouth.

Kolya leaned back, unzipped his jeans. He had a full erection. "You're out of your fuckin' league, bitch." He cut her bra and panties away, climbed back on top of her, all the time keeping tight hold of her hair. Abby fought him as hard as she could, but she was overpowered.

He grabbed her by the throat, applied pressure. "You point a gun at me?"

Kolya spread her legs with his other hand, settled his heavy body between them. "You're gonna like this, Mrs ADA. Too bad you won't be able to tell your friends about it."

As Abby felt the world pull away, she heard something click onto the bed next to them, something metallic. It sounded as if something had fallen from the ceiling, but she couldn't be sure what it had been.

Kolya stopped for a moment, looked up at the ceiling, then at the bed. On it were five small-caliber bullets. Kolya looked into Abby's eyes. And knew.

Before he could make a move, Kolya grunted once, a wet animal sound. Abby's face was suddenly bathed in a warm, viscous liquid. Some of it went into her mouth and nose. The taste made her gag, making her head pound, but bringing her back from the edge. Her world went bright red.

It was blood. Her face was now covered in it.

In her near-delirium, Abby thought it was her own blood, but when she looked at Kolya, she saw that his face was frozen in a rictus of pain, the muscles on his neck were corded and taut. Something was growing from his throat. Something silver and flat. Kolya fell on Abby in a quivering lump, and Abby now saw the shape of a man standing at the foot of the bed.

It was Aleks. He had stabbed Kolya from behind, and now the spasming man was on top of her, the huge knife protruding from the back of his neck. A second later, Aleks leaned over, pulled out the knife.

"*No!*" Abby screamed.

With all her strength she pushed Kolya off her. He rolled onto the bed, onto the floor, both of which were now drenched with blood.

"*What have you done?*"

Abby scrambled to her feet, the world spinning out of control. She tore a pillowcase from the bed, balled it, and put it over the hole in Kolya's throat. Blood pumped from the wound, soaking the floor beneath Kolya's head. His body jerked once, twice, then fell still. Abby kept pressure on the wound, but she knew it was too late. He was dead.

Abby glanced at Aleks. He stood in the doorway to the bedroom. His face offered no expression. Not anger, not remorse, not even satisfaction. He looked like a bird of prey, surveying his territory. Abby now realized Aleks had found her gun when he had been upstairs on his own earlier. He had unloaded it.

For a long time Abby couldn't move. Then she realized her nakedness. She pulled one of the drapes from the rod, gathered it, wrapped it around her, the twin horrors of the past few minutes sinking in.

"Where . . . where are the girls?" she asked. Her voice sounded small, defeated, distant.

Aleks turned his head, looked at her. For a moment she wasn't sure he knew who she was.

"Clean yourself up," he said. "We are leaving in twenty minutes."

FORTY-ONE

The police officer was nervous. He was young, no more than twenty-two or so. His partner was a little older. Maybe his FTO, Michael thought, his field-training officer. Once the older cop had assessed that there was no imminent danger in the parking lot of the Squires Inn, he had told the other two patrol cars they could move on.

The young officer had worked it by the book, first asking for identification, then patting Michael down.

Michael had explained who he was, and that he was here investigating a case.

The officer had looked at Michael's outfit, perhaps wondering why a Queens County prosecutor was wearing maroon golf slacks and a raincoat that were both clearly two sizes too big for him. If he was wondering, he said nothing about it. But Michael knew the mindset, even for a young cop. Something was off. And when something was off, it did not right itself.

"And why don't you have any ID, sir?"

"It's in my golf bag," Michael said. "I got this call about a witness going squirrelly on us and I just jumped in the car."

The officer looked at the blue Ford, then back. He glanced at his partner, who just shrugged.

According to the officer, a call had come in on 911 of two

men fighting in the parking lot of the Squires Inn Motel. Michael said he knew nothing about it.

Michael snuck a glance at his watch. He had missed the call from Kolya.

"Could you wait right here for me?" the officer asked. He pointed to the rear of the Ford. Michael moved to the back of the car.

"Sure."

As Michael approached he noticed a thin trickle of blood coming from the lid of the trunk. He moved from the left rear fender to the trunk, leaned against it.

As the young officer communicated on the radio, he looked from the laptop in his cruiser, to Michael, back. It seemed to take forever. Michael glanced again at his watch. He was now a full five minutes past the deadline.

The officer got out of the car.

"Sorry about this, Mr Roman. You know how it is. You get the call you have to check it out."

"I understand."

The kid looked at him for a few more seconds, then around the parking lot, at the motel itself, still not really comprehending the situation. Michael knew he would have crazier days than this.

"Have a good day, sir."

Michael wondered how the uniformed officers had gotten the call. Had Kolya's cousin seen the altercation from the office? Had she seen what happened and called Kolya, and now something had happened to Abby, Charlotte and Emily?

He glanced at his watch a third time. There was no point going back inside.

He slipped into the Ford, turned over the engine. Under the seat was Omar's pistol and cellphone. He was glad the incident with the police had not progressed to a search of the vehicle. A few moments later he pulled out of the parking lot, and merged into traffic.

He headed home.

FORTY-TWO

Aleks had not intended to let Kolya live, but neither had he expected it to end like this. He hated it when things got messy, and this was as messy as it could be.

He had owed Kolya's father Konstantine many debts — indeed, the man had saved his life on more than one occasion — but the son held no power over him, had earned no such arrears.

While Abby took a shower, Aleks dragged Kolya's body into the clothes closet. The bedroom was all but coated with blood, and moving the heavy, lifeless form streaked even further a deep crimson into the light-colored carpeting.

He went through Kolya's pockets, taking the dead man's cellphone, but leaving his wallet, which was connected to a belt loop via a silver chain. He opened the phone, checked the list of recently placed calls. The last call to the motel was more than forty minutes ago. Aleks hit the redial. The phone at the motel rang twice, three times, four times, five. Michael Roman was no longer there. If he was, he would certainly have answered the phone. Aleks scrolled down the list until he came to Omar's cellphone number. Figuring that Omar had Kolya on his caller ID list, Aleks took out one of his prepaid cellphones. He dialed Omar's number. The phone rang once, twice . . .

*

. . . three times. Michael stared at the phone in his hands. The readout said the call was coming from a private number. He turned on the radio, then the heater, cranking the fan to high. He opened his window. On the fifth ring he answered. He kept his mouth a few inches away from the phone, answered.

"Yeah."

Silence from the other end. "Are you still at the motel?"

It was Aleks. He was calling Omar. He was calling Omar to see if Michael was still under lock and key. *Why hadn't Kolya placed the call?* Michael tried to remember Omar's voice. It was deep. He hoped the background noise covered him. "Yeah."

Another hesitation. This time Michael heard the girls talking in the background. They were with Aleks. His heart shattered.

"Do not come here Mr Roman," Aleks said. "If you do you will not like what you find."

"Listen," Michael said. "Just tell me what you want. You can have everything I have. Just don't hurt my family."

For a moment, Michael thought Aleks might have hung up. He had not. "If you come here you will drown in your family's blood."

The phone clicked. The connection was broken.

Michael slammed his fist into the dashboard three times. He pushed the speedometer to eighty.

They were ready. The woman had packed a pair of bags for herself and the girls, as well as some food. Everything Aleks needed was in his leather shoulder bag. The gear was stacked near the front door.

In a moment Aleks would collect the girls from the backyard, explaining to them that they were going on a little journey. They would take Kolya's SUV. They would find somewhere to hide for just a few hours, until midnight, then they would head for the Canadian border.

By this time tomorrow they would be in Canada, and he would be one step closer to becoming deathless. By this time tomorrow the woman would be dead, and Anna and Marya would be his. This had not gone as smoothly as he would have liked, but there was nothing to be done about that now.

You'll never get them out of the country. Someone is going to catch you.

Perhaps Abigail was right. He touched the two empty crystal vials on the chain around his neck. If they closed in on him and the girls, he knew what he had to do.

For now, though, he still had his daughters, and there were no obstacles on the horizon.

Then the doorbell rang.

Abby looked out the front window. In the drive was a late-model dark sedan. She had not heard anyone drive up, and she always did. She was attuned to the sounds around her house. But the horror of this day, as well as the throbbing pain in her head, made it impossible.

She looked at Aleks. He said nothing, but rather glanced through the back window at the girls. He stepped into the hallway, out of sight.

Abby crossed the foyer, opened the door. On the porch was a tall, slender black woman in a dark suit. The woman had the look of authority. Abby knew the demeanor, the posture, and she was suddenly even more frightened.

Through the screen door Abby said "Yes?"

"Are you Abigail Roman?"

"Yes."

The woman held up a badge wallet. A gold shield. NYPD. "My name is Detective Desiree Powell. I'm with Queens Homicide. May I come in for a moment?"

It took all of Abby's strength and concentration not to look anywhere but the detective's eyes. "Can I ask what this is about?"

"I just have a few routine questions. May I come in?"

"I'm terribly busy right now."

The woman put her hand on the screen door handle. Abby let go. The woman smiled, opened the door, stepped inside. She did a quick perusal of the entrance, living room, the stairs leading to the second floor. "I know your husband, Michael. We've worked a few cases together," the woman said. "By the way, he's not here by any chance, is he?"

"No," Abby said. "He's in court today."

Powell glanced at her watch. "They're adjourned for the day, I believe. I called his office and they said he's gone for the day. Would you happen to know where he is right now?"

"I'm afraid I don't."

Powell gave a closer look at the living room, its décor. "You have a lovely home."

Here comes the bullshit, Abby thought. She had to find a way to get this woman out of her house. "Thank you. Now if —"

"Are you all right?"

Abby instinctively touched her face. She had iced it down, and the swelling was not as noticeable as she thought it was going to be. "I'm fine. Got whacked with a tennis ball this afternoon."

Powell nodded, clearly not believing the story. She was a cop. She encountered a lot of married women who walked into doors, tripped in the shower, slipped on the ice. As a nurse, Abby had met her share, too.

"I've never played. Always wanted to. Have you been playing long?"

"Just a few years," Abby said.

"Are your girls here?"

"Yes." She pointed out the back window. Charlotte and Emily were sitting at the picnic table in the backyard.

Powell looked out the window. "Oh my. They're adorable. Michael talks about them all the time. How old are they?"

"They just turned four."

"Can I ask what their names are?"

"Charlotte and Emily."

Powell smiled. "Like the Brontë sisters."

"Like the Brontë sisters."

Powell stepped further into the house. "You're probably wondering what this is all about."

"Yes. In fact, we were just about to leave in a few minutes."

Powell glanced at the bags by the door. Two lilac nylon duffels, two bags of groceries, and a man's leather messenger bag. "Going on a trip?"

"Yes," Abby said. "We're going to visit my parents."

"Oh yeah? Whereabouts?"

Abby took a short step towards the door, the kind of move you make when you are trying to usher someone out of your house. "They're in Westchester County. Near Pound Ridge."

"Oh, it's beautiful up there. Especially this time of year." Powell angled her body in front of Abby, her back now to the hallway leading to the kitchen. She pointed at the man's leather bag. "Is Michael coming with you?"

"He's going to meet us up there."

Powell nodded, held Abby's gaze for a moment. She wasn't buying any of this. She took a notebook out of her pocket, flipped it open. "Well, I won't keep you too long." She glanced at a page of her book. "Do you know a woman named Sondra Arsenault?"

The name was familiar to Abby. She couldn't immediately place it. She also knew, from five years of living with a prosecutor, that the best way to handle this was to plead memory loss. "I'm not sure. Who is she?"

"She's a social worker," Powell said. "She lives over in Putnam County with her husband James."

"The names don't really ring a bell."

"They have twin girls. Just like you."

Abby knew that this detective would not be asking these questions unless she already had the answers. And she now knew what this was about. "I'm sorry. I don't know them."

"Okay," she said. "What about a man named Viktor Harkov?"

Abby brought her hand to her mouth, trying to keep the emotion inside. She couldn't. It was all about to come tumbling out, and there didn't seem to be anything she could do about it. She could still smell the dead man on her, could still taste the blood. She leaned forward, whispered: "You have to help us. He's here. In the house."

"Who's here?"

In that moment Abby saw a shadow move behind Powell, a darting grey silhouette on the wall. It was Aleks. In his hand was Abby's .25 semi-automatic pistol. There was no doubt in Abby's mind that he had reloaded it.

Abby looked over the detective's shoulder. "Don't."

Powell understood.

She spun around.

Before Detective Desiree Powell turned fully, she saw the soft yellow muzzle flash, heard three quick blasts. She felt as if she had been mule-kicked in the side of the chest, the pain roaring through her body like a white-hot freight train. The air was pummeled from her lungs. She felt herself falling backwards.

She hit the floor hard, the pain in her chest turning an icy cold, her legs falling numb. She looked at the ceiling, the patterns in the stippled finish starting to swirl, to coalesce into a Dali dreamscape.

For a moment, she smelled the sea, heard the waves crash onto the beach on Montego Bay, heard the unmistakable lilt of the steel drum.

Then the darkness drew her down, into the long night.

Lucien, she thought, the light fading. *You were wrong, my sweet boy.*

I did *hear it.*

Aleks stood over the woman. Abby had collapsed in the corner of the room. It was one thing to kill Kolya. He was a liability from the start. No one knew where Kolya was, or where he was expected to be. No one would be looking for him here.

It was something entirely different with a police officer. Even in Estonia you did not do this, if you could avoid it. Where there was one there were many, and it would not be long before there were more. The detective had mentioned Viktor Harkov's name. They would soon make the connection to the missing girls, and perhaps they would get a tape from the cameras at the post office, seeing him with Anna and Marya. If that happened, they would be looking for him. He had to move.

He took the handcuffs from the fallen detective's belt, along with her keys.

They would leave right now.

FORTY-THREE

Michael parked the blue Ford on Creekside Lane. He had stopped on the way, pulling off the road about a mile from his house, back into the part of the woods that had once been a campground. He left Omar Cantwell's body there, covered in leaves and compost. The man was still alive.

As Michael walked through one of the still-vacant lots in the new development south of his house, he saw a man he knew only as Nathan. Nathan and his wife had just moved into the neighborhood a few weeks ago. Michael waved; Nathan waved back.

There was something in Michael's stride that told Nathan there would be no stopping and chatting today. As a prosecutor, Michael knew well that everything that had happened this day, everything that *would* happen this day, went into a timeline, a continuum of impressions, facts, assumptions, interpretations. And, ultimately, testimony.

I spoke to Mr Roman at the motel, the officer would say. *He seemed very agitated.*

I saw him walking through the woods, Nathan would say.

Moments later Michael reached the top of the hill, just a few feet from the property line behind his house, his blood burning in his veins. He tried to banish from his mind the possible horrors of what had happened here, what he might find.

If you come here, Mr Roman, you will drown in your family's blood.

The back of the house offered no clues. He could see Abby's car in the driveway, but no further. But that didn't mean there were no other cars. There were a pair of turnarounds about twenty feet from the garage.

He was just about to go back down the hill, and circle around to the side of the house, when he saw something to his right, a flash of gold in the late afternoon sun. He turned, his hand moving to the weight of the pistol in his pocket.

It was Charlotte. Charlotte was standing right there. She was picking dandelions, putting them into a little jar. *Right in front of him.* For a crazy moment, Michael thought he might be hallucinating. How could this be? Had it all been some kind of insane hoax? No. He had seen Viktor Harkov's body. That was real.

Michael put the revolver into the back of his waistband. He edged to the top of the hill, slipped behind a tall maple at the rear of the property.

Charlotte looked up, saw him. "Daddy!"

Charlotte dropped the dandelions and ran across the yard. Michael got down on his knees and embraced her.

"Baby!" he said. He felt the tears well up in his eyes. It had only been a few hours, but it seemed like years since he had seen her. He pulled back, looked into her eyes. "Are you okay?"

"I am," she said. Formal, proper Charlotte.

"Where are Mommy and Emily?"

Charlotte pointed over her shoulder, toward the house. Michael took her by the hand, positioned the two of them behind a hedge, so that they would not be visible from the back windows. "Are they okay?"

Charlotte nodded.

"What about . . . the man?" Michael asked. He did not know how to put this. He did not want to make things worse. "Is that man still here?"

Charlotte thought for a moment. It looked as if something passed behind her eyes, something dark. Then she brightened, nodded again.

"Is it just him?"

"Yes," she said. "The other man left, I think."

"Okay, baby," Michael said. He held her again, taking a quick inventory. There were no visible bruises. It did not appear as if Charlotte had been crying, nor did she pull back because something hurt. "Okay."

Michael stood, held his daughter's hand. He glanced around the yard. Everything appeared to be the way he had left it that morning. He peered around the hedge. There was no movement. Michael decided he would take Charlotte to the car, and come back.

"Let's go for a walk, okay?"

Charlotte glanced at the house, back. "Where are we going?"

"We're going to see Shasta. You like Shasta, right?"

"I do."

"Do you know exactly where Mommy and Emily are now?"

Charlotte shook her head.

"What about the man? Do you know exactly where he is?"

Charlotte seemed to zone out on this question. Michael was just about to ask again when he saw a shape appear near the left side of the house, next to the garage. Michael got down low, peered through the hedges. It was Emily. She was standing at the corner of the house, looking out toward the woods. A few seconds later Michael saw Abby.

Before he could stop himself, Michael stood, took a step out from behind the hedges, bringing Charlotte along. Abby saw him. She shook her head. Michael could see her mouth the word *no*.

A second later a man stepped around the corner. Michael knew it was Aleks. He was tall, broad shouldered. He wore a black leather coat.

The two men saw each other and, in that moment, knew each others' souls.

Michael looked at Abby. He could see the tears coursing down her cheeks. For a sickening moment the three of them looked like a family – father, mother, daughter. They looked like a suburban family in the yard of their suburban home, perhaps getting ready to leave for a day at the beach, or a picnic.

Then Michael saw a gleam of silver. There, in the man's hand, just a few inches from Emily's head, was a large knife. The man pulled Emily close to him. Michael's blood ran cold.

He did not know how long they stood there on opposite ends of the property. No one moved. Michael had to make a decision, the hardest of his life. He did not know if it was the right decision, but it seemed to be the only one.

He scooped Charlotte into his arms, lifted her into the air, held her close, and began to run down the hill. He almost slipped when they reached a narrow section of the creek, his leather-soled shoes slipping on a slippery rock. He found his balance as they forded the shallow water. Michael was certain he heard footsteps approaching rapidly behind them, the snapping of fallen branches and plodding on leaves, but he knew he could not stop.

Moments later they reached the back of the Meisner property. Michael put Charlotte down, and together they ran across the backyard, skirting the garden. They reached the back patio and the sliding door. Michael banged on the glass. Within moments Zoe came into the dining room, looked at them. At first it appeared as if she did not know Michael, but soon recognition dawned. She crossed the room, slid open the glass door.

"Michael," she said. "How nice."

Zoe Meisner was a widower in her sixties. She lived for her garden, her dog, and community fundraisers. In that order.

Shasta came loping up. She was a big golden Lab, and when she reached the end of the living-room carpet, momentum and a hefty diet propelled her across the quarry tile of the foyer, sliding, trying to maintain balance. She stopped just short of knocking Charlotte over.

The dog wagged its tail and began to lick Charlotte's face. Charlotte giggled, and it loosed something in Michael's chest. The sound of his daughter laughing. He realized he had all but begun to think he would never hear that sound again.

Michael caught his breath, tried to appear normal. "Uh, Zoe, I was wondering if I could ask you a small favor."

"Of course," she said. "Why don't you come on in? Would you like some tea?"

"No," Michael said. "No thanks. I was wondering, could you watch Charlotte for just a few minutes?"

Zoe looked him up and down, perhaps for the first time noticing the clothes he was wearing, and the dirt and mud along the cuffs of his maroon golf slacks, slacks that Michael found himself unconsciously hitching every few seconds. He hoped the gun did not fall out of his waistband.

"Are you all right?" Zoe asked.

"I'm fine," Michael said. "Just kind of a . . . crazy day."

In addition to being the town's resident expert on all things organic, Zoe Meisner was the repository of neighborhood gossip. She gave Michael a skeptical glance, then looked at Charlotte, who was busy petting the dog.

"Of course," she said.

"I won't be long," Michael said, half out the door already.

"No hurry," Zoe said. "Take your time."

Michael crossed the yard, and headed back up the hill.

The backyard was empty when Michael again reached his house. This time he came in on the southern end of the property, in the area behind the shed and the garage, from where he could see the side door. He saw no one. He glanced at the windows. The drapes behind the large picture window in the back of the house were closed; the horizontal blinds in the window over the kitchen sink were lowered. He saw no lights, no shadows. The vertical blinds, which hung over the sliding glass door, were only half drawn. He glanced at the side of the house. In order for him to see if Abby's car – or any car – was still in the driveway, he would have to move across the yard. He would be visible from any and all windows in the back.

Michael tried to slow his breathing, his heart. For a few mad moments he could not remember the layout inside his own house. It seemed to be blocked.

Moreover, he did not know how many *people* were in his house. He did not know if Aleks and Kolya were the only two people doing this to them. But he knew he could no longer wait.

He sidled up to the northern edge of the property, then along the side of the house. He edged up to the window in the first floor bedroom, the bedroom they used as an office. He saw no one inside.

He inched along the back wall of the house, pushed open the

sliding glass door, drew the weapon, then thought better of it. He put it back into the waistband of his slacks. He stepped into the house.

The kitchen was empty. Two juice glasses sat on the table. Michael glanced around the room, trying to take it all in. He wanted to call out, but stopped himself. He looked at the refrigerator magnets, the letters and numbers he and Abby often used to teach the girls new words. It was a pretty strict rule, a daily routine. Every day Abby would choose a word, and she and the girls would go over it, sometimes looking it up online or in the big dictionary in their home office. Abby would always leave the word in place until Michael got home. Many times the girls would be waiting for Michael at the door when he returned from work, dragging him excitedly into the kitchen to teach him the new word.

Today there were no words spelled out. The letters were all bunched together at the top of the door, a jumble of nonsense. A pair of numbers had been dragged to the bottom.

Michael sidled up to the living room, peered in. Another empty room. One of the dining room chairs had been positioned in front of the sliding glass door.

A lookout position? Michael wondered.

He crossed the foyer, moved silently up the steps. He peered into the bathroom. The shower curtain was pulled open. The room was empty. He looked into the girls' room. The beds were made, the room tidy as always. He edged down the hallway and caught a whiff of something at the back of his throat that tasted like warm brass. He looked into the master bedroom.

The room was covered in blood.

"Oh my God. *No!*"

The bed sheets were bunched in the middle of the bed, the TV had fallen off the dresser, things were scattered all over the room. There was blood on the walls, the ceiling. The room where he slept, where he made love to his wife, was an abattoir. He steadied himself against the wall. He saw a thick rut of scarlet leading from the foot of the bed over to the closet. He took the gun in his unsteady hand, eased open the closet door.

There, inside, was Kolya. There was no point in trying to determine if he was still alive. His face was a bloated plum, crusted with blood. There was a gaping wound in his neck.

Michael ran down the stairs, taking them two at a time, the madness all but overtaking him. He quickly crossed the living room and was just about to enter the kitchen, when he almost tripped over something on the floor. He stopped, looked down. It was the body of Desiree Powell.

He lurched into the kitchen and vomited in the sink.

Aleks had Abby and Emily. Gone. And his house was strewn with corpses.

Michael looked out the front window. At the bottom of the hill, just visible through the trees, he could see a car turning into the drive, the unmistakable dark blue of a city police car.

Michael knew that even if the police believed him – and there was little chance of that, considering that Michael himself, if the positions were reversed, would have a hard time believing he had nothing to do with these crimes – it would cause two courses of action. One, he would be taken into custody. Two, the police department, not to mention the FBI and the Crane County sheriff's office would kick into high gear to locate Abby, Emily, and the man who was terrorizing his family.

And who knew what would happen if the police found Aleksander Savisaar?

No. He would turn himself in, but not until Abby and Charlotte and Emily were with him. He had to be in the same

room with his family. He would never believe in the world
again until that moment.

He glanced out the window. Marco Fontova was just
getting out of his car. The good news was that he was alone.
He had not brought in the troops. Not yet.

Michael ran to the back door, looked around the yard, the
area behind the house. No cops. He heard the doorbell ring as
he slipped outside, the revolver now a dead weight in his
pocket, his mind a jumble of dark scenarios.

There was no way to lock the sliding glass door from the
outside. He would have to leave it open. He glanced back into
the house. He could see Desiree Powell's feet from the patio,
and knew it would be all the probable cause Fontova would
need to enter.

Michael sprinted across the yard, ran down the hill, leaping
over fallen trees. He forded the creek at a low point, being
careful not to slip on the rocks, all the while expecting to hear
a gunshot. A few moments later he made it through the woods
to the Meisner house. He picked up Charlotte, telling Zoe
Meisner nothing. She would hear the sirens soon enough.

Five minutes later, with Charlotte strapped into a seatbelt
in the front seat with him, he left Eden Falls, and headed for
the 102, and Ozone Park. There was only one place to go.
There was only one man who could help him.

FORTY-FOUR

"Des."

Lucien stood on the corner, his blinding white smile a beacon in the steamy dusk of a Kingston summer night. His two skinny chums – a pair of funny *bwois* who never brought luck or favor – poked him in the ribs.

Jealous, she thought. Who wouldn't be? She was a princess.

Inside, butterflies took to the breeze. From somewhere came the sound of Peter Tosh's "Glass House".

"Des."

Detective Desiree Powell opened her eyes. It was not Lucien. It was Marco Fontova. If her chest had not been on fire, if it did not feel as if someone had deposited a grand piano on her ribs, and then weighted that down with anvils, and then had the entire New York Rangers team work out on it, she might have laughed. She passed out again, but could not find Lucien.

Gone.

She drifted back. It took a while to find a sound within her. "How long have I been out?" she asked. Her voice sounded like someone else's, like an old scratchy recording from the Twenties.

Fontova looked at his watch. His face betrayed his fear, his concern for her. It was sweet. "I don't know."

"Why did you look at your watch if you don't know?"

"I don't know."

"Am I bleeding out?"

Fontova shook his head. "No."

There was someone standing behind Fontova, a blond female paramedic, too young and pretty to be in this line of work. As Powell struggled to sit up, the young EMT told her to stay down, but it wasn't going to happen. Fontova helped Desiree into a sitting position. With a great deal of pain she leaned against the wall. The room began to spin and, for a moment, she felt the nausea creep. She took a moment, waited it out. She then reached behind her. Something was wrong. "Where're my cuffs?"

Fontova looked away, then back. He was never good at telling her bad news. "I think they were taken," he said. "Your badge too."

"Mother*fucker.*"

Fontova raised an eyebrow. "I think that might be two dollars."

"Mother is not a swear word."

"I think it's the intent, though."

The sickness came over her in a foul rush. Powell choked back the bile. She glanced to her left, saw the Kevlar vest they had taken off her. It was ripped and dented. "Jesus."

"You okay?" Fontova asked.

Powell just glared at him.

"Okay. Well. There's something you should see."

"Where?"

Fontova pointed at the steps. Powell looked up. "That might take a while. Like maybe a week."

"Hang on," Fontova said. He stood up, took the stairs two at a time, probably in an attempt to show off to the pretty blond paramedic. When he returned a few minutes later, he held his cellphone in front of him. Powell glanced at the screen. There, in living color – mostly red – was a dead male body, slumped in a closet. It looked like his face had been carved by a meat slicer.

"Jesus Christ."

"The bedroom looks like a slaughterhouse."

Powell looked more closely at the small screen. The DOA could have been anyone. "Is it Michael Roman?"

Fontova shook his head, held up an evidence bag. In it was an oversized leather wallet, connected to a chain. "His name was Nikolai Udenko."

"Did you run him?"

Fontova nodded. "Small timer. Did a stretch at Rikers for assault. No wants or warrants."

"Then why is he dead in this pretty house?"

Fontova had no answer.

"Ma'am?"

Powell glanced over at the paramedic. She hated being called ma'am, but this kid looked twenty-four, and Powell figured it was the right term. "Yeah?"

"I should really take a look at those ribs."

Ten minutes later, while an EMT team wrapped her damaged – probably broken – ribs, Powell tried to put it all together.

Since she'd gotten the assignment, she was certain she had the starting point of this case. She believed it was the point where all homicide investigations began, that being with the murder itself. Elementary this, no?

No. Not always.

"We got a call from the 105," Fontova said, sitting at the dining-room table, looking the other way while Desiree Powell – wearing just her bra on top – got swaddled in Ace bandages. "It seems that a uniformed officer talked to a man up there at one of the pay-and-play motels along Hempstead. They'd gotten a call of two men fighting in the parking lot."

"What about it?" All three words hurt. Powell winced. The paramedic helped her slip her blouse back on.

"The officer said the guy did not have any ID on him, but identified himself as a Queens prosecutor."

"A prosecutor?"

Fontova nodded. "The guy said his name was Michael Roman."

"*Okay.*"

"They checked him out, let him slide. But the officer said they pulled around the back of the motel and watched the guy drive away. He was driving a 1999 Ford Contour."

"He run the plate?"

Fontova looked at his notes. "Yeah. It comes back to a company called Brooklyn Stars."

"What the hell is that, a Roller Derby Team?"

"Small car dealership in Greenpoint. Probably a chop shop. I checked it out. Guess who owns the place?"

Powell would have thrown up her hands if it wouldn't have sent her into paroxysms of agony. "I am in a world of hurt. Don't make me guess."

"Nikolai Udenko."

"Our friendly neighborhood DOA?"

"The same."

Powell glanced out the window. Her chest was aflame. But that didn't stop the wheels from turning.

"So let me get this straight. We've got a torture homicide up in the 114, the victim a shady lawyer tied to ADA Michael Roman – a man who I might add was spotted this afternoon on Hempstead Avenue, driving a car that belonged to a man we just found sliced and diced in the aforementioned Mr Roman's lovely suburban house."

"Yep."

"A house inside which I talked to his rabbit-eyed wife before taking three —"

"Four."

"Four slugs to the vest." Powell shifted her weight in the chair. For some reason, learning about the fourth shot made her ribs even worse. "And now the wife and daughters are gone."

"In the wind."

Powell thought it might take a calculator to add all this up. "Some fuckery this."

"That's exactly what I was gonna say, but I gave that word in all its forms up for Lent."

Fontova held up a second evidence bag, this one containing what looked to Powell like a .25 semi-auto.

"That was my ticket to heaven?" Powell asked.

"Yep."

"That bitty thing? I'm almost embarrassed." The truth was, a .25 could drop you just like a .38, depending on the load. Powell thanked the Lord it was only a twenty-five. At the range at which she had been shot, the vest might not have saved her if it had been anything bigger.

"I called in the serial number," Fontova said. "And it turns out this here belly gun is registered to none other than one Abigail Reed Roman, RN, thirty-one, of Eden Falls, New York."

Powell just looked at her partner. "Now, you're just a handbook of police procedure aren't you?"

"Tell the world, *chica*."

"Well I may not know much, but I'm sure of one thing," Powell said, struggling to her feet.

"What's that?"

"I know *she* didn't pull the trigger."

*

As the shooting team headed up to Eden Falls, Powell got on her cellphone to Lieutenant John Testa, the commanding officer of the Queens Homicide Squad. Testa was a supple sixty, with a full head of silver hair and burnished little grey eyes that could make you confess to something you never did. He had an unrequited thing for Desiree, and therefore she could usually wrap him around her finger. After assuring her supervisor that she was fine (she was not), and pleading with him to not pull her in (she hated begging), she told him the facts as they knew them. Except in detail about how her chest felt like she had been kicked for a forty-nine-yard field goal and it hurt to even hold the cellphone. Testa caved, let her stay on the street.

As promised, five minutes later, he issued an arrest warrant for Michael Roman.

FORTY-FIVE

Michael drove two miles under the speed limit, coming to a full stop at stop signs and red lights. He was usually a careful driver, especially with the girls in the car, but today there were more reasons to be cautious. He did not know if there were wants and warrants on him yet. He had to be where he was going, but he had to get there.

The horror of what he had found inside his house roiled within him. The place where his children played, where he had thought his family was protected, was shrouded in blood. Right now a madman had his wife and one of his children. And that madman could be anywhere in the city.

He had gotten on Henry Hudson Parkway heading south, frantically scanning both the side and rear-view mirrors, trying to see if Aleks was following him. For the first few miles, he concentrated on looking for Abby's car. He saw no champagne-colored Acuras. Then it occurred to him that Aleks might have had his own car, a car unknown to Michael. He had not been able to see the length of the driveway.

He called Abby's brother Wallace, first at his office, then at his house in Westchester. Wallace said he had not spoken to Abby since the birthday party, and Michael did not sense that Wallace was under any kind of duress. Wallace Reed could negotiate multimillion dollar contracts with foreign investors, but when it came to confrontations he was not the coolest egg in the dozen. Michael doubted he would have even been able to talk if a psychopath was holding him hostage.

Michael then called Abby's parents house in Pound Ridge. He got Charles Reed's answering service and, after identifying himself to the satisfaction of the efficient young woman on the phone, was told that the Reeds were currently on a plane between Alexandria, Egypt and Madrid. They were not expected back for another ten days.

The security around the gated community in which Abby's parents lived was tighter than Quantico, and Michael doubted that Abby and her captor would have been able to bluff their way past.

Still, Michael did not know what kind of network this madman had in place, how many bolt-holes he might have around the city, the county, the country.

Michael knew that Desiree Powell was one of the best detectives in Queens Homicide and, for her to have had probable cause to enter the house, given all the surrounding circumstances of the case as it sat — combined with the facts that no one would be able to contact Michael and Abby Roman, not at the office, not at the clinic — it would not be long before they put two and two together.

There was only one reason Powell had showed up in Eden Falls, and that was because she had made the connection between Michael and Viktor Harkov.

They stopped at the red light on Northern Boulevard at 82nd Street. The sun was warm, the sky was gemstone blue, and people walked with a spring in their step. It was all too surreal. It had never been darker in Michael's heart.

Since leaving Eden Falls Charlotte had not said a word. She was sitting in the passenger seat, her hands folded in her lap, looking out the window. Michael had no idea what had happened in his house, had no idea what Charlotte had seen. It appeared that she had not been crying. That was the only positive thing.

As they waited for the light to turn green, Charlotte turned slightly in her seat, scanned the messy back seat. She looked at Michael.

"Whose car is this, Daddy?"

Her tiny voice roused Michael from his black reverie. "Uh, it belongs to a friend of mine."

"Which one?"

"You've never met him, honey. It's somebody I work with."

Charlotte wrinkled her nose.

"What's wrong?" Michael asked.

"It smells funny."

She was right. Michael had smelled it the moment he had dumped Omar in the park. The man had soiled himself.

"Where are we going?"

"We're going to see another a friend of mine. A friend of *ours*."

Charlotte didn't ask who the friend was this time. Emily would have, but not Charlotte. Once Charlotte sensed a pattern developing, she tried to find a way around it. "Are Mommy and Em going to be there?"

Michael looked over at his daughter. The open window had blown her hair into her eyes. He reached over, smoothed his daughter's hair. "No, baby. We're going to meet up with them later."

Michael went silent for a few moments, organizing his thoughts. He knew he had to ask. The possibilities were eating him from the inside. "That man back at the house," he began, not knowing how he was going to broach the subject. "The tall man. Was he nice?"

Charlotte just shrugged.

"He didn't . . . hurt you or Emily or Mommy did he?"

Charlotte hesitated for a moment, and Michael's heart began to sink. Then, "No."

There were a million more questions, but there was no way to ask them without scaring Charlotte even further. He would have to get the answers on his own.

As they drove down 94th Street Michael rehearsed what he would say to Dennis McCaffrey, his boss. He had placed a call to the office and found, as expected, that McCaffrey was still there. Michael visualized pulling into the back lot, leading Charlotte down the sidewalk. She had never been to his office. What a first visit this would be.

When they turned onto Roosevelt Avenue, they pulled directly behind a NYPD sector car, lights flashing. The entire street was blocked.

Michael looked past the police car. Ahead was a fender bender, probably a little worse. Two cars sat at right angles to each other. A second police car sat in front of the scene. A patrol officer was directing cars around it.

As they approached the officer who was diverting traffic, Michael pulled his cap down low, put on a pair of gradient lens sunglasses that were sitting on the back seat. The shades were a woman's style, and looked far too feminine, but this was New York. Michael chanced a glance, peering over the top of the frames. The police officer on the street was only ten feet away now, looking straight at him. Was he made? Would the cop draw his weapon, command Michael to get out of the car and lay down on the pavement?

Michael had spent so much time on the other side of things, garnering so little sympathy for the criminals and their mindset, that –

The cop held up his hand. Stepping in front of the car,

nearly at the hood. Michael glanced in the rear-view mirror. There was no one behind him. If he slipped the transmission into reverse, floored it, he could back up the twenty or so feet needed to get away. They could get a few blocks, get out, and take the subway.

The cop was just a few feet away now.

Michael eased the gearshift into reverse, trying not to make it obvious. The cop still had his hand up. Michael was just about to put his foot on the gas when a vehicle turned the corner and drove up behind him, a dark SUV. He was blocked in.

The cop eased up to Michael's window, twirling his finger in a circular motion, indicating to Michael that he should roll down his window. Michael thought of the illegal handgun under the seat, the blood in the trunk of the car. He heard the next few seconds unfold in his mind.

Can I see your license and registration, please?

I'm sorry. I don't have them with me.

You have no identification with you?

No, sir.

Is this your car, sir?

No.

Please step out.

"Good afternoon," the officer said. He was in his late forties, a veteran patrol officer. Michael knew a lot of men who were on the job more than twenty-five years, men who never took the test, men who were not consumed by advancement. They were savvier in many ways then half the detectives out there.

"Good afternoon."

The cop looked at Michael, at Charlotte, at the back seat. Cops of this experience could take in an entire scene in seconds. "You know your front license plate is about to fall off. It's hanging on by one screw."

Michael felt a cool wave pass over him. "Oh, I'm sorry. I didn't know."

"That plate falls off, someone picks it up, they could use it for all manner of nefarious purposes."

"I understand."

The officer held him in his cop stare for a few more seconds – direct, street-hardened, unconvinced. This was his nature. He then looked over at Charlotte. "What's your name, little darling?"

Charlotte beamed. "Charlotte Johanna Roman."

The cop smiled, winked at Michael. Michael took a breath, held it. He knew if this cop decided to run the plate, it would not come back registered to anyone named Roman.

"That's a lot of name for such a little girl," the officer said.

Charlotte nodded. She loved to say her full name.

The cop gazed up the street. He tapped his hand on the roof of the car. "Get that taken care of right away, sir."

"I will. Thank you, officer."

As the cop walked away, Michael rolled up his window, finally exhaling.

The cop spoke into his two-way, stood to the side, held up his hand again, stopping traffic. Twenty feet up the street a concrete truck pulled out of an alley blocking the road. The cop turned his back on Michael, waved the truck along.

When Michael looked again in the rear-view mirror, his blood froze in his veins. The man driving the black SUV behind him was Aleksander Savisaar. Michael's eyes instinctively went to the passenger. It was Abby.

They had followed him from Eden Falls.

Michael scanned his mirrors. He was blocked. He couldn't go forward, and he couldn't back up. Should he tell the police? Should he just jump out of the car and tell the police that the man in the H2 had kidnapped his wife and daughter and was responsible for a number of homicides?

Too much could happen in the blink of an eye. He thought of Viktor Harkov, and Kolya, and Desiree Powell. He thought of the knife. He couldn't take the chance.

The concrete truck ambled to the curb ahead of him. The cop blew his whistle, waved Michael on. Not knowing what else to do, Michael reached forward, and turned the car off. The cop waved again. When Michael didn't move the cop looked at him with impatience. He walked back over.

Michael opened the door, slid out. Out of the corner of his eye he could see the figures in the car behind him. No one moved.

"Something wrong?" the cop asked.

Michael threw his hands up. "Stalled."

"Try it again."

Michael gestured to Charlotte. She slid across the front seat, took his hand. "I'm afraid the battery's dead. I had to jump it just a few minutes ago. It's not going to start. I'm going to have to push it."

The cop shook his head. He glanced up the street at the other officer directing traffic. By the time he turned back they were joined by someone.

It was Aleks. He was standing right next to them.

"Need a hand?" Aleks asked.

The cop turned, sized the big man up. For police officers, whenever citizens get out of their vehicles, in the middle of the street, without being asked, it was a red flag. Now this cop had two citizens in the middle of the street. He looked over Aleks's shoulder, at the woman and the little girl in the driverless SUV. "No," the cop said. "We've got it under control, sir."

At this close range, Michael could see that Aleks was about

his age. His eyes were a pale blue; he had a scar on his left cheek. They stood, wordlessly assessing each other. Between them stood the police officer. The *armed* police officer.

Would Aleks take this chance? Michael wondered. He gripped Charlotte's hand tightly, eased a step backward.

"I really don't mind," Aleks said. As he took a step forward, Michael and Charlotte retreated yet another step, angling themselves behind the police officer.

"Sir, please return to your vehicle," the officer said. "We can handle this."

Michael and Charlotte edged toward the curb and the sidewalk. Aleks did not move. Michael saw Aleks's right hand descend, saw his forefinger touch the hem of his coat. The moment drew out. The officer stiffened, nearing a state of heightened alert. He turned fully to Aleks. "Sir, I'm not going to ask you again. Please get back in your vehicle."

Aleks put his hands out, palms up, as if to say: *Sorry, I was just trying to help*.

As Aleks did this, the right side of his coat fell open. Michael – and the police officer – both saw the large knife on Aleks's hip.

The officer put a hand on his weapon. "Sir, please turn around and put your hands on the car. Do it now!"

Aleks glanced at the gun, at Michael, at the officer. He backed up a foot. The cop spoke into the microphone on his shoulder. A few anxious seconds later he received a reply. Michael knew all the codes. There were other officers on the way.

In this moment Michael and Charlotte stepped onto the sidewalk. Michael glanced at the SUV, at Emily, saw her lift her hands, bunch her sweater at her neck, shiver, as if she was freezing. It was a funny gesture, an inside joke between Michael and his daughter.

When Michael was small, he used to stand for minutes on end in front of the refrigerator, door open, never being able to make up his mind about what he wanted. His mother, ever trying to save a few pennies here and there on electricity, would always say to him: "Would you like me to get you a sweater?"

The routine continued with Michael and Emily, who was the same way Michael was as a child.

But why is she doing that now? Michael wondered.

Before he could think about it further, hell came to the street. It all happened at once. A woman on the sidewalk screamed as the officer unsnapped his holster. Before the cop could clear his weapon, Aleks had the knife off his hip. In a blur he slashed the police officer, the long blade catching the cop on the right side of his neck. Bright red blood fountained high into the blue sky. The officer staggered back against the car, his eyes wide with surprise and horror. Aleks cut him again, this time from shoulder to shoulder. The cop slid to the ground, slicking the car behind him.

For Michael, everything slowed. He heard another woman on the other side of the street start screaming. In the distance he heard car horns blow. Someone, hanging out of one the windows above, yelled "Hey!"

The other officer arrived on the scene, and seemed to take a moment to realize what he was looking at. He started to draw his weapon, but it was too late. Aleks pivoted, and kicked the man just below his jaw, splintering the young officers' teeth. The officer crashed back into the Ford. As he was falling to the ground, Aleks slashed him with the knife. It opened a large wound in the man's chest. In seconds his blue shirt was black with blood.

Michael and Charlotte backed quickly away from the scene on the street, working their way through the gathering crowd.

Sirens blared in the near distance. The older officer, now on the pavement, his face and hands covered in blood, raised his weapon and fired at Aleks, but the shot went wide, smashing into the side of his sector car. More screams as Aleks came in low and kicked the weapon from the man's hand. It skittered beneath a parked car.

Aleks, clearly disoriented, spun in place, the huge knife in front. He backed toward the SUV. On the sidewalks people were running, scattering. Aleks spun 360, looking for Michael in the hysterical crowd. He found him nearly fifty feet away, separated by scores of people.

Aleks and Michael looked at each other. A pair of sector cars were now just a half-block away. They would be on the scene in seconds, weapons drawn.

Aleks jumped back in the SUV. He put it in reverse, floored it, burned white smoke from the tires. He backed up all the way to 94th Street, and spun out, nearly causing an accident. Seconds later the SUV was gone.

Michael turned, continued up the avenue, as quickly as he could without running. Charlotte did her best to keep up. When they got to the alley, he scooped Charlotte into his arms.

They ran down Roosevelt Avenue – Michael all the while waiting to hear footsteps behind him. Moments later they came to the Junction Avenue subway stop, and boarded a train.

FORTY-SIX

Abby was handcuffed to the inside of the car door. She held Emily's hand, tried to focus. There had been many times in her career when chaos ruled the ER, when the waiting room was full, as were the four bays. Blood, bedlam, misery, pain. Dealing with it was a matter of triage, a process of prioritizing the injured for treatment according to the seriousness of their condition.

That's what she had to do right now. She knew what she wanted – for all of this to be over, for she and the girls and Michael to be safe – but that was the end of things. She had to figure a way to get there.

She had to prioritize.

The horrors were compounding. First Kolya, then Detective Powell. Then the police officers on the street. She had heard the sirens before they had gone a block. She envisioned the next few minutes, the image of the police surrounding them, guns drawn. There was the possibility that none of them – Aleks, Emily or herself – were going to survive.

Barreling down the street, running both stop signs and red lights, sending cars careening, Abby could smell the brute rage coming off Aleks. The steering wheel was sticky with drying blood. He drove quickly but expertly through traffic on 94th

Street toward Lamont Avenue.

Abby heard the sirens closing in. Just a few blocks away. When they reached Lamont Avenue Aleks pulled the SUV down an alley, behind a four-story apartment building. He cut the engine.

The police cars passed the alley, the sound reverberating between the brick walls. Aleks got out of the SUV, left the door open, began to pace. His eyes were manic, crazed.

"Where is he going?" he screamed.

Emily started at the sound. Abby put her arm around her daughter. "I don't know," Abby said.

"*Where is he taking her?*"

Aleks swarmed to the front of the SUV. He stared up at the sky for a moment, thinking. The sound of a slamming door behind the building made him spin on his heels. Abby tried to see what was happening, but because of the handcuffs she could not turn all the way.

"He will *not* take my daughter!" he yelled.

Abby now saw someone walking up the alley. There were two other cars parked in the back. A delivery van for the auto parts store on the corner, and a late-model Lincoln.

As the man approached, Abby saw that he was middle-aged man carrying a bag of groceries. He stopped and stared at Aleks, perhaps debating about stepping in and speaking to this demented man yelling at the woman and child.

In an instant Aleks was across the alleyway. The man went pale. He dropped his groceries.

"What are you looking at?" Aleks screamed. "Do you have business with me?"

"I'm not . . . I don't —"

"No you do not." Aleks looked up the alley, toward the street, back at the man. He pointed at the Lincoln. "Is this your vehicle?"

The man just stared. Aleks drew his knife. He held the tip beneath the man's chin. Abby could see a slight trickle of blood.

"No!" Abby screamed.

"Last time. Is this your vehicle?"

The man's eyes rolled back. Abby knew the signs. She feared the man might be going into shock. "Yes," he said softly.

"Give me the keys."

The man slowly reached into his pocket. He pulled a few things out: a handkerchief, a pack of gum, a few dollars in cash. No keys.

Aleks spun on his heel, swung his leg around, kicking the man in his chest. The man slammed against the brick wall, and folded to the ground. Aleks took the knife, sliced open the man's pockets. He soon found the keys, then dragged the man behind the Dumpster. He returned to the SUV, pulled all the bags from the back and put them in the Lincoln. He unlocked Abby's handcuffs, picked up Emily. They got in the Lincoln.

Aleks cuffed Abby to the door handle, then jumped in the vehicle. He started the car, studied the GPS screen on the console. Something seemed to register. He tore open the bag on the seat, pulled out the files he had taken from the house. Abby saw the phases of her life flash by. The deed to the house, her nursing certificate, her marriage license. Soon Aleks took out a photo. He scanned the document, then punched numbers into the GPS.

He pulled into traffic.

Abby knew where they were going. Aleks was not going to give up. Neither was she. She would find her moment.

FORTY-SEVEN

They took the subway to the 82nd Street station, where Michael flagged a cab. When they arrived at their destination, in Ozone Park, Michael paid the fare, looking up and down the street. They had not been followed.

He took Charlotte's hand in his. Before she got out of the cab, she put something in the pocket of her pink fleece jacket, something she had been holding.

"What do you have there?" Michael asked.

Charlotte took the item back out of her pocket, handed it to her father. It was a carved marble egg. Michael angled it to the sun to get a better look at the intaglio. It was a bizarre tableau – chickens, ducks, rabbits, and a needle.

"Where did you get this?" Michael asked, although a dark feeling inside gave him his answer. She had gotten it from Aleks.

Charlotte just shrugged.

"I'll keep it for a little while, okay?"

Charlotte nodded. Michael closed the car door.

Michael and Charlotte approached the side door of the

house on 101st Street— a two-story 1920s colonial, maroon siding over beige stone. Michael pressed the doorbell next to the casing. There was a small camera overhead watching them, along with a pair of heavily built men leaning against a car across the street. The men were smoking, chatting softly, watching Michael and his daughter.

After a few seconds the door opened, and Solomon Kaasik welcomed them inside.

Michael had not seen Solomon in almost a year. He had been in Chicago attending a five-day conference the day Solomon was released from Attica.

On the occasion of his release, Michael had sent Solomon a case of Türi – the exquisite Estonian vodka – along with a gift basket from La Guli's. They had spoken on the phone twice, both times ending the conversation with Michael's promise to see the man soon and resume their monthly chess game. One day led to the next, months passed, and Michael had still not seen his father's oldest friend, the man who had avenged the murder of his parents when society could not.

He was not prepared for what he saw when Solomon Kaasik opened the door.

Solomon was dying.

The two men wordlessly embraced. To Michael, Solomon felt like dry kindling. Michael had been meaning to call, to come by. *Life takes over*, he thought. Now it had taken everything.

He looked at Solomon. What had once been robustness and health was now the pall of the grave. He had lost seventy-five pounds. His face was thin and pallid, gaunt. In the corner of the room, next to an easy chair blanketed in an afghan – an afghan Michael remembered his mother knitting for Solomon when he was sentenced to Attica – sat an oxygen tank.

"Mischa," Solomon said. "*Minu poeg.*"

My son.

"This is my daughter Charlotte," Michael said.

With great effort Solomon got down onto one knee, holding Michael's arm to steady himself. Charlotte did not shy away from the old man.

"Say hello to Mr Kaasik," Michael said.

"Hi," Charlotte said.

Solomon considered the girl for a few moments. He put a knotted finger to her cheek, then stood up again. It took three attempts. Summoning all available strength and dignity, Solomon moved, ghost-like, unaided, across the room to his kitchen. He turned to Charlotte. "Would you like some juice?"

Charlotte looked at her father. Michael nodded.

"Yes, please," she said.

Solomon opened the fridge, removed some freshly squeezed orange juice. He poured a glass with a trembling hand.

While Charlotte sat at the dining-room table, crayon in hand, a sheaf of blank paper before her, Michael spoke to Solomon. Beginning with the murder of Viktor Harkov, continuing to the horror he had found at his house, and ending with the bloody confrontation on the street.

Solomon looked out the window, at the traffic on 101st Street. He glanced back at Michael. "The man from the motel," he said softly. "This Omar. Where is he?"

Michael told him.

Solomon rose, walked to the door. Michael heard the old man speaking to someone. A moment later Michael saw one of the men who had been in front of the house get into a step van on the street, take off.

Solomon returned. A long silence passed. Then, "What are you going to do, Mischa?"

Michael did not have an answer.

"I can put a man at your side," Solomon continued. "A very experienced man."

Michael had thought about this. Indeed, it was probably one of the reasons he had reached out. He decided against it. He knew that these were hard, violent men, and he could not take the chance of a confrontation.

"No," Michael said. "But there is something you can do for me."

Solomon listened.

"I need to know if someone knows this Aleksander Savisaar. I need to know what I'm up against."

"Savisaar."

"Yes."

"He is Estonian?"

"Yes."

"*Alt eestlane?*"

"I don't know." It was true. Michael did not know if Aleks was born in Estonia or not.

Solomon closed his eyes for a moment. Michael looked at him, remembering for a moment how big the man once was, how he had filled a room, his thoughts. He struggled to his feet, this time allowing Michael to help him.

"I will make a call."

Solomon moved slowly across the room, to one of the spare bedrooms. He closed the door. Michael looked out the window. He saw no police cars. He looked above the buildings, toward the skyline of the city. His wife and daughter could be anywhere. New York had never seemed larger or more forbidding.

Although it was probably only ten minutes, it seemed like

an hour before Solomon returned. His face looked even more bloodless, as if he had received some terrible news. Michael was not braced for this.

"Did you find anything out?"

"Yes." Solomon crossed the room to his bookshelves. "This man is from Kolossova. He was in the army in the first wave in Chechnya."

"And lived to tell."

"And lived to tell," Solomon repeated. "He is well known in eastern Estonia. A *roimar*. My cousin has had dealings with him." Solomon turned, supported himself against the bookcase. He looked Michael in the eye. "There is no easy way to say this."

"Then I suggest you just say it."

Solomon took a long moment. "Charlotte and Emily are his children."

Michael felt hot and cold at the same time, dizzied. Every slot in which he had tried to fit the events of this day now made perfect, horrifying sense, a wisdom he did not want. Aleksander Savisaar was here to take his daughters back. "Are you sure of this?"

Solomon nodded gravely.

Michael got up, began to pace. He considered that this news provided one thin ray of light, as discomforting as it may be at its core. If Aleksander Savisaar believed Emily was his daughter, perhaps it meant he would not harm her. On the other hand, it made Abby expendable, but maybe not until he got to where he was going.

"They say he consorted with a girl in Ida-Viru County," Solomon continued. "An *ennustaja*. She bore him three children, but one was stillborn."

The facts roared through Michael's mind like a runaway locomotive. Three place settings. Three candy bars. Three everything.

"An *ennustaja*?" Michael asked. "A fortune-teller?"

Solomon nodded.

Everything began to fall into place, all the explanations of how Charlotte and Emily were far more in tune with each other, far more perceptive than even the brightest twins. Could it be that the girls were prescient, just like their biological mother? Had they inherited this? Was clairvoyance their legacy?

Ta tuleb, Michael thought. *He is coming.*

They *knew*.

"There is more, I'm afraid," Solomon said. The words chilled Michael's blood.

Solomon turned, unsteadily, and made his way over to a glass-enclosed bookcase. In it was a collection of leather-bound editions. He opened the case, searched for a few seconds, then removed a small, scuffed book. He leafed through it, then turned to Michael, a thousand miseries in his damp eyes. "Koschei," he said. "Do you remember the story?"

The name was familiar to Michael. It walked the far horizon of his childhood memories. It had something to do with a boogeyman.

"It is an old tale," Solomon said. "I used to read it to you when you lived on Ditmars. You got scared, but you never wanted me to stop. The story of Koschei the Deathless was your favorite."

Bits and pieces of the tale came floating back.

"You used to think Koschei lived in your closet. You used to wake up your parents every night with your nightmares. Then your father and I rewired the closet and put that light fixture inside. You were never afraid again."

Until now, Michael thought.

"What does this have to do with this Savisaar?" he asked.

Solomon seemed to choose his words carefully. "He is insane,

Mischa. He believes himself to be Koschei. He believes he is going to live forever. And it has something to do with the girls."

Michael tried to process it all. He remained silent. Now that he had an idea what this was all about, he might find a way to fight it.

Solomon nodded. "What can I do for you, Mischa?"

"I want you to watch Charlotte. I can't think of anywhere in the world where she would be safer at this moment."

Solomon turned to the window, made a signal to one of the men on the street. The man got on his cell, and within thirty seconds a car pulled up, and two other men got out. They walked toward the backyard. Solomon turned back to Michael, reached into his pants pocket, handed Michael a single key. "You will take this car. It is the silver Honda, parked three doors down."

Michael took the key, stood, pulled off his oversized raincoat. "I could use some clothes, too."

Solomon pointed to one of the bedrooms. Michael rose, crossed the room, opened the door. Inside, stacked floor to ceiling, were a hundred sealed cardboard boxes: electronics, small appliances, expensive liquors. Michael found a box of Guess jeans, rummaged through them until he found his size. There were also a dozen boxes of Rocawear hoodies. He found his size, slipped it over his head. In the corner of the room was a flat screen TV, tuned to channel 7, volume low.

The news came when Michael was at the door. It was a breaking story. His heart fell. Beneath the talking head was a headline.

QUEENS PROSECUTOR SOUGHT IN HOMICIDE

Onscreen was his "executive" photo, the one taken by the office, the one that was featured on the DA's office website.

Next to it was a live shot of his house. A pair of Eden Falls sector cars flashed their lights.

Michael walked out of the bedroom, sat on the chair next to Charlotte's. He looked at the table. On it was the piece of paper she had been working on, practicing writing 0 through 9. The numbers were all drawn in precise rows. The sight of his daughter's diligent work almost made Michael break down. But there was something else about the drawings that caught his eye, and his attention. Charlotte had used two different crayons drawing the numbers. In all four rows of numbers, all but two of the numerals were drawn in black crayon. The only two numbers drawn in red crayon were the 6 and the 4.

Michael sat on the chair next to Charlotte's. "That's very good," Michael said. He turned Charlotte's chair to face his. "Honey, I need to go out for awhile. *Onu* Solomon is going to watch you."

Although Charlotte had never met Solomon, Michael's use of the Estonian word for uncle, and its affection, was known to her.

"Is that okay?" Michael said.

"It's okay."

Michael held his daughter close. "My big girl." He sat back, looked her in the eye. "I'm going to go pick up Mommy and Em, and then we'll all go out to dinner. I won't be long at all. Okay?"

Charlotte nodded. She then reached over, picked up the page with the numbers, handed it to Michael. Michael looked back into her eyes. She seemed to drift, to be in some sort of trance. He had seen this before, usually at a time when she and Emily were separated.

"What is it honey?"

Charlotte said nothing. Instead, she began to hum a song. Michael didn't recognize it. It sounded like a classical theme.

"Charlotte," Michael said. "Tell Daddy."

His daughter continued to stare off into the distance, a void into which Michael could not see. She stopped humming.

"Anna is sad," she said.

Anna, Michael thought. The nightmare fable of his youth came flooding back. *The girl in the story.*

Michael scanned the piece of paper in his hand, the numbers. It was the same two numbers on the refrigerator door at home. *Familiar* numbers.

That's what Emily meant when she pretended to be cold, he thought. She wanted him to look at the refrigerator. She was trying to tell him something, and Michael now knew what it was.

FORTY-EIGHT

He moved through the farmhouse, the kinzbal on point. He had taken the dagger off a dead Chechen, a young soldier no more than eighteen. The smell of decomposing flesh filled his head, his remembrance.

The house had many rooms, each filled with a different light.

For the past few years he had slipped in and out of time, a place unfettered by memory, a place that had, at first, both frightened and unnerved him, but one that had now become his world. He saw the walls of the stone house rise and fall, in one moment constructed of raw timber and mortar, at other moments open to the elements, the trees and sky, the rolling hills that sloped gently to the river. He felt the floor beneath his feet transform from hard-packed dirt to fine quarry tile, back to soft grass. All around him he heard hundreds scream as they fled the heat and blood and insanity of war, the madness soon giving way to the serenity of the graveyard, all of it subsumed in time present, time past, time yet to unfold.

He looked at the old woman dying on the kitchen floor, the taste of her blood fresh and metallic on his tongue. All at once he felt the earth tremble beneath his feet, saw the shadow of enormous things move in the grey miasma, then clear, revealing a pastoral scene of rich and painful splendor.

He saw a young woman sitting by the river. She had a long, slender neck, delicate arms. Even from behind he knew so many things about *her. He knew that she, like himself, was ageless. Next to her were two other rocks, unoccupied.*

As he approached he realized he could no longer smell the stench of the dead and dying. The air was now suffused with the scent of honeysuckle and grape hyacinth. The young woman turned and looked at him. She was a heart-stopping beauty.

"Mis su nimi on?" *Aleks asked. He wasn't sure if she spoke Estonian.*

She answered his question. "Anna."

"What's wrong?"

Anna looked at the river, then back. "Marya is sad."

Nearby, Aleks heard the rumble of a vehicle, the sound of a blaring horn. When he looked at the woman he discovered that she was now a little girl, no more than four. She looked up at him with pride, with longing, her blue eyes shining, her soul an unpainted canvas.

He smelled flour and sugar and blood, the hunger within him rising. He sensed someone near.

An intruder.

They were no longer alone.

Aleks raised his knife, and stepped into the shadows.

FORTY-NINE

Michael stood in the alley behind the building at 64 Ditmars Boulevard. In his mind he saw the numbers on the drawing Charlotte made, the numbers on the refrigerator.

The last time he stood in this place, a time when his heart had been whole and he felt safe in this world, he was nine years old. That day he had played stickball with four of his friends from the neighborhood. Later that night, the night two men walked in the front door and murdered his parents, his whole world fell apart. He had been piecing it back together ever since.

Michael put his ear to the door, listened. Nothing.

Since Abby had bought the building, they'd had all the locks changed and upgraded, putting deadbolts on every door, bars on all the basement and first-story windows.

Michael turned the knob, bumped the door with his shoulder. Solid. He would not be breaking down the door, nor would he be defeating the new lock. He scanned the area for something with which he could break the window pane, saw a broken umbrella sticking out a trashcan. He took it out, fed it through the narrow bars on the door, tapped the pane twice. On three he hit the glass. It smashed. Michael listened to the interior of the space. He was met with a thick brown silence. After a few moments he reached in, scraping his hand on the too-narrow opening, cutting his palm on the broken glass. He turned the lock.

Michael looked both ways and, seeing he was alone, pushed open the door. He stepped into the abandoned bakery, into the dark dominion of his past.

FIFTY

For Detective Desiree Powell it was a long shot. She hated long shots. If all her players were still in New York City, it would only leave five boroughs, hundreds of neighborhoods, tens of thousands of streets, and a hundred thousand buildings to search. Not to mention the world that existed underground – subways, basements, tunnels, catacombs. So she made a command decision. She had to put herself and her team somewhere.

This was why she made the big money, just enough to keep her in subway tokens and Jimmy Choo knock-offs.

She parked at the corner of Steinway Street and 21st Avenue, scanned the block, the long row of red-brick row houses, the small stores interspersed between, each with a colorful sign trumpeting their wares and services. There was a drama unfolding in each one of them, she thought, life-altering comedies and tragedies and farces that, to the outside world, would proceed unexamined, unknown. Until some unexpected horror descended, and they called the police.

Was the theater of Michael Roman's tragedy unfolding in one of these buildings? Or had the curtain already fallen?

She shifted in her seat. Her ribs were getting worse. She had taken six Tylenol already. She would need the hard stuff before the day was over.

When she looked in her side-mirror she saw Fontova come running up, out of breath. Bracing herself against a fresh sword of agony, Powell opened the door, gently slid out of the car.

"You hear about the two cops on Roosevelt?" Fontova asked.

An "officer needs assistance" call had gone out over the radio twenty minutes ago. Powell had not heard the details. "What about them?"

Fontova bent over, catching his wind. Sufficiently recovered, he continued. "Uniformed officer was directing traffic around an accident on 98th Street. A car stalled, and when they were just about to push it, a guy jumped out a car behind the stalled car. He pulled a knife and cut two cops."

"Jesus Christ. How bad?"

"Both are on the way to the hospital. One of the officers got a shot off, but he missed."

"They have the cutter?"

Fontova shook his head. "Took off. There's a BOLO on the vehicle and the doer. White male, thirties, tall. Driving a black H2."

"Shouldn't be too hard to spot."

"It gets better."

"Doesn't it always?"

Fontova reached into the inside pocket of his suit coat, took out the composite sketch of the man who had broken into the Arsenault house.

"You're shitting me," Powell said.

"Not," Fontova said. "And two witnesses put a woman and a little blond girl in the H2 with the cutter. And dig this."

Powell just listened.

"The stalled car was a blue Ford Contour."

Powell's head began to spin. "*Our* BOLO? The one Michael Roman drove away from that motel?"

"Yep. Other wits said they saw another man and another little girl running from the scene."

"Did we get a description on the man?"

"Not a good one."

"Got to be Roman, right?"

"This is what I'm thinking."

"What happened to the car?"

"The 114 has it. Still on the scene."

Powell glanced down the road, towards Ditmars Boulevard, back at her partner.

"Where?"

He thumbed over his shoulder. "Two blocks up. They also found an H2 behind a building off Lefferts."

"This is the center of the world today."

Fontova nodded.

Powell closed her eyes for a moment, began to connect the dots. A few moments later she opened her cellphone, called it in. They would set up a perimeter.

This section of Queens, near Astoria Park, was made up of row houses and small retail establishments. There was a large contingent of Greek immigrants in the neighborhood, but over the years Italians, Poles, and eastern European immigrants had moved into the area, and their influence could be seen on the variety of awnings and flags and stores.

By the time Powell and Fontova pulled onto the block there were a half-dozen sector cars in position, a dozen or so uniformed officers fanning out. They began to knock on doors, talk to people on the street. Powell and Fontova split up. It was a warm, early evening, and the sidewalks were congested.

Powell did her best to keep up with Marco Fontova and the rest of the team, but she knew she would be lagging far behind. The first person she talked to was a man standing in front of a pager store. Black, sixties, salt-and-pepper goatee, silver hoops in both ears. He may have been a player once, right around when the Chi-Lites had hits.

"How you doing?" Powell asked.

The man looked her up and down, smiled lasciviously. Real dreamboat. Powell wanted to shoot him in the ribs, see how he liked it.

"It's all good, baby," the man said.

Powell no longer had her badge, but she did have her NYPD ID. She took it out and clipped it to her pocket. Suddenly, it was *no* good, baby. The man was now afflicted with blindness, deafness, muteness, and amnesia. Powell asked the questions anyway, moved on.

The sixth time was a charm. A pair of skateboard rats, skinny white kids, about fourteen, idling in front of a corner smoothie shop. One had on a T-shirt that read *Alien Workshop*. The other wore a lime-green Mizuno bicycle jersey. Powell held forth a photograph of Michael Roman.

"Have either of you seen this man?"

They both looked at the photo. "Hard to say," said lime green.

"He might be with a girl," Powell said. "A little blond girl."

"Oh yeah, yeah," *Alien Workshop* said. "He just ran by here a little while ago." He squinted at the photo. "He's a lot older than that, though."

"Which way?"

He pointed toward the park.

"The little girl was with him?"

"Yeah."

Powell got on her two-way, dispatched four officers to Astoria Park. She continued down the street, each step a fresh stiletto in her side. She walked past bagel shops, unisex salons, an open fruit-and-vegetable stand, past a trade fair, a laundromat. The massive police presence in the neighborhood had drawn attention, but it had not shut down commerce.

Between 32nd and 33rd Streets, about a block from the Astoria Ditmars subway stop, Powell stopped. Two reasons. The fact that she couldn't walk anymore was the main. The other was that something was nagging her, besides her aching torso, something that walked the edge of her recall like a rearranged melody. She stood on the street, scanning the buildings, the windows, the people. She had walked a beat on these streets a long time ago, an area that stretched from the park all the way to Steinway, back in the day when community policing meant shoe leather and Pepsodent.

Across the street was a Greek travel agency, a Jackson Hewitt office, a nail salon.

What the hell was nagging her about this stretch of Ditmars?

She held her ID high, limped across the street. Thankfully, traffic slowed. Some people actually came to a full stop.

Powell walked into the nail salon. A girl behind the counter looked up from a magazine.

"Help you?"

The girl was about twenty, with blunt-cut, multicolored hair, a set of dazzlingly bright spangled nails. There were no customers in the shop.

"Have you got Internet access?" Powell asked.

Nothing. Powell tapped the ID on her chest. The girl looked from the ID to Powell's eyes. Powell asked again, this time speaking a little more slowly, enunciating every word.

"Have . . . you . . . got . . . Internet access?"

Now the girl looked at her as if she were from another planet. Maybe the Alien Workshop. "Of course." She turned the LCD monitor on the counter to face Powell, then slid the keyboard and mouse forward.

"Have you got a stool, something I can sit on?"

Another pause. Powell was beginning to wonder if there was some sort of drug-induced time delay in here, one caused by a long-term exposure to nail-salon chemicals. The girl caught on, slid off her stool, picked it up, and walked it around the counter.

"Thank you," Powell said. She eased onto the stool, opened a web browser. She searched again for the *New York* article on Michael Roman. Her eyes blazed down the page. She found the paragraph she had been looking for, and finally located the itch. She got on her two-way, raising Fontova. A few minutes later he walked into the nail shop. By that time, Powell had navigated to an overhead map of the surrounding ten-block area.

Powell briefed her partner. Fontova looked at the map.

"Okay," Powell began. "We have the initial crime scene here." She put a virtual pushpin in the building that housed Viktor Harkov's office. "We have the Ford Contour last seen in Roman's possession here, which is also where our cutter attacked two police officers. And lastly we find the H2 in which our alleged psycho made his temporary escape abandoned here."

Powell leaned back, looked at the locations. "Now, I love this part of the city. Don't get me wrong. But what the fuck is so special about Astoria, and especially this here little slice of heaven around Ditmars?"

She slipped a dollar into Fontova's hand. He took it without comment.

"I don't know."

"I think I do."

Powell maximized the other browser window, the one displaying the *New York* article. She pointed to the screen, at the paragraph that mentioned Michael Roman's childhood, about how his parents were murdered in their place of business, a place called the Pikk Street Bakery, a place that Michael Roman and his wife had purchased a few years earlier.

A place located at 64 Ditmars Boulevard.

FIFTY-ONE

The old feelings rushed over him in a dizzying flourish. It wasn't just a remembrance of his time spent here, a recollection of carefree childhood, a home movie unspooling in his mind, but rather a feeling that he was once again nine years old, still running down this hallway to help his father accept deliveries of flour and sugar, large boxes of bottled molasses, dried fruits and fresh-roasted nuts. The aroma of just-baked bread still lived in the air.

Since the Pikk Street Bakery had closed only a few retail tenants had tried to make a go of the space. Michael knew that, for a short while, a company offering orthotic and prosthetic services rented the first floor. After that, a natural foods store. Neither enterprise flourished.

The back hallway was just as Michael remembered it, its hardwood flooring worn in the center, a pair of Sixties-era light fixtures overhead. He proceeded down the hallway by feel, hugging the wall. A nail protruding from the plaster caught his sweatshirt, tearing the fabric, scratching his skin.

When he reached the doorway before the front room he stopped. He tried to calm himself, quiet his breathing. He slowly peered around the corner, into the room that once held the bakery's office. As a child he had been forbidden to play in this room, only entering when his mother was doing the books, the mysterious paperwork that seemed to hold adults in its dark thrall once a month. He recalled once being punished for leaving a lemon ice to melt on the desk. Now the room was musty, abandoned. In the dim light he could make out shapes. A pair of dun-colored file cabinets, an old metal desk on its side, a pair of packing crates.

He continued a few feet down the hallway into the front room. When they purchased the building, Abby visited with the realtor, and told Michael that the previous tenants had removed most of their furniture, had even made a half-hearted attempt at cleaning. Michael looked across the room. The front windows were soaped, making the translucent light otherworldly. Dust motes hazed the room.

Michael eased his way up the steps, each tread echoing that horrible day, the dry wood protesting his presence, the sounds and smells vaulting him back in time. He could all but hear the noise of firecrackers going off in the street outside, some of them, he learned, the sounds of the gunfire that had shattered his family.

He reached the top of the stairs, looked down the hallway. The door to the bathroom had been removed. Scant light came in through the barred window. He turned to his parents' bedroom. He recalled the day his father and Solomon painted the room, a hot summer day in July, the sound of a Mets game in the background, fading in and out on old transistor radio. Solomon had gotten drunk that Sunday afternoon, and rolled paint over half the window before Peeter had been able to stop him. The glazing was still flecked with blue.

Sweat slid down Michael's back, his skin pimpled with gooseflesh. The air was close and damp and silent. He crossed the hallway to the space that was once his bedroom. He pushed open the door, the old hinge giving a squeal of complaint. He could not believe how small the room was, how it had, at one time, in the fictional world of his child's mind, been his tundra, his castle, his western plains, his fathomless ocean. There was no bed, no dresser, no chair. Against one wall were a pair of cardboard boxes, coated with years of filth.

He closed his eyes, recalled the moment – seven o'clock exactly, the time the bakery closed. He had had nightmares about the scenario for years, had even felt a pang of terror at the times when he happened to glance at a clock at exactly seven. In his dreams he saw shadows on the walls, heard footsteps. It all coalesced at this moment. The horror in his closet, the two men who had killed his mother and father, the man who now had his wife and daughter.

Michael stopped, opened his eyes, and suddenly realized it was not a dream. The footsteps were real. He felt the slight buckle of the floorboards, the change in the air, and knew that someone was right behind him. Before he could take the gun from his pocket, a shadow filled the room.

Mischa, he heard his mother say. *Ta tuleb.*

Then there was fire inside his head, a supernova of orange and scarlet pain.

Then, nothing.

FIFTY-TWO

It took a while to realize where he was, *when* he was. Reality sifted back, laced with the thudding agony in his head.

When his eyes adjusted to the light, he took in the scene. He was in the front room of the bakery, sitting in a chair, next to Abby. In front of them was one of the small wooden café tables that used to be near the window of the bakery. Michael could see some of the names still carved into the surface.

On the table was a gun.

Emily sat on the other side of the room, the side on which the three counters of the bakery once were. The glass cases were long gone, but the two large ovens still stood against the back wall. Next to them were dismantled tables, chairs, bookshelves. There was no electricity, no overhead fixtures, but in the thin light slicing through the grimed front windows, Michael could see his daughter clearly. She was perched on a dusty pillow, one of three.

Michael turned to Abby. Her hands were taped behind her, around a copper water pipe bolted to the wall. Her eyes were wide, terrified. She had a gag stuffed in her mouth. Michael's hands were handcuffed in front of him, but he was not otherwise restrained in any way.

A moment later Aleks emerged from the shadows. He stood behind Emily. "You've interrupted my plans," he said.

Michael eyed the weapon on the table. He shifted himself in the chair, opened his mouth to speak, but found that the words would not come. If he'd ever needed a closing argument it was now.

"The police are already at my house," Michael said. "You can't possibly get away with this. They'll figure it out. They'll be here."

"They are already here." Aleks reached into his pocket, pulled something out, threw it on the floor in front of Michael and Abby. It was a gold detective badge. Powell's shield. "Where is Marya?"

"I can't tell you," Michael said.

In an instant Aleks was across the room, the folds of his leather coat snapping in the still air. "*Where is she?*" He pulled Abby's head back, put the knife to her throat.

"Wait!"

Aleks said nothing, did not take the blade from Abby's throat. His eyes had morphed from a pale blue to almost black.

"She's . . . she's with a friend," Michael said.

"Where?"

"It's not far."

"*Where?*"

"I'll tell you. Just please . . ."

After a long moment, Aleks withdrew the knife. He reached into his pocket, took out a cellphone. He handed it to Michael. "I want you to call this friend. Put it on speakerphone. I want to hear my daughter's voice."

Michael took the phone in his shackled hands, dialed Solomon's number. When it began to ring, Michael put it on speaker. In a moment, Solomon answered.

"It's Mischa," Michael said. "Everything's fine, *onu*. It's all over."

Solomon said nothing.

"Can you put Charlotte on?"

Again, a hesitation. Then, Michael heard Solomon's show, shambling footsteps. A few seconds later: "Daddy?"

At the sound of Charlotte's voice, Michael saw Emily pick up her head. She still looked to be under some sort of spell, but the sound of her sister's voice brought her to the moment.

"Yes, honey. It's me. Mommy's here, too."

"Hi, Mommy."

Abby began to cry.

"Are you coming to get me?" Charlotte asked.

"Soon. We'll be there really soon. Can you put *Onu* Solomon back on the phone, please?"

Michael heard the transfer.

"Mischa," Solomon said. "You are coming to collect her?"

Michael knew he had to give Solomon a heads up, but he didn't know how to do it. Speaking in Estonian would not help.

"No," Michael said. "I'm going to send someone."

"Someone from your office?"

"No," Michael said. He glanced at the gold badge on the floor. "A detective. A detective from Queens Homicide will be coming by to get her. I hope that's okay."

"Of course," Solomon said.

Aleks crossed the space, picked up the badge, put it in his pocket.

"His name is Detective Tarrasch," Michael said.

Michael glanced at Aleks. He did not react to the name.

"I will be ready," Solomon said.

I will be ready, Michael thought. Not *I will be waiting*. Solomon knew there was something wrong. *Tarrasch* was a chess term, a variation on the French Defense Solomon had taught Michael in the 1980s. If Michael knew Solomon, he knew that the old man was already preparing to send Charlotte to another location.

Before Michael could sign off, Aleks took the phone from his hands, closed it. He crossed the room, and began to put things into a shoulder bag.

Michael looked at Emily. With the index finger of her right hand, she touched the floor, and drew a straight line in the dust.

A few miles away, in a small house in Ozone Park, Charlotte Roman sat at the dining-room table, a fresh white sheet of typing paper in front of her, a rainbow of stubby crayons awaiting her muse. In the background, the television played *Wheel of Fortune*.

Charlotte surveyed the choices of colors. She picked up a black crayon and began to draw. At first she drew a long horizontal line across the bottom of the page, stretching from one edge to the other. She hesitated for a moment, then continued, drawing first the right side of what would be a rectangle, then the left. Finally, she began to complete the shape, carefully connecting the two sides at the top . . .

. . . creating the ridge line of the roof, though Emily Abigail Roman was far too young to know what a ridge line was. To her it was just the top of the house. She ran her small finger through the dust, keeping the line as straight as possible. Underneath the ridge line she made two smaller rectangles, these of course being the windows. Each window had a cross in the center, which made four smaller windows. Beneath the windows . . .

. . . she drew a pair of even smaller rectangles, wide and thin, which were flower boxes. Charlotte put down the black crayon and picked up the red one. It was almost halfway gone, but that was okay. Gripping the small crayon tightly, she made little red tulips in the flower boxes, three flowers in each. When she was satisfied, she picked up the green crayon, and filled in the stems and leaves. All that was left to do was the front door. She selected a brown crayon . . .

. . . and made a doorway in the dust. With one final poke of her tiny finger, she made the doorknob. A door was useless without a doorknob. Emily Roman looked at her drawing. There was one last touch. She reached forward, and swirled her finger over the chimney. The last little curlicue was the smoke.

FIFTY-THREE

Aleks paced back and forth. He spoke rapidly, drifting from Estonian to Russian to English. He held his knife in his right hand, and as he turned he tapped it against his right leg, slicing the black leather of his coat. To Michael, who had seen his share of unhinged defendants, Aleks was clearly coming apart.

Aleks stood directly in the front window, his back to the room.

"Things go full circle in this life, do they not, Michael Roman?"

Michael stole a glance at Abby. She was rocking back and forth, pulling on the pipes behind her.

"What do you mean?" Michael asked.

Aleks turned to face them. "This place. I can smell the yeast in the air. Once it is in the air, it never leaves, you know. I've heard of a bakery in Paris, a shop known for its sourdough breads, that has not used an active culture for more than a hundred years." He turned to glance at Emily, back. "Do you think things remain? Things like energies, spirits?"

Michael knew he had to keep Aleks talking. "Maybe. I —"

"Were you here when it happened? Did you see it?"

Michael now knew what he was talking about. He was talking about the murder of Peeter and Johanna Roman. "No," Michael said. "I didn't see it."

Aleks nodded. "I read about you. About the incident with the car bomb."

Michael said nothing.

"You were supposed to die that day, yet you did not. Have you ever questioned this?"

Only every day since, Michael thought. "I don't know," he said, hoping to find some common ground with this madman. "Maybe I was destined for something else. Maybe something better."

"Yes," Aleks said. "Destiny." He began to pace back and forth again, now behind Emily. Out of the corner of his eye Michael could see that Abby had begun to work the copper pipe from its mooring. "Tell me. When you were about to die, how did it feel?"

"It felt like nothing," Michael said. "It happened too fast."

"No," Aleks said. "It is the longest moment of your life. It can last forever."

Michael saw the pipe budge a little more, saw the duct tape on Abby's wrists begin to fray. Aleks circled behind Emily.

"It was in a place not unlike this that it all began for me," Aleks said. "I know the feeling. To be brought to the edge of the abyss, and to emerge unscathed. I do not think it was an accident that you came to care for Anna and Marya. I believe it was ordained. Now I must take them home."

Before he could stop himself, Michael rose from the chair. The words just seemed to tumble out. "I won't let you!"

Michael glanced again at Emily, at the drawing she had made in the dust. He could not make it out from where he was.

"You should know about their mother," Aleks continued, moving closer to Emily. "A beautiful young girl. An *ennustaja* of magnificent power. Elena. She was merely a child when I first saw her. She was the spirit of the grey wolf." Aleks pointed at the table in front of Michael. "There are two bullets in that weapon. I want you to pick it up."

Michael froze. "No."

"I want you to pick it up *now*!"

Slowly, Michael picked up the pistol. It felt heavy, leaden in his hand. Was it loaded? And if it was, why was Aleks doing this? Michael wondered if he could point it at Aleks, and pull the trigger.

No, he thought. He could not take the chance. Aleks was too close to Emily. "What do you want me to do?"

"There is only one choice. I am going to leave with my daughter, and I cannot take the risk that I will be stopped."

Michael had no idea what the man meant by *one choice*. He remained silent.

"First, you will take the weapon, point it at Abigail's head, and pull the trigger."

Michael's heart plunged. "*What?*"

"Then you will take your own life. You see, it will be seen as a murder/suicide, the logical actions of a man who killed the lawyer who illegally worked for him, then a young thug with whom he had done business. Not to mention the police detective who came to investigate. In your madness, seeing no way out, you brought your wife here, to the site of your life's greatest tragedy, and took both your lives."

Michael's mind began to reel. Abby sobbed. "That's . . . that's not going to happen."

Aleks crouched down behind Emily. "Maybe there is another choice for you." He took one of the small, empty glass vials from the chain around his neck, placed it on the floor in front of Emily. He held the tip of the knife just inches from the back of the little girl's head. "There are other ways for Anna to come with me."

Abby screamed into the gag in her mouth. She began to rock back and forth violently, pulling on the pipe.

"We do not live in your world," Aleks said, glancing at his knife. "These things cannot hurt us."

"No."

"The choice is between your life and Anna's. What are you willing to do for her?"

"Don't . . ." Michael lifted the pistol.

"Are you willing to trade your life for hers?"

"*Stop!*"

"Put the gun to Abigail's head, Michael. If you love this child you will not hesitate." He moved the knife even closer.

"*Wait!*" Michael screamed.

Emily looked up at him. In that moment Michael saw his daughter as a teenager, a young woman, an adult. It all came down to this moment.

"Make your choice now, Michael Roman," Aleks said.

Michael knew what he had to do. Aleks was right. There really was no choice.

FIFTY-FOUR

There had been other suitors over the years, many interlopers in their lives. Once, in a small village in Livonia, a young boy had dared speak with him about his daughter, Marya. The boy claimed to be the son of the town's bailiff. This was after the second siege of Reval. Led by Ivan the Terrible, there was a sickness in the air, a state of lawlessness that swept the towns of Dünaburg, Kokenhausen and Wendenthe, and Aleks had dispatched the boy with no consequence.

Marya had been nearly seventeen at the time, a young woman of incomparable beauty. As she and Anna flowered to womanhood, they had begun to manifest small differences, not only in their person- alities, but also in their looks. From a few yards away, to most people, they were indistinguishable from each other — their honey-colored hair, their flawless skin, their clear-blue eyes. But a father knows his children.

And now this man. A man who claimed to be their father. Another intruder.

Aleks stood outside the church, a bitter wind cutting along the ridge that led to the banks of the river. Anna sat before him, wrapped in fur. At her feet was a bundle, a swaddled, stillborn infant.

Aleks looked at the imposters.

Next to the dead child sat the grey wolf; primordial silver eyes set deep into the smooth dome of his head.

"Do it now," he said. "Or I will do it for you."

The grey wolf bayed.

The man raised the weapon, and pointed it at the woman's head.

FIFTY-FIVE

The building was a three-store commercial block on Ditmars near Crescent, home to a bodega, a dry cleaner, and the shuttered space on the end. There was a driveway to the right, leading behind the building. Next to it was a six-suite, two-story apartment building. Powell had been by this block many times, but like so much of New York, she hadn't noticed it.

Above the storefronts were living quarters. Along the block the windows on the upper floors were open, some with sheer curtains billowing out in the warm spring evening, some with the sounds of dinner being prepared, the evening news blaring its tragedies.

Powell stepped up to the front entrance. It was covered by a rusted steel riot gate. The windows were soaped, all but opaque. Everything seemed benign, empty, peaceful. Had she been wrong about this? She had gotten reports from her teams every minute or so. There had been no sign of Michael Roman or the girls, no sign of their cutter.

Fontova came around the corner. He had gone to check the back entrance to the building.

"Anything?" Powell asked.

"The window in the back door is broken."

"Recently?"

"Yeah. The glazing doesn't look weathered."

"Any vehicles?"

"No, but there's no glass laying on the ground in front of the door."

"It was broken from the outside."

"Yeah. And it's got blood on it."

The two detectives looked at each other with understanding. "Let's get some backup here."

Fontova lifted the handset to his mouth, and called it in.

That's when they heard the gunshots.

FIFTY-SIX

The blasts were deafening in the confined space. Michael was stunned at how easy it was to do what he had done, how little pressure was needed to pull the trigger, how short the journey between life and death. He had talked about it for many years, had sat in judgment and conclusion of those who had said things like "it just went off," and "I didn't mean to shoot him," never having any understanding of the process.

Now, having pulled the trigger, he knew it wasn't that hard. The difficult part was making the decision to aim the weapon.

Michael had pointed the gun at the ceiling and fired the rounds. He kept pulling the trigger, but it seemed that Aleks had told him the truth. There were only two bullets in the gun. Michael ejected the magazine and threw the two parts in different directions.

As soon as the echo of the gun blast began to fade, Aleks stood. Michael could see in his eyes a fierce determination to bring this all to a close. He strode with slow deliberation toward Abby, the knife at his side.

"You have made a mistake," Aleks said. "You could have made this far less painful for your wife, for yourself, but you chose to defy me. To defy your destiny."

He stopped in front of Abby, raised the knife. There was nothing Michael could do to stop him.

"*Isa!*" Emily screamed.

In that second – a moment where Emily cried out the word *father* in Estonian –Aleks turned, looked at Emily. Michael knew there would never be another moment. He ran at Aleks, hitting him full force in the side, knocking him backwards. The two men crashed into the drywall with a bone-jarring force. Aleks righted himself, and lashed out with his fist, catching Michael high on the left side of his head, stunning him, showing him flashes of bright white light behind his eyes. Michael went down to the hardwood floor, but was able to roll, absorbing most of the impact with his shoulder. He sprang to his feet, and was now face to face with Aleks. Aleks slashed at the air between them, closing the distance little by little. The blade came in high, but Michael sidestepped. He caught the blade flat on his upper arm.

Michael backed across the room, toward his daughter. In the background he could hear Abby screaming into her gag, the sound of the metal pipes clanging as she struggled ferociously to break free. Michael was breathing hard, the blows he had taken to the head were clouding his vision. Aleks slashed at him again, this time slicing open the back of Michael's right hand. As Michael pulled away, he stumbled over something on the floor, momentarily losing his balance.

Aleks lunged toward Emily. With all rational thought beyond him, Michael righted himself and threw his body between them. The knife carved into the left side of Michael's stomach, slicing away a large flap of skin and flesh. Michael fell back into the wall, the pain a searing lava flow down his right side. He felt his leg go numb, slid down the wall, his hands groping for purchase. He found one of the dismantled table legs leaning in the corner.

As Aleks moved again toward Emily, Michael struggled to his knees, clawed his way to his feet. He raised the table leg high, and brought it around in an almost complete arc, hitting Aleks on the side of his head, stunning him. The sound of the impact was loud, the long rusted bolt fastened at the top of the table leg cut deep into Aleks's scalp. Aleks's eyes rolled into his head as he staggered back and went down, blood now seeping from the head wound. Michael brought the bludgeon down twice more, all but shattering Aleks's right knee.

Michael limped across the room, lifted his cuffed hands over Emily's head, picked her up, the right side of his body now grown ice cold. He glanced behind them, at the front door of the bakery. It was locked with a deadbolt, secured by iron bars. No exit. Aleks was between them and the back door. He was trying to get to his feet.

Michael looked at Abby. Her eyes told him all he needed to know. She wanted him to get out with Emily while he could.

Filled with a suffocating fear, with no way out, Michael held Emily close, and lurched toward the steps leading to the second floor. He angled his body against the handrail for balance. One step, two, three. Each effort drained him of energy, leaving slick scarlet footprints on the worn treads. Moments later he heard Aleks mount the stairs behind them, dragging his fractured leg.

"You will not *take* her!" Aleks screamed.

The knife came down, splintering the dry steps, just inches behind Michael's feet.

"She is my daughter!"

Again the knife descended, this time tearing at the hem of Michael's jeans, the hot blade cutting through the heel of his shoe.

When the two wounded men reached the top, Aleks swung the knife in a whistling arc, nearly taking off the newel post on the landing. The blade missed Emily's head by inches.

Michael turned the corner at the top of the stairs, his sense memory propelling him down the short hallway to his old bedroom. He burst through the door, ran toward the window, nearly slipping in his own blood.

He put Emily down at the far side of the room. He knew the door had a slide bolt, and if he could just make it back, he could bolt the door, and it would give him a few precious seconds to break the window and get the attention of someone on the street.

But when he turned back to the door, Aleks was there. He lunged at Michael, the knife out front. At the last second Michael was able to dodge the full force of the blade, but it sliced into his left shoulder. Michael shrieked in pain as Aleks turned and came at him again. This time Michael warded off the blow as Aleks slammed into him, the momentum of the attack propelling them both into the closet door, knocking it off its hinges, choking them in the dust and soot of decades. The two men fell to the floor, struggling for control. Michael grabbed his attacker by the wrist, trying to hold off the knife, but Aleks was too strong.

As Aleks brought the blade ever closer to his throat, Michael sensed something brushing his cheek, something in the debris on the floor of the closet. He flashed on a mental image, the drawing Emily had made in the dust, the crude sketch of a little house, a cottage with a chimney and smoke.

Good night, my little nupp.

It was something that lived in Michael's heart, his memory: his mother on the fire escape, a warm, summer evening, the skyline of Manhattan before them like a glittering promise.

Next to him was his mother's knitting basket. The basket with the Estonian cottage embroidered on its side.

Michael felt the knife tip nearing his Adam's apple. With all his strength he pushed Aleks away from him, buying seconds. His hands still cuffed, he tore the knitting bag open, groped inside, felt the needle, the vintage twelve-inch Minerva steel needle his mother used for lace.

As Aleks came in for the kill, Michael summoned the final vestige of his strength. He did not have time for thought. He swung the needle up with all his power, plunging it into Aleks's left temple.

Aleks screamed and staggered back, blood gushing from the wound.

Michael tried to stand, to cross the room to Emily, but his legs would not hold him. A darkness began to descend. The last image Michael had was Aleks staggering across the room, red eyes bulging in their sockets, spinning wildly, blood spraying the walls, his voice a rutting animal sound.

I'm sorry, my love, Michael thought as the last of his strength left him, the light wavering, then falling dim. *I'm sorry*.

FIFTY-SEVEN

Abby pulled furiously at the copper pipe. The tape had dug deep into her wrists, and she could barely feel her hands. But she could not stop. The rusted pipes moaned and groaned under her efforts, but she could not seem to break the welded fittings.

She recalled her training, the resource of how to face crises, how to pull a twenty-four-hour shift, from where to summon strength and energy and focus. She closed her eyes, saw Charlotte and Emily in their little cribs on that day in South Carolina, the look on Michael's face.

With one last burst of force she broke free. The severed copper pipe sprayed water high into the air. She pulled the duct tape from her wrists, her mouth, ran across the room searching frantically for something, anything she could use as a weapon. She spotted Aleks's shoulder bag in the corner. She fell upon it, tore it open. At the bottom were four loose bullets, the rounds Aleks had taken from the magazine of Kolya's gun. Abby pulled them from the bag, then began to search the nearly dark room for the weapon. She crawled on her hands and knees, more than once slipping in the blood. The sounds had ceased coming from upstairs, and the silence was even more terrifying than the sounds.

She soon found the .9 mm pistol underneath the old oven.

She tried to remember where Michael had thrown the magazine. She couldn't recall.

Think Abby.

Think!

Michael had thrown the weapon to the right, the clip to the left. Abby stood where Michael had been standing, followed the trajectory with her eyes. To her left was a stack of wooden moving pallets. She ran across the room, began lifting the heavy pallets, pushing them to the side, her fear and frustration coursing through her like an electric current. When she lifted the last pallet she heard the metallic clank. In the dim light she saw the magazine. She fell to her knees, loaded the bullets into the magazine, her fingers slick with blood and sweat.

"*Isa!*" Emily screamed again from upstairs.

"Oh, my baby!" Abby said. She jammed the magazine into the gun, chambered a round, ran up the steps.

When she reached the second floor, and looked into Michael's old bedroom, she saw a tableau she knew would haunt her forever. The room was covered with blood. Emily sat in the corner, just beneath the windows, her hands folded in her lap. She was shaking. Aleks was slumped against the wall near the closet, a long needle protruded from his temple, leaking blood. His eyes were closed.

Then there was Michael. Michael was on the floor, face down. The back of his shirt was covered in blood. Abby ran over to him, put down the gun, and tried to put pressure on the wound, but it felt too deep.

Oh God, Michael! Please don't die! Please!

From somewhere in the distance she heard sirens, shouting. Perhaps it was in another world, another life.

The phone, she thought. Aleks had a phone. She crossed the room, began to rummage in Aleks's coat pockets. She went through them all, found nothing. It must have fallen out downstairs. Before she could get to her feet Aleks opened his eyes. He rocked forward, struggled to his feet, lifted her high into the air. He threw her into the wall. Plaster crumbled, exploding into the room in a cloud of dust.

"*Tütred!*" Aleks screamed as he fell back to his knees, and began to creep across the room, toward Emily. He crawled on his stomach, using the knife, sticking it in the floor, pulling himself forward in a sheet of glossy blood.

"Em!" Abby shouted. "Come to Mommy. Run!"

Emily was frozen. She did not move. Abby looked around frantically, found the gun in the morass of her blurred vision. She picked it up as Aleks edged ever closer.

"No!" Abby yelled. "*No!*"

Abby held the gun out in front of her, hands trembling. Sweat salted her eyes. Aleks was now just a few feet from Emily.

"*Stop!*"

Aleks brought himself to his knees. Choking back blood, he raised the knife over his head.

The booming roar of the gun shook the room, stealing all sound. The bullet slammed into Aleks's back, blowing a large hole in his chest. He fell to the floor, driving the long needle deep into his skull. The metal snapped. He rolled onto his back, his eyes wide, feral, disbelieving.

At the moment his eyes drifted shut, Abby saw something creep over his face, something dark, like the passing of a violent storm.

He was crossing over, becoming. He smelled the wet fur, felt the warm breath on his face. He turned his head. The grey wolf sat next to him — young and strong and full of life.

Behind the wolf was the gate to his home. The gate was open, the road to the house covered in pine needles, the air sweet with the fragrance of cornflower. He knew that if he could just get inside, Anna, Marya, and Olga would be waiting for him.

He saw a shadow near the gate. A man in a black leather coat, a garment a few sizes too large. The man was young, but not so young that he had not already crossed the devil's path. There was a finger missing from his right hand. In the dying light Aleks could just make out the young man's face, and in it he saw himself.

In it he saw eternity.

Abby sensed someone else in the room. She spun around, gun raised. Behind her was a woman in an attack stance, holding an automatic weapon. From the barrel of the woman's pistol curled a thin ribbon of smoke. Abby pointed the gun at the woman, but the woman did not back up, did not recoil. Neither did she lower her gun.

The woman spoke to her. In the aftermath of the thundering echo of the gun blast, Abby could not make out the words.

Somehow Abby knew the woman, the voice, but she could not place her. All she knew was that this was not over. The woman was there to take her daughter.

"No," Abby said. She cocked the pistol. "You can't have her!"

"It's okay," the woman said. "You can put the gun down."

A man stepped up behind the woman. Abby could see the man, too, had a weapon in his hand. He held it at his side. He was nervous, and his eyes shifted back and forth.

"It's over," the woman said softly, lowering her weapon. She slipped it into her shoulder holster. "Please, put down the gun."

The sirens drew closer. More footsteps. They were coming up the stairs.

"Please," the woman repeated. "Put the gun down, Mrs Roman."

Abby looked at the woman's eyes, heard her words.

Mrs Roman.

Detective Desiree Powell took a few steps forward, never taking her eyes off the pistol in Abby Roman's hand. To those whose only experience with a moment like this was watching *Law & Order* or reading about it in a book, Powell had a message. The longer you stare into a steel barrel, the worse it gets. No one ever takes it in their stride.

She gently eased the weapon away, handed it to Fontova. She heard the young detective exhale loudly.

"It's over," Powell said softly. "It's all over."

Abby Roman slid to the floor. She gathered herself to her trembling little girl with one arm, positioned her body to protect her husband. Powell had seen a lot of carnage in her time, a lot of fatal and near-fatal injuries. Michael Roman did not look good.

With weapons secured, Fontova stepped out the door. As paramedics rushed inside, Desiree Powell found her own way to the floor. She'd had two guns pointed at her on this day. She'd like to say she was getting used it, but she hoped she would never reach that place.

In her twenty-four years on the NYPD, she had drawn her weapon four times, fired it twice. Today was her first kill. She was kind of hoping to make it one more year without reaching that milestone, but it was not meant to be. When she had gotten out of bed that morning, she did not know that by the end of her tour she would be part of this exclusive club.

While the paramedics tended to the living, Powell closed her eyes.

Outside the window, the city of New York went about its business; traffic swept along, oblivious, heading toward the majestic bridges – the Triborough, the 59th Street, the

Williamsburg – toward the island of Manhattan with its steel and glass riddles, dark fingers in a gloaming sky. Powell had read once that more than forty million people came into New York City every year, each with their own dreams and thoughts and ideas on how to solve the city's many mysteries.

Some, Desiree Powell knew too well, by the grace or wrath of God, never leave.

FIFTY-EIGHT

The street was crowded with kids and parents. Easter in Astoria was a magical time, a time when Michael's father would relent and let him go down to La Guli's, the legendary pastry shop on Ditmars near 29th Street. Once there, money in hand, Michael had to make a decision between a pignoli tart or a *sfogliatelle*. Life was never easy.

On this Easter Sunday Michael lay in bed, eyes closed, the maddening aromas of baking ham, new potatoes, and peas with mint owning his senses.

When he opened his eyes he was more than a little startled to see a woman leaning over his bed. She was going to kiss him. It wasn't Abby.

Instead of kissing him, the woman lifted his left eyelid, shone a bright light in.

He was in the hospital. The horrors came flooding back.

The girls.

Michael tried to sit up. He felt a pair of strong hands on his shoulders. As he eased back down, images came floating toward him. The paramedics loading him on the ambulance, the sound of the sirens, the lights of the operating theater. He recalled the pain coming and going, felt the weight on his chest and abdomen. He saw his wife and daughters sitting on a bench at Cape May. Behind them a dark wave rose.

He slept.

*

The room was filled with flowers. Abby stood at the foot of the bed. Tommy was next to her.

"Hey," Tommy said.

Tommy looked older. How long had he been gone? Years? No, Michael thought. It was just the stress. Abby's face was drawn and pale, too. Her eyes were rimmed in red.

Michael closed his eyes for a minute. He saw the monster standing over Emily, the knife near her throat.

"The girls," Michael said weakly. His voice was barely a whisper.

Abby looked away for a moment. Michael's heart turned to ice. She looked back. "They're . . . they're fine. They're staying with my brother. They don't seem to remember much."

Michael wished it were the case for him. "Is that good or bad?" Each word seemed to drain an equal measure of his energy.

Abby paused for a while. In the hallway people in blue scrubs were running somewhere. "I don't know."

"The man," Michael managed. "Aleks."

"He's dead."

"Did you . . . ?"

Abby's eyes were wet. She shook her head. "No."

It was enough. Michael slept.

Michael felt new needles in his arms. He tried to swallow, and realized it was easier than it had been . . . when? Before. Earlier. What had been in his throat was gone.

He slept.

Two days later they raised his bed. He dozed for a while, and when he awoke he swung his gaze to the chair by the window. For some reason, Desiree Powell was sitting there. Her right arm was in a sling. Michael knew enough to know that there were going to be many legal complications from what had happened. He was fully prepared for the consequences of his actions. The dead man at his house, the two police officers on the street. Omar. But maybe not. Maybe Desiree Powell was just an hallucination.

No. The drugs weren't that good. She was real.

"Counselor," she said. "Welcome back."

Michael nodded at the glass of water on his tray. Powell looked out at the hallway, back. Perhaps he wasn't supposed to have water. She stood, and with her good hand lifted the straw to his lips. The cool water was every desire Michael had ever known.

"I thought you were dead," Michael said. His voice was weak and raspy.

"No such luck."

Another sip. "What happened?"

"I'll spare you all the details for now. But what put me in this device – which, by the way, doesn't go with any of my outfits – is that I took four in the vest. Broke two ribs."

"In my house?"

Powell nodded.

"I'm sorry."

Powell shrugged. "Just another sunny day in paradise."

Although it was not the time or the place for it, Michael had to know. Over the past twenty-four hours he had envisioned ten futures. Nine of them were bad. "What's going to happen?"

Powell took a few moments. "That's a question for your office, not mine, Michael. But I can tell you the forensics are all coming back good. It was the bad guy's knife that killed Nikolai Udenko. We found GSR on his hand, his prints on the grip of your wife's pistol. Plus we have a dozen witnesses who saw what he did on the street with the two officers."

There was going to be more, Michael knew. Powell was nothing if not thorough.

"Get better," she said. "We'll talk."

Powell stood, walked over to the window. After a few moments she turned back to him. Michael noticed that, for the first time since he had met her nearly ten years earlier, she was wearing jeans and an NYPD sweatshirt. It must have been casual Friday. If it was Friday. "You've been through this before," Powell said.

"What do you mean?"

"I mean, with that car bomb and all. Almost getting your ticket punched."

Michael nodded.

"So, let me ask you something."

"Sure."

Powell walked back across the room, sat down. "How many times can you cheat the devil?"

Michael glanced out the window. The trees were in full bloom, the sky was a crystal blue. In the distance the river sparkled with diamonds. He looked back at the detective. There was only one answer. "As many times as you can."

When Powell left, Michael slept. When he awoke, it was dark. He was alone.

Over the next two months Michael Roman grew to hate physiotherapy. More so, he came to hate the physiotherapists. They were all about twenty-six, perfectly fit, and they all had names like Summer and Schuyler. On any given day, after his fifth set of power squats, he had a few other choice names for them.

Slowly, he began to regain his strength and balance, returning to a form that was probably in many ways better than he was before.

During his convalescence, they stayed at Abby's parents' estate in Pound Ridge. They hired a company to come in and clean the Eden Falls house, but both Michael and Abby knew they would not be able to live there again. Whatever had been there for them was gone, dissolved in an acid of evil and darkness that no amount of disinfectant could mask. Michael had no idea what they were going to do, or where they were going to go, but for the moment that was secondary.

The Ghegan trial went forward in early July, helmed by a third-year ADA. Michael briefed the young man on the case and, with about an hour before opening statements, Falynn Harris showed up in courtroom 109. Two days later, after only four hours of deliberation, the jury returned a verdict of manslaughter. Ghegan was sentenced to fifteen years in prison. It wasn't what Michael had hoped for, what the city deserved, but Ghegan was off the street. The young ADA came to see Michael the day after sentencing. In his eyes Michael saw so much. Mostly himself, a few years ago.

In mid-August Michael returned, alone, to the Eden Falls house. He was still using a cane now and then, but for the most part he was independent. As he approached the house he saw something attached to the column next to the front door. His heart fluttered. Closer inspection revealed it was a decal, a stencil in the shape of a bright yellow daisy. Michael glanced around. There were no other decals, just this solitary, cheerful plastic flower on the column. Next to it was taped a small envelope. Michael opened it. Inside was a note card and a photograph. Michael looked at the picture first, an image of a young couple sitting on the stoop of a brownstone. By the look of the cars on the street it was probably the mid-Nineties. The man, who wore a Kelly green florist's smock, was lean and handsome. He had a twinkle in his eye. The woman had fine features, light-brown hair pinned up with plastic barrettes. The baby – a toddler, really – sat on the man's knee. There was no mistaking those sad eyes.

Michael looked at the note. On the back was a slip of paper. He turned it over. It was a receipt for the daisy decals. He had to laugh. She was informing him that she hadn't shoplifted these. He read the note.

I just wanted to tell you that I think I know what it means, now. Zhivy budem, ne pomryom. (I looked up the spelling. ☺)

It means that everything is going to be all right.

Be well all of your days.

Falynn xo

Michael folded the note, put it into his pocket.

After a few long moments he turned, and walked away from the house. He never went inside again.

FIFTY-NINE

A year after the horrible incidents in Eden Falls and Astoria, New York, a young woman stood across the street from the Pikk Street Café. Even there, on the corner, the air was rich with the aromas of cinnamon and marzipan and dark chocolate.

Inside, the owner of the café, a man of just thirty-six years, but one whose sandy hair was already shocked with grey, stacked boxes in the back room. There was never enough space.

At just after nine AM, after the morning rush had subsided, he stepped behind the counter. There were three customers at the tables, each lost in their coffee, their pastries, their copies of that morning's *Eesti Ekspress*.

When they decided to move to Estonia, they knew that Michael would never again practice law. The day he was to return to the Queens County District Attorney's office, he stood in Dennis McCaffrey's office, surrounded by his colleagues and friends. Because there had been no hard evidence that Michael had broken the law, no charges were filed regarding the adoption of the girls.

But there would always be a wariness surrounding Assistant District Attorney Michael Roman. And the DA's office – any DA's office – could not afford a cloud of suspicion. He tendered his resignation that day.

And although they had both taken a blitz Berlitz course in Estonian, it was Abby who excelled. She applied to the Estonian government, and within six months would take the first of two boards she would need to work as a nurse in this country.

As for the art of baking, Michael found that he took to it like a natural. He recalled watching his father in front of the ovens, the choreography of an artisan, a master of his craft. Michael was far from perfecting his *pirukad*, but was beginning to get repeat customers.

When he finished filling the lunch orders for the nearby hotels, he poured himself a cup of coffee. The girls were sitting at a table in the front window, giggling, as always, with some private, mysterious knowledge. When Michael looked out the window he saw a woman standing on the corner, watching the girls. His senses alerted, as they would forever be when it came to Charlotte and Emily, he moved closer. When he saw the young woman's face his heart stuttered, as if he had suddenly found the second half of a long-forgotten locket.

The woman noticed him, raised a delicate hand to wave.

Michael ran out the front door of the bakery, but by the time he reached the corner, the woman was gone, lost in the crowd of commuters and tourists on Pikk Street.

When he stepped back inside, Abby was waiting for him by the door.

"Did you see that woman?" he asked. "The blond woman in the red coat?"

"She was just in," Abby said. "She was sitting in the corner." She pointed to the table by the radiator.

Michael crossed the room. On the table sat a white napkin, and on it was drawn a beautifully detailed pencil rendering of a hillside cemetery. In the center was a small cross. There was no headstone, no name, but Michael knew whose resting place it was, and what it meant.

They say he consorted with a girl in Ida-Viru County. An ennustaja. *She bore him three children, but one was stillborn.*

"Something wrong?" Abby asked, stepping beside him.

Michael considered telling his wife. Instead, he put the napkin in his pocket, and said:

"It's a beautiful day. Let's close a little early."

A few hours later they sat on the shore at Pirita Beach, not far from the Olympic Yachting Centre, the host site of the 1980 Moscow Olympics. The wind was strong, and the air a little chilly – the beaches of Tallinn did not get crowded until late June – but the water glistened and the breeze carried the pledge of another summer.

After lunch the girls walked down to the water. Back to back, with little tree branches in hand, they made drawings in the wet sand. Charlotte etched something that looked like a mountain. Emily drew a horse. Or maybe it was a camel.

Michael gazed out over the Gulf of Finland. In the six months before they left the states, the girls had gone through intense counseling. According to the therapists, there did not appear to be any lasting trauma from the events of spring, 2009, but there existed the possibility that one day the terror they had experienced would return. Only time would tell.

Later, as they packed their things and headed to the car, Michael turned to look one last time at the sand drawings, but found that the tide had already come in and washed them away.

That evening, in the small flat over the café, with the girls fast asleep, and his wife engrossed in a book beside him, Michael held the napkin the woman had left on the table, and considered his beliefs, his faith in this life, and the knowledge that there was no eternity, no forever.

For the Roman family – Michael, Abby, Charlotte, and Emily – there was only now.

EPILOGUE

December. Snow fell gently over eastern Estonia, coating the hills, dusting the tall, imperial pines. The young man with a finger missing from his right hand stood looking out the window of a house set atop a hill in Kolossova. He had read about what happened on the Internet. The newspapers said that Aleksander Savisaar was some kind of monster, that he had terrorized a family in New York City.

Villem Aavik knew the truth.

When Savisaar left more than a year ago, he told Villem many things, had entrusted him with a great many responsibilities, not the least of which was the care of the house, the grounds, the animals. With both parents dead, Villem saw Savisaar as much more than just a father figure. He was the thing of myth. He was *vennaskond*.

Villem looked at the wall of knives in the study, each one a work of art. He took one from the rack, opened it, fingered the blade.

He had read all the books in the small library, knew all the names: Baba Yaga, Koschei Besmertney, Baš Čelik, Ivan, Marya, Anna, Olga. He had listened many times to Stravinsky's *The Firebird*, his confidence growing with each hearing. He had memorized every note from Rimsky-Korsakov's opera *Kashchey the Immortal*.

Immortal, he thought. He was young, just sixteen, but the idea enthralled him.

Forever.

He looked out the window again, at the blackness of the winter night. He had lost the finger in a foundry accident, but the fable would ultimately be whatever he said it was. He had already begun to visit Savisaar's accounts along the Narva, dealing with the provincial *roimar* who at first did not take him seriously. Villem Aavik made an example of one man in a farm village near Värska. In time his legend would precede him.

And there would be time enough. There was a girl in a nearby town, a girl they say will one day be *ennustaja*. She was only eleven years old, but already people were bringing to her their tales of unfaithful husbands, dying mothers, and lottery dreams.

One night, when the rue flowers were in bloom, and the Narva River ran silent, he would visit her.

Villem sat before the fire, his stomach full, the house and grounds secure. In a few days, a new year would begin.

Outside, in the soundless white of the countryside, a pair of silver eyes watched. And waited.

ACKNOWLEDGMENTS

I would like to thank Meg Ruley, Peggy Gordijn, Jane Berkey, Christina Hogrebe, Don Cleary, and everyone on the front line at the Jane Rotrosen Agency; thanks to Kate Elton, Jason Arthur, Susan Sandon, Rob Waddington, Trish Slattery, Oli Malcolm, Jay Cochrane, Louisa Gibbs, Emma Finnigan, Lucy Beaumont, Claire Round, Chrissy Schwartz, and all at Random House UK; thanks to Darin Brannon and Tiina Fischgrund; and a special thanks to Robert Masters, Esq. of the Queens County District Attorney's Office, and Detective Rick Torelli, NYPD. As always, *grazie mille di cuore*, Pop.

Coming soon … Richard Montanari's terrifying new novel

THE ECHO MAN

Read on for an exclusive extract…

MAN
All seems evil until I
Sleepless would lie down and die.

ECHO
Lie down and die.

–William Butler Yeats
Man and the Echo

PROLOGUE

For every light there is shadow. For every sound, silence.

From the moment he got the call, Detective Kevin Francis Byrne knew this would be a night that changed his life forever, a night that would take him to a place where evil had lumbered unseen from its lair, walked briefly in the world, then disappeared, leaving behind only darkness.

"You ready?"

Byrne glanced at Jimmy. Jimmy was just a few years older, but there was something in the man's eyes that held wisdom, a hard-won experience that transcended time spent on the job and spoke, instead, of time earned. They'd known each other for a long time, but this was their first full tour as partners.

"I'm ready," Byrne said.

He wasn't.

They got out of the car and walked to the front entrance of the sprawling, well-tended Chestnut Hill mansion. Here there was history at every turn, a neighborhood plotted at a time when Philadelphia was second only to London as the largest English speaking city in the world.

This night the language was death.

The first officer on the scene, a rookie named Timothy Meehan, stood inside the foyer, cloistered by coats and hats and scarves perfumed with age, just beyond the reach of the brisk autumn wind cutting across the grounds.

Byrne had been in Officer Meehan's shoes a handful of years earlier, and remembered well how he'd felt when detectives arrived, the tangle of envy and relief and admiration. Chances were slight that Meehan would one day do the job Byrne was about to do. It took a certain breed to stay in the trenches, especially in a city like Philly, and most uniformed cops, at least the smart ones, moved on.

Byrne signed the crime scene log and stepped into the warmth of the atrium, taking in the sights, the sounds, the smells, knowing he would never again walk into this place for the first time, never again breathe an air so red with violence. He looked into the kitchen, saw the blood-splattered killing room, scarlet murals on pebbled white tile, the torn flesh of the victim jigsawed on the floor.

While Jimmy called for the medical examiner and crime scene unit, Byrne walked to the end of the entrance hall. The officer standing there was a veteran patrolman, a man of fifty, a man content to live without ambition. At that moment Byrne envied him. The cop nodded toward the room on the other side of the corridor.

And that's when Kevin Byrne heard the music.

She sat in a chair on the opposite side of the room. The walls were covered with a forest of green silk; the floor, an exquisite burgundy Persian. The furniture was sturdy, in the Queen Anne style. The air smelled of jasmine and leather.

Byrne knew the room had been cleared, but he scanned every inch of it anyway, perhaps looking for unseen monsters. In one corner stood an antique curio case with beveled glass doors, its shelves arrayed with small porcelain figurines. In another corner leaned a beautiful maple cello. Candlelight shimmered on its golden surface.

The woman was slender and elegant, in her late twenties.

She had burnished russet hair down to her shoulders, eyes the color of polished copper. She wore a long black gown, sling-back heels, pearls. Her make-up was a bit garish, theatrical some might say, but it flattered her delicate features, her lucent skin.

When Byrne stepped fully into the room the woman looked as if she had been expecting him, as if he might be a guest for Thanksgiving dinner, some discomfited cousin just in from Allentown or Ashtabula. He was neither. He was there to arrest her.

"Can you hear it?" the woman asked. Her voice was soft, almost adolescent in its pitch and resonance.

Byrne glanced at the crystal CD case resting on a small wooden easel atop the expensive stereo component. *Chopin: Nocturne in G Major*. He then looked closely at the cello. There was fresh blood on the strings and fingerboard, as well as on the bow lying on the floor. It appeared she had played afterwards.

The woman closed her eyes. "Listen," she said. "The blue notes."

Byrne listened. He has never forgotten the melody, the way it both lifted and shattered his heart.

A few moments later the music stopped. Byrne waited for the last sound to feather into silence.

"I'm going to need you to stand up now, ma'am," he said.

When the woman opened her eyes Byrne felt something flicker in his chest. He had met all types of people in his time on the streets of Philadelphia, from soulless drug dealers, to oily con men, to smash and grab artists, to hopped-up joyriding kids. He had never before encountered anyone so detached from the crime they had just committed. In her eyes Byrne could see demons shift from shadow to shadow.

The woman rose, turned to the side, put her hands behind

her back. Byrne took out his handcuffs, slipped them over her slender white wrists, clicked them shut.

She turned to face him. They stood in silence now, just a few inches apart, strangers not only to each other, but also to this grim pageant, and all that was to come.

"I'm scared," she said.

Byrne wanted to tell her that he understood. He wanted to say that we all have moments of rage, moments when the walls of sanity tremble and crack. He wanted to tell her that she was going to pay for her crime, probably for the rest of her life – perhaps even *with* her life – but that while she was in his care she would be treated with dignity and respect.

He did not say these things.

"My name is Detective Kevin Byrne," he said. "It's going to be all right."

It was November 1, 1990.

Nothing has been right since.

PART ONE:
ALLEGRO

MONDAY OCTOBER 25

Can you hear it?

If you listen closely, there, beneath the clatter of the lane, beneath the ceaseless hum of man and machine, you will hear the sound of the slaughter, the screaming of peasants in the moment before death, the plea of an emperor with a sword at his throat, the quiet agony of a child left to die in a frozen field.

Can you hear it?

Step onto hallowed ground, where madness has made the soil fertile with blood, and you will hear it: Nanjing, Thessaloniki, Warsaw.

If you listen closely it is always there, never fully silenced, not by prayer, by law, by time. The symphony of the world, and its history of crime, is the slow, sepulchral music of the dead.

There.

Can you hear it?

I hear it. I am the one who walks in shadow, ears tuned to the night. I am the one who hides in rooms where murder is done, rooms that will never be quieted, each corner forever sheltering a whispering ghost. I am the one who hears fingernails scratching granite walls, the drip of blood onto scarred tile, the hiss of air drawn into a mortal chest wound. Sometimes it all becomes too much, too loud, and I must let it out.

I am the Echo Man.
I hear it all.

On Monday morning I rise early, shower, take my breakfast at home. I step onto the street. It is a glorious fall day. The sky is clear and crystalline blue, the air holds the faint smell of decaying leaves.

As I walk down Pine Street I feel the weight of the three killing instruments at the small of my back. I watch the eyes of passersby, or at least those who will meet my gaze. Every so often I pause, eavesdrop, listening to the sounds of the past. In Philadelphia there are many places where Death has lingered. I collect these sounds the way some men collect fine art, or war souvenirs, or lovers.

Like many who have toiled in the arts over the centuries my work has gone largely unnoticed. That is about to change. This will be my *magnum opus*, that by which all such works are judged forever. It has already begun.

I turn up my collar and continue down the lane.

Zig, zig, zig.

I rattle through the crowded streets like a white skeleton.

At just after eight am I enter Fitler Square, finding the expected gathering — bikers, joggers, the homeless who have dragged themselves here from a nearby passageway, the businessmen adrift on their Machiavellian plots, scanning their PDAs and Wall Street Journals with cautious attention. Some of these homeless will not live through the winter. Soon I will hear their last breaths.

I stand near the ram sculpture at the eastern end of the park, watching, waiting. Within minutes I see them, mother and daughter. They are just what I need.

I walk across the square, sit on a bench, take out my newspaper, halve and quarter it. The killing instruments are uncomfortable at my back. I shift my weight as the sounds begin to amass: the flap and squawk of *pigeons congregating around a man eating a bagel, a taxi's horn, the thump of a bass speaker. I look at my watch. It is time, and time is short. Soon my mind will be full of screams and I will not be able to do what I need to do.*

I glance at the young mother and her baby, catch the woman's eye, smile.

"Good morning," I say.

The woman smiles back. "Hi."

The baby is in an expensive jogging stroller, the kind with a rainproof hood and mesh shopping basket beneath. I rise, cross the path, glance inside the pram. It is a girl, dressed in a pink flannel one-piece and matching hat, swaddled in a snow white blanket. Bright plastic stars dangle overhead.

"And who is this little movie star?" I ask.

The woman beams. "This is Ashley."

"Ashley. She is beautiful."

"Thank you."

I am careful to not get too close. Not yet. "How old is she?"

"She's four months," the woman says. "Well, three months and twenty-six days to be precise."

"Four months is a great age," I reply with a wink. "I may have peaked around four months. I think it's all been downhill after that."

The woman laughs.

I'm in.

I glance back inside the stroller. The baby smiles at me. Or at least in my direction. In her face I can see so much. But it is not sight that drives me. The world is full of beautiful images, breathtaking vistas, all mostly forgotten by the time the next vista presents itself. I have stood before the Taj Mahal, Westminster Abbey, the Grand Canyon. I once spent an afternoon in front of Picasso's Guernica. All these images faded into the dim corners of memory within a short period of time. Yet I recall with clarity the first time I heard someone scream in anguish, the yelp of a dog struck by a car, the dying breath of a young officer bleeding out on a hot sidewalk.

"Is she sleeping through the night yet?"

"Not quite," the woman says.

"My daughter slept through the night at two months. Never had a problem with her at all."

"Lucky."

I reach slowly into my right coat pocket, palm what I need, draw it out. The mother is standing just a few feet away, on my left. She does not see what I have in my hand.

The baby kicks her feet, bunching the blanket. I wait. I am nothing if not patient. I need the little one to be tranquil and still. Soon she calms, her bright blue eyes scanning the sky.

With my right hand I reach out, slowly, not wanting to alarm the mother. I place a finger into the center of the baby's left palm. She closes her tiny fist around my finger, gurgles. Then, as I had hoped, she begins to coo.

In that moment all other sounds cease. In that moment it is just the baby, and this sacred respite from the dissonance that fills my waking hours.

I touch the Record button, keeping the microphone near the little girl's mouth for a few seconds, gathering the sounds, collecting a moment which will be gone in an instant.

Time slows, lengthens, like a lingering coda.

A few moments later I withdraw my hand. I do not want to stay too long, nor alert the mother to any sense of danger. I have a full day ahead of me, and cannot be deterred.

"She has your eyes," I say.

She does not, and it is obvious. But no mother ever refuses such a compliment.

"Thank you."

I glance at the sky, at the buildings that surround Fitler Square. It is time. "Well, it was lovely talking to you."

"You, too," replies the woman. "Enjoy your day."

"Thank you," I say. "I'm sure I will."

I reach out, take one of the baby's tiny hands in mine, give it a little shake. "It was nice meeting you, little Ashley."

Mother and daughter giggle.

I am safe.

A few moments later, as I walk up Pine Street, toward Seventeenth, I pull out the digital recorder, insert the mini-plug for the earbuds, play back the recording. Good quality, a minimum of background noise. The baby's voice is precious and clear.

As I slip into the van and head to South Philadelphia I think about this morning, how everything is falling into place.

Harmony and melody. These things live inside me, side by side, violent storms on a sun blessed shore.

I have captured the beginning of life.

I will now record the end.

The Rosary Girls

Richard Montanari

Only a killer hears their prayers . . .

In the most brutal killing crusade Philadelphia has seen in years, a series of young Catholic women are found dead, their bodies mutilated and their hands bolted together. Each clutches a rosary in her lifeless grasp.

Veteran cop Kevin Byrne and his rookie partner Jessica Balzano set out to hunt down the elusive killer, who leads them deeper and deeper into the abyss of a madman's depravity. Suspects appear before them like bad dreams – and vanish just as quickly. While the body count rises, Easter is fast approaching: the day of resurrection and of the last rosary to be counted . . .

'Be prepared to stay up all night' James Ellroy

'A specialist in serial killer tales . . . a wonderfully evocative writer' *Publishers Weekly*

arrow books

ALSO AVAILABLE IN ARROW

The Skin Gods

Richard Montanari

No one can hear you scream . . .

Philadelphia is blistering in the summer heat and detectives Kevin Byrne and Jessica Balzano prowl the streets with growing unease. Suddenly, a series of crimes shatters the restless city. A beautiful secretary is slashed to death in a grimy motel shower; a street hustler brutally murdered with a chainsaw. Piece by piece, a sickening puzzle presents itself: someone is recreating famous Hollywood murder scenes and inserting the clips into videos – for an unsuspecting public to find.

Investigations reveal a violent world of underground film, pornography and seedy nightclubs, hidden to all but the initiated. None of *The Actor*'s victims are as innocent as they appear, though, and Kevin and Jessica soon discover they're not just chasing a homicide suspect. They are stalking evil itself . . .

arrow books

Broken Angels

Richard Montanari

Evil prays upon the fallen . . .

When the first body is found, mutilated and strangled on the river-bank, Philadelphia homicide detectives Kevin Byrne and Jessica Balzano suspect yet another random case of urban violence. Then it happens again. And again.

Carefully dressed and posed, each victim seems to tell a story so gruesome that Byrne and Balzano struggle at first to make sense of the killer's dark and twisted imagination. But when they stumble upon a collection of old fairy tales, the fragile link between the murders suddenly becomes clear – and with it the terrifying conclusion of the killer's plan.

Desperately, they try to anticipate the madman's next move, but as the body count rises, the killing spree spirals out of control . . .

arrow books

ALSO AVAILABLE IN ARROW

Play Dead

Richard Montanari

A serial killer is on the loose. No one is safe . . .

Philadelphia homicide detectives Kevin Byrne and Jessica Balzano's
first assignment from the Cold Case files is the brutal murder of a
young runaway. The lifeless body of Caitlin O'Riordan was found
carefully posed in a glass display case in the desolate Philadelphia
Badlands but, as Byrne and Balzano rapidly discover, she was just
the first pawn in the killer's twisted game . . .

A mysterious phone call leads them on a scavenger hunt for
another victim who has been dismembered, her body parts left in
three boxes in the basement of a deserted house. More clues lead
to other victims and, as the body count rises, Byrne and Balzano
come to realise that the homicidal mastermind plans to complete
seven depraved tricks in his dark and dangerous magic act.

With Balzano increasingly obsessed by a case that haunts her, and
Byrne struggling with a loss of his own, the stakes are mounting.
But this is one game they can't afford to lose . . .

arrow books

Kiss of Evil

Richard Montanari

He's watching. He's waiting. He'll stop at nothing . . .

Christmas is just around the corner; the season of peace and goodwill. But this year, for Detective Jack Paris, the Christmas spirit is eclipsed by the hunt for a sadistic and twisted serial killer . . .

When an accused murderer is acquitted on a technicality then found dead of an apparent suicide, a spree of brutal murders terrorises the citizens of Cleveland. This vicious and vengeful killer tortures his seemingly unrelated victims in unimaginably violent ways, leaving them all with a strange symbol carved into their flesh.

When Detective Paris discovers that these murders are the grim handiwork of one maniac obsessed with the dark side of the ancient religion, *Santeria*, he's pulled into a web of danger and sexual deviance. Jack must catch the killer before he kills again. But on Christmas Eve, Jack finds himself right where the homicidal maniac wants him: questioning his loyalties, facing an impossible choice, with the barrel of a gun pointing at his temple and the whole world watching . . .

'Told at breakneck pace, with more than one truly frightening villain, and a protagonist whose tenacity in the face of evil makes him a hero for our times, you turn the pages as if your very life depends on it' *Daily Mail*

arrow books